ALSO BY LEN DEIGHTON

SPY LINE

SPY LINE

a novel by

Len Deighton

ALFRED A. KNOPF

NEW YORK

1989

THIS IS A BORZOI BOOK
PUBLISHED BY ALFRED A. KNOPF, INC.

Grateful acknowledgment is made to PolyGram International
Publishing, Inc., for permission to reprint an excerpt from
"Make Believe," music by Jerome Kern and lyrics by Oscar
Hammerstein II. Copyright 1927 by PolyGram International
Publishing, Inc. Copyright renewed. International copyright
secured. All rights reserved. Used by permission.

Library of Congress Cataloging-in-Publication Data
Deighton, Len, [date]
Spy line.
Second in a trilogy, preceded by Spy hook.
I. Title.
PR6054.E37S68   1989   823'.914   89-45302
ISBN 0-394-55179-6

Manufactured in the United States of America

FIRST AMERICAN EDITION

SPY LINE

Chapter 1

G lasnost is trying to escape over the Wall, and getting shot with a *silenced* machine gun!" said Kleindorf. "That's the latest joke from over there." He spoke just loudly enough to make himself heard above the strident sound of the piano. His English had an American accent that he sometimes sharpened.

I laughed as much as I could, now that he'd told me it was a joke. I'd heard it before, and anyway Kleindorf was hopeless at telling jokes: even good jokes.

Kleindorf took the cigar from his mouth, blew smoke at the ceiling, and tapped ash into an ashtray. Why he was so finicky I don't know; the whole damned room was like a used ashtray. Magically the smoke appeared above his head, writhing and coiling, like angry gray serpents trapped inside the spotlight's beam.

I laughed too much, it encouraged him to try another one. "Pretty faces look alike, but an ugly face is ugly in its own way," said Kleindorf.

"Tolstoy never said that," I told him. I'd willingly play the straight man for anyone who might tell me things I wanted to know.

"Sure he did; he was sitting at the bar over there when he said it."

Apart from regular glances to see how I was taking his jokes, he never took his eyes off his dancers. The five tall, toothy girls just found room on the cramped little stage, and even then the one on the end had to watch where she was kicking. But Rudolf Kleindorf—or "Der grosse Kleiner," as he was more usually known—evidenced the truth of his little joke. The dancers—smiles fixed and eyes wide—were distinguished only by varying cellulite and different choices in hair dye, while Rudi's large lopsided nose was surmounted by amazingly wild and bushy eyebrows. The permanent scowl and his dark-ringed eyes made unique a face that had worn out many bodies, not a few of them his own.

I looked at my watch. It was nearly four in the morning. I was dirty, smelly, and unshaven. I needed a hot bath and a change of clothes. "I'm tired," I said. "I must get some sleep."

Kleindorf took the large cigar from his mouth, blew smoke, and shouted, "We'll go on to 'Singing in the Rain'; get the umbrellas!" The piano stopped abruptly and the dancers collapsed with loud groans, bending, stretching, and slumping against the scenery like a lot of rag dolls tipped from a toybox. Their bodies were shiny with sweat. "What kind of business am I in, where I am working at three o'clock in the morning," he complained as he flashed the gold Rolex from under his starched linen cuffs. He was a moody, mysterious man and there were all manner of stories about him, many of them depicting him as bad-tempered and inclined to violent rages.

I looked round "Babylon." It was gloomy. The fans were off and the place smelled of sweat, cheap cosmetics, ash, and spilled drinks, as all such places do when the customers have departed. The long chromium-and-mirror bar, glittering with every kind of booze you could name, was shuttered and padlocked. His clients had gone to other drinking places, for there are many in Berlin which don't get going until three in the morning. Now Babylon grew cold. During the war this cellar had been reinforced with steel girders to furnish a shelter from the bombing, but the wartime concrete seemed to exude chilly damp. Two blocks away, down Potsdamerstrasse, one of these shelters had for years provided Berlin with cultivated mushrooms until the health authorities condemned it.

It was the "carnival finale" that had made the mess. Paper streamers webbed tables still cluttered with wine bottles and glasses. There were balloons everywhere—some of them already wrinkled and shrinking—cardboard beer mats, torn receipts, drinks lists, and litter of all descriptions. No one was doing anything to clear it all up. There would be plenty of time in the morning to do that. The gates of Babylon didn't open until after dark.

"Why don't you rehearse the new show in the daytime, Rudi?" I asked. No one called him Der Grosse to his face, not even me, and I'd known him almost all my life.

His big nose twitched. "These bimbos work all day; that's why we go through the routines so long after my bedtime." It was a stern German voice, no matter how colloquial his English. His voice was low and hoarse, the result no doubt of his devotion to the maduro-leaf Havanas that were aged for at least six years before he'd put one to his lips.

"Work at what?" He dismissed this question with a wave of his cigar.

"They're all moonlighting for me. Why do you think they want to be paid in cash?"

"They will be tired tomorrow."

"Yah. You buy an icebox and the door falls off, you'll know why. One of these dolls went to sleep on the line. Right?"

"Right." I looked at the women with new interest. They were pretty, but none of them were really young. How could they work all day and half the night too?

The pianist shuffled quickly through his music and found the sheets required. His fingers found the melody. The dancers put on their smiles and went into the routine. Kleindorf blew smoke. No one knew his age. He must have been on the wrong side of sixty, but that was about all he was on the wrong side of, for he always had a huge bundle of high-denomination paper money in his pocket and a beautiful woman at his beck and call. His suits, shirts, and shoes were the finest that Berlin outfitters could provide, and outside on the curb there was a magnificent old Maserati Ghibli with the 4.9-liter engine option. It was a connoisseur's car that he'd had completely rebuilt and kept in tune so that it could take him down the Autobahn to West Germany at 170 mph. For years I'd been hinting that I would enjoy a chance to drive it, but the cunning old devil pretended not to understand.

One persistent rumor said the Kleindorfs were Prussian aristocracy, that his grandfather General Freiherr Rudolf von Kleindorf had commanded one of the Kaiser's best divisions in the 1918 offensives, but I never heard Rudi make such claims. Der Grosse said his money came from "car-wash parlors" in Encino, southern California. Certainly not much of it could have come from this shabby Berlin dive. Only the most intrepid tourists ventured into a place of this kind, and unless they had money to burn they were soon made to feel unwelcome. Some said Rudi kept the club going for his own amusement, but others guessed that he needed this place, not just to chat with his cronies but because Rudi's back bar was one of the best listening points in the whole of this gossip-ridden city. Such men gravitated to Rudi and he encouraged them, for his reputation as a man who knew what was going on gave him an importance that he seemed to need. Rudi's barman knew that he must provide free drinks for certain men and women: hotel doormen, private secretaries, telephone workers, detectives, military government officials, and sharp-eared waiters who worked in the city's private dining rooms. Even Berlin's police officials—notoriously reluctant to use paid informants—came to Rudi's bar when all else failed.

How Babylon kept going was one of Berlin's many unsolved mysteries. Even on a gala night, alcohol sales didn't pay the rent. The sort of people who sat out front and watched the show were not big spenders: their livers were not up to it. They were the geriatrics of Berlin's underworld: arthritic ex-burglars, incoherent con men, and trembling forgers; men whose time had long since passed. They arrived too early, nursed their drinks, leered at the girls, took their pills with a glass of water, and told each other their stories of long ago. There were others, of course: sometimes some of the smart set—Berlin's *Hautevolee,* in fur coats and evening dress—popped in to see how the other half lived. But they were always on their way to somewhere else. And Babylon had never been a fashionable place for "the young"; this wasn't a place to buy smack, crack, angel dust, solvents, or any of the other powdered luxuries that the Mohican-haircut crowd bartered upstairs on the street. Rudi was fanatically strict about that.

"For God's sake, stop rattling that ice around. If you want another drink, say so."

"No thanks, Rudi. I'm dead tired, I've got to get some sleep."

"Can't you sit still? What's wrong with you?"

"I was an hyperactive child."

"Could be you have this new virus that's going around. It's nasty. My manager is in the clinic. He's been away two weeks. That's why I'm here."

"Yes, you told me."

"You're so pale. Are you eating?"

"You sound like my mother," I said.

"Are you sleeping well, Bernd? I think you should see a doctor. My fellow in Wannsee has done wonders for me. He gave me a series of injections—some new hormone stuff from Switzerland—and put me on a strict diet." He touched the lemon slice floating in the glass of water in front of him. "And I feel wonderful!"

I drank the final dregs of my Scotch, but there was no more than a drip or two left. "I don't need any doctors. I'm all right."

"You don't look all right. You look bloody ill. I've never seen you so pale and tired-looking."

"It's late."

"I'm twice your age, Bernd," he said in a voice that mixed self-satisfaction and reproof. It wasn't true—he couldn't have been more than fifteen years older than me—but I could see he was irritable, and I didn't argue about it. Sometimes I felt sorry for him. Years back, Rudi had bullied his only son into taking a regular commission in the Bundeswehr. The kid had done well enough, but he was too soft for even the modern army. He'd taken an overdose and been found dead in a barrack room in Hamburg. The inquest said it was an accident. Rudi never mentioned it, but everyone knew that he'd blamed himself. His wife left him, and he'd never been the same again since losing the boy: his eyes had lost their sheen; they'd become hard and glittering. "And I thought you'd cut out the smoking," he said.

"I do it all the time."

"Cigars are not so dangerous," he said and puffed contentedly.

"Nothing else, then?" I persisted. "No other news?"

"Deputy-Führer Hess died . . ." he said sarcastically. "He used to live in Wilhelmstrasse—number forty-six. After he moved to Spandau we saw very little of him."

"I'm serious," I persisted.

"Then I must tell you the real hot news, Bernd: you! People are saying that some maniac drove a truck at you when you were crossing Waltersdorfer Chaussee. At speed! Nearly killed you, they say."

I stared at him. I said nothing.

He sniffed and said, "People asked what was a nice boy like Bernd Samson doing down there where the world ends.

Nothing there but that ancient checkpoint. You can't get anywhere down there: you can't even get to Waltersdorfer,
there's a Wall in the way."

"What did you say?" I asked.

"I'll tell you what's there, I told them, memories." He
smoked his cigar and scrutinized the burning end of it as a
philatelist might study a rare stamp. "Memories," he said
again. "Was I right, Bernd?"

"Where's Waltersdorfer Chaussee?" I said. "Is that one
of those fancy streets in Nikolassee?"

"Rudow. They buried that fellow Max Busby in the grave-
yard down there, if I remember rightly. It took a lot of wheel-
ing and dealing to get the body back. When they shoot
someone on their side of the Wall, they don't usually prove
very cooperative about the remains."

"Is that so?" I said. I kept hoping he'd insist upon my
having another shot of his whisky, but he didn't.

"Ever get scared, Bernd? Ever wake up at night and fancy
you hear the footsteps in the hall?"

"Scared of what?"

"I heard your own people have a warrant out for you."

"Did you?"

"Berlin is not a good town for a man on the run," he said
reflectively, almost as if I weren't there. "Your people and the
Americans still have military powers. They can censor mail,
tap phones, and jail anyone they want out of the way. They
even have the death penalty at their disposal." He looked at
me as if a thought had suddenly come into his mind. "Did you
see that item in the newspaper about the residents of Gatow
taking their complaints about the British Army to the High
Court in London? Apparently the British Army commander in
Berlin told the court that since he was the legitimate successor
to Hitler he could do anything he wished." A tiny smile, as if
it caused him pain. "Berlin is not a good place for a man on
the run, Bernd."

"Who says I'm on the run?"

"You're the only man I know who both sides would be pleased to be rid of," said Rudi. Perhaps he'd had a specially bad day. There was a streak of cruelty in him, and it was never far from the surface. "If you were found dead tonight there'd be ten thousand suspects: KGB, CIA, and even your own people." A chuckle. "How did you make so many enemies, Bernd?"

"I don't have any enemies, Rudi," I said. "Not that kind of enemies."

"Then why do you come here dressed in those old clothes and with a gun in your pocket?" I said nothing, I didn't even move. So he'd noticed the pistol; that was damned careless of me. I was losing my touch. "Frightened of being robbed, Bernd? I can understand it, seeing how prosperous you are looking these days."

"You've had your fun, Rudi," I said. "Now tell me what I want to know, so I can go home and get some sleep."

"And what do you want to know?"

"Where the hell has Lange Koby gone?"

"I told you, I don't know. Why should I know anything about that shmuck?" It was not a word a German uses lightly: I guessed they'd had a row, perhaps a serious quarrel.

"Because Lange was always in here and now he's missing. His phone doesn't answer and no one comes to the door."

"How should I know anything about Lange?"

"Because you were his very close pal."

"Of Lange?" The sour little grin he gave me made me angry.

"Yes, of Lange, you bastard. You two were as thick . . ."

"As thick as thieves. Is that what you were going to say, Bernd?" Despite the darkness, the sound of the piano, and the softness with which we were both speaking, the dancers seemed to guess that we were quarreling. In some strange way there was an anxiety communicated to them. The smiles were slipping, and their voices became more shrill.

"That's right. That's what I was going to say."

"Knock louder," said Rudi dismissively. "Maybe his bell push is out of order." From upstairs I heard the loud slam of the front door. Werner Volkmann came down the beautiful chrome spiral staircase and slid into the room in that demonstratively apologetic way that he always assumed when I was keeping him up too late. "All okay?" I asked him. Werner nodded. Kleindorf looked round to see who it was and then turned back to watch the weary dancers entangle umbrellas as they danced into the nonexistent wings and cannoned against the wall.

Werner didn't sit down. He gripped a chair back with both hands and stood there waiting for me to get up and go. I'd been at school, not far from here, with Werner Jacob Volkmann. He remained my closest friend. He was a big fellow, and his overcoat, with its large curly astrakhan collar, made him even bigger. The ferocious beard had gone—eliminated by a chance remark from Ingrid, the lady in his life—and it was my guess that soon the mustache would go too.

"A drink, Werner?" said Rudi.

"No thanks." Although Werner's tone showed no sign of impatience, I felt bound to leave.

Werner was another one who wanted to believe I was in danger. For weeks now he'd insisted upon checking the street before letting me take my chances coming out of doorways. It was carrying caution a bit too far, but Werner Volkmann was a prudent man; and he worried about me. "Well, good night, Rudi," I said.

"Good night, Bernd," he said, still looking at the stage. "If I get a postcard from Lange, I'll let you put the postmark under your microscope."

"Thanks for the drink, Rudi."

"Anytime, Bernd." He gestured with the cigar. "Knock louder. Maybe Lange is getting a little deaf."

Outside, the garbage-littered Potsdamerstrasse was cold and snow was falling. This lovely boulevard now led to nowhere but the Wall and had become the focus of a sleazy district where sex, souvenirs, junk food, and denim were on sale. Beside the Babylon's inconspicuous doorway, harsh blue fluorescent lights showed a curtained shopwindow and customers in the Lebanese café. Men with knitted hats and curly mustaches bent low over their plates, eating shreds of roasted soybean cut from the imitation shawarma that revolved on a spit in the window. Across the road a drunk was crouched unsteadily at the door of a massage parlor, rapping upon it and shouting angrily through the letter box.

Werner's limp was always worse in the cold weather. His leg had been broken in three places when he surprised three DDR agents rifling his apartment. They threw him out of the window. That was a long time ago, but the limp was still there.

It was while we were walking carefully upon the icy pavement that three youths came running from a nearby shop. Turks: thin, wiry youngsters in jeans and T-shirts, seemingly impervious to the stark cold. They ran straight at us, their feet pounding and faces contorted into the ugly expressions that come with such exertions. They were all brandishing sticks. Breathlessly the leader screamed something in Turkish that I couldn't understand, and the other two swerved out into the road as if to get behind us.

My gun was in my hand without my making any conscious decision about needing it. I reached out and steadied myself against the cold stone wall as I took aim.

"Bernie! Bernie! Bernie!" I heard Werner shout with a note of horrified alarm that was so unfamiliar that I froze.

It was at that moment that I felt the sharp blow as Werner's arm knocked my gun up.

"They're just kids, Bernie. Just kids!"

The boys ran on past us, shouting and shoving and jostling as they played some ritual of which we were not a part. I put away my gun and said, "I'm getting jumpy."

"You overreacted," said Werner. "I do it all the time." But he looked at me in a way that belied his words. The car was at the curbside. I climbed in beside him. Werner said, "Why not put the gun in the glove compartment?"

"Because I might want to shoot somebody," I said, irritable at being treated like a child, although by then I should have become used to Werner's nannying. He shrugged and switched the heater on so that a blast of hot air hit me. We sat there in silence for a moment. I was trembling; the warmth comforted me. Huge silver coins smacked against the windscreen glass, turned to icy slush, and then dribbled away. It was a red VW Golf that the dealer had lent him while his new BMW was being repaired. He still didn't drive away: we sat there with the engine running. Werner was watching his mirror and waiting until all other traffic was clear. Then he let in the clutch and, with a squeal of injured rubber, did a U-turn and sped away, cutting through the back streets, past the derelict railway yards to Yorckstrasse, and then to my squat in Kreuzberg.

Beyond the snow clouds the first light of day was peering through the narrow lattice of morning. There was no room in the sky for pink or red. Berlin's dawn can be bleak and colorless like the gray stone city which reflects its light.

My pad was not in the part of Kreuzberg that is slowly being yuppified with smart little eating places, and apartment blocks with newly painted front doors that ask you who you are when you press the bell push. Kreuzberg 36 was up against the Wall: a place where the cops walked in pairs and stepped carefully over the winos and the excrement.

We passed a derelict apartment block that had been patched up to house "alternative" ventures: shops for bean sprouts and broken bicycles, a cooperative kindergarten, a feminist art gallery, and a workshop that printed Marxist books, pamphlets, and leaflets; mostly leaflets. In the street outside this block—dressed in traditional Turkish clothes, face obscured by a scarf—there was a young woman diligently spraying a slogan on the wall.

The block in which I was living had on its façade two enormous angels wielding machine guns surrounded by men in top hats standing under huge irregular patches of color that was the underpainting for clouds. It was to have been a gigantic political mural called "The Massacre of the Innocents," but the artist died of a drug overdose soon after getting the money for the paint.

Werner insisted upon coming inside with me. He wanted to make sure that no unfriendly visitor was waiting to surprise me in my little apartment, which opened off the rear courtyard. "You needn't worry about that, Werner," I told him. "I don't think the Department will locate me here, and even if they did, would Frank find anyone stouthearted enough to venture into this part of town?"

"Better safe than sorry," said Werner. From the other end of the hallway there came the sound of Indian music. Werner opened the door cautiously and switched on the light. It was a bare low-wattage bulb suspended from the ceiling. He looked round the squalid room; the paper was hanging off the damp plaster, and my bed was a dirty mattress and a couple of blankets. On the wall was a tattered poster: a pig wearing a policeman's uniform. I'd done very little to change anything since moving in; I didn't want to attract attention. So I endured life in this dark hovel: sharing—with everyone living in the rooms around this *Hinterhof*—one bathroom and two primitive toilets, the pungent smell of which pervaded the whole place. "We'll have to find you somewhere better than this, Bernie." The Indian music stopped. "Somewhere the Department can't get you."

"I don't think they care any more, Werner." I looked round the room, trying to see it with his eyes, but I'd grown used to the squalor.

"The Department? Then why try to arrest you?" He looked at me. I tried to see what was going on in his mind, but with Werner I could never be quite sure.

"That was weeks ago. Maybe I've played into their hands. I've put myself in prison, haven't I? And they don't even have the bother or the expense of it. They are ignoring me like a parent might deliberately ignore some child who misbehaves. Did I tell you that they are still paying my salary into the bank?"

"Yes, you told me." Werner sounded disappointed. Perhaps he enjoyed the vicarious excitement of my being on the run and didn't want to be deprived of it. "They want to keep their options open."

"They wanted me silenced and out of circulation. And that's what I am."

"Don't count on anything, Bernie. They might just be waiting for you to make a move. You said they are vindictive."

"Maybe I did, but I'm tired now, Werner. I must get some sleep." Before I could even take my coat off, a very slim young man came into the room. He was dark-skinned, with large brown eyes, pockmarked face, and close-cropped hair, a Tamil. Sri Lanka had provided Berlin's most recent influx of immigrants. He slept all day and stayed awake all night, listening to ragas on a cassette player. "Hello, Johnny," said Werner coldly. They had taken an instant dislike to each other at the first meeting. Werner disapproved of Johnny's indolence; Johnny disapproved of Werner's affluence.

"All right?" Johnny asked. He'd appointed himself to the role of my guardian in exchange for the German lessons I gave him. I don't know which of us had the best out of that deal: I suspect that neither of us gained anything. He'd arrived in

East Berlin a zealous Marxist, but his faith had not endured the rigors of life in the German Democratic Republic. Now, like so many others, he had moved to the West and was reconstructing a philosophy from ecology, pop music, mysticism, anti-Americanism, and dope.

"Yes, thanks, Johnny," I said, "I'm just going to bed."

"There is someone to see you," said Johnny.

"At four in the morning?" said Werner and glanced at me.

"Name?" I said.

Suddenly there was a screech from across the courtyard. A door banged open and a man staggered out backward and fell down with the sickening thud of a head hitting the cobbles. Through the dirty window I could see by the yellow light from an open door. A middle-aged woman—dressed in a short skirt and a bra—and a long-haired young man carrying a bottle came out and looked down at the still figure. The woman, her feet bare, kicked the recumbent man without putting much effort into it. Then she went inside and returned with a man's hat and a coat and a canvas bag and threw them down alongside him. The young man came out with a jug of water and poured it over the man on the ground. The door slammed loudly as they both went back inside.

"He'll freeze to death," said the always concerned Werner. But even as he said it the figure moved and dragged itself away.

"He said he was a business acquaintance," continued Johnny, who remained entirely indifferent to the arguments of the Silesian family on the other side of the yard. I nodded and thought about it. People announcing themselves as business acquaintances put me in mind of cheap brown envelopes marked "confidential," and are as welcome. "I told him to wait upstairs with Spengler."

"I'd better see who it is," I said.

I plodded upstairs. This sort of old Berlin block had no

numbers on the doors, but I knew the little musty room where Spengler lived. The lock was long since broken. I went in. Spengler—a young chess-playing alcoholic whom Johnny had met after being arrested at a political demonstration—was sitting on the floor drinking from a bottle of apple schnapps. The room smelled noticeably more foul than the rest of the building. Sitting on the only chair in the room there was a man trying not to inhale. He was wearing a melton overcoat and new string-backed gloves. On his head he had a brown felt hat.

"Hello, Bernd," said Spengler. He wore an earring and steel-rimmed glasses. His hair was long and very dirty. His name wasn't really Spengler. No one knew his real name. Rumors said he was a Swede who had exchanged his passport for the identity papers of a man named Spengler so that he could collect welfare money, while the real Spengler went to the U.S.A. He was growing a straggling beard to assist the deception.

"You looking for me?" I asked the man in the hat.

"Samson?" He got to his feet and looked me up and down. He kept it formal: "How do you do. My name is Teacher. I have a message for you." His precise English public-school accent, his pursed lips and hunched shoulders displayed his distaste for this seedy dwelling, and perhaps for me too. God knows how long he'd been waiting for me; top marks for tenacity.

"What is it?"

"I . . ."

"It's all right," I told him. "Spengler's brain was softened by alcohol years ago." A dazed smile crossed Spengler's white face as he heard and understood my words.

The visitor, still doubtful, looked round again before picking his words carefully. "Someone is coming over tomorrow morning. Frank Harrington is inviting you to sit in. He guarantees your personal freedom."

"Tomorrow is Sunday," I reminded him.

"That's right, Sunday."

"Thanks very much," I said. "Where?"

"I'll collect you," said the man. "Nine o'clock?"

"Fine," I told him.

He nodded goodbye without smiling and eased his way past me, keeping the skirt of his overcoat from touching anything that might carry infection. It was not easy. I suppose he'd been expecting me to shout with joy. Anyone from the Field Unit—even a messenger—must have sniffed out something of my present predicament: disgraced ex–field agent with a warrant extant. Being invited to the official interrogation of a newly arrived defector from the East brought an amazing change of status.

"You're going?" Werner asked after the front door banged. He was watching over the balcony to be sure the visitor actually departed.

"Yes, I'm going," I said.

"It might be a trap," he warned.

"They know where to find me, Werner," I said, making him the butt of my anger. I knew that Frank had sent his stooge along as a way of demonstrating how easy it was to pick me up if he felt inclined.

"Have a drink," said Spengler, from where he was still sprawled on the floor. He pushed his bent glasses up on his nose and prodded the buttons on the machine he was holding so that the little lights flashed. He'd finally found new batteries for his pocket chess computer, and despite his alcoholic daze he was engaging it in combat. Sometimes I wondered what sort of genius he would be if he ever sobered up.

"No thanks," I said. "I've got to get some sleep."

Chapter 2

Take me to a safe house blindfolded and I'd know it for what it was. Werner once said they smelled of electricity, by which he meant that smell of ancient dust that the static electricity holds captive in the shutters, curtains, and carpets of such dreary, unlived-in places. My father said it was not a smell but, rather, the absence of smells that distinguishes them. They don't smell of cooking or of children, fresh flowers or love. Safe houses, said my father, smelled of nothing. But reflexes conditioned to such environmental stimuli found hanging in the air the subtle perfume of fear, a fragrance instantly recognized by those prone to visceral terror. Somewhere beyond the faint and fleeting bouquet of stale urine, sweat, vomit, and feces there is an astringent and deceptive musky sweetness. I smelled fear now in this lovely old house in Charlottenburg.

Perhaps this young fellow Teacher smelled something of it too, for his chatter dried up after we entered the elegant mirrored lobby and walked past the silent concierge, who'd come out of the wooden cubicle from where every visitor was inspected. The concierge was plump, an elderly man with gray hair, a big mustache, and heavy features. He wore a Sunday churchgoing black three-piece suit of heavy serge that had gone shiny on the sleeves. There was something anachronistic about his appearance; he was the sort of Berliner better suited to cheering Kaiser Wilhelm in faded sepia photos. A fully grown German-shepherd dog came out of the door too. It growled at us. Teacher ignored dog and master and started up the carpeted staircase. His footfalls were silent. He spoke over his shoulder. "Are you married?" he said suddenly, as if he'd been thinking of it all along.

"Separated," I said.

"I'm married," he said in that definitive way that suggested fatalism. He gripped the keys so tight that his knuckles whitened.

The wrought-iron baluster was a delicate tracery of leaves and flowers that spiraled up to a great glass skylight at the top of the building. Through its glass came the colorless glare of a snow-laden sky, filling the oval-shaped stairwell all the way down to the patterns of the marble hall but leaving the staircase in shadow.

I had never been here before or even learned of its existence. As I followed Teacher into an apartment on the second floor, I heard the steady tapping of a manual typewriter. Not the heavy thud of a big office machine, this was the light patter of a small portable, the sort of machine that interrogators carry with them.

At first I thought the interrogation—or "debriefing," as they were delicately termed—had ended, that our visitor was waiting to initial his statement. But I was wrong. Teacher took me along the corridor to a sitting room with long windows one of which gave on to a small cast-iron balcony. There was a view of the bare-limbed trees in the park and, over the rooftops, a glimpse of the figure surmounting the dome of the eighteenth-century palace from which the district gets its name.

Most safe houses were shabby, their tidiness arising out of neglect and austerity, but this anteroom was in superb condition, the wall coverings, carpets, and paintwork cared for with a pride and devotion that only Germans gave to their houses.

A slim horsey woman, about thirty-five years old, came into the room from another door. She gave Teacher a somewhat lackluster greeting and, head held high, she peered

myopically at me and sniffed loudly. "Hello, Pinky," I said.
Her name was Penelope but everyone had always called her
Pinky. At one time, in London, she'd worked as an assistant
to my wife, but my wife had got rid of her. Fiona said Pinky
couldn't spell.

Pinky gave a sudden smile of recognition and a loud
"Hello, Bernard. Long time no see." She was wearing a cock-
tail dress and pearls. It would have been easy to think she was
one of the German staff, all of whom always looked as if they
were dressed for a smart Berlin-style soirée. At this time of the
year most of the British female staff wore frayed cardigans and
baggy tweed skirts. Perhaps it was her Sunday outfit. Pinky
swung her electric smile to beam upon Teacher and in her
clipped accent said, "Oh well, chaps. Must get on. Must get
on." She rubbed her hands together briskly, getting the circulation going, as she went through the other door and out into
the corridor. That was something else about safe houses: they
were always freezing cold.

"He's inside now," said Teacher, his head inclining to
indicate the room from which Pinky had emerged. "The shorthand clerk is still there. They'll tell us when." So far he'd
confided nothing, except that the debriefing was of a man
called Valeri—obviously a cover name—and that permission
for me to sit in on the debriefing was conditional upon my
not speaking to Valeri directly or joining in any general
discussion.

I sank down onto the couch and closed my eyes for a
moment. These things could take a long time. Teacher
seemed to have survived his sleepless night unscathed, but I
was weary. I was reluctant to admit it, but I was too old to
enjoy life in a slum. I needed regular hot baths with expensive
soap and thick towels and a bed with clean sheets and a room
with a lock on the door. To some extent I was perhaps identi-
fying with the mysterious escaper next door, who was no
doubt desirous of all those same luxuries.

I sat there for nearly half an hour, dozing off to sleep once or twice. I was woken by the sound of an argument coming not from the room in which the debriefing was taking place but from the room with the typewriter. The typewriting had stopped. The arguing voices were women's; the argument was quiet and restrained in the way that the English voice their most bitter resentments. I couldn't hear the actual words, but there was a resignation to the exchange that suggested a familiar routine. When the door opened again, an elderly secretary they called "the Duchess" came into the room. She saw me and smiled; then she put two dinner plates, some cutlery, and a brown paper bag, inside which some bread rolls could be glimpsed, onto a small table.

The Duchess was a thin and frail Welshwoman, but her appearance was deceptive, for she had the daring, stamina, and tenacity of a prizefighter. God knows how old she was: she had worked for the Berlin office for countless years. Her memory was prodigious, and she also claimed to be able to foretell the future by reading palms and working out horoscopes and so on. She was unmarried and lived in an apartment in Dahlem with a hundred cats, and moon charts and books on the occult, or so it was said. Some people were afraid of her. Frank Harrington made jokes about her being a witch, but I noticed that even Frank would think twice before confronting her.

The arrival of the dinner plates was a bad sign: someone was preparing for the debriefing to continue until nightfall. "You're looking well, Mr. Samson," she said. "Very fit." She looked at my scuffed leather jacket and rumpled trousers and seemed to decide that they were occasioned by my official duties.

"Thank you," I said. I suppose she was referring to my hungry body, drawn face, and the anxiety that I felt, and no doubt displayed. Usually I was plump, happy, and unfit. An angry cat came into the room, its fur rumpled, eyes wide, and manner agitated. It glared around as if it were some unfortunate visitor suddenly transformed into this feline form.

But I recognized this elderly creature as Jackdaw. The Duchess took it everywhere, and it slumbered on her lap while she worked at her desk. Now, dumped to the floor, it was outraged. It went and sank its claws into the sofa. "Jackdaw! Stop it!" said the Duchess, and the cat stopped.

"Would you like a cup of tea, Mr. Samson?" she asked, her Welsh accent as strong as ever.

"Yes. Thank you," I said, gratified that she'd recognized me after a long time away.

"Sugar? Milk?"

"Both, please."

"And you, Mr. Teacher?" she asked my companion. She didn't ask him how he drank it. I suppose she knew already.

Drinking tea with the Duchess gave me an opportunity to study this fellow Teacher in a way that I hadn't been able to the night before. He was about thirty years old, a slight, unsmiling man with dark hair, cut short and carefully parted. The waistcoat of his dark-blue suit was a curious design, double-breasted with ivory buttons and wide lapels. Was it a relic of a cherished bachelorhood, or the *cri du coeur* of a man consigned to a career of interminable anonymity? His face was deeply lined, with thin lips and eyes that stared, revealing no feelings except perhaps unrelieved sadness.

While we were drinking our cups of tea, the Duchess spoke of former times in the Berlin office and she mentioned the way that Werner Volkmann had made an hotel off Ku-Damm into a "cozy haven for some of the old crowd." She knew Werner was my close friend, and that's probably why she told me. Although she intended nothing but praise, I was not sure that her description augured well for its commercial success, for most of the "old crowd" were noisy and demanding. They were not the sort of customers who would do much for the profit-and-loss account. We chatted on until, providing an example of the sort of considered guess that had helped her reputation for sorcery, she said that I'd be invited to go inside in ten minutes' time. She was almost exactly right.

I went in quietly. Two men sat facing each other at either side of the superb mahogany dining table. Its surface was protected by a sheet of glass. Around it there were eight reproduction-Hepplewhite dining chairs, six of them empty, except that one was draped with a shapeless blue jacket. A cheap cut-glass chandelier was suspended over one end of the table, revealing that the table had been moved away from the window, for even here in Charlottenburg windows could prove dangerous. One of the men was smoking. He was in shirtsleeves and loosened tie. The window was open a couple of inches, so that a draft made the curtain sway gently but didn't disperse the blue haze of cigarette smoke. The distinctive pungent reek of coarse East German tobacco took me by the throat. Smoking was one of the few pleasures still freely available in the East, and there was neither official disapproval nor social hostility toward it over there.

The man called Valeri was quite elderly for an active agent. His high cheekbones and narrow eyes gave him that almost Oriental appearance that is not unusual in Eastern Europe. His complexion was like polished red jasper, flecked with darker marks and shiny like a wet pebble found on a beach. His thick brown hair—darkened and glossy with dressing—was long. He'd combed it straight back, so it covered the tops of his ears to make a shiny helmet. His eyes flickered to see me as I came through the door, but his head didn't move, and his high-pitched voice continued without faltering.

Sitting across the table from him, legs crossed in a languid posture, there was a fresh-faced young man named Larry Bower, a Cambridge graduate. His hair was fair and wavy, and he wore it long in a style that I'd heard described as Byronic, although the only picture of Byron that I could call to mind showed him with short back and sides. In contrast to the coarse, ill-fitting clothes of Valeri, Bower was wearing a well-tailored fawn saxony check suit, soft yellow cotton shirt, Wykehamist tie, and yellow pullover. They were speaking German, in which Larry was fluent, as might be expected of a man with a German wife and a Rhineland beer-baron grandfather named Bauer. In an armchair in the corner a gray-haired clerk bent over her notebook.

Bower raised his eyes to me as I came in. His face hardly changed, but I knew him well enough to recognize a fleeting look that expressed his weariness and exasperation. I sat down in one of the soft armchairs, from which I could see both men. "Now, once again," said Bower, "this new Moscow liaison man." As if reflecting on their conversation, he swung round in his chair to look out of the window.

"Not new," said Valeri. "He's been there years."

"Oh, how many years?" said Bower in a bored voice, still looking out of the window.

"I told you," said Valeri, "four years."

Bower leaned forward to touch the radiator as if checking to see if it was warm. "Four years."

"*About* four years," Valeri replied defensively.

It was all part of the game: Bower's studied apathy and his getting facts wrong to see if the interviewee changed or misremembered his story. Valeri knew that, and he did not enjoy the mistrust that such routines implied. None of us did. "Would you show me again?" Bower asked, pushing a battered cardboard box across the table.

Valeri opened the box and searched through a lot of dog-eared postcard-sized photographs. He took his time in doing it, and I knew he was relaxing for a moment. Even for a man like this—one of our own people, as far as we knew—the prolonged ordeal of questioning could tighten the strings of the mind until they snapped.

He got to the end of the first batch of photos and started on the second pile. "Take your time," said Bower, as if he didn't know what a welcome respite it was.

Until four years before, such identity photos had been pasted into large leatherbound ledgers. But then the KGB spread alarm and confusion in our ranks by instructing three of their doubles to select the same picture, in the same position on the same page, to identify a man named Peter Underlet as a spy, a KGB colonel. In fact, Underlet's photo was one of a number that had been included only as a control. Poor Underlet. His photo should never have been used for such purposes. He was a CIA case officer, and since case officers have always been the most desirable targets for both sides, Underlet was turned inside out. Even after the KGB's trick was confirmed, Underlet never got his senior position back: he was posted to some lousy job in Jakarta. That had all happened at the time my wife, Fiona, went to work for the other side. If it was a way of deflecting the CIA's fury and contempt, it worked. I suppose that diversion suited us as much as it did the KGB. At the time I'd wondered if it was Fiona's idea: we both knew Peter Underlet and his wife. Fiona seemed to like them.

"This one," said Valeri, selecting a photo and placing it carefully on the table apart from the others. I stood up so that I could see it better.

"So that's him," said Bower, feigning interest, as if they'd not been through it all before. He picked up the photo and studied it. Then he passed it to me. "Handsome brute, eh? Know him, by any chance?"

I looked at it. I knew the man well. He called himself Erich Stinnes. He was a senior KGB man in East Berlin. It was said that he was the liaison man between Moscow and the East German security service. It must have been a recent photo, for he'd grown fatter since the last time I'd seen him. But he still hadn't lost the last of his thinning hair, and the hard eyes behind the small lenses of his glasses were just as fierce as ever. "It's no one I've ever seen before," I said, handing the picture back to Bower. "Is he someone we've had contact with?"

"Not as far as I know," said Bower. To Valeri he said, "Describe the deliveries again."

"The second Thursday of every month . . . The KGB courier."

"And you saw him open it?" persisted Bower.

"Only the once, but everyone knows. . . ."

"Everyone?"

"In his office. In fact, it's the talk of Karlshorst."

Bower gave a sardonic smile. "That the KGB liaison is sniffing his way to dreamland on the second Thursday of every month? And Moscow does nothing?"

"Things are different now," said Valeri adamantly, his face unchanging.

"Sounds like it," said Bower, not concealing his disbelief.

"Take it or leave it," said Valeri. "But I saw him shake the white powder into his hand."

"And sniff it?"

"I was going out of the room. I told you. I shut the door quickly, I wasn't looking for trouble."

"And yet you could see it was white powder?"

"I wish I'd never mentioned the damned stuff." I had him sized up now. He was a typical old-time communist, one of the exiles who'd spent the war years in Moscow. Many such men had been trained for high posts in the Germany that Stalin conquered. What was the story behind this one? Why had he come to work for us? Blackmail? Had he committed some crime—political or secular—or was he not of the hard stuff of which leaders are made? Or was he simply one of those awkward individuals who thought for themselves?

"No comment," said Bower in a tired voice and looked at his watch.

Valeri said, "Next week I'll watch more carefully."

I noticed Bower stiffen. It was a damned careless remark for an active agent to make. I was not supposed to discover that this Valeri was a double, going in and out regularly. It was the sort of slip of the tongue that kills men. Valeri was tired. I pretended not to have noticed the lapse.

Bower did the same. He should have noted it and cautioned the man, but he gave an almost indiscernible shake of the head to the shorthand clerk before turning his eyes to me. Levelly he asked, "Is that any use?" It was my signal to depart.

"Not as far as I can see."

"Frank wanted you to know," he added, just in case I missed the message to get out of there and let him continue his difficult job.

"Where is he?"

"He had to leave." Bower picked up the phone and said they'd break for lunch in thirty minutes. I wondered if it was a ploy. Interrogators did such things sometimes, letting the time stretch on and on to increase the tension.

I got to my feet. "Tell him thanks," I said. He nodded.

I went out to where Teacher was waiting in the anteroom. He didn't say "All right?" or make any of the usual polite inquiries. Interrogations are like sacramental confessions: they take place, and are seen to take place, but no reference to them is ever made. "Are you returning me to Kreuzberg?" I asked him.

"If that's where you want to be," said Teacher.

We said our goodbyes to the Duchess and went downstairs to be let out of the double-locked front door by the guardian.

The streets were empty. There is something soul-destroying about the German *Ladenschlussgesetz*—a trade-union-inspired law that closes all the shops most of the time —and, right across the land, weekends in Germany are a mind-numbing experience. Tourists roam aimlessly. Residents desperate for food and drink scour the streets hoping to find a Tante Emma Laden where a shopkeeper willing to break the law will sell a loaf, a chocolate bar, or a liter of milk from the back door.

As we drove through the desolate streets, I said to Teacher, "Are you my keeper?"

Teacher looked at me blankly.

I asked him again. "Are you assigned to be my keeper?"

"I don't know what a keeper is."

"They have them in zoos. They look after the animals."

"Is that what you need, a keeper?"

"Is this Frank's idea?"

"Frank?"

"Don't bullshit me, Teacher. I was taking this town to pieces when you were in knee pants."

"Frank knows nothing about you coming here," he said mechanically. It contradicted everything he'd previously said, but he wanted to end the conversation by making me realize that he was just obeying instructions: Frank's instructions.

"And Frank keeps out of the way so that he can truthfully tell London that he's not seen me."

Teacher peered about him and seemed unsure of which way to go. He slowed to read the street signs. I left him to figure it out. Eventually he said, "And that annoys you?"

"Why shouldn't it?"

"Because if Frank had any sense he'd toss you onto the London plane, and let you and London work it all out together," said Teacher.

"That's what you'd do?"

"Damned right I would," said Teacher.

We drove along Heer Strasse, which on a weekday would have been filled with traffic. Every now and again there had been a dusty glint in the air as a flurry offered a sample of the promised snow. Now it began in earnest. Large spiky flakes came spinning down. Time and time again the last snow had come, and still the cold persisted, reminding those from other climates that Berlin was on the edge of Asia.

In what was probably an attempt to impress me with his knowledge of Berlin, Teacher turned off and tried to find a shortcut round the Exhibition Grounds. Twice he came to a dead end. Finally I took pity on him and directed him to Halensee. Then, as we got to Kurfurstendamm, he sat back in his seat, sighed, and said, "I suppose I am your keeper."

"And?"

"Frank might like to hear your reactions."

"Berlin is the heroin capital of the world," I said.

"I read that in *Die Welt*," said Teacher.

I ignored the sarcasm. "It all comes through Schönefeld Airport. Those bastards make sure it keeps moving to this side of the Wall."

"If it *all* comes here, then it makes sense that someone might try sending a little of it back," said Teacher.

"Stinnes is top brass nowadays. He'd have a lot to lose. I can't swallow the idea that he's having an army courier pick up consignments of heroin—or whatever it is—in the West."

"But?"

"Yes, there is a but. Stinnes knows the score. He's spent a lot of time in the West. He's an active womanizer, and some types of hard drugs connect with sexual activity."

"Connect? Connect how?"

"A lot of people use drugs only when they jump into bed. I could perhaps see Stinnes in that category."

"So I tell Frank you think it's possible."

"Only possible; not likely."

"A nuance," said Teacher.

"Once upon a time this fellow Stinnes was stringing me along. . . . He told me he wanted to come across to us."

"KGB? Enrolled? Work for us?"

"That's what he said."

"And you swallowed it?"

"I urged caution."

"That's the best way: cover all the exits," said Teacher. He was not one of my most fervent admirers. I suspected that Frank had painted me too golden.

"Anyway: once bitten, twice shy."

"I'll tell Frank exactly what you said," he promised.

"This is not the way to Kreuzberg."

"Don't get alarmed. I thought I'd give you lunch before you go back to that slum." I wondered if that too was Frank's idea. Mr. Teacher didn't look like a man much given to impulsive gestures.

"Thanks."

"I live in Wilmersdorf. My wife always has too much food in the house. Will that be okay?"

"Thanks," I said.

"I've given my expenses a beating this month. I had a wedding anniversary."

By the time we arrived in Wilmersdorf, the streets were wrapped in a fragile tissue of snow. Teacher lived in a smart new apartment block. He parked in the underground car park that served the building. It was well lit and heated: luxury compared with Kreuzberg. We took the elevator to his apartment on the fourth floor.

He rang the bell while opening the door with his key. Once inside he called to his wife, "Clemmie? Clem, are you there?"

Her voice replied from somewhere upstairs, "Where the hell have you been? Do you know what time it is?"

"Clemmie—"

She still didn't appear. "I've eaten my lunch. You'll have to make do with an egg or something."

Standing awkwardly in the hall, he looked at the empty landing and then at me and smiled ruefully. "Egg okay? Clemmie will make omelettes."

"Wonderful."

"I've brought a colleague home," he called loudly.

His wife came down the stairs, skittish and smiling. She was worth waiting for: young, long-legged, and shapely. She touched her carefully arranged hair and flashed her eyes at me. She looked as if her makeup was newly applied. Her smile froze as she noticed some flecks of snow on his coat. "My God! When does summer come to this damned town?" she said, holding him personally responsible.

"Clemmie," said Teacher after she'd offered her cheek to be kissed, "this is Bernard Samson, from the office."

"The famous Bernard Samson?" she asked with a throaty chuckle. Her voice was lower now and her genial mockery was not unattractive.

"I suppose so," I said. So much for Teacher's ingenuous inquiry as to whether I was married. Even his wife knew all about me.

"Take off your coat, Bernard," she said in a jokey, flirtatious way that seemed to come naturally to her. Perhaps the dour Teacher was attracted to her on that account. She took my old coat, draped it on a wooden hanger marked Disneyland Hotel, Anaheim, California, and hung it in an antique walnut closet.

She was wearing a lot of perfume and a button-through dress of light-green wool, large earrings, and a gold necklace. It was not the sort of outfit you'd put on to go to church. She must have been six or eight years younger than her husband, and I wondered if she was trying to acquire the pushy determination that young wives need to survive the social demands of a Berlin posting.

"Bernard Samson: secret agent! I've never met a real secret agent before."

"That was long ago," said Teacher in an attempt to warn her off.

"Not so long ago," she said archly. "He's so young. What is it like to be a secret agent, Bernard? You don't mind if I call you Bernard, do you?"

"Of course not," I said awkwardly.

"And you call me Clemmie." She took my arm in a gesture of mock confidentiality. "Tell me what it's like. Please."

"It's like being a down-at-heel private eye," I said, "in a land where being a private eye will get you thirty years in the slammer. Or worse."

"Find something for us to eat, Clemmie," said Teacher in a way that suggested that his acute embarrassment was turning to anger. "We're starved."

"Darling, it's Sunday. Let's celebrate. Let's open that lovely tin of sevruga that you got from someone I'm not allowed to inquire about," she said.

"Wonderful idea," said Teacher and sounded relieved at this suggestion. But he still did not look happy. I suppose he never did.

Clemmie went into the kitchen to find the caviar while Teacher took me into the sitting room and asked me what I wanted to drink.

"Do you have vodka?" I asked.

"Stolichnaya, or Zubrovka or a German one?" He set up some glasses.

"Zubrovka."

"I'll get it from the fridge. Make yourself at home."

Left alone, I looked around. It is not what guests are expected to do, but I can never resist. This was a small but comfortable apartment with a huge sofa, a big hi-fi, and a long shelf of compact discs—mostly outmoded pop groups—that I guessed were Clemmie's. On the coffee table there was a photo album, the sort of leatherbound, tasseled one in which people record an elaborate wedding. It bulged with extra pictures and programs. I opened it. Every page contained photos of Clemmie: on the athletic field, running the thousand-meter, hurdling, getting medals, waving silver cups. The pages were lovingly captioned in copperplate writing. Tucked into the back, she was to be seen in already yellowing sports pages torn from the sort of local newspaper that carries large adverts for beauty salons and nursing homes. In all the pictures she looked so young: so very, very young. She must have been here looking through it when she heard us at the door: and then rushed upstairs to put on fresh makeup. Poor Clemmie.

The apartment block was new and the walls were thin. As Teacher went into the kitchen, I heard his wife speak loudly: "Jesus Christ, Jeremy! Why did you bring him here?"

"I didn't have cash or I would have taken us all to a restaurant."

"Restaurant . . . ? If the office hear all this, you'll be in a row."

"Frank said give him lunch. Frank likes him."

"Frank likes everyone until the crunch comes."

"I'm assigned to him."

"You should never have agreed to do it."

"There was no one else."

"You told me he was a pariah, and that's what you'll end up as if you don't keep the swine at arm's length."

"I wish you'd let me do things my way."

"It was letting you do things your way that brought us to this bloody town."

"We'll have a nice long leave in six months."

"Another six months here with these bloody krauts and I'll go round the bend," she said.

There was the sound of a refrigerator door closing loudly, and of ice cubes going into a jug.

"You don't have to put up with them," she said. Her voice was shrill now. "Pushing and elbowing their way in front of you at the checkouts. I hate the bloody Germans. And I hate this terrible winter weather that goes on and on and on. I can't stand it here!"

"I know, darling." His voice remained soft and affectionate. "But please try."

When he returned he poured two large measures of vodka and we drank them in silence. I suppose he knew how thin the walls were.

It was not an easy lunch. We consumed 250 grams of Russian sevruga virtually in silence. With it we had rye bread and vodka. "The spring catch," said Teacher knowledgeably as he tasted the caviar. "That's always the best."

Unsure of an appropriate response to that sort of remark, I just said it was delicious.

Clemmie's mascara was smudged. She responded minimally to her husband's small talk. She wouldn't have a drink: she kept to water. I felt sorry for both of them. I wanted to tell them it didn't matter. I wanted to tell her it was just the Berlin Blues, the claustrophobic time that all the wives suffered when they were first posted to "the island." But I was too cowardly. I just contributed to the small talk and pretended not to notice that they were having a private and personal row in silence.

Chapter 3

K eep going!" I told Teacher as he began to slow down to let me out of the car.

"What?"

"Keep-going keep-going keep-going!"

"What's the matter with you?" he said, but he kept going and passed the car that had attracted my notice. It was parked right outside my front door.

"Turn right and go right round the block."

"What did you see? A car you recognize?"

I made a prevaricating noise.

"What, then?" he persisted.

"A car I didn't recognize."

"Which one?"

"The black Audi . . . Too smart for this street."

"You're getting jumpy, Samson. There's nothing wrong, I'll bet you. . . ."

As he was speaking, a police car cruised slowly past us, but Teacher gave no sign of noticing it. I suppose he had other things on his mind. "Perhaps you're right," I said. "I am a bit jumpy. I remember now, it belongs to my landlady's brother."

"There you are," said Teacher. "I told you there was nothing wrong."

"I need a good night's sleep. Let me off on the corner. I must buy some cigarettes."

He stopped the car outside the shop. "Closed," he said.

"They have a machine in the hallway."

"Righto."

I opened the car door. "Thanks for sharing your caviar. And tell Clemmie thanks too. Sorry if I outstayed my welcome." He'd let me have a hot shower. I felt better but couldn't help wondering if the grime was going to block the drain. I was grateful. "And best wishes to Frank," I added as an afterthought.

He nodded. "I was on the phone to him. Frank says you're to keep away from Rudi Kleindorf."

"Forget about the good wishes."

He gave a grim little smile and revved the motor and pulled away as soon as I closed the door. He was worried about his wife. I took a deep breath. The air was thick with the stink from the lignite-burning power stations that the DDR have on all sides of the city. It killed the trees, burned the back of the throat, and filled the nostrils with soot. It was the *Berlinerluft*.

I let Teacher's car go out of sight before cautiously returning down the street to rap on the window of the red VW Golf. Werner reached over to unlock the door, and I got into the back seat.

"Thank God. You're all right, Bernie?"

"Why wouldn't I be?"

"Where have you been?" Werner was good at hiding his feelings, but there was no doubt about his agitated state.

"What does it matter?" I said. "What's going on?"

"Spengler is dead. Someone murdered him."

Bile rose in my throat. I was too old for rough stuff: too old, too involved, too married, too soft.

"Murdered him? When?"

"I was going to ask you," said Werner.

"What's that mean, Werner? Do you think I'd murder the poor little sod?" Werner's manner annoyed me. I'd liked Spengler.

"I saw Johnny. He was looking for you, to warn you that the cops were here."

"Is Johnny all right?"

"Johnny is at the Polizeipräsidium answering questions. They're holding him."

"He has no papers," I said.

"Right. So they'll put him through the wringer."

"Don't worry. Johnny's a good kid," I said.

"If he has to choose between deportation to Sri Lanka or spilling his guts, he'll tell them anything he knows," said Werner with stolid logic.

"He knows nothing," I said.

"He might make some damaging guesses, Bernie."

"Shit!" I rubbed my face and tried to remember anything compromising Johnny might have seen or overheard.

"Get down, the cops are coming out," said Werner. I crouched down on the floor, out of sight. There was a strong smell of rubber floor-mats. Werner had moved the front seats well forward to give me plenty of room. Werner thought of everything. Under his calm, logical, and conventional exterior there lurked an all-consuming passion, if not to say obsession, with espionage. Werner followed the published, and unpublished, sagas of the cold war with the same sort of dedication that other men gave to the fluctuating fortunes of soccer teams. Werner would have been the perfect spy: except that perfect spies, like perfect husbands, are too predictable to survive in a world where fortune favors the impulsive.

Two uniformed cops walked past, going to their car. I heard one of them say, *"Mit der Dummheit kämpfen Götter selbst vergebens"*—"With stupidity the gods themselves struggle in vain."

"Schiller," said Werner, equally dividing pride and admiration.

"Maybe he's studying to be a sergeant," I said.

"Someone put a plastic bag over Spengler's head and suffocated him," said Werner after the policemen had got into their car and departed. "I suppose he was drunk and didn't make much resistance."

"The police are unlikely to give it too much attention," I said. A dead junkie in this section of Kreuzberg was not the sort of newsbreak for which press photographers jostle. It was unlikely even to make a filler on an inside page.

"Spengler was sleeping on your bed," said Werner. "Someone was trying to kill *you.*"

"Who wants to kill me?" I said.

Werner wiped his nose very carefully with a big white handkerchief. "You've had a lot of strain lately, Bernie. I'm not sure that I could have handled it. You need a rest, a real rest."

"Don't baby me along," I said. "What are you trying to tell me?"

He frowned, trying to decide how to say what he wanted to say. "You're going through a funny time; you're not thinking straight any more."

"Just tell me who would want to kill me."

"I knew I'd upset you."

"You're not upsetting me, but tell me."

Werner shrugged.

"That's right," I said. "Everybody says my life is in danger but no one knows from who."

"You've stirred up a hornets' nest, Bernie. Your own people wanted to arrest you, the Americans thought you were trying to make trouble for them, and God knows what Moscow makes of it all. . . ."

He was beginning to sound like Rudi Kleindorf; in fact, he was beginning to sound like a whole lot of people who couldn't resist giving me good advice. I said, "Will you drive me over to Lange's place?"

For a moment he thought about it. "There's no one there."

"How do you know?" I said.

"I've phoned him every day, just the way you asked. I've sent letters too."

"I'm going to beat on his door. Perhaps Der Grosse wasn't kidding. Maybe Lange is playing deaf: maybe he's in there."

"Not answering the phone and not opening his mail? That's not like Lange." Lange was an American who'd lived in Berlin since it was first built. Werner disliked him. In fact, it was hard to think of anyone who was fond of Lange except his long-suffering wife—and she visited relatives several times a year.

"Maybe he's going through a funny time too," I said.

"I'll come with you."

"Just drop me outside."

"You'll need a ride back," said Werner in that plaintive, martyred tone he used when indulging me in my most excruciating foolishness.

When we reached the street where John "Lange" Koby lived, I thought Werner was going to drive away and leave me to it, but the hesitation he showed was fleeting, and he waved away my suggestions that I go up there alone.

Dating from the last century, it was a great gray apartment block typical of the whole city. Since my previous visit, the front door had been painted and so had the lobby, and one side of the entrance hall had two lines of new tin post boxes, each one bearing a tenant's name. But once up the first staircase all attempts at improvement ceased. On each landing a press-button timer switch provided a dim light and a brief view of walls upon which sprayed graffiti declared the superiority of soccer teams and pop groups, or simply made the whirls and zigzag patterns that proclaim that graffiti need not be a monopoly of the literate.

Lange's apartment was on the top floor. The door was old and scuffed; the bell push had had its label torn off as if someone had wanted the name removed. Several times I pressed the bell but heard no sound from within. I knocked, first with my knuckles and then with a coin I found in my pocket.

The coin gave me an idea. "Give me some money," I told Werner.

Obliging as ever, he opened his wallet and offered it. I took a hundred-mark note and tore it gently in half. Using Werner's slim silver pencil, I wrote "Lange—open up you bastard" on one half of the note and pushed it under the door.

"He's not there," said Werner, understandably disconcerted by my capricious disposal of his money. "There's no light."

Werner meant there was no light escaping round the door or from the transom. I didn't remind him that John Lange Koby had been in the espionage game a very long time indeed. Whatever one thought of him—and my own feelings were mixed—he knew a thing or two about fieldcraft. He wasn't the sort of man who would pretend he was out of town while letting light escape from cracks around his front door.

I put a finger to my lips, and no sooner had I done so than the timer switch made a loud plop and we were in darkness. We stood there a long time. It seemed like hours, although it was probably no more than three minutes.

Suddenly the door bolts were snapped back with a sound like gunshots. Werner gasped: he was startled, and so was I.

Lange recognized that and laughed at us. "Step inside, folks," he said. He held out his hand, and I gave it the slap that he expected as a greeting. Only a glimmer of light escaped from his front door. "Bernard! You four-eyed son of a bitch!" Looking over my shoulder, he said, "And who's this well-dressed gent with false mustache and big red plastic nose? Can it be Werner Volkmann?" I felt Werner stiffen with anger. Lange continued, not expecting a reply. "I thought you guys were Jehovah's Witnesses! The hallelujah peddlers been round just about every night this week. Then I thought to myself, 'It's Sunday, it's got to be their day off!' " He laughed.

Lange read my written message again and tucked the half-banknote into the pocket of his shirt as we went inside. In the entrance there was an inlaid walnut hallstand with a mirror and hooks for coats, a shelf for hats, and a rack for sticks and umbrellas. He took Werner's hat and overcoat and showed us how it worked. It took up almost all the width of the corridor, and we had to squeeze past it. I noticed that Lange didn't switch on the light until the front door was closed again. He didn't want to be silhouetted in the doorway. Was he afraid of something, or someone? No, not Lange: that belligerent old bastard was fearless. He pushed aside a heavy curtain. The curtain was in fact an old gray Wehrmacht blanket, complete with the stripe that tells you which end is for your feet. It hung from a rail on big wooden rings. It kept the cold draft out and also prevented any light escaping from the sitting room.

There was only one big comfortable room in which to sit and watch television, so Lange used it as his study too. There were bookshelves filling one wall from floor to ceiling, and even then books were double-banked and stuffed horizontally into every available space. An old school-desk near the window held more books and papers and a big old-fashioned office typewriter, upon which German newspapers and a cup and saucer were precariously balanced.

"Look who finally found out where we live," Lange said to his wife in the throaty Bogart voice that suited his American drawl. He was a gaunt figure, pens and pencils in the pocket of his faded plaid shirt, and baggy flannel trousers held up by an ancient U.S. Army canvas belt.

His wife came to greet us. Face carefully made up, hair short and neatly combed, Gerda was still pretty in a severe, spinsterish style. "Bernard, dear! And Werner too. How nice to see you." She was a diminutive figure, especially when standing next to her tall husband. Gerda was German; very German. They met here in the ruins in 1945. At that time she was an opera singer, and I can remember how, years later, she was still being stopped on the street by people who remembered her and wanted her autograph. That was a long time ago, and now her career was relegated to the history books, but even in her cheap little black dress she had some arcane magic that I could not define, and sometimes I could imagine her singing Sophie in *Der Rosenkavalier* the way she had that evening in 1943 when she brought the Staatsoper audience to its feet and became a star overnight.

"We tried to phone," explained Werner apologetically.

"You are looking well," said Gerda, studying Werner with great interest. "You look most distinguished." She looked at me. "You too, Bernard," she added politely, although I think my long hair and dirty clothes disturbed her. "Would you prefer tea or coffee?" Gerda asked.

"Or wine?" said Lange.

"Tea or coffee," I said hurriedly. Each harvest Gerda made enough plum wine to keep Lange going all year. I dread to think how much that must have been, for Lange drank it by the pint. It tasted like paint remover.

"Plum wine," said Lange. "Gerda makes it."

"Do you really, Gerda?" I said. "What a shame. Plum wine brings me out in spots."

Lange scowled. Gerda said, "Lange drinks too much of it. It's not good for him."

"He looks fit on it," I pointed out; considering that this huge, aggressive fellow was in his middle seventies, or beyond, was almost enough to convert me to Gerda's jungle juice.

We sat down on the lumpy sofa while Mrs. Koby went off to the kitchen to make some tea for us. Lange hovered over us. He'd not changed much since the last time I'd seen him. In fact, he'd changed very little from the ferocious tyrant I'd worked for long, long ago. He was a craggy man. I remember someone in the office saying that they'd rather tackle the north face of the Eiger than Lange in a bad mood, and Frank Harrington had replied that there was not much in it. Ever since then I'd thought of Lange as some dangerous piece of granite: sharp and unyielding, his topsoil long since eroded so that his rugged countenance was bare and pitiless.

"What can I do for you boys?" he said with the urgent politeness with which a shopkeeper might greet a customer arriving a moment or two before closing time.

"I need advice, Lange."

"Ah, advice. Everybody wants it; nobody takes it. What can I tell you?"

"Tell me about the Wall."

"What do you want to know?"

"Escaping. I'm out of touch these days. Bring me up to date."

He stared at me for a moment as if thinking about my request. "Forget glasnost," said Lange. "If that's what you've come here to ask me. No one's told those frontier guards about glasnost. They are still spending money improving the mine fields and barbed wire. Things are still the same over there: they still shoot any poor bastard who looks like he might want to leave their part of town."

"So I hear," I said.

"Then where do I start?"

"At the beginning."

"Berlin Wall. About a hundred miles of it surrounds West Berlin. Built Sunday morning, August 1961 . . . Hell, Bernard, you were here!"

"That's okay. Just tell me the way you tell the foreign journalists. I need to go through it all again."

A flicker of a smile acknowledged my gibe. "Okay. At first the hastily built Wall was a bit ramshackle, and it was comparatively easy for someone young, fit, and determined to get through."

"How?"

"I remember the sewers being used. The sewers couldn't be bricked off without a monumental engineering job. One of my boys came through a sewer in Klein-Machnow. A week after, the Wall went up. The gooks had used metal fencing so as not to impede the sewage flow. My guys from this side waded through the sewage to cut the grills with bolt cutters and got him out. But after that things gradually got tougher. They got sneaky: welded steel grids into position and put alarms and booby traps down there, put them under the level of the sewage so we couldn't see them. The only escapers using the sewers that I heard of in the last few years were both East German sewage workers who had the opportunity to loosen the grid well in advance."

"So then came the tunnels," I said.

"No, at first came all the scramble escapes. People using ladders and mattresses to get across places where barbed wire was the main obstacle. And there were desperate people in those buildings right on the border: leaping from upstairs windows and being caught in a *Sprungtuch* by obliging firemen. It all made great pictures and sold newspapers, but it didn't last long."

"And cars," said Werner.

"Sure, cars, lots of cars—remember that little bubble car
. . . some poor guy squeezed into the gas-tank space? But they
wised up real fast. And they got rid of any Berlin kids serving
as *Grenztruppen*—too soft, they said—and brought some real
hard-nosed bastards from the provinces, trigger-happy country boys who didn't like Berliners anyway. They soon made
that sort of gimmick impossible."

"False papers?"

"You must know more about that than I do," said Lange.
"I remember a few individuals getting through on all kinds of
Rube Goldberg devices. You British have double passports
for married couples, and that provided some opportunities for
amateur label fakers, until the gooks over there started stamp-
ing 'traveling alone' on the papers and keeping a photo of
people who went through the control to prevent the wrong
one from using the papers to come back."

"People escaped in gliders, hang gliders, microlites, and
even hot-air balloons," said Werner helpfully. He was looking
at me with some curiosity, trying to guess why I'd got Lange
started on one of his favorite topics.

"Oh, sure," said Lange. "No end of lunatic contraptions,
and some of them worked. But only the really cheap ideas
were safe and reliable."

"Cheap?" I said. I hadn't heard this theory before.

"The more money that went into an escape, the greater
the number of people involved in it, and so the greater the
risk. One way to defray the cost was to sell it to newspapers,
magazines, or TV stations. You could sometimes raise the
money that way, but it always meant having cameramen hanging around on street corners or leaning out of upstairs windows. Some of those young reporters didn't know their ass
from their elbow. The pros would steer clear of any escapes
the media were involved with."

"The tunnels were the best," pronounced Werner, who'd
become interested in Lange's lecture despite himself.

"Until the DDR made the hundred-meter restricted area all along their side of the Wall, tunnels were okay. But after that it was a long way to go, and you needed ventilation and engineers who knew what they were doing. And they had to dig out a lot of earth. They couldn't take too long completing the job, or the word would get out. So tunnels needed two, sometimes three dozen diggers and earth movers. A lot of bags to fill; a lot of fetching and carrying. So you're asking too many people to keep their mouth shut. You trust a secret to that many people and, on the law of averages, at least one of them is going to gossip about it. And Berliners like to gossip."

I said nothing. Mrs. Koby came in with the tea. Upon the tray there was a silver teapot and four blue cups and saucers with gilt rims. They might have been heirlooms or a job lot from the flea market at the old Tauentzienstrasse S-Bahn station. Gerda poured out the tea and passed round the sugar and the little blue plate with four chocolate "cigarettes." Lange got a refill of his plum wine: he preferred that. He took a swig of it and wiped his mouth with a big wine-stained handkerchief.

Lange hadn't stopped: he was just getting going. "Over there, the Wall had become big business. There was a department of highly paid bureaucrats just to administer it. You know how it is: give a bureaucrat a clapboard doghouse to look after and you end up with a luxury zoo complete with an administration-office block. So the Wall kept getting bigger and better, and more and more men were assigned to it. Men to guard it, men to survey it and repair it, men to write reports about it, reports that came complete with cost estimates, photos, plans, and diagrams. And not just guards: architects, draftsmen, surveyors, and all the infrastructure of offices with clerks who have to have pension schemes and all the rest of it."

"You make your point, Lange," I said.

He gave no sign of having heard. He poured more wine and drank it. It smelled syrupy, like some fancy sort of cough medicine. I was glad to be allergic to it. He said, "Wasteful, yes, but the Wall got to be more and more formidable every week."

"More tea, Bernard," said Gerda Koby. "It's such a long time since we last saw you."

If Gerda thought that might be enough to change the subject, she was very much mistaken. Lange said, "Frank Harrington sent agents in, and brought them out, by the U-Bahn system. I'm not sure how he worked it: they say he dug some kind of little connecting tunnel from one track to the next so he could get out in Stadtmitte, where the West trains pass under the East Sector. That was very clever of Frank," said Lange, who was not renowned for his praise of anything the Department did.

"Yes, Frank is clever," I said. He looked at me and nodded. He seemed to know that Frank had deposited me in the East by means of that very tunnel.

"Trouble came when the gooks got wind of it. They staked it out and dumped a pineapple down the manhole just as two of Frank's people were getting ready to climb out of it. The dispatching officer was blown off his feet . . . and he was two hundred yards along the tunnel! Frank wasn't around: he was apple-polishing in London at the time, telling everyone about the coming knighthood that he never got."

I wasn't going to talk about Frank Harrington; not to Lange, I wasn't. "So the diplomatic cars are the only way," I said.

"For a time that was true," said Lange with a wintry smile. "I could tell you of African diplomats who put a lot of money into their pockets at ten thousand dollars a trip with an escapee in the trunk. But a couple of years ago they stopped a big black Mercedes with diplomatic plates at Checkpoint

Charlie and fumigated it on account of what was described as 'an outbreak of cattle disease.' Whatever they used to fumigate that car put paid to a thirty-two-year-old crane operator from Rostock who was locked in the trunk. They say his relatives in Toronto, Canada, had paid for the escape."

"The guards opened the trunk of a diplomatic car?" asked Werner.

"No. They didn't have to," said Lange grimly. "Maybe that poison gas was only intended to give some young escaper a bad headache, but when the trunk was opened on this side the fellow inside was dead. Hear about that, Bernard?" he asked me.

"Not the way you tell it," I admitted.

"Well, that's what happened. I saw the car. There were ventilation holes drilled into the trunk from underneath to save an escaper from suffocating. The guards must have known that, and known where the vents were."

"What happened?" asked Werner.

"The quick-thinking African diplomat turned around and took the corpse back to East Berlin and into his embassy. The corpse became an African national by means of predated papers. Death in an embassy: death certificate signed by an African medico, so no inquiries by the East German police. Quiet funeral. Buried in a cemetery in Marzahn. But here's the big boffola. Not knowing the full story, some jerk working for the Foreign Affairs Committee of the Volkskammer thinks a gesture of sympathy is required. So—on behalf of the government and people of the DDR—they send an enormous wreath in which the words 'peace, trust, and friendship' are made from miniature roses. It was only on the grave for a day or two; then it was discreetly removed by someone from the Stasi." Lange laughed loudly. "Cheer up, Bernie," he said and laughed some more.

"I thought you'd have good news for me, Lange. I thought things had eased up."

"And don't imagine going through Hungary or Czecho-slovakia is any easier. It's tight everywhere. When you read how many people have been killed crossing the Wall, you should add on the hundreds that have quietly bled to death somewhere out of sight on the other side."

"That's good tea, Gerda," I said. I never knew whether to call her Mrs. Koby or Gerda. She was one of those old-fashioned Germans who prefer all the formalities: on the other hand, she was married to Lange.

"Bringing someone out, Bernie?" said Lange. "Someone rich, I hope. Someone who can pay."

"Werner's brother-in-law in Cottbus," I said. "No money, no nothing."

Werner, who knew nothing of any brother-in-law in Cott-bus, looked rattled, but he recovered immediately and backed me up gamely. "I've promised," said Werner and sat back and smiled unconvincingly.

Lange looked from one of us to the other. "Can he get to East Berlin?"

"He'll be here with his son," Werner improvised. "For the Free German Youth festival in summer."

Lange nodded. Werner was a far better liar than I ever imagined. I wondered if it was a skill that he'd developed while married to the shrewish Zena. "You haven't got a lot of time, then," said Lange.

"There must be a way," said Werner. He looked at his watch and got to his feet. He wanted to leave before I got him more deeply involved in this fairy tale.

"Let me think about it," said Lange as he got Werner's coat and hat. "You didn't have an overcoat, Bernie?"

"No," I said.

"Aren't you cold, Bernard?" said Gerda.

"No, never," I said.

"Leave him alone," said Lange. He opened the door for us, but before it was open wide enough for us to leave he said, "Where's the other half of that banknote, Bernard?"

I gave it to him.

Lange put it in his pocket and said, "Half a banknote is no good to anybody. Right, Bernie?"

"That's right, Lange," I said. "I knew you'd quickly tumble to that."

"There's a lot of things I quickly tumble to," he said ominously.

"Oh, what else?" I said as we went out.

"Like there not being a Freier Deutsche Jugend festival in Berlin this summer."

"Maybe Werner got it wrong," I said. "Maybe it was the Gesellschaft für Sport und Technik that have their festival in East Berlin this summer."

"Yeah," said Lange, calling after us in that hoarse voice of his, "and maybe it's the CIA having a gumshoe festival in West Berlin this summer."

"Berlin is wonderful in the summer," I said. "Just about everyone comes here."

I heard Lange close the door with a loud bang and slam the bolts back into place with a display of surplus energy that is often the sign of bad temper.

As we were going downstairs Werner said, "Is it your wife, Fiona? Are you going to try to get her out?"

I didn't answer. The time switch plopped and we continued downstairs in darkness.

Vexed at my failure to answer him, Werner said somewhat petulantly, "That was my hundred marks you gave Lange."

"Well," I explained, "it's your brother-in-law, isn't it?"

Chapter 4

S ome men are born hoteliers, others strive to acquire hotels, but Werner Volkmann was one of those rare birds
who have hotels thrust upon them. It would be difficult to
imagine any man in the whole world less ready to become a
hotel manager than my good friend Werner Volkmann. His
dedication to Tante Lisl, the old woman who had brought him
up when he was orphaned, compelled him to take over from
her when she became too old and sick to continue her despotic
reign.

It was not a sumptuous establishment, but the neighbor-
hood could hardly be more central. Before the war it had been
Lisl's family home, set in the fashionable New West End. In
1945 the division of the city between the Russians and the
Western Allies had made Der Neuer Westen the center of
"capitalist Berlin."

Werner was making changes but sensitive to Lisl's feelings, for she was still in residence and monitored every new
curtain and every drip of paint; the modifications did little to
change the character of this appealing old place, where so
much of the interior was the same as it had been for fifty years
or more.

After we left Lange Koby's apartment that evening, I let
Werner persuade me to move into his hotel. There was little
reason to suffer the dirt and discomfort of my Kreuzberg slum
now that Frank Harrington had demonstrated his office's abil-
ity to put a finger out and reach me anytime they chose.

Before going to bed, Werner offered me a drink. We

walked through the newly refurbished bar—there was no one else there—to the small office at the back. He poured me a big measure of Scotch whisky with not much soda. Werner drank soda water with just a splash of Underberg in it. I looked around. An amazing transformation had taken place, especially pleasing for anyone who'd known Werner back in the old days. It had become a den, and Werner's treasures had miraculously resurfaced. There was a lion's head: a moth-eaten old fellow upon whose wooden mounting some drunken wag had neatly inscribed *Felis leo venerabilis*. Next to it on the wall hung an antique clock. It had a chipped wooden case, upon the front panel of which a bucolic scene was unconvincingly depicted. It ticked loudly and was eight minutes slow, but it was virtually the only thing he possessed which had belonged to his parents. Hanging from the ceiling there was the model Dornier flying boat that Werner had toiled so long to construct: twelve engines, and if you lifted up each and every cowling the engine detail could be seen inside. I remember Werner working on those tiny engines; he was in a vile temper for over a week.

We'd done no more than say how well Lange looked and what a fierce old devil he was when Ingrid Winter came into the room.

"Bernie is staying here with us," Werner said rather more sadly than I would have hoped, but, then, Werner was like that.

Ingrid had come into the room without my noticing. "Oh, that's good," she said. It would be easy to see Ingrid as a timid, self-effacing spinster, for she was always willing to appear in this guise. Her graying hair, which she did nothing to tint, her quiet voice, and her style of floral-patterned woolen dresses all contributed to this picture. But even on our short acquaintance I'd discovered that Ingrid was a creature of fortitude and strength. Werner had discovered the same thing, and more, for the relationship between them was close. "That

woman was here again," she told Werner in a voice tinged
with disapproval.

"The Duchess?"

"The Englishwoman. The secretary . . . the one you said
was a busybody."

Werner looked at me and grinned self-consciously.
"What did she want?"

"The Duchess likes it here," I interjected. "She hopes it's
becoming a sort of club for the people she knows."

Werner's face tightened. Ingrid was watching him as I
spoke, but her face showed no emotion, not even reflecting
that of Werner. Werner looked at me and said, "Ingrid thinks
there is more to it than that."

"What sort of more?"

"I told her about Frank," said Werner as if that would
explain everything. When I didn't react he added, "Frank
wants to use this place. It's obvious."

"It's not obvious to me, Werner," I said. "Use it how?"

Werner poured himself more soda water and added no
more than a drop of Underberg, which only just colored it. He
took a sip of it and said, "I think Frank has ordered his people
to come here. They'll return to the office and report to him
every word they hear and everything they see. It will all go on
file." This mild paranoia—complete with his rather endearing
picture of Frank's rigorous and capable administration—provided a perfect example of Werner's ingrained Germanic
thinking. In fact, Frank was typically English. Idle and conge-
nial, Frank was an easygoing time-server who'd muster neither the energy nor the inclination to organize such a venture.

Werner, on the other hand, was provincial and narrow-
minded in the way that Germans are prey to being. These
differing attitudes were fundamental to their enmity, but I
would never tell either of them what I thought. Werner would
have been horrified: he always thought of himself as a cosmo-

politan liberal. But of course all wealthy well-traveled bigots make that claim.

"As long as they pay cash for their drinks," I said.

This flippancy did not please Werner. "I don't mind Frank's people coming here, but I don't want them to monopolize the place and try to turn it into some awful sort of English pub. And anyway, Bernie," he added in a very quiet, measured voice, as if talking to a small child, "if you're here, they'll spy on you."

Any difficulty I might have had in answering Werner was removed by Ingrid. I had a feeling she was not listening to us very carefully. Perhaps she was already familiar with Werner's suspicions about the Departmental personnel transmogrifying his bar. During a lapse in the conversation she said, "There is something else. I heard them talking about Bernard. And about his wife."

My wife! My wife! Now she had all my attention and I wanted to hear all about it. She said that the Duchess had come into the bar in the early evening. She'd ordered a gin and tonic and read the *Daily Express*. Werner had recently started to provide the hotel with French and English, as well as German, daily papers, impaling them upon wooden *Zeitung-hälter*, and hanging them alongside the coat rack. Two other Department people—a man and a woman—came in soon afterward and invited the Duchess to join them.

I recognized Ingrid's description of the second woman of this trio. The voice, the Burberry scarf, the horseshoe-shaped diamond brooch. It was Pinky: there was only one Pinky, and thank God for that. Her daddy owned race horses, Mumsie hunted foxes, and her brother's nightclub adventures were regularly chronicled in the gossip columns. I remembered her when she'd come to work in the Department. She was newly divorced from "Bang-bang" Canon, a captain in the Horse Guards who went into insurance. She said she couldn't stand the sight of him in mufti, but that might have been her sense of humor. Pinky started using her maiden name again when Bang-bang went to prison for fraud.

From across the other side of the bar, Ingrid had heard Pinky say in her shrill home-counties voice, "When a man loses his wife it looks like carelessness, darling." And laughing loudly and calling for another drink.

"What about the telephone?" the man asked. Long, fair, wavy hair parted high, almost center. Check-patterned suit and mustard-colored shirt. Larry Bower, taking Pinky in for a drink on their way back from a hard day's work at the safe house in Charlottenburg.

Pinky said, "His phones were tapped from the first moment walked out. That's the drill. The transcripts go to Frank."

"Eventually they'll fire him," said Bower.

Pinky said, "You know how the Department works, darling: they have to make sure about him. It will take time. They'll get rid of him when it suits them."

"I never met her," said Bower. "What sort of woman was she?"

The Duchess answered the question: "Very beautiful. But I could never understand why she married him. Every man who clapped eyes on her wanted her; she has a sort of magic, I suppose. Some women are lucky like that."

"I never got to know her," said Pinky. "No one did. She wasn't a woman's woman, if you know what I mean."

"I think she spent a lot of money on clothes," said the Duchess. "But in all fairness I have to say that she could wear an old sweater and jeans and make herself look like . . ."

"A film star?" supplied Bower.

"No," said Pinky. "Never like a film star. She wasn't brainless, darling! Men can't abide the notion that beautiful women can be brainy. But they can."

"Yes, but what sort of woman was she really?" said Bower. "Everyone's talking about her, but no one seems to really know her."

"An absolute cow!" answered Pinky.

"Sometimes an absolute cow can be a good wife," said the Duchess.

"Oh, no!" said Pinky. "She made his life a misery. Everyone knew that."

"He seems to be managing without her," said Bower.

"He's something of a play actor," said the Duchess sadly. "He always has been."

"He can put down a few," said Bower.

"I've never seen him drunk," said the Duchess.

"Have you not, darling? My goodness, yes, but he can hold it. Let's face it, he was never really one of us, was he?" said Pinky.

"He hasn't got a bean, you know," said the Duchess.

"But there were no papers missing?" said Bower.

Pinky said, "Not as far as anyone can see . . . But who knows what was copied."

"She phoned Frank, you say?" the Duchess asked.

"Early this morning, at his home," said Pinky, who seemed to know everything. "I don't know how she had that number. It's changed regularly."

"You don't think that she . . . and Frank . . ." said Bower.

"Having it off with Frank?" Pinky's laugh ended in a giggle. "Good old Frank! Not my type, darling, but it's astounding how the ladies zero in on the poor old thing." Then, in a more serious voice, "No, I don't think there could be anything like that."

"Not in the dim and distant past?" said Bower.

"No, not even in the dim and distant past." This time the Duchess answered, firmly closing that door.

"So did Frank tell him?" said Bower.

"Tell hubby?" Pinky said. "About the phone call? . . . No. And no one knows what she said. We just know that Frank canceled all his appointments and ordered his car brought round the front . . . driving himself. No one knows where he went. Of course Frank's sudden departure may have nothing to do with it. You know what Frank is like. He might have just decided to spend the day with his army cronies or play golf or something."

"I just hope," said the Duchess, "that it's not all going to start all over again."

"Drinky for Pinky, darling," said Pinky to Bower.

Bower said, "All what start all over again?"

"You'll soon know," said the Duchess. "Life becomes hell for everyone once one of these security purges begins. Internal Security arrive and it's questions, questions, questions."

"Drinky for Pinky, darling. Drinky for Pinky."

"The same again three times," Bower called across the bar to Ingrid. Then five cheerful Australians came in; they were on some government-financed jaunt, buying ten thousand hospital beds or something of that sort. They'd spent all day at a residential complex where internationally renowned architects had competed to produce the world's ugliest apartment blocks. The Aussies needed a drink and, pleased to hear English spoken after a long day, joined the Duchess and her friends for a boozy evening. The conversation turned to lighter matters, such as why the Germans invaded Poland.

I thanked Ingrid for passing on to me the gist of this conversation she'd overheard. Then I quickly downed another stiff drink and went up to bed.

I had my usual room. It was a tiny garret at the top of the house, the sort of place which inspired Puccini to orchestrate Mimi's demise. It was a long walk to the bathroom. The floral wallpaper's big flowers and whirling acanthus leaves had gone dark brown with age, so that the pattern was almost invisible, and there in the corner was the little chest of drawers that had once held my stamp collection, my homemade lock picks, and the secret hoard of Nazi badges which my father had forbidden me to collect.

The bed was made up ready for me. There was a pair of

pajamas wrapped round a hot-water bottle. It was all as if Werner had guessed that it was just a matter of time before I saw sense.

I undressed and got into bed, put my pistol in my shoe so I could reach it easily, and went straight off to sleep. I must have been very tired, for I had plenty to stay awake and worry about.

Chapter 5

Lisl's hotel—or perhaps what I should more appropriately call Werner and Ingrid's hotel—did not run to phones in every room. The next morning at eight o'clock there was a tap at the door. It was Richard, one of Lisl's employees whom Werner had kept on. "Herr Bernd," he said. "A gentleman phoned, Herr Bernd. Herr Teacher. He comes here. Twelve hours sharply." He was a nervous young man who had come to Berlin, as many such German youngsters came, to avoid being drafted into the Bundeswehr. He got a job at Lisl's and met a girl, and now he had no plans to return to his parents in Bremen. Every now and again his father phoned to ask if Richard was "keeping out of trouble." Usually the phone calls came late at night, and usually his father sounded drunk.

Sometimes I wished Richard would not persist in using English when speaking to me, but he was determined to improve his languages. His ambition was to work on the reception desk of some very big luxury hotel, but he'd asked me not to reveal this to Lisl. So I kept his secret and I answered him in English, telling him that I would be having lunch downstairs and that if my visitor, Herr Teacher, was early he should put him in the bar and invite him to join me for lunch.

Richard said, "It is exactly as you say, Herr Bernd." He blinked nervously. He had a comprehensive store of phrases that he could deliver in reasonable English. His problem lay in putting these fragments together so that the joins didn't show.

"Thank you, Richard."

"You are hotly welcome, Herr Bernd. Have a nice day."

"You too, Richard," I said.

Once awake, I was overcome with a desperate need for a cup of hot strong coffee. So at nine-fifteen I was sitting in the dining room—the breakfast room was being completely re-done—with Lisl, who was waving her hand to obtain a pot of coffee from Klara. The faithful Klara wore an old-fashioned starched white apron with lacy edges on the bib. Lisl invariably referred to her as *das Dienstmädchen,* as if she were a newly employed teenage serving girl, but Klara was amazingly old. She was thin and wiry, a birdlike creature with bright little eyes and gray hair drawn back into a tight bun at the nape of her neck, a style in vogue when she was young. She was bent from a lifetime of hard work, having toiled for Lisl since long before the house became a hotel.

"And this time," Lisl told Klara emphatically, "put less coffee in the pot."

"Some people like strong coffee," I told Lisl, but Lisl waved a hand to tell Klara to pay no heed to me.

When Klara was out of earshot, Lisl explained in a loud and earnest voice, "She wastes coffee. It's so expensive. Do you know how much I pay for that coffee?"

From the corner of my eye I saw Klara turn her head to hear better what Lisl was saying. I was about to reply that it was time that Lisl stopped thinking about such things and left the account books to Werner and Ingrid. But the last time I'd said something like that, it unleashed upon me an indignant tirade forcefully assuring me that she was not too old to know how the hotel should be run. I suppose Werner and Ingrid had found some way of handling Lisl, for she gave no sign of resenting any of the changes they'd made.

This dining room, for instance, had been totally refurbished. All the paneling had been stripped back to the natural wood, and the nondescript prints had been junked in favor of some contemporary water colors: Berlin street scenes by a local artist. They went well with a cruel George Grosz drawing which was the only item retained from the former decoration. The picture had always hung beside this table—which was near a window that gave onto the courtyard—and this was where Lisl liked to sit for lunch. One of Lisl's more spiteful critics once said she was like a George Grosz drawing: black and white, a person of extremes, a jagged caricature of Berlin in the thirties. And today this obese woman, with her long-sleeved black dress and darkly mascaraed penetrating eyes, did look the part.

The coffee came, and Klara poured some into my cup. It was a thin brew with neither aroma nor color. I didn't remark on it, and Lisl pretended not to notice that it had come at all. Lisl sipped some milk; she wasn't drinking coffee these days. She was very slowly working her way through a red apple with a piece of Swiss Emmenthaler and a slice of black rye bread. Her arthritic old hand—pale and spotted and heavy with diamond rings—held a sharp kitchen knife and cut from the apple a very small piece. She took it between finger and thumb and ate carefully, making sure that she didn't smudge her bright-red lipstick.

"Werner has his own ideas," said Lisl suddenly. She said it as if we'd both been talking about him, as if she were replying to a question. "Werner has his own ideas, and he is determined."

"What ideas?"

"He has been back through the records, and is using that word-process machine to write letters to all the people who have stayed here over the last five years or more. Also, he keeps a record of all the guests, their names, their wives' names, and what they liked to eat, and any problems we have had with them."

"Excellent," I said. She pulled a face, so I said, "You don't think that's the way to do it?"

"For years I have run the hotel without such things," said Lisl. She didn't say it *wasn't* the way to do it. Lisl would sit on the fence until Werner's new ideas were tested. That was Lisl's way. She didn't like to be proved wrong.

"Werner is very clever at business affairs," I said.

"And the bridge evenings," said Lisl. "Frank Harrington's people come for the bridge evenings. The British like bridge, don't they?"

"Some of them."

Lisl laughed grimly. She could usually thrash me at bridge. When she laughed her huge frame wobbled and the glossy satin dress rippled. She reached up and touched the corner of her eye with her little finger. It was a delicate gesture with which she tested the adhesion of her large false eyelashes. "Werner is like a son to me."

"He's very fond of you, Lisl," I said. I suppose I should have told her that Werner loved her, for the sort of sacrifices Werner was making to run this place left no doubt of that.

"And loves the house," said Lisl. She picked up another little piece of apple and crunched it noisily, looking down at her plate again as if not interested in my response.

"Yes," I said. I'd never thought of that before, but Werner had been born here, during the war. It was the home in which he grew up as a tiny child. The house must have even more sentimental associations for him than it did for me, and yet in all our conversations he'd never expressed any feelings about the place. But how selfish of me not to see what was now so obvious. "And you have your niece here too," I said.

"Ingrid." Lisl cleared her throat and nodded. "She is my niece."

"Yes," I said. Since Lisl had repeatedly told anyone who would listen that Ingrid was her sister's illegitimate daughter, and therefore was *not* her niece, I interpreted this admission as substantial progress for Ingrid.

"Are you going somewhere?" she asked truculently. "You keep looking at your watch."

"I'm going to the bank. There should be money waiting for me, and I owe money to Frank."

"Frank has plenty of money," said Lisl. She shifted about in her chair. It was her way of dismissing both Frank's generosity as a lender and my integrity in reimbursing him. As I got up to go she said, "And I must get you to sort out all that stuff of your father's some time."

"What stuff?"

"There's a gun and a uniform full of moth holes—he never wore it except when they ordered him to wear it—and there's the cot your mother lent to Frau Grieben across the street, and books in English—Dickens, I think—the footstool, and a mattress. Then there's a big bundle of papers: bills and that sort of thing. I would have thrown it all away, but I thought you might want to sort through it."

"What sort of papers?"

"They were in that old desk your father used. He forgot to empty it. He left in a hurry. He said he'd be back and collect it, but he forgot. You know how absent-minded he could be sometimes. Then I started using that room as storage space and I forgot too."

"Where is it all now?"

"And account books and bundles of correspondence. Nothing important, or he would have written and asked me for it. If you don't want it I'll just throw it all out, but Werner wants me to clear everything out of the storeroom. It's going to be made into a bathroom."

"I'd like to sort through it."

"That's all he thinks about—bathrooms. You can't rent a bathroom."

"Yes, I'd like to sort through it, Lisl."

"He'll end up with *fewer* bedrooms. So how will that earn more money?"

"When can I look at it?"

"Now, don't be a nuisance, Bernd. It's locked up and quite safe. That room is crammed full of all sorts of junk, and there's nowhere else to put it. Next week . . . the week after. I don't know. I just wanted to know if you wanted it all."

"Yes, Lisl," I said. "Thank you."

"And buy me the *Guide Michelin* for France. The new one! It's just come out. I don't want the old one, mind."

"The Michelin hotel guide to France!" For years now Lisl had rarely emerged from the hotel except to go to the bank. Since the heart attack she hadn't even done that. "Are you going to France?" I asked. I wondered if she had some crazy plan to visit her sister Inge, who lived there.

"Why shouldn't I go to France? Werner's running things, isn't he? They keep telling me to go away for a rest."

Werner was thinking of putting Lisl into a nursing home, but I could see no way of explaining that to her. "The new *Michelin France,*" I said. "I'll get one."

"I want to see which are the best restaurants," said Lisl blithely. I wondered if she was joking, but you couldn't always be sure.

I spent the rest of the morning strolling along Ku-Damm. The snow had gone, and the sunlight was diamond-hard. The clouds were torn to shreds to reveal jagged shapes of blue, but under such skies the temperature always remains bitterly cold. Soviet jet fighters were making ear-splitting sonic bangs, part of the systematic harassment that capitalism's easternmost outpost was subjected to. After a visit to the bank, I browsed in the bookshops and looked round Wertheim's department

store. The food counters in the basement sold all sorts of
magnificent snacks. I drank a glass of strong German beer
and ate a couple of Bismarck herrings. For an hour the prospect of a lunch meeting that would be discordant, if not to
say an outright conflict, was forgotten. My problems vanished.
Around me there were the ever-cheerful voices of Berliners.
To my ears their quips and curses were unlike any others, for
Berlin was home to me. I was again a child, ready to race back
along the Ku-Damm to find my mother at the stove and father
at the lunch table waiting for me at the top of that funny old
house that we called home.

Time passes quickly when such a mood of contentment settles
the mind. I had to hurry to get back to Lisl's for noon. When
I went into the bar there was no sign of Teacher. I sat down
and read the paper. At half past twelve a man came in and
looked around to find me, but it was not Teacher: it was the
Berlin resident, Frank Harrington. He took off his hat. "Bernard! How good to see you." His manner and his warm
greeting gave no clue to the reason for this change of plan,
and I immediately decided that his presence was in some
way connected with the enigmatic exchange that Ingrid had
overheard.

Perhaps it was Frank's paternal attitude to me that made
his behavior so unvarying. I do believe that if I surprised Frank
by landing on his side of the moon unexpectedly he would not
be startled. Nonchalantly he'd say, "Bernard! How good to
see you," and offer me a drink or tell me I was not getting
enough exercise.

"I heard you were out of town, Frank."

"London overnight. Just one of the chores of the job."

"Of course." I tried to see in his face what might be in
store, but Frank's wrinkled face was as genial as ever. "I went
to the bank this morning," I said. "I have a draft to repay the

thousand pounds you let me have." I gave it to him. He folded
it and put it in his wallet without reading it.

He wet his lips and said, "Do you think your friend
Werner could conjure up a drink?" His feeling that this might
be beyond Werner's abilities, or that Werner might be dis-
posed to prevent him having a drink, was evident in his voice.
Coat still on, hat in hand, he looked round the room in a way
that was almost furtive. Frank had never been fond of Lisl or
Werner or the hotel. It seemed his unease at being here was
increased now that Werner had taken charge.

"Klara!" I said. I did not have to speak loudly, for the old
woman had positioned herself ready to take Frank's hat and
coat. "A double gin and tonic for my guest."

"Plymouth gin with Schweppes?" said Klara, who apparently knew better than I did what Frank drank. She took
Frank's trench coat, felt hat, and rolled umbrella.

"Yes, Plymouth with tonic," said Frank. "No ice." He
didn't immediately sit down in the chair I had pulled out for
him but stood there, preoccupied, as if unable to remember
what he'd come to tell me. He sighed before sinking down
onto the newly chintz-covered banquette. "Yes, just one of the
chores of the job," he said. "And it's the sort of task I could
be very happy without at this time." He looked tired. Frank
was somewhere in his middle sixties. Not so old perhaps, but
they'd asked him to stay on at a time when he'd got all ready
to retire. From that time onward some of the zeal had gone
out of him.

Or perhaps that was just my fancy, for today Frank had
the sort of appearance that almost restored my faith in the
British public-school system. He radiated fidelity, trustworthi-
ness, and good breeding. His hair was wavy and graying, but
not so wavy that he looked like a ladies' man and not so gray
that he looked like he couldn't be. Even the wrinkles in his face
were the sort of wrinkles that made him look like a good-
natured outdoorsman. And of course Frank had a valet to

press his Savile Row suits and polish his hand-sewn shoes and make sure his Jermyn Street shirts had exactly the right amount of starch in the collars.

"You heard about my son?" He was rummaging through his pockets. The question was put in that casual manner and tone of voice that, with a certain sort of Englishman, indicates a matter of vital importance.

"No," I said. "What about him?" Frank had never made any secret of his hope that his son would find a place in the Diplomatic Service. He'd prepared the ground well in advance. So, when the boy came down from Cambridge with the declared intention of getting a commercial pilot's license, Frank still didn't take it too seriously. It was only after he'd seen him flying the routes for a few years that Frank reluctantly faced the fact that his son was going to live a life of his own.

"Failed his medical."

"Frank, I'm so sorry."

"Yes, for an airline pilot that's a sentence of death. He said that to me on the phone. 'It's a sentence of death, Dad.' Until that very moment I don't think I understood what that damned flying job meant to him." Frank wet his lips nervously; I knew that I was the first person to whom he'd confided his true feelings. "Flying. It must be so boring. So repetitious." This was of course exactly the superior attitude that his son had so resented, and which had created the insurmountable barrier between them. "Not much of a job for a fellow with a good degree, I would have thought." He looked at me quizzically and then realized that I didn't have a college degree of any kind.

"What will he do?" I asked hurriedly to cover his discomfort.

"He's still in a state of shock," said Frank and gave a little laugh, trying to hide the distress he felt at the abrupt ending of his son's career.

"It will be all right," I said, improvising as I went. "They'll find him a ground job. He'll end up with a seat on the board." I knew that such a tedious administrative job would be something that Frank would really approve.

"There are too many of them," said Frank. "Too many unemployed aviators who don't know anything except how to drive an airbus. He'd be no damned use behind a desk, Bernard, you know that." Frank had been going through his pockets in a distracted way; finally he brought out a yellow oilskin tobacco pouch. From his top pocket he got out his cherry-wood pipe and blew through it experimentally before he snapped open the pouch.

"I'm not sure they permit smoking in here any more, Frank," I said.

"Nonsense." He sat down and began pushing tobacco into the bowl of his pipe and pressing it down with his thumb.

Klara brought Frank's gin and tonic. As she set it down before him, she saw his pipe and said, *"Hier darf nicht geraucht werden, Herr Harrington."*

"Fiddlesticks!" said Frank.

Despite Frank's devastating smile, Klara waggled a finger at him and said, *"Die Pfeife! Die Pfeife ist strenglich verboten!"*

Frank kept smiling and said nothing. Klara looked at me and pulled a fierce face that asked me how Lisl would deal with such a dilemma. Then she shrugged her shoulders and marched off. I don't think Klara cared very much whether guests smoked in the dining room: she'd done her duty as laid down by Lisl; that was enough.

Perhaps Klara's warning took effect, for Frank continued to toy with his smoking equipment but did not light up. At first I thought Frank's mind was still wholly occupied with the consequences of his son's failure to pass his pilots' medical, but there was something else. "But I bring good news for you, Bernard," he said.

"What's that, Frank?" I said.

"You're free." Perhaps my face didn't show the joy that he'd anticipated, for he added, "Free to go to England. All charges dropped. No board to face, not even a tribunal."

"I see," I said.

"I don't think you understand what I'm telling you. All charges against you are to be dropped."

"I thought you said they *had been* dropped."

"You're in a captious mood today, Bernard."

"Perhaps. But which is it?"

He coughed. Was it a sign of nervousness, the way the interrogation teams said, or was it something that came with that damned pipe tobacco? "A couple of formalities still remain. Nothing more, I assure you."

"Either/or," I said. "Did London send you to hold a pistol to my head?" I looked out of the window. The blue sky had only been a brief interlude, a deception. Now it had clouded over and looked like more snow, or, with the thermometer going up, rain.

"Come along, Bernard. It's nothing like that."

"What formalities?"

He tapped the table with his pipe. "Well, we wouldn't want you selling your memoirs to one of the Sunday papers." He smiled as if the restriction were upon something outrageous like leaping from the topmost pinnacle of Big Ben holding an umbrella. "We don't want you starting an action in the High Court." Another big smile.

"Wait a minute, Frank. Action in the High Court? I couldn't do that if I was still working for the Department." I looked at him: his expression was unchanging. I said, "Was that order for my arrest just some bizarre way of getting rid of me? Did they want me to run? Was someone half hoping that I might go East?"

"God forbid!" A gust of air rattled the windows like some demon trying to break in. Despite the double windows, the noise of the wind continued low and undulating, crooning a lament.

"From the Department's point of view, that would make things easier, wouldn't it? If I ran East I'd be labeled a defector. . . . For their reputation, that would be marginally better than having me in an English courtroom, or even facing a military court in Berlin."

"Bernard, please. They are simply asking for a signed supplementary agreement, covering the matters of confidence, contract, and official secrets, and so on. Formalities, just as I said."

"Are you telling me I'm fired? Is that the 'final solution' to the Samson problem? I'm to be tightly gagged and put out to grass?"

"Hold your horses, Bernard."

"Then tell me, Frank. But tell me straight."

"They want you to resign. . . . They suggest you give a year's notice. You'll work the year normally."

"Severance pay? Pension rights?"

"To be agreed."

"Oh, I see the hand of Morgan in this one. I work a year relegated to some remote job where nothing classified will pass across my desk. If I behave myself and keep my mouth shut, and sign a hundred forms to make sure I can't say a word to anyone without dire consequences, then I will tiptoe offstage and get my pension. But if I shake, rattle, and roll during that twelve months, I'm cut off without the proverbial penny."

"These matters always have two sides, Bernard."

"But am I right?"

"That would be one way of looking at it. But I hope you'll see that it's good for you too. It's a chance to cut loose from an impossible situation."

"The answer is no," I said.

"Wait a minute, Bernard."

"I've done nothing dishonest. They know that. Jesus! When Fiona took off, I faced positive vetting teams from the Ministry of Defence and the Cabinet Office. They pronounced me clean, and I am still. That's why they have dropped this lunatic plan of arresting me. The lawyers have told them that there is no case for me to answer. Not even here in occupied Berlin, where they can virtually invent their own laws. If they'd arrested me in England, I would have been headline news, and by now the Department would be looking damned stupid."

"Well, yes," said Frank with what might have been a sigh. "In fact, I understand the Deputy discussed you, and the order to arrest you, with someone from the Attorney General's office."

"And came out with his arse in a sling."

"I don't know what was said." He was looking down and giving all his attention to his tobacco pouch. Frank's position as Berlin Head of Station had brought him into many head-on collisions with London Central. He couldn't entirely conceal his pleasure at the hash London had made of this whole business. That he was being asked to pull their coals from the fire must have made it even more piquant.

"I'm not resigning," I told him. "I'll work the year, as they suggest, but only if I continue in the same job. If in twelve months' time the Department still wants my head, we'll talk about compensation then."

"I don't see the difference, Bernard."

"Don't you, Frank? The difference is that if I resign now it's like admitting that I've done something wrong: that I've sold secrets to a foreign power or taken the office pencils home. If they employ me normally for another year, it will be a tacit admission that I was wrongly accused."

"They won't like that answer," said Frank. "They are very keen to get it settled very quickly." The wind came again, fiercer now. When the wind abated, it would rain.

"I'll bet they are. Well, we can get it settled very quickly, if that's what they want. I'll fax my story to *The New York Times.*"

For a moment Frank didn't react. Then he rubbed his face and said, "Don't make jokes like that, Bernard. I shudder to think of the damage that would be inflicted upon all of us if you did something silly."

"Okay, Frank. I'll stop making jokes like that, but you tell London that it's my deal or nothing."

He kept his voice low and measured. "I don't know anyone who has your knowledge—and your instinct—for what's happening here, Bernard. Your time in the field added to time on the German Desk in London makes you a key person, and so a prime target. You've seen the Department at work since you were on your father's knee. Surely you can see why they worry so much."

"Yes, Frank. So you tell London that it's my deal or nothing."

"They'll not be threatened, Bernard."

"That has a sinister ring to it, Frank."

"Did it? I'm truly sorry, that's not at all what I intended to convey. I was trying to point out that your approach is ill-considered. Their offer is made in good faith. Must you throw it back into their face?"

"I'm not resigning."

"Go back to London. I'll arrange everything. Go to the office and work normally. Let the resignation issue stand for the time being, while I talk to the old man."

"There remains the question of Fiona," I said.

Frank flinched as if I'd struck him. "We can't discuss your wife."

"I've got to know whether Fiona defected or went over there continuing to work for the Department."

Frank stared at me; his face was like stone, without even a flicker of sentience.

I said, "Very well: you can't tell me officially, and I

understand that, Frank. But it's my wife. I've got to know."

I waited for him to frame an answer that would comply with his sense of propriety, but he still didn't speak.

"Fiona was sent, right? She's working for us still?" In Frank's face was the same Frank I'd known since childhood, but those pitiless eyes revealed a Frank that I'd always said did not exist. Yet this tough, unbending reaction to my question did not cause me to hate him: on the contrary, it made me want his help and assistance even more. That, of course, was the secret of Frank's success over these many years; I'd taken a long time to discover it. "Right?" I seemed to see in his eyes an affirmative. I felt sure that Frank wouldn't allow me to harbor the dangerous belief that Fiona was innocent if she was really a dedicated opponent.

After what seemed an age, Frank said, "I forbid you to discuss Fiona with me or with anyone else. I told you I would do my best to find out what you want to know. Meanwhile, you must keep completely silent. Put her out of your mind."

"Okay."

"And mean it."

"I said okay."

Frank relaxed a little. He said, "I take it you'll want to go to London as soon as possible?" I nodded. "You must have a lot of things to attend to."

He looked at me for a moment before putting his hand in his pocket and setting a foolscap-sized white envelope on the table in front of me.

I looked at him and smiled. He'd outmaneuvered me and been so confident about being able to do so that he'd brought the airline ticket with him. "Checkmate in three moves, eh, Frank?" I smiled and tried not to sound too bitter.

"I thought you would want to see Gloria and the children as soon as possible." He touched the ticket and moved it a fraction of an inch closer to me. "You'll be with them tonight. Go into the office tomorrow and work as usual. I'll phone you at home to tell you what's happening." He was careful to keep any note of triumph out of his voice. From his tone and demeanor you'd have thought we were fellow sufferers with the same misfortune.

"Thanks, Frank," I said, picking up the ticket. "What happened to our colleague Teacher today?"

"You won't regret it, Bernard. I'm giving you good advice, the sort your dad would have given you." A pause as he breathed deeply and no doubt congratulated himself upon getting a chance to change the subject. "Teacher. Yes. A spot of bother," said Frank, picking up his pipe and touching it to his lips. "His wife skedaddled. An awfully nice girl. Extremely intelligent. Clementine: gorgeous-looking creature, wonderful figure. Ever meet her?"

I nodded. Frank had a sharp eye for desirable young females with wonderful figures. His eyes stared into the distance as he remembered her.

"She went off with some flashy Yankee film producer. Met him for the first time ten days ago. Women are so impulsive, aren't they? What provokes a young wife to such a headstrong act?" The wind had dropped now. The sky had darkened. At any moment it would rain.

"Poor old Teacher," I said. "He seemed to be very fond of her." Now I realized why the beautiful Clemmie had become so agitated when I had lunch there on Sunday. Never mind her shouting about my being a pariah; my guess is that she thought the Department had got wind of her plans and sent me to spy on her.

"This wretched American has taken her to a film festival in Warsaw. Warsaw! Alarm bells started ringing, I can tell you. London overreacted: the telex got red hot! 'Do this; don't do that; disregard previous message; provide present whereabouts.' You know. Luckily Mrs. Teacher must have realized what trouble she was causing us. She phoned me from her hotel in Warsaw and explained, in guarded terms, that it was just a domestic rift. She had, she said, fallen in love for the very first time. Deep sighs and all. Says she'll never go back to her husband. They plan to fly on to a film festival in Japan, and then to America. She wants to live in Beverly Hills. She said that I was not to worry." Frank blew through his pipe and gave me a worried smile. "So I'm not worrying."

So that was what the Duchess and Co. had been so excited about. They'd been talking about the Teachers, not about me and Fiona. "And London?"

"London Central have professional worriers on the staff. But there's no way we can have our chaps lock their wives in the broom cupboard while they're out at work, eh?" He began to push tobacco into the bowl of his pipe. "It's a pity in some ways we can't."

There was the gentle noise of rain dabbing the windows. At first there were huge raindrops that came at measured intervals, but soon the drops dribbled and joined and made rivulets and bent the trees and distorted the outside world beyond recognition.

Chapter 6

I am not paranoid. That is to say, I am not paranoid to the extent of distrusting everyone around me. Only some of them. When I went into the office next morning, all seemed normal: too normal. After I'd finished looking at my own desk, I was summoned upstairs. Dicky Cruyer, German Desk supremo and my immediate superior, was in a singular mood that I could almost describe as jovial.

"Good morning, Bernard!" he said and smiled. He was a slim, bony man with pale complexion and a golliwog-style head of curly hair that I suspected he regularly had permed.

During my few weeks of living rough in Berlin, I'd reconciled myself to the idea that I would never again see this office. Never again see England, in fact. So now I looked round Dicky's office and marveled at it as if seeing it all for the first time. I examined anew the magnificent rosewood table that Dicky used instead of a desk, and behind it the wall filled with photos, mostly of Dicky. I inspected the soft black leather Eames chair and matching footstool and the slightly mangy lion's skin on the floor, which I noticed he'd positioned less obtrusively. I looked at it all with a feeling of wonder.

"I hope you're in a mood for hard work," said Dicky. "There is plenty to do, now your holiday is over." He leaned forward, elbows on table with fingertips touching. He was in shirtsleeves with bright-red braces and a floral-patterned bow tie. The Deputy had objected to Dicky's denim and leather, and now he wore suits in the office, but the newly acquired loud ties and bright braces were a subtle erosion of these dress restrictions.

I looked at him. "Yes, I am." He smiled. Did he really think I'd been on holiday? There was no way I could tell from his warm, relaxed, friendly smile. But the way he touched his fingertips together in a rapid succession of staccato taps betrayed what I judged to be an underlying nervousness.

"The Deputy Controller Europe wants a powwow at ten-thirty. You'd better come along too. Take notes."

"What about?" The Deputy Controller Europe was an Australian named Augustus Stowe. Dicky imperfectly concealed his envy of Stowe and usually referred to him by his title, with sarcastic emphasis, as if the position Stowe occupied was self-evidently unsuited to the man's abilities. This attitude to Stowe, complete with whispered doubts about his competence, was shared by some of Dicky's immediate circle. Stowe, a formidable childhood prodigy, had stayed on to teach logic at Perth University, and some now slightingly referred to him as "Dr. Stowe," as if a man with a doctorate was too unworldly for the Department.

"There are a number of things," said Dicky vaguely. It was Dicky's way of admitting that he hadn't the slightest idea. I suspected that Dicky was intimidated by Stowe, who had a savage temper when any shortcomings were uncovered, and so Dicky's meetings with him were sometimes less than convivial. "Coffee?"

"Yes, please." Whatever shortcomings Dicky had, they did not extend to his talent for self-preservation or to his coffee. Chagga, from Mr. Higgins' new shop in Duke Street. Dicky sent motorcycle messengers to collect it. One day someone would ask what urgent secret dispatches were coming in aromatic brown packets from Mr. Higgins two or three times a week.

"Capital!" said Dicky as his secretary brought in a polished wooden tray with steaming glass jug, the Spode chinaware and creamer. The cups contained hot water: Dicky said warmed cups were a vital contribution to the flavor. He tipped the hot water into a bowl and poured out his own coffee first. When tasting it, he frowned with eyes half closed and jug held poised. "Even better than the last lot," he pronounced.

"Is Stowe gunning for me?" I asked.

"He's gunning for someone," said Dicky.

Dicky looked out of his window while he drank. The weather system that had Berlin still gripped in winter temperatures had loosened its hold on England, where a succession of highs had provided enough warmth to coax the trees into bud and bathe the streets in a deceptively golden morning sunlight. It was a false summer, the sort of day when a man leaves home without an overcoat and comes back with pneumonia.

At ten-thirty I made my way to the room of the Deputy Europe. I remembered this room when it was decorated to the

expensive and somewhat avant-garde taste of Bret Rensselaer—chrome, glass, black leather, and deep carpet—but now
all that was gone. To say it was bare would be a gross under-
statement. It was even without floor covering. The walls still
had the coat of gray-green underpaint that marked Bret's
departure. Where once there had been an exquisite Dürer
now hung the standard portrait photo of the Queen. Stowe's
desk was a metal one of the sort used in the typing pool, and
his chair was of the back-breaking design that the Ministry of
Works used to discourage visitors from sitting too long in the
reception area downstairs.

Dicky Cruyer was already there. He'd put his jacket on
over his bright-red braces, which I interpreted as a gesture of
deference. Possibly their meeting had started earlier. Dicky
liked to arrange an opportunity for a confidential chat before
the real business started. He was perched on a metal chair with
uneven feet, so that it moved a fraction of an inch when he
shifted his weight. All three of the visitors' chairs in this room
had the same defect. I'd heard someone say the Deputy Controller had arranged for the chairs to be bent, but I thought
it unlikely that Stowe required any such psychological devices
for discomfiting his visitors.

Augustus Stowe had jet-black hair. As well as supplying
an abundant mustache, this same black hair grew from inside
his ears and straggled from his nostrils; it appeared in tufts on
his cheeks, and great tangles of it covered the backs of his
hands. Strange, then, that he was so bald. The carefully
combed hair, and the sideburns, only emphasized the perfect,
shiny pink dome of his head.

"No good sitting there scratching your arse, Dicky. Some
bugger will have to go," said Stowe with the antipodean di-
rectness of manner that had earned him few friends in the
Department. "You could go yourself," he suggested in a way
that implied that this would be a last and desperate resort.

"Leave it with me, Gus," said Dicky.

Although it wouldn't be his style to comment on such a thing, I had the feeling that Stowe didn't like being called Gus. I wondered if Dicky failed to realize this, or whether it was deliberate provocation. "No, Dicky," said Stowe. "When I leave things with you, they end up back in my tray six weeks later—flagged urgent."

Dicky pressed his fingers against his thin, bloodless lips, as if suppressing a temptation to smile at such a good joke. "Bernard could go," Dicky offered. "He could manage it."

"Manage it!" scoffed Stowe in his flat Australian growl. "Of course. That's just what I've been saying. Any bloody fool could manage it."

"Bernard knows Vienna," said Dicky.

It wasn't true by any means, but I didn't contradict Dicky, and he knew I wouldn't. It simply wasn't done to contradict your boss in front of a superior. "Do you, Bernard?" said Stowe. There was a fat old fly buzzing round his head. He waved it away with a rather regal gesture.

"I was there with Harry Lime," I said.

Stowe gave me a brief and disparaging smile. "Vienna is only part of it," he said. He was not an easy man to fool, although perhaps that wouldn't have been so evident to anyone meeting him for the first time. Stowe was wearing a gray three-piece suit of curious weave, a lumpy knitted tie, and zip-sided high boots. All of his clothes looked like theatrical costume rummaged from the hamper of some long-defunct repertory company. Even his wristwatch was of unusual trapezoid shape, its crystal discolored brown, so that to see the time he had to bring his wrist up close to his face.

To peer at his watch, he'd taken off his heavy tortoiseshell glasses. The stylish spectacles were an incongruous aspect of Stowe. One would have expected him to wear small circular gold-rimmed glasses, bent, and perhaps secured with a piece of flesh-colored sticking plaster. These spectacles were expen-

sive and modern, and after looking at his wristwatch he bran-
dished them as if wanting to make the most of them.

"And Bernard has good Russian," said Dicky.

"They will all speak English," Stowe said, looking again
at his watch.

"Not amongst themselves," said Dicky. "Bernard will be
able to understand what they say to each other."

"Ummm," said Stowe. "What's the time?" He was twisting the crown of the watch to adjust the hands.

"Ten-fifty-two," said Dicky.

"You're not empowered to make any concessions,"
Stowe told me solemnly. "Listen to what these hoodlums have
to say. If you think it's all baloney, come back and say so. But
no deals. And come straight back. No sightseeing tours on the
blue Danube, or tasting the May wine at the *heuriger* houses in
Grinzing. Right?" Even Stowe could not resist telling us he'd
been there.

"Of course," said Dicky. The fly buzzed round Dicky now.
Dicky gave no sign of noticing it, and it flew away.

"And, lastly, I don't want any of our bloody Yankee
friends mixed up in it," said Stowe as he opened a folder and
turned its pages. Dicky looked at me and gave me a fleeting
smile. I saw then that Dicky was not intimidated as much as
discomposed by Stowe. He didn't know whether to respond
with Stowe's same barroom vernacular or keep him at his
distance with deference and good manners.

"How would they get mixed up in it?" asked Dicky.

Stowe referred to his notes. The fly alighted on a page
and walked insolently across the heading. "They'll be on to
any of our people arriving in Vienna. They'll be on to them
right away." With a surprising speed, his hand shot forward.
His fingers flicked and closed tightly upon the fly, but when
he opened his fingers there was no fly.

"Do you think so, Gus?" said Dicky.

He gave a crafty smile. "I'm bloody sure so. I worked with

the Yanks in Korea. Corps Headquarters. I know what they're like." He wiped his hand on his trouser leg just as if the remains of the fly had been upon it. Perhaps it itched.

"What *are* they like?" said Dicky, dutifully providing the cue for which Stowe waited.

Stowe looked at Dicky and sniffed in the contemptuous manner of a practiced lecturer. "It is in the character of the average American, an aspect of his history, that he is curious by nature, resourceful by upbringing, and empirical by training," said Stowe. "In other words: Yanks are nosy, interfering bastards. Stay clear of them." He made an unsuccessful grab at the fly, and then waved at it angrily as it flew away. "And I don't want one of you big spenders checking into the Vienna Hilton with your dark glasses on, and asking the desk clerk if they have a night safe and telex facilities. Got it?"

Dicky, whose tastes for expense-account high living were directed more to the grandeur of the Imperial, nodded agreement.

Stowe must have guessed from the look on my face that Dicky hadn't told me much about the subject under discussion. In fact, Dicky had told me nothing. Stowe said, "You're having one of those off-the-record meetings with people from the other side." Facing my blank look, he added, "Russkies, I mean. Don't ask me who or how or where, because I'm not allowed to tell you."

"Yes, sir," I said.

"Top priority, so we can assume they have some bloody complaint to whine about. There will be threats too, if I know anything about the way these bastards operate. Stonewall all the time, and don't get ruffled."

"Is it something Vienna Field Unit could do?" I asked as diffidently as I was able. "I've never known any of them to become even slightly ruffled."

Stowe touched his bald head very delicately, almost as if he were smoothing his hair. He must have thought the fly had settled upon his head, but in fact it was tramping across his desk. For a moment he seemed to forget the conversation we were having; then he looked at me. "I told you: we've got to avoid the Yanks." His eyes fixed on me, and he added, "Vienna is packed with Yanks. . . . CIA, I mean."

So it wasn't tourists or encyclopedia salesmen he was worried about. "Why would the CIA be interested?" I asked. "Or do you mean we are going to send someone to Vienna for every off-the-record contact?"

Slowly a smile came to Stowe's face. It was not much of a smile, but what it lacked in joy it made up for in guile. "Very good, Bernard!" he said, and there was in his voice a note of approval that I had not heard before. "Very good!" He turned his head to share the fun with Dicky. Dicky gave a dutiful smirk that revealed that he didn't know what the hell was going on. I recognized it easily: it was one of Dicky's standard expressions.

But soon I saw that Stowe's pleasure was feigned, the way he reacted to what he judged to be insubordinate questioning. Speaking slowly, Stowe said, "I know the CIA are interested, Bernard, because a little bird told me. And if I'm told to make sure such events go smoothly in the future, maybe I *will* send someone to Vienna every time. And it might bloody well be you. Would you like that, Bernard?"

I didn't answer. Dicky smiled to show that now he knew what Stowe was talking about. Helpfully he said, "So you think the Vienna CIA will try to interfere, Gus?"

"I *know* they bloody will," he said. "Brody, the Vienna Station Chief, is an old sparring partner of mine. He'll screw this one up for us if he gets half a chance."

"And he knows it's on?" I asked.

"Joe Brody is a tough old bastard," said Stowe. "And he's very good at guessing."

Stowe stared at me and nodded his head. I wondered if that was intended to be some special warning for me.

"What do you make the time now?" Stowe asked while he was tapping his watch. Dicky told him, having consulted an elaborate wristwatch that had a tachometer, a perpetual calendar programmed to allow for leap years until the year 2100, and a little moon that waxed and waned. Stowe growled and hit his old timepiece with the flat of his hand, as if punishing it for failing to meet requirements.

Dicky got to his feet. "Okay, Gus. I'll come back to you with some ideas tomorrow." As Stowe opened his mouth to object, Dicky said, "Or perhaps this afternoon."

"Jesus Christ, Dicky," Stowe said. "I know how jealously you guard your little realm, and about this overdeveloped *amour-propre* that is a byword of all dealings with German Desk. But if you think I don't know you went to the Deputy D-G last week demanding Bernard's return because he was the only man for this job, you'd better think again."

Dicky's face went bright red with anger, or with embarrassment, or perhaps a combination of those emotions, over which English gentlemen have been supposed to exercise complete control. No doubt my presence added to his discomfort. "Did Sir Percy tell you that?" Dicky stammered.

"A little spy told me," said Stowe abrasively. Then: "Yes, what do you think Sir Percy and I talk about at the briefings, except what all you bloody controllers go sniveling to him about?"

Dicky was standing now, and he gripped the back of the chair he'd been occupying, like a prisoner in the dock. Flustered, he said, "I merely said . . . confirmed . . . that is . . . I told Sir Percy no more than I told you . . . that . . ."

"That Bernard could manage it? Yes, right. Well, why come in here pretending you hadn't already gone above my head?" The fly appeared, did a circuit, and went into a holding pattern around Stowe's cranium.

"I assure you that using Bernard was not my idea," said Dicky indignantly. Stowe smiled grimly.

So that was it. This meeting had been called specifically to stage a Departmental brawl, and it was now evident that the clash was not really about who should attend an off-the-record meeting with a KGB delegation. This bare-knuckle contest was calculated to rebuff some rash attempt by Dicky to assail Stowe's territory. It was my bad luck to be the blunt instrument that Stowe had chosen to beat upon Dicky's head.

In the manner of the English, Dicky's voice had grown quieter as he became angry. Now he weighed his words carefully as he went into an involved explanation. Dicky was so offended that it made me wonder if he was telling the truth. In that case it would mean that the Deputy had arranged my recall, and pretended that it was at Dicky's request, to conceal the fact from Stowe.

I was determined to get out of this quarrel. "May I get back to my desk?" I asked. "I'm expecting an important phone call." Stowe waved a hand in the air in a gesture that might have signaled agreement to my leaving the room but might have been rejecting something Dicky was saying. Or might have been a bid for the fly.

As I was leaving the room, Stowe's words overlaid Dicky's, and Dicky said, "Look here, Gus, I give you my solemn word that Bernard wasn't mentioned . . ." and then sat down again as if he was going to be there a long time.

With a sigh of relief, I stepped out into the corridor. The fly came with me.

That evening I was very happy to get back to my little house in Balaklava Road. Until now I had not felt much affection for this cramped and inconvenient suburban house, but after my cold and lonely bed in Berlin it had become a paradise. My unexpected arrival the previous evening had been discounted. Tonight was to be my welcome home.

The children had painted a bright banner—"Welcome

Home Daddy"—and draped it across the fireplace, where a real fire was flickering. Even though half of me was a Berliner, the sight of a coal fire always made me appreciate the many subtle joys of coming home. My wonderful Gloria had prepared a truly miraculous meal, as good as anything any local restaurant could have provided. She'd chilled a bottle of Bollinger. I sat in our neat little front room with the children squatting on the carpet and demanding to hear about my adventures in Berlin. Gloria had told them only that I was away on duty. After a couple of glasses of champagne on an empty stomach, I invented an involved story about tracking down a gang of thieves, keeping the narrative sufficiently improbable to get a few laughs.

I was more and more surprised at the manner in which the children were maturing. Amongst their ideas and jokes— comparatively adult and sophisticated, for the most part— the evidence of some childish pleasure would break in. Requests for a silly game or a treasure hunt or infantile song. How lucky I was to be with them while they grew up. What misplaced sense of patriotic duty persuaded Fiona to be elsewhere? And was her choice of priorities some bounden commitment that enslaved only the middle classes? I'd grown up amongst working-class boys from communities where nothing preceded family loyalty. Fiona had inflicted her moral obligations upon me and the children. She had forced us to contribute to her sacrifice. Why should I not feel grievously wronged?

A timer pinged. Effortlessly Gloria led the way into the dining room, where the table was set with our best china and glass. When the dinner came, it was delicious. "Would champagne be all right with the whole meal?" "Can a fish swim?" Another bottle of Bollinger and a risotto made with porcini. After that there was baked lobster. Then a soft Brie with French bread. And, to finish, huge apples baked with honey and raisins. A big jug of rich egg custard came with it. It was a perfect end to a wonderful meal. Sally sorted out each and every raisin and arranged them all around the edge of her plate, but Sally always did that. Billy counted them—"Rich man, poor man, beggarman, thief"—to foretell that Sally would marry a beggarman. Sally said she'd always hated that rhyme, and Gloria—optimist, feminist, and mathematician—rejected it as inaccurate on the grounds that it gave a girl only one chance in four of a desirable partner.

The children were both in that no-man's-land between childhood and adult life. Billy was dedicated to motorcars and beautiful handwriting. Sally was chosen to play Portia in *Julius Caesar* and gave us her rendition of her favorite scene. Her teddy bear played Brutus.

> *Within the bond of marriage, tell me, Brutus,*
> *Is it excepted I should know no secrets*
> *That appertain to you?*

Dismissing the marital prophecy, we all declared it to be a memorable family occasion.

"The children are old enough now to enjoy celebrating together as a family," said Gloria after they had been put to bed. She was standing looking into the dying embers of the open fire.

"I'll never forget this evening," I said. "Never."

She turned. "I love you, Bernard," said Gloria, as if she'd never said it before. "Now, before I sit down, do you want a drink or anything?"

"And I love you, Gloria," I said. I'd resisted voicing my feelings for too long, because I still felt a tinge of guilt about the difference in our ages, but my time away from her had changed things. Now I was happy to tell her how I felt. "You are wonderful," I said, taking her hand and pulling her down to sit with me on the sofa. "You work miracles for all of us. I should be asking you what I can do for you."

Her face was very close. She looked sad as she put a hand on my cheek as if touching a statue—a precious statue, but a statue nevertheless. She looked into my eyes as if seeing me for the very first time and said, "Sometimes, Bernard, I wish you would say you loved me without my saying it to you first."

"I'm sorry, darling. Did the children thank you for that delicious meal?"

"Yes. They are lovely children, Bernard."

"You are good for all of us," I said.

"I got all the food from Alfonso's," she confessed in the little-girl voice she affected sometimes. "Except the baked apples. I did the baked apples myself. And the egg custard."

"The baked apples were the best part of the welcome home."

"I hope the best part of the welcome home is yet to come," she said archly.

"Let's see," I said. She switched out the light. It was a full moon, and the back garden was swamped with that horrid blue sheen that made it look like a picture on television. I hate moonlight.

"What is it?"

"It's good to be home," I said, staring at the ugly little garden. She came up behind me and put her arm round me.

"Don't go away again," she said. "Not ever. Promise?"

"I promise." This was no time to reveal that Dicky and Stowe had got a little jaunt to Vienna lined up for me. She might have thought that I welcomed the prospect, and the truth was that I had some irrational dread of it. Vienna was not a big city and never has been: it is a little provincial town where narrow-minded peasants go to the opera, instead of the pig market, to exchange spiteful gossip. At least that's the way I saw it: in the past Vienna had not been a lucky town for me.

Chapter 7

I remember telling a young probationer named MacKenzie that, the more casual the briefing was, the more hazardous the operation you were heading into. It was the glib sort of remark that one was tempted to provide to youngsters like MacKenzie, who hung upon every word and wanted to do everything the way it was done in the training school. But I was to be given plenty of time to think about the truth of it. When, afterward, I considered the way in which I'd been brought into the Vienna operation, I inclined to the view that Stowe had been given no alternative: that he was instructed to choose me to go.

The operation was called Fledermaus—not Operation Fledermaus, since it had been decided that the frequency rate of the word "operation," and the way in which it was always followed by a code name, made it too vulnerable to the opposition's computerized code-breaking.

Certainly Fledermaus was cloaked in Departmental secrecy. These BOA—Briefing on Arrival—jobs always made me a little nervous, there being no way of preparing myself for whatever was to be done. It seemed as if the determination to keep this task secret from the Americans had resulted in a strictness of documentation, a signals discipline, and a delicacy of application that were seldom achieved when the aim was no greater than keeping things secret from the KGB.

I flew to Salzburg, a glittering toy town dominated by an eleventh-century fortress with a widely advertised torture chamber. The narrow streets of the town are crammed with

backpack tourists for twelve months of every year, and post-
cards, ice creams, and souvenirs are readily available. My
hotel—like almost everywhere else in Austria—was not far
from a house in which the seemingly restless Wolfgang Ama-
deus Mozart had resided.

My arrival had been timed to coincide with an important
philatelic auction, and I checked into the hotel together with
a dozen or more stamp dealers who'd come in on the same
flight. Their entries in the book showed a selection of home
addresses including Chicago, Hamburg, and Zurich. On the
reception desk a cardboard sign depicted a youthful Julie Andrews, arms outstretched, singing "The Sound of Music
tour—visit the places where the film was shot." Behind the
desk sat a fragile-looking old man in a black suit and stiff
collar. He used a pen that had to be dipped in an inkwell and
rocked a blotter upon each entry.

The hotel was gloomy, spacious, and comfortable. It was
the old-fashioned sort of grand hotel still to be widely found
in Austria, and the sweet synthetic scent of polish hung in the
air: an indication of manual work. An ancient elevator, crafted
of brass and mahogany, lurched upward inside a wire box with
a wheezing sound and sudden rattles that persuaded me to use
the stairs for the duration of my visit. There was even a man
in black waistcoat and green baize apron to carry my bag.

An Austrian named Otto Hoffmann had met me at the
airport and made sure I got a comfortable room in the hotel.
"At the back, overlooking the river," he said in his powerful
Austrian accent, and a chilly draft hit me as he opened the
window and peered out to be sure the water was still there.
"No traffic noise, no smells of cooking, no noise from the
terrace café. Tip the porter ten schillings." I did so.

Hoffmann was about forty years old, a short, hyperactive
man with merry little eyes, turned-up nose, and smiling
mouth. His manner, plus his large forehead, his pale unwrin-
kled skin, the way his small features were set in his globular

head, and his sparse hair, all gave him the appearance of an inebriated baby. I don't know how much Hoffmann had been told about Fledermaus, but he never mentioned that name. He knew that my cover story of being a stamp dealer was completely untrue, and he'd obviously been chosen for his knowledge of philately.

"And now I shall buy you a drink," he said as he closed the inner window and put his hand on the radiator to be sure the furnace was working. He meant a cup of weak tea. Because he kept his money in his back pocket, in a large roll secured with a rubber band, he had a disconcerting habit of tapping his behind to make sure his money was still there. He did this now.

He briefed me while we were sitting in the hotel lounge. It was a cavernous place with a celestial dome where angels cavorted and from which hung an impressive cut-glass chandelier. Around the walls there were potted plants set between other small tables and soft chairs where fellow guests, unable or unwilling to face the crowded streets, sat drinking lemon tea in tall glasses together with the rich pastries or gargantuan fruit-and-ice-cream concoctions that punctuate the long Austrian days.

He ordered two teas and a rum baba. He told me they were delicious here, but I was trying to give up rum babas.

"The auction sale consists almost entirely of Austrian and German material," he told me. "Of course the biggest market for that is Austria and Germany, but there will be American dealers, bidding as high as the present exchange rate of the dollar permits. Also, there will be compatriots of yours from London. London is an important trading center for philatelic material, and there are still many important German and Austrian collectors there. Mostly they are refugees who fled the Nazis and stayed in England afterward."

The waitress brought our order promptly. The tea came in a glass, its elaborate silver-plated holder fitted with a clip from which a spoon was suspended. She put two large chunks of lemon on the table and splashed a generous amount of an alcoholic liquid upon a shiny sponge cake which bore a crown of whipped cream. "Are you sure . . . ?" Hoffmann asked again. I shook my head. The waitress scribbled a bill, put it on the table, and sped away.

"And what am I doing here?" I asked, keeping my voice low.

He frowned. Then, as he understood me, he twitched his nose. On the table he had two beautiful catalogues. He passed one to me. It was an inch thick, its colored cover, magnificent art paper, and superbly printed illustrations making it look more like an expensive book of art reproductions than a commercial catalogue. They must have cost a fortune to produce. He opened it to show me the pictures of stamps and old envelopes, tapping the pages as some picture caught his attention. "Most of the really good items are from the old German states. Württemberg and Braunschweig, with a few rarities from Oldenburg, Hannover, and so on. Here too are some choice things from old German colonies: mail from China, Morocco, New Guinea, Togo, Samoa."

As he leafed through the catalogue, Herr Hoffmann lost the thread of his conversation. His eyes settled upon one page of the catalogue. "Some of these Togo covers sound wonderful," he said in an awed voice and read the descriptions with such concentration that his lips quivered. But he tore himself away from the wonderful offerings to show me the auction schedule printed on the inside cover. The hours—eight o'clock in the morning until approximately three o'clock in the afternoon, with an hour off for lunch—were listed to show the numbered lots that would be offered in each session. There were several thousand lots for the sale, which would last five days. "Some rich collectors employ agents to come to the auction and buy selected items on their behalf. The agent gets a nice fee. You will be such a person."

"Why don't they bid by post?"

He gave a slight grin. "Some collectors are suspicious of these auctions. When you bid by post, the amount you authorize the auctioneer to spend is supposed to be your tiptop offer. The auction house undertakes to charge you no more than one step above the next-best bid." He squeezed lemon into his tea and chased a pip around with his spoon but, after testing the side of his glass with his fingertips, decided it was too hot to drink.

"And?"

He gave another sly grin; his face slipped naturally into this expression, so that it was hard to know whether he was amused or not. "Whenever I bid by post, it always seems that someone has mysteriously kept bidding right up to one step below my maximum offer. I find I always pay the whole of whatever I bid." He picked up his fork and looked at his cake with the concentration a demolition expert gives to placing dynamite.

"So collectors have agents who make sure the bids and the bidders are real?" I said.

"Exactly. Even then it is difficult to know if there is a swindle. Sometimes there will be an auction official on the phone taking phone bids and the auctioneer will have in front of him the postal bids. It is difficult to be sure exactly what is happening." His conversation had been marked by the little smiles, but now he became serious as he took his fork and ate a section of his rum baba. "The pastry chef is Viennese," he confided as he savored it.

"And what else will the agent have to do?"

"He should have examined the lots for which he is going to bid, to make sure they are not damaged, or repaired, or forgeries."

"Are there many forgeries about?"

"There are some lots in this auction with estimated prices of about one hundred thousand U.S. dollars. That is a great deal of money by any standards. Many people pay less than that for the lease of a house to live in."

"You make your point, Mr. Hoffmann," I said. "But don't the auction houses have experts? Don't they know enough about stamps to recognize a forgery?"

"Of course they do. But auction houses get their percentage of the sale price. What inducement do they have for detecting a forgery? And what do they do then—accuse their customer of dishonesty? If the forgery is sold, they get a nice share of the money. If they reject it, they lose a customer and make an enemy and lose their percentage too." He stopped abruptly and ate some cake. Two men who'd been sitting at a nearby table had got up and were walking out. They were Americans, to judge by their clothes and their voices, neatly dressed, with fresh faces and polished shoes.

"You make them all sound like a lot of crooks," I said.

"I hope I don't. I know dealers I would trust my life to. But it is a precarious trade," said Hoffmann and smiled as if that was what he liked about it. I had the feeling that the idea of selling forgeries did not offend him in the way that it should have done. I wondered if he was in some way connected with the forgeries that the Department commissioned from time to time. Reading my mind perhaps, he gave me a sly grin.

"Are the people here all dealers?"

He looked round the sepulchral lounge. Waitresses, in formal black dresses and white starched aprons, padded silently to and fro across the white marble floor with trays of teas and cakes. The men, a mixed collection but for the most part middle-aged or elderly, were bent low, scribbling annotations in their catalogues and whispering conspiratorially to each other, rather as we were. "I know most of them," he said.

"And all men?"

"Yes, I don't know of one important female stamp dealer. There are virtually no female collectors, even. Should a woman inherit a collection, she sells almost immediately: you can depend upon it." He decided his tea was cool enough to drink and tasted it.

I was flipping through the catalogue. "How do they decide the estimated price?" I asked.

"Don't take much notice of that," he said. "That's just to whet your appetite. The estimated prices are far below what the auctioneer expects to get."

"How much below?"

"There is no way to answer such a question. Auction houses vary. Crazy things happen. Sometimes two agents arrive, both instructed with buy bids."

"What is a buy bid?"

"It means buy at any price."

"At any price?"

"The craving—the reckless lust—that some collectors show for an item they particularly want is difficult to believe. Some collectors become unbalanced; there is no other word to describe it." He fastidiously wiped his fingers on the napkin and then brought from his pocket a small folder of tough clear plastic. Inside it there was a used envelope (or what I'd learned to call a "cover") with a stamp (or what I'd learned to call an "adhesive") on it. "Look at that."

He handed me a white envelope adorned with quite an assortment of stamps and postmarks. Smudged and discolored, it had been readdressed twice and was such a mess that I would probably have thrown it straight into the waste bin had I found it on my desk. It meant nothing to me, but I looked at it with the kind of reverence he obviously expected of me. "Most attractive," I said.

"A man went to prison for that," said Hoffmann. "A respected man, chief clerk in an insurance office. He was a customer of mine: nearly fifty years old, with three children and a pensionable job. He had a decent little collection. I'd provided quite a lot of the things myself. He was knowledgeable about his own specialty. He regularly gave talks, and

displayed his stamps to philatelic societies. Then he heard that
a well-known collector had died and he knew that this cover
was amongst the collection. It would be the gem that com-
pleted his collection. He asked me if I could find out when it
was coming on the market. He was determined. By a lucky
chance, I knew about it. I guessed the widow would dispose
of everything: they always do. You don't like to go sniffing
round too soon. It upsets the family. On the other hand, if you
wait too long some other dealer will go in there and pick up
the whole collection . . . buy it up for nothing sometimes,
when the relatives don't know what they have inherited. There
are some unscrupulous people in this business, I can tell you."

"I'm beginning to believe it," I said.

"Is there something wrong with your tea?"

"No. It's delicious."

"You're not drinking it."

"I'll get around to it."

"The widow was a rich woman. The collection was unim-
portant to her. When I went there and asked her about the
collection, she decided to make me her agent, to value, and
then sell, the whole lot of it. It put me in a difficult position
in respect of the other collector, but I never really considered
that he was seriously in the market for it anyway. There are
only thought to be four or five covers like that one. The last
time one of them was auctioned, it fetched fifty thousand
dollars, and that was almost ten years ago. Even if this one
fetched no more than that one did, my insurance-company
friend just didn't have access to that sort of money."

I looked at the cover. "Fifty thousand dollars?" Could it
be true?

Hoffmann nodded. No smile this time. They were serious
people, these philatelists. "In this year's catalogue the adhesives alone are listed at nearly that—of course catalogue values don't mean a lot, but I have a prospect in Munich. . . . He's
phoned me three times about it. He is becoming demented

with the thought of owning it and insists that I let him see it.
. . . I am interested in hearing his assessment of its value. He
spends a lot on his collection."

"And your insurance friend?"

"The fool! He stole the money from his company. Filed
a false claim, forged a check, and made it payable to himself.
Can you believe it? He was detected immediately. Pleaded
guilty. His company said they had to prosecute him: there
were too many other employees who might try the same trick.
They were right, of course, and he knows that. I went to see
him yesterday."

"In prison?" I handed the cover back to Hoffmann.

"Yes, in Graz. I gave evidence for him at the trial. I said
he was honest and of good character, but of course the evidence said he was a thief."

"He must have been pleased to see you," I said.

"I'm selling his collection too. He's flat broke now; the
lawyers took his last penny. He's selling everything." Hoffmann put the cover back into his pocket.

"Aren't you nervous about carrying a valuable thing like
that?"

"Nervous? No."

"What was the sentence?"

"My client?" He spoke through a mouthful of baba.

"The insurance man."

He took his time in swallowing cake and then took some
tea. "Five years. I took him a color photo of that cover." He
tapped his pocket. "And the prison governor gave him special
permission to have the picture in his cell." Hoffmann sipped
tea. "The joke is that I'm beginning to think it's a forgery. In
which case it's worthless." He laughed down at his plate as if
trying to resist it but finally ate the last of the cake.

"Did you know that right from the start?"

"Not for sure." He wiped his lips.

"You suspected it?"

"I put it under the ultraviolet light. You can't be too careful. Then I took it to someone who knows. I'm still not certain one way or the other." He drank more tea. "Are you sure you wouldn't like a cream cake? They are delectable here, as light as a feather."

"No thanks."

"It's a weakness of mine," he confessed. He'd finished the baba but left a huge blob of thick cream on the side of his plate. "Not even apple strudel?"

"No."

"You go into the auction and bid for Lot Number 584. It will come up in the morning, at about ten o'clock, but it would be safer if you were there a little early." I looked at him. I recognized that this was my briefing: London Central had sent me here to buy. "Pay cash for it. It is estimated at one thousand schillings. I will leave you three thousand Austrian schillings; that should be enough. Take it to Vienna and phone von Staiger. You've heard of the Baron, I suppose?"

"No," I said.

He looked surprised. "You won't actually meet him, but there will be instructions for you." He passed me a visiting card. Its printed content consisted only of Staiger's name and title and the description "Investment Consultant." In minuscule handwriting a Vienna address had been added in pencil. The use of aristocratic titles was illegal in Austria, but Staiger, like many others, seemed not to care about that.

From his back pocket Hoffmann took his roll of money and counted out the Austrian notes. With it there was a small printed receipt form, of the sort sold in stationery shops. "Sign there, please," he said.

I signed for the money. "You won't be at the auction tomorrow?"

"Alas, no. I go to Munich tonight." He smiled as he made sure my signature was legible and put the receipt away in his wallet. "Hold up one of the number cards to bid. Sit at the front, where the auctioneer can see you, and then no one else in the room knows you are bidding. Your lot will be ready for collection about five minutes after you've bought it. By paying cash, you won't have to establish your credit or say who you are."

"Will I be seeing you again?"

"I don't think so," he said. He waved a spoon at me.

"Is there anything else you are going to tell me?"

"No," he said. "From this point onward Baron Staiger runs the show." He used his fork to scoop up the huge dollop of cream and put it in his mouth. There was a look of pure bliss on his face as he held it on his tongue and then swallowed it. "You haven't drunk your tea," he said.

"No," I said.

He got up and clicked his heels as he said goodbye. I sat there for a few minutes more, sipping my tea and looking round the room. I noticed he'd left me with the bill.

I took the catalogue he'd left for me and strolled out onto the terrace that overlooked the river Salzach. It was too chilly for anyone else to be seated there, but I relished the idea of being alone.

I looked up Lot Number 584. It came in the section of the auction designated "Deutsches Reich Flugpost—Zeppelin-belege" and was written in that unrestrained prose style used by men selling time-share apartments on the Costa Brava.

Lot 584. Sieger Katalog 62B. Brief. Bunttafel IV. ÖS 1,000,— 1930 Südamerikafahrt, Paraguaypost. Schmuckbrief mit Flugpostmarken, entwertet mit violettem Paraguay-Zeppelin-Sonderstempel "Por Zeppelin" dazu violetter Paraguay-Flugpoststempel 16. 5. Brief nach Deutschland, in dieser Erh. ungewöhnl. schöner und extrem seltener Beleg, Spitzenbeleg für den grossen Sammler.

From which I gathered that the 1930 cover illustrated in color on Plate 4 was expected to fetch one thousand Austrian schillings. It had been sent from Paraguay on the *Graf Zeppelin* airship with all the necessary postal formalities, and, that having become a great philatelic rarity, it was available as centerpiece for some "big collector."

The color photo showed a well-preserved light-blue envelope with several different rubber stamps and adhesives, addressed to a Herr Davis in Bremen. It didn't look like anything worth a thousand schillings.

As I was sitting there by the river and staring up at the Hohensalzburg fortress, which blocked off half the skyline, the glass doors swung open and a man joined me on the terrace. At first he seemed unaware of my presence. He walked across to the metal balcony and checked how far there was to fall, the way most people do.

As the man turned to obtain a better view of the castle across the river, I had a chance to study him. It was one of the Americans I'd seen earlier. He was dressed in a short forest-green hunter's coat, fashionably equipped with big pockets, straps, and loops. His hair was streaked with gray and neatly trimmed, and on his head he wore a smart loden cap. He spoke without preamble: "When I visited Mozart's birthplace yesterday, it was one of the greatest experiences of my life." He had a rich cowboy voice that belied his declared emotion. "Number nine Getreidegasse: ever been there?"

"Once . . . a long time back," I said.

"You need to go real early," he went on. "It soon gets to be full of these pimple-faced backpackers drinking Coke out of cans."

"I'll watch out for that," I said and opened my catalogue hoping he'd go away.

"Mozart gets himself born on the third floor, and that's inconvenient, so they only let you look at the museum downstairs. It's kind of dumb, isn't it?"

"I suppose so."

"I really go for Mozart," he said. *"Così fan Tutte* has got to be the ultimate musical experience. Sure, critics go for *Don Giovanni*, and Mozart's wife, Constanze, said the maestro rated *Idomeneo* number one, but *Idomeneo* was his first smash hit. The sort of box-office receipts *Idomeneo* rang up in Munich made young Wolfgang a star. But *Così* has real class. Consider the psychological insight, the dramatic integrity, and the musical elegance. Yes, sir, and it is sweet, sweet all the way through. I play *Così* in the car: I know every note, every word. My theory is that those two girls weren't fooled by the disguises: they wanted to have fun swapping partners. That's what it's really about: swapping. Mozart couldn't make that clear, because it would have been too shocking. But think about it."

"I will," I promised.

"And shall I tell you something about that great little guy? He could compose in his head: reams of music. Then he'd sit down and write it all out. And, do you know, he'd let his wife prattle on about her tea parties and be saying 'So what did you say?' and 'What did she tell you?' And all the time he'd be writing out the score of a requiem or an opera or a string quartet, keeping up a conversation at the same time. How do you like that?"

"It's not easy to do," I said feelingly.

"I can see you want to get back to your catalogue. I know there's some kind of big-deal stamp collector's shindig in the hotel. But I never reckoned you as a stamp collector, Bernie."

I tried not to react suddenly. I slowly raised my eyes to his and said, "I collect airmail covers."

He smiled. "You don't recognize me, do you, Bernie?"

I tried to put his face into a context but I couldn't recognize him. "No," I said.

"Well, no reason you should. But I remember seeing you when I used to share an office with Peter Underlet, and then

Underlet went to Jakarta and I went to Bonn and worked for Joe Brody. Jesus, Bernie. Have you forgotten?"

"No," I said, although I had forgotten. This man was a stranger to me.

"On vacation, huh?"

"I had a few days' leave due."

"And you came to Salzburg. Sure, screw the sunshine. This is the spot to be if you are looking for a chance to get away from it all. Are you . . ." He paused and delicately added, ". . . with anyone?"

"All alone," I said.

"I wish we could have had dinner together," said the man regretfully. "But I have to be back in Vienna tonight. Tomorrow I'm on the flight to Washington, D.C."

"Too bad," I said.

"I just had to make this pilgrimage," he said. "Sometimes there are things you just have to do. Know what I mean?"

"Yes," I said.

"Well, good luck with the stamp collecting. What did you say it was . . . Zeppelinpost?"

"Yes," I said, but of course I hadn't told him that. I'd just said airmail.

He waved and went back through the doors to the lounge. If he'd been sent by Joe Brody with the task of making me squirm, he'd done rather well. I closed the catalogue and resumed my contemplation of the grim gray walls of Festung Hohensalzburg on the far side of the river. I needed a belly laugh. Perhaps, after I'd had a stiff drink, I'd stroll across town, catch the funicular up to the fortress, and take a look round the torture chamber.

Chapter 8

I didn't eat dinner in the hotel. I found a charming little place near the Mozart statue, or it might have been near the Papageno fountain or the Mozart footbridge. I heard the music of an accordion playing a spirited version of "The Lonely Goatherd" and went in. The interior was done in dark wood paneling with red check tablecloths. It was almost empty. On the walls there were shiny copper pans together with the actual marionettes that had been used to perform the Mozart operas in the world-famous Marionettentheater. Or maybe they were plastic replicas. The waiter strongly recommended the breaded pork schnitzel but, as my mother told me, you should never trust a man in lederhosen. It took several glasses of the local Weizengold wheat beer to help me recover. The accordion music was on tape.

I got back to the hotel late. There were men everywhere: some standing about in the lobby, others drinking solemnly in the bar, and all of them eyeing each other warily. I knew they were stamp dealers, for I could detect the ponderous gravity that so often attends the first evening when men are gathered together for business purposes.

Even the serious drinkers were quiet. A group near the bar were speaking in that stilted German that is usually the sign of the expatriate. One said, "I don't know why people say the Austrians are venal; it took them more than a century to discover how much money they could make out of Mozart."

His companion shushed him. Rightly so, for even his quiet voice was audible on the other side of the hotel. Then suddenly there was loud shuffling and squeaking noise from the revolving doors and into the lobby there came two young couples. They had gleaming complexions and perfect wavy hair. Their clothes were chic and expensive, and the women wore glittering jewelry, and they all had that boisterous self-confidence with which the wealthy are so often endowed. They were not stamp dealers. Everyone turned to see them, for their sudden entrance into the somber hotel lobby was unwelcome, like noisy, brightly colored TV advertisements interrupting the soft nostalgia of an old black-and-white film.

They must have sensed the feelings their unexpected appearance had provoked, for they became quieter and their movements more composed as they made their way across the marble floor. The lift was not working, so they went up the grand staircase to their rooms. The eyes of every man followed the progress of the glamorous people, the women with their long dresses decorously lifted as they ascended the stairs, the young men murmuring together.

I looked around for the mysterious American but there was no sign of him. I had done enough for one day: I went to bed. As I put my head on the pillow, a clock began to chime eleven, and soon another one joined in.

The auction started exactly on time, as most things do in that part of the world. It was all Zeppelin mail today, starting with the earliest examples, mail of the "pioneer" airships *Viktoria Luise* and the *Schwaben*. Then came one postcard from the airship *Deutschland* which bore the airship company's red stamp, and the bidding just kept going and going until it reached the sky. There were three men after the card, and the room went silent as the auctioneer just kept his litany of numbers going with glances from one side to the other. The bidding stopped suddenly as two of the men seemed to decide simultaneously that there was no longer a margin of profit left.

Crack, went the hammer, and the reaction was a sudden shuffle of tense muscles and released breaths. They were all writing the price into their catalogues. This would set a higher value for such items and would mean a reappraisal of their stocks.

The room wasn't crowded, but there was a continuous flow of people as specialists interested in particular items came in and took part in some spirited bidding and then went to drink coffee in the glassed-in sidewalk café, or out on the terrace to smoke and chat with their colleagues.

They must have been running a bit behind time that morning, for the auctioneer kept glancing at his watch and there seemed to be a general tendency to hurry things along.

As the auction reached 1914, and the wartime Zeppelins, there was something of an exodus that left only a couple of dozen specialists. Whether this was because the First World War items were a neglected part of the stamp collector's world, or because this particular auction contained poor examples, I had no way of knowing. But when the auctioneer announced the beginning of a Hungarian collection of *Graf Zeppelin* mail, sold by order of the executor of the deceased man's estate, almost every chair was taken, and there were some who preferred to remain standing at the very back.

I was ready well before Lot 584 was offered for sale. Face down on the table in front of me there was a large white card printed with a big black number 12. That was my number, and when the bidding for 584 began I tipped it up so that it was visible to the auctioneer. For a fraction of a second he met my eyes to tell me that I was in the auction, and increased the bid accordingly. Behind me there must have been a dozen or more bids offered somewhat mechanically. The price kept going up, and it was hard to know whether my raised card made any difference. The auctioneer looked into the distance and deliberately gave no clue as to where the bids were coming from.

The bidding slowed. That first flurry of bids had gone, leaving more serious ones. "One thousand nine hundred!" he called, and as the total increased each bid was a bigger jump. Suddenly we were into bigger bids. I tipped the card to keep the bidding going, but someone behind me was interested too. We were now at double the estimated price, and the bids were still coming!

The auctioneer didn't look surprised. That morning there had been other things to surprise him more: items ignored and items fetching three or four times their estimates. I tried to remember how much cash I had in my wallet over and above the money that Hoffmann had left with me. "Two thousand five hundred!" They were hundred-schilling increments now, and still going.

"Two thousand six hundred!" Behind me there were two other people bidding for the damned envelope. I turned but could not see either of my rivals.

"Two thousand nine hundred!" The auctioneer was looking at me now, an eyebrow lifted. I showed my bidding card again, and he lifted his eyes to somewhere at the back of the room.

"Three thousand . . ." And even before he said it, he was looking over my head and saying, "Three one . . . Three two . . ."

His eyes came back to me. I held the card resolutely upright, and his eyes passed discreetly over me and to the room. "Three three . . . Three four . . . Three five . . ." He hadn't even brought his eyes back to me. There must be two of them fighting it out. And they weren't slowing. I turned to see the room. One of the auction officials was standing in the corner at a telephone. He lifted his hand. So it was a phone-in customer who was bidding against me, plus someone at the back of the room.

"Three thousand seven hundred schillings!"

Some sort of pause had come in the bidding, for the auctioneer's eyes came back to me. "Three thousand seven hundred schillings at the back of the room," he said.

I nodded. The auctioneer said, "Three eight at the front of the room."

From somewhere behind me I heard a German voice say, "Three nine," and then another German voice say, "Four thousand on the phone."

"Four thousand one hundred at the back of the room," said the auctioneer. And then, immediately, "Four two . . . three . . . four, five." Even the auctioneer was surprised. "Four thousand six hundred at the back of the room."

He was looking at me. I nodded. He looked up and said, "Four . . ." and then said, "Five thousand one hundred schillings to the back of the room."

I turned to get a proper look at who was bidding and was in time to see the man at the telephone wave a hand to indicate the bidder had stopped.

"For the second time: five thousand one hundred schillings," said the auctioneer, looking at me quizzically.

I lifted the numbered card. "Five two at the front."

For a moment I thought the bidding had stopped. I was relieved. If I turned out all my pockets and persuaded the hotel to take an English check, I might put together that amount of cash. Then the auctioneer said, "Five three . . ." and then, without looking in my direction at all, he said, "Five four . . . Five five."

Someone else had joined the bidding, and before I could catch my breath the price was at six thousand Austrian schillings.

The auctioneer was tapping his hammer again. "For the third time . . ." I shook my head. "Gone!"

Once again the Department had given their orders and then so arranged things that the man in the field could not carry them through. I put the numbered card in my pocket as a souvenir and got to my feet. I wanted to see the man who now owned what I'd been sent here to buy.

He made no attempt to avoid detection. He looked sixty-ish; wavy hair, a bit overweight, but physically rather trim. He was wearing a Black Watch tartan jacket and dark slacks with a spotted bow tie. His neatly trimmed gray beard and gold-rimmed bifocals all added up to an American college professor on sabbatical. He was leaning against the edge of a table, and as he saw me he smiled and edged his way past the other men to join me. I waited for him.

"Oh boy! I wondered what was happening," he said in English with a soft American accent. "I thought you maybe had a buy bid too."

"No," I said. "I had a limit."

"And am I glad you did. We could have gone through the ceiling. Can I buy you a drink?"

"Thanks," I said.

"I haven't seen you around before."

"I work in London," I said.

As we reached the door, he asked one of the auction staff where he could pick up his purchase and was told to go to the cashier's office—a room on the ground floor at the back of the hotel. It was all well organized, and evident that the same firm held auctions here regularly.

"Jesus, look at that rain, and it's becoming hail," he said as we walked past the bookstall and along the corridor.

There was a line waiting outside the cashier's office when we got there. We joined the line. "It was a good item, but I've seen better," said the man, continuing with the conversation. "My name is Johnson, Bart Johnson. I work in Frankfurt, but I come from Chicago. Are you a Zeppelinpost expert?"

"No," I said.

He looked at me and nodded. "Well, *Graf Zeppelin* is a kind of hero for me. I was always crazy about airships. It started when I was a kid and someone gave me a piece of fabric from the *Shenandoah,* which crashed in Ohio in 1925. I've still got it, framed on the wall. Yes, back in my office I keep a file on everything. And I looked up Berezowski's *Handbuch der Luftpostkunde.* . . . You know that, of course?"

"I'm not sure I do."

"Jesus, I depend on Berezowski even more than I rely on the *Sieger Katalog.* " In his hands he had a catalogue and a blue folder containing clippings and handwritten notes. He flipped it open to refer to it.

I sensed that some reaction was expected so I said, "Do you really?"

"Berezowski's 1930 book is a classic for this kind of reference. It's been reprinted: you can still buy copies. I'll give you an address and you can get one mailed. But in the clippings I came across an article that Dr. Max Kronstein wrote in the *Airpost Journal* in January 1970. He says the Paraguay post office refused to accept International Reply Coupons; *that's* why Paraguay mail is so rare. The only mail with Paraguay adhesives came from residents—foreign residents."

"That's very interesting," I said.

"Yes, isn't it." He flipped the file closed and put a gold pencil into his pocket. "And ever since Sieger listed the mail to Europe as being worth ten percent more than mail to the U.S.A., our customers prefer it. In fact, I looked up Kummer: he says that only sixty items went to the U.S.A. and about a hundred and eighty to Europe, so I'd say it was the other way around. Mind you, you can never be sure, because mail sent to Europe might have been destroyed by the war, while items in American collections remained safe." He kept a finger in the file, as if it might be necessary for him to prove these contentions to me by references to it.

"Yes," I said.

"Sure. I know. I mustn't go on so much. You seem kind of disappointed. Was it for your own collection?"

"No, it was just a job."

"Well, don't take it to heart, fella. There's a whole lot more Zeppelinpost out there waiting to be bought. Right?" I nodded. He stroked his beard and smiled. The line moved forward as some dealers emerged from the office with their purchases.

"Say, who was that character I saw you talking with on the terrace yesterday?"

"An acquaintance," I said.

"What's his name?"

"I've been trying to remember," I said. "I thought he was with you."

"Thurkettle," he supplied. "He said his name was Ronnie Thurkettle. So he's not a buddy of yours?"

"I hardly know him." Now I remembered the name, but his face was still not familiar to me.

"Say, what kind of work does that guy do? He's not in the stamp business, is he? I used to see him in Frankfurt and all around, but I never figured what kind of job he has."

"Works for the State Department," I said. "But that's all I know about him."

"He buttonholed me yesterday. He came on real friendly, but he just wanted to pick my brains about Zeppelinpost. He doesn't know the first thing about airmail. He was expecting me to explain the catalogue to him. I told him to go and get a good book on the subject. I'm not about to give lessons to guys like him: he's not my kind. Know what I mean?"

"How did he take it?"

"Take it? He backed off and changed the subject. He's not a friend of mine. No way. I just used to see him around when I was in public relations. Frankfurt—I'd see him at those little shindigs the contractors give to entertain visitors, cute little weenies on a stick and diluted martinis. You know. I guessed he was with the government. Washington is written all over him: right? But I thought maybe he was a civilian with the army."

"No," I said. "State."

"I stay well away from those guys. They bring trouble, and I don't need it." The line moved again, until we were at the front. A soft buzzer sounded, and the security guard signaled for us to go in. There was not much room in the cashier's office. A morose clerk looked through a small metal grille. Behind him there was a girl with a table piled with philatelic covers and cards in transparent plastic and a cashbox full of checks and money of all denominations. "Johnson's the name. Johnson, Bartholomew H.," said my companion. "Lot 584. Six thousand schillings. I have an account with you." The room had an unfamiliar smell, like incense. Maybe it was the clerk's after-shave. Or the money.

The man behind the grille turned the pages of the book. "What number?" he asked.

"Lot 584." Johnson now had a thick bundle of Austrian money in his hand. He riffled it. It seemed as though all these stamp dealers liked cash.

"There must be a mistake," said the man behind the grille.

"Johnson, Bartholomew H. I have an account. Six thousand schillings. If you want cash, I have it here." He flip-flopped the wad of money and said, "I'm not going to spend ten thousand schillings before getting on the plane this afternoon."

The clerk said, "Lot 584 went for six thousand two hundred schillings. A telephone bid."

"No, sir!" said Johnson. "I got it."

"You have made a mistake, sir," said the man behind the grille.

"*You've* made the mistake, buddy. Now, give me my cover."

"I'm sorry."

"I insist. It's mine! Now, let me have it." He was angry.

"I'm afraid it's no longer here," said the clerk. "It went off with a lot of other material. It's for a very well-known client."

"What am I?" said Johnson angrily.

"I'm sorry you are disappointed, sir," he said. "But there is really nothing I can do, and there are many other customers waiting."

"How do you like that?" He shouted so loudly that the security man looked round the door, but the steam was going out of him.

"Let's get out of here," I said, a number-one rule amongst the people I work with being: Never get tangled with the law.

"You haven't heard the last of this!" Johnson said to the man behind the grille.

"I'm very sorry, sir. I really am."

Once out in the corridor again, we both became objects of curiosity for those who had heard Johnson shouting. He brushed the front of his suit self-consciously and said, "Come on. Let's get a drink."

"Good idea," I said.

It took him several minutes to recover his composure. He seemed really rattled. If it was all an act it was an Oscar-worthy performance. Once seated at the counter in the bar he said, "What the hell was that all about? You were there. You saw me get that damned cover. Or am I going nuts?"

"You're not going nuts," I said.

"Did you tell me your name?"

"No, I didn't."

"I'm not going nuts," said Johnson. "It's these Austrians who are going nuts. Give me a double Scotch," he called to the barman. He raised his eyes and I nodded. "Make it two double Scotches."

"Let me pay," I said. "I suddenly seem to have a lot of cash."

"Me too," he said and laughed. "I've got to get out of here; these people drive me crazy. Want a ride to the airplane? Or have you got a car?"

"When?"

"I'm catching the seven o'clock plane to Vienna," he said, and I told him that would suit me just fine. The whisky calmed him down. I let him talk about his stamps while I made appropriate interjections and thought about other things.

Later I walked upstairs with him. His room was near the stairs, and mine along the same corridor. As he let himself into his room he said, "I'll take a bath and maybe grab a sandwich. See you in the lobby about five-thirty?"

"Right," I said.

Then, as his door closed, I heard him say, "Well, what about that?" and I wondered what he was referring to. But by that time I'd grown used to his spirited disposition and decided that he was talking to himself.

There was plenty of time. I wondered whether to phone London and tell them that someone else had bought the cover but decided to put it off for an hour or two. By that time I'd be speaking to a Duty Officer rather than to Dicky or Stowe.

I went to the window and stared down at the rain-swept street. The tourists were indomitable. Buttoned tight in long, brightly colored plastic coats, their feet encased in transparent overshoes, with hoods with drawstrings tightened to reveal small circles of grim red faces, they trekked past like combat-hardened veterans resolutely moving up to the fighting line. I got a glass from the bathroom and poured myself a shot of duty-free Scotch. I'd promised Gloria not to touch the hard stuff while I was away this time, but that was not taking into account the fiasco in the auction room, and the way in which I would soon have to explain my failure.

I kicked my shoes off, stretched out on the bed, and dozed. All day—like an errant poodle tugging its leash—my mind had tried to explore some other time and place. And yet these fugitive memories remained fuzzy, gray, and unfocused. It was when I closed my eyes and relaxed that my memories sniffed out what had been bothering me all day.

"Deuce" Thurkettle! Jesus Christ, how could I ever have forgotten Deuce Thurkettle, even if he now preferred to be known as Ronnie? I'd never known him, but his dossier was something not to be forgotten.

"Deuce" not in the sense of runner-up, quitter, or coward, the way the word is sometimes used, nor a "pair" in a poker game. This man was "Deuce" because of the barbaric double murder for which he'd gone to prison. Deuce Thurkettle came to Berlin after being released from some high-security prison in Arizona, where he was serving a life sentence for murder in the first degree.

Perhaps it was a long, dull afternoon after too much Southern-fried chicken when some bright young fellow sitting behind a desk in Langley, Virginia, had got this brilliant idea of sending a convicted murderer into Berlin on a tourist visa, to get rid of a troublesome KGB agent who had so far eluded all attempts to incriminate him.

I remembered the Deuce Thurkettle file and the way I'd read it all the way through without pause. I suppose to some extent I read it because I was not supposed to see it. It was a CIA document buried deep in the dank, dark place where the CIA buried their secrets. Or that's where it should have been. Poor old Peter Underlet had taken it home with him. He had shown it to me one evening after the two of us had dinner—and two bottles of lovely Château Beychevelle 1957—in his apartment. I could recollect each page of that bizarre insight into the cloistered mentality of the administrator: ". . . and Thurkettle's knowledge of electronic timing devices, sophisticated locks, modern handguns, and explosives, added to his proved physical resources, qualify him as an outstanding field agent."

Underlet had opened the file to that page of a long report from Langley before he slammed the whole thing onto my knees. "Look at that," said Underlet bitterly. "That's what those shits in Washington think about field agents. Without any training or experience this murdering bastard becomes a field agent overnight—an outstanding field agent, it says there."

I remember Underlet slumping back in the armchair and drinking his wine and saying nothing while I read the file right through. Deuce Thurkettle; how could I have forgotten him? The first of a trio of hit men who came unbidden and unwelcome to the CIA offices of Europe during that unhappy period.

Afterward—weeks afterward—we talked about it again. By that time I had become more indignant about the morality of Washington, D.C., than about what the episode revealed of the desk man's feelings about field agents.

I was no longer stretched out; I was sitting up in bed, fully aware of the racing pulse and tension that come when the mind is on the verge of remembering some important image. What happened to those three jailbirds? All three were given the elaborate new identities that later became the reward for mafiosi who turned state's evidence. Thurkettle: Thurkettle. There was speculation that he murdered a supermarket tycoon in Cologne—a man with whose wife Thurkettle had a love affair. I wasn't sure that was Thurkettle. Had Thurkettle's name been in any of those "most wanted—confidential" lists? My memory could just not get hold of it.

By now I was on my feet. I paced the room, knowing beyond any doubt that it all added up to a conclusion that would seem obvious when the questions were asked. Obvious, that is to say, to the questioner.

I decided to ask Johnson some more questions: about

Thurkettle and anything else that emerged. I put on my shoes and went down the corridor to knock at the door of Johnson's room. There was no response. I turned the knob and found the door unlocked.

Inside, the bedroom was empty. A clean shirt, underclothes, and socks were laid out on the bed, in the careful way a valet might arrange clothes for a fastidious employer. From the bathroom there came the sound of water running. The door was closed. Johnson called, "Put it down on the table. There's a tip there for you."

"It's not room service: it's me," I said.

"You're early, aren't you?" His voice was distorted like that of a man cleaning his teeth.

"That guy Thurkettle. I remembered something about him."

"Give me fifteen minutes." There was a splutter, as if the tooth cleaning was proceeding energetically.

Okay, I thought, everything is normal. I went back to my room. I don't know how long I sat there before the sound of the explosion made me jump out of the chair and run for the door. Afterward the newspapers said the Forensic Department estimated it at three hundred grams of explosive, but that amount would have taken the bathroom door off, and maybe the wall and me too.

But it was a loud bang all the same, and that unmistakable stink of explosive came rolling down the corridor to meet me. My mind went blank. Experience said hide under the bed; curiosity made me wonder what had happened.

For better or worse, I hurried along the corridor and into Johnson's room. I went to the bathroom and grabbed the handle as the door fell off its hinges. I don't know what kind of explosive they'd used, but the inside of the bathroom was black with soot and dirt. Maybe that had come from something else. The washbasin was the center of the damage: the mirror had disappeared, except for a couple of splinters dangling from the fixing screws. Below it, looking like some example of modern sculpture, the blue china pedestal remained in position, supporting one elegant slice of basin.

What remained of Johnson was on the floor, face up and twisted between the water-closet bowl and the bidet. There were appalling burn marks on the torso, and his clothes were scorched. There was very little blood; the heat of the explosion had cauterized the blood vessels. Around him there were hundreds of pieces of broken chinaware. I didn't have to look twice to know what had happened. His hand was only a stump, and what was left of him above the neck was wet and shiny and spread all over the marble floor.

It was the electric-razor bomb, an old trick, but I'd never seen the results of one before. Find out what model of razor your victim uses, fill one with any decent plastic explosive— shaping it for something really directional—and fit a neat little detonator (made in Taiwan—please state on order form whether 110 v. or 220 v.), and he'll obligingly hold it to his head and switch on the electricity!

Poor Johnson. Behind me excited voices indicated that people were crowding into the bedroom now, so I slid back amongst them, vociferously asking everyone what had happened. Johnson. Had there been someone waiting for him when he went into his room? Was that remark, "Well, what about that?," rhetoric, or had he been talking to a visitor, someone like Deuce Thurkettle, whose "knowledge of electronic timing devices, sophisticated locks, modern handguns, and explosives, added to his proved physical resources, qualify him as an outstanding field agent?"

And if Thurkettle was the killer, why? Or, to turn the whole thing on its end: was Thurkettle some sort of deep-cover operator for whom a bizarre background story of a murder conviction had been fabricated? If so, who killed Johnson, if Johnson was his real name? And all the time another part of my mind was telling me that London Central would not expect me to phone them now. Not even Stowe would expect me to make contact, not with this mess to extricate myself from, and the likelihood of the Austrian police listening to phone calls. Despite everything, I was somewhat comforted by that reprieve.

Chapter 9

My plane took off from Salzburg Airport in a Wagnerian electric storm that lit up the Alps with great flashes of blue light and thunder that shook the world. Rain beating upon the metal skin was audible over the Muzak, and the plane slewed and yawed as it fought the gusting winds and climbed through the narrow path between the mountains.

I still had to get the horrific vision of that torn-apart body out of my mind. With nothing to read except the flight magazine, I took the stamp catalogue from my bag and looked again at the cover I'd failed to get. I studied the picture closely and tried to understand what demon drove men to amass expensive collections of these pretty little artifacts. The color photo was so realistic that it seemed almost as if I could lift it from the page. Using the scissors of my Swiss army knife, I cut out the illustration and put it in my wallet.

It was late when we descended for the landing in Vienna. The storm had passed over, and the stars were shining in a moonless sky. The address that Hoffmann had provided for me was in the Inner City. I looked again at the map of Vienna that I'd picked up from the airline counter. It was a brightly colored depiction of the city—with isometric drawings of such buildings as the Imperial Palace—garlanded with adverts for such diversions as a "revue bar," a "contact club sauna," and "private escort services," all captioned in German, Arabic, and Japanese. Close study of the map revealed that my destination was a side street off Kärntner Strasse, a well-known thoroughfare which runs from the Opera Ring—which surrounds the Inner City—to St. Stephan's Cathedral at its center.

It was dark when the taxi dropped me outside the huge shape of the State Opera House just after the curtain descended on the final act of *Der Barbier von Sevilla*. Many doors opened simultaneously, so that yellow rectangles of light fell out onto the pavement. Then people emerged, not many at first, just a dozen or so, silently exploring the rain-shiny streets with an air of disoriented caution, as intergalactic voyagers might emerge from a huge stone spaceship. From inside there came the muffled roar of applause. Moments later the ensemble's final bow released a flood of people, and these were clamorous and elated. A swirling press of them swept across the forecourt and the pavement and into the road with no thought of the traffic, laughing and calling to each other, like upper-class felons unexpectedly released from imprisonment.

"*Fussgängerzone,*" explained the driver, executing an illegal U turn and positioning his cab ready for the homegoing crowds, who were already raising their arms to hail him. "You have to walk from here." By now the street was filled with people dressed in the sort of amazing fur coats and evening clothes that are *de rigueur* when Germans or Austrians attend a cultural event. A group of such overdressed operagoers besieged the cab as it came to a stop and began bidding for it in loud voices that quickly became an argument between competing groups.

I paid off the driver and pushed my way through the hordes of people who were still spewing from the opera-house doors. But as I progressed, the crowds thinned, for few people were heading into the narrow streets of the city center. Soon

I was alone, and my footsteps echoed as I walked past the dark shops and closed cafés. Downtown Vienna goes to sleep early.

The address I wanted was in a narrow, ill-lit *Gasse,* an alley of antique shops, their façades neglected and dilapidated in that way that only the most exclusive antique shops are. Through the gloomy shopwindows, rich Oriental rugs, polished furniture, and old glassware gleamed. The door for one shop displayed a brass plate with the discreet legend "Karl Staiger." I pushed the bell. It was a long time before there was any response. Even then it was an upstairs window being opened, and closed again shortly afterward.

I could see through the shopwindow as eventually a dim light came on at the back of the shop, silhouetting the furniture and the shape of the short, plump man who picked his way through the display to the door. It took him some time to release the bolts and security locks on the shop door. He allowed the door to open only to the extent that the security chain permitted. Through the gap he called, "Yes? What is it?"

"I'm looking for Baron Staiger," I said. "I have come from Salzburg." There was a sigh. The door was closed while the chain was taken off the hook.

When he opened the door to look at me, I saw it was Otto Hoffmann himself. I had every excuse for not recognizing him sooner, for this was a more sober fellow than the jolly little man who'd given me three thousand Austrian schillings and a lecture on philately in Salzburg. Now he was dressed up in stiff shirt and formal bow tie, wearing over it a colorful embroidered smoking jacket. He stared at me for a moment without replying. It was almost as if he were trying to find reasons to send me away. But, grudgingly, he said, "Hello, Samson." It was not a warm welcome. "I told you to phone."

"It wasn't possible to phone."

"Why not?"

"I had no change," I said facetiously.

"You'd better come in. Here in Vienna I'm von Staiger." His accent was the same: pure Viennese, right down to the "ih" instead of "ich." He let me step inside the shop, and I waited while he went through the rigmarole of securing the front door again.

He switched out the light in the shop and led the way to the very back and up the narrow wooden staircase. From the basement there came those smells of bonding materials, freshly shaved wood, and polish that together distinguish the workshop. The three upper floors were given over to living quarters. On the staircase there were engravings and embroidery in antique frames, and on the landing was a fine oak commode in pristine condition. It seemed that some of these rooms doubled as showrooms. As we got near the top of the house, I could hear music, and a smell of cooking—or, rather, the legacy of some former meal preparation—replaced the more acrylic odors from the basement. "I have company," explained Staiger. "Put your coat on the rack and leave your bag here. We will talk later."

"Okay."

At the top of the house, two small rooms had been made into one, and there were about a dozen people there. They were all dressed in an extravagant fashion that in London I might have mistaken for fancy costume. The women wore lots of jewelry and décolletage dresses, one of them smoke-colored silk with tiered flounces, and another spectacular design was trimmed with antique lace. The men were in evening-dress suits with vivid cummerbunds, or sashes, and some of the older men wore medals.

This fellow Baron Staiger had none of the merriment I'd seen in Hoffmann in Salzburg. He made no attempt to introduce me to his guests, listlessly addressing those who had noticed our entrance with the words, "This is Mr. Samson, a

friend from Salzburg." I was damp. The heavy rain had pene-
trated my trench coat, and my baggy old suit had creases in
all the wrong places. They looked at me without enthusiasm.

In the corner a pianist was wrestling with George Gersh-
win, and they were both losing. After my entrance he played
a few desultory bars of waltztime and then gave a smile as if
he knew me. The piano stopped soon after that. I had the
feeling that my entrance had spoiled the *gemütlich* atmosphere.

The waiter bore down. Asked what I'd like to drink, and
hearing there was no hard liquor, I took the *Gspritzter* and
stood around waiting for everyone to go home. I could not
avoid the impression that Staiger wanted to be distanced from
me in every way, for, after making sure I had a drink in my
hand, he moved to a group on the other side of the room.

"So you live in Salzburg now?" asked someone from behind me. I turned and saw it was the piano player, who in the
better light I now realized with a shock was someone I knew.

Jesus Christ! It was a malevolent reptile named Theodor
Kiss, who preferred to be called Dodo. The last time I'd seen
him, he was threatening to tear me to pieces and was equipped
with the means to do so. Now he smiled sweetly, his long white
hair giving him a rather august appearance despite the un-
pressed dinner suit. He was a vicious old man, a Hungarian
who'd changed sides when Germany lost the war and carved
a new career with the victors. "No, do you?" I replied.

"Vienna, actually. I have a wonderful new apartment. I
decided to move. . . . The south of France has become so
. . . so vulgar."

"Is that so?" I could see the new red scar tissue across
Dodo's scalp: the wound made when Jim Prettyman felled him
and probably saved my life.

"And how is my darling Zu?" He was a friend of Gloria's
family.

I mumbled something about her being well.

He knew I didn't want to talk with him, but he enjoyed

persisting. "I studied in Vienna, of course. The city is like a home to me—so many old friends and colleagues."

I nodded. Yes, indeed: plenty of old colleagues here for a onetime Nazi like Dodo. The waiter offered us a tray with dabs of Liptauer cheese on small shapes of toast. I popped a couple in my mouth. I'd had no food on the plane.

"Vienna is the most beautiful city in the world," said Dodo. "And so *gemütlich!* Do you like the opera?"

I was eventually rescued from the conversation by a man who asked me if I was a newspaper reporter. Dodo moved away. The newcomer was thickset, with a little beard of the sort called a Vandyke, although on him it looked somewhat Mephistophelian. I answered that I wasn't, and he seemed content that I shouldn't be. He raised an arm to indicate a large painting: a grotesque arrangement of abstract shapes in primary colors. "You like it?" he asked.

"What is it?"

"It is modern art," he said with a patronizing drawl. "Do you know what that is?"

"Yes. Modern art is what happened when painters stopped looking at girls."

"Really?" he said coldly. "Is that not *Kulturbolschewismus?*" It was a low blow. "Cultural Bolshevism" was the name the Nazis coined to condemn anything other than the state-approved social realist art.

"I'm getting to like it," I said in my usual cowardly way. "Are you a painter?"

"Andras Scolik!" He clicked his heels and bowed from the neck. "I write music," he said. "Viennese music."

"Waltzes?"

"Waltzes!" he said disdainfully. "Of course not! Real music!"

"Oh, yes," I said. I caught the attention of a passing waiter, and this time I had local champagne. It tasted just like the *Gspritzer.*

"No," he said, "I didn't write 'The Yodeler' or shepherd songs like 'In the Salzkammergut Folk Are Gay.' I hope that doesn't disappoint you too much."

"No," I said.

"It is a battle against history," he said. "We Austrians do everything to excess, don't we?"

"No," I said.

"Yes, we do. Foreigners laugh at us. Our national costume is comic, our version of the German language is incomprehensible, our cuisine indigestible, our bureaucracy indomitable. Even our landscape and our climate are absurd and extreme. Mountains and snow! How I hate it all. Ask a foreigner to name a famous Austrian and he says Julie Andrews."

I was not expecting to arouse such fervor. I tried to calm him down. "I was thinking of Mozart," I said hurriedly.

It seemed only to infuriate him more. "Don't talk to me of Mozart. This damned country is enslaved by his memory. We musicians are prisoners of Mozart and his wretched eighteenth-century music. Tum-titty-tum-titty-tum-tum-tum. I despise Mozart!"

"I thought everyone liked Mozart," I said.

"The English like him. That anemic eighteenth-century music suits the bloodless English temperament."

"Perhaps that's it," I said, having given up hope of cooling his temper.

"Dead composers! They only like dead composers. When Mozart was alive, they seated him with the servants: one place above the cooks but well below the valets. That's what they do to musicians when they are alive."

"You don't really despise Mozart, do you?" I asked him.

"Tum-titty-tum-titty-tum-tum-tum."

"Consider," I said authoritatively, "the psychological insight, the dramatic integrity, and the musical elegance."

"Rubbish! Why did that foolish boy waste so much time

with German operas—toy music—couldn't he see that the
future of opera was rooted in the sublime genius of the Itali-
ans? Listen to *La Traviata*. You will hear passion . . . profound
human feelings as expressed by the lush sound of a full-sized
orchestra and scored by a composer of real genius who understood the art of singing in a way that little Mozart never
could."

"Andras!" called someone from the other side of the
room. "Could you settle an argument over here?"

The angry musician bowed stiffly from the neck and, spilling a few drops of his wine, took his leave of me with all the
formalities. I sipped my drink and looked round. There was
a distinct heightening of atmosphere in the room. Instead of
that jaded weariness that so often attends the mourners at a
dying party there was a feeling of expectancy, but what was
expected I could not guess.

I examined the room. It would seem to have been cleared
of some of its furniture in preparation for this gathering.
Some faded rectangles on the wall revealed the places from
which large pictures had been removed and replaced with
smaller ones. Those few items of furniture remaining were
choice antiques, inlaid occasional tables and a sideboard of
Hepplewhite style. But my attention went to a set piece at one
end of the room. It had obviously been arranged to captivate
some rich client. Three lovely chairs designed in the stark and
geometrical Secessionist style, and behind them two superb
posters by Schiele. I went to get a closer look at the chairs. My
reluctant host must have seen me admiring his wares, for he
was smiling as he came toward me with a bottle of champagne
in his hand.

"I hope Andras was not too abusive," said Staiger. He
filled my glass. He seemed reconciled to my gate-crashing his
party.

"He was most informative."

"Are you with the Diplomatic Corps?" This time there

was a smile and a twitch of the nose. "Or is London Central sending us a more subtle type of man these days?" Staiger was a decade younger than me, and yet he could get away with such a remark without inciting anger or resentment. Baron Staiger of Vienna, and Herr Hoffmann of Salzburg, and God knows what in the other places he went, was provided with more than his full share of that Viennese *Zauber* that the rest of the world called "schmaltz."

He said, "Andras has had a disappointing evening, I'm afraid. He has spent ten years trying to get his string quartet performed. Tonight it was. His loyal friends went, but there were not enough of us to fill the hall." He sipped his drink. "Worse still, I think Andras realized that his composition wasn't really very good."

"Poor Andras," I said.

"His parents own the Scolik Konditorei," said Staiger sardonically. "Know it? Each afternoon old ladies stand in lines to devour that superb Scolik poppy-seed strudel with a big dollop of Schlagobers. It is like owning a gold mine. The strudel will help him survive his crisis of confidence."

"Is that what he's having?"

"Strudel?" he asked mockingly. "No, you mean a crisis of confidence. Tomorrow he will face the music critics," said Staiger. "And Vienna breeds a savage race of critics."

"Karl!" said a small, sharp-featured woman who soon made it evident from her manner that she was Staiger's wife. Ignoring me, she said, "Anna-Klara has arrived, Karl." She touched his arm. I wondered if she knew about her husband's other lives. Perhaps she thought I was a part of them.

Staiger smiled in a satisfied way. "She has? *Kolossal!*" I was later to discover that he considered this lady's visit a social coup of some magnitude. He looked round to make sure that there was no aspect of the room that would disgrace him in the eyes of this renowned visitor, and found only me. For a moment I thought he would hide me in a cupboard, but he swallowed, looked at his wife apologetically, and—as if explaining his predicament—said, "When the guests have gone home, I have some work to do with *Doktor* Samson." He smoothed his thinning hair as if checking that it was in place.

The wife looked at me and nodded grimly. She knew I wasn't really a *Doktor;* a real *Doktor* would have been called "Baron," and a real Baron "Prince." That's how things worked in Austria. I smiled but she didn't respond. She was a dutiful Austrian wife, who let her husband make decisions about his work. But she didn't have to like his down-at-heel workmates. "Here comes Anna-Klara," she said.

The arrival of the guest of honor was what they had all been waiting for. This soprano had been performing at the opera that night, and when she came into the room it was an entrance befitting the reverence that this assembled audience afforded her. She swept in with a flourish of the long, flowing skirt. Her yellow hair was piled high and glittering with jewels. Her makeup was slightly overdone, but that was *de rigueur* for someone who'd hurried from the opera stage.

Her fellow guests greeted her with a concerted murmur of awe and devotion. With the Staigers at her side, the *gnädige Frau* went from one to another of them like a general inspecting a guard of honor. Here, bowing low, was a *Doktor Doktor* and a *Frau Doktor,* his wife; the bureaucrat's wife—*Frau Kommerzialrat*—gave a sort of a curtsy, and the *Hofrat*—court adviser for a Hapsburg emperor long since dead and gone—kissed her hand. Anna-Klara had gracious words for all of them, and special compliments for Andras Scolik and the string-quartet performance she'd missed. Scolik brightened. Anna-Klara had praised him. Art is long. And, after all, there was always the strudel.

It was a bravura performance, and with impeccable instinct Anna-Klara stayed for only one glass of champagne before departing again. Once she had gone, the party broke up quickly.

It was midnight when I sat down with Karl Staiger in his office at the back of the shop. All the church clocks in Vienna were proclaiming the witching hour. The room smelled of varnish, and Staiger opened the window a fraction despite the bitter-cold night outside. Then he moved a lot of unopened mail from where it was leaning against an antique carriage clock and compared the time with that on his wristwatch. It was a beautiful clock, its face decorated with dancing ladies. The movement ticked happily inside the glass-sided case. He nodded proudly at me, as a father might smile to see his child play the piano for guests. Satisfied, he moved more books and papers to clear a space on his desk, where a green-shaded lamp made a perfect circle of light upon a pink blotter.

"What happened?" said Staiger.

"I haven't got it," I said. I had no intention of talking to him about the death of Johnson, or mentioning Thurkettle and his possible role in the murder.

"Haven't got what?" He had his arms loaded with books.

From my jacket pocket I produced my wallet, and I laid the colored photo of the cover exactly in the center of the pool of light. "This," I said, smoothing it out. "I haven't got this."

He put the books on a cupboard and looked down at the photo. Then, without speaking, he took the bundle of unopened mail propped against the clock. Going quickly through it, he chose a packet that bore the large and impressive-looking labels of a courier company. It was a small padded bag secured with metal staples. He tore it open with an effortless twist and shook the contents from it.

Onto the table slid a blue envelope with Paraguay stamps and Zeppelin marks: the same cover as that depicted in the color photo upon which it fell.

"But I've got it," said Staiger with a satisfied smile.

"What's the story?" I picked up the cover that had caused so much trouble and probably brought about the amiable Johnson's death. I turned it in my hands. It seemed such a useless piece of paper to be sold for such a high price.

"I only know what I can read between the lines," he said. "But I think the Americans sent someone to buy it over your head. I had to get on to one of the biggest dealers in Vienna— an old friend—and ask him to get it at all costs."

"He must have phoned his bids."

"There was no time for anyone to get to Salzburg."

"The room bidder was chiseled, the auction was rigged. At least, that bid was."

"These things happen," said Staiger. "I had no idea the Americans would try to intervene, or I would have given you more cash. But it turned out all right. I was told to get it; I got it." He picked up the cover and held it against the light.

"Is there something inside?"

"Usually there is some stiffening to protect such covers, a piece of card, sometimes one that advertises some long-forgotten stamp dealer." But while saying this he got from the drawer of his desk a beautiful ivory letter opener and tapped it against his open hand. "You know that the best items in the sale were from a private collection put together in the nineteen thirties by a famous Hungarian airpost dealer named Zoltan Szarek. He was the author of the 1935 *Szarek Airpost Manual,* long out of print. Now that the Szarek collection is broken up, it is the end of one of the world's greatest." He turned the letter opener round. One end of it concealed a tiny penknife blade. He opened the blade and to my surprise cut the precious Paraguay envelope open.

Having seen the sort of passion that these philatelic objects aroused in men like Staiger, I was amazed at this vandalism. But there was a surprise to come, for inside the blue envelope were two passport-sized photos. The photos were obviously recent ones. The people had grown older since the last time I'd seen them, and the photos were dull and lacking in true blacks because they were printed on that sort of gray-toned photo paper that is used in countries that can't afford much silver. He placed them on the blotter in front of me. "Anyone you know?"

Two people stared back at me: a man and a woman. One was a Russian KGB man who operated under the name of Erich Stinnes. The photo was a more formal version of the one Bower had shown me in Berlin. The other was my wife.

That was not all. The "stiffener" was provided by the presence of two small identity cards. They were pink: both printed on a typical example of the coarse stock standard for Eastern Europe's endless flood of official paperwork. Each was a specific journey visa: one person, one journey, one admission to the Socialist People's Republic, one exit. The rubber stamp was that of the Statni Tajna Bezpecnost, Czechoslovakia's Secret Security Organization. One card bore Staiger's photo, the other mine.

Chapter 10

The region of Czechoslovakia that borders Austria's northern frontier is Moravia. Somewhat surprisingly, it is a short drive from downtown Vienna. Or would have been, had we not run into the Haydn Festival. Once at the border, we'd passed through the Austrian controls with no more than a moment's pause while Staiger waved his papers at them. But the Czechoslovak checkpoint was a different matter entirely.

It is a busy place, for it lies on the direct route from Vienna to Prague, and beyond that Berlin. Here, through the gap between Alps and Carpathians, the wind from the Russian steppe brings sudden drops in temperature and bites through even the warmest of clothes to chill the bones. As well as the cars, on this day about twenty or so articulated heavy trucks from all corners of Europe were lined up nose to tail. Inside their vehicles, windows tightly closed, the drivers dozed, chatted, and read, patiently waiting their turn in the large gray-painted hut where the cargo manifests and vehicle documentation were slowly read, incessantly queried, and reluctantly rubber-stamped by uniformed bureaucrats, beady-eyed men with inky fingers and regularly oiled guns.

Baron Staiger, a.k.a. Otto Hoffmann, this morning wearing a wavy brunette toupee, had collected me from the Vienna hotel where I'd spent the night after leaving his home. We were in a white jeeplike Subaru, and somewhat conspicuous amongst the exotic collection of Eastern Bloc vehicles. There were mud-spattered Ladas, smelly two-stroke Wartburgs, a Skoda cabriolet repainted bright pink, and a wonderful old Tatraplan with a long fin marking the air ducts of the rear engine compartment. With imperious disregard of the other drivers, Staiger drove to the head of the line and parked carelessly alongside the glass-sided box from which half a dozen Czech officials surveyed the landscape with impassive disdain.

Staiger said, "Wait in the car," and went over to engage the sentry in animated talk while tapping the pink identity cards. Whatever dialect the sentry spoke, Staiger seemed to speak it too, for the response was warm and immediate. The sentry nodded at Staiger and looked up and waved in the direction of a large green car on the Czech side of the border. Two men in civilian clothes hurried over to Staiger. They were tall, bulky men in trench coats, the sort of men who want everyone to know they work for the First Section of the STB, that most effective of all the East European secret-police services, which—significantly, perhaps—chose an ancient Prague monastery as its headquarters. The barrier was immediately raised.

"All okay," said Staiger as he climbed back into the driver's seat, bringing with him a breath of chill winter air.

"All okay," I echoed. "Well, that's a nice change."

"What?"

"All that tomfoolery with the stamp auction . . . and at the end it went wrong," I said.

"It's a regular route for our documents," he said smugly. "The Prague office arranged it; usually it goes like clockwork."

"Maybe someone should tell them that we live in the age of quartz crystals," I said.

"The Americans were bidding against us. They got wind of what was happening. The Vienna CIA office sent a man with a pocketful of money."

"And that's not the way we work," I said bitterly, remembering my inadequate allotment of schillings.

"No one can outbid the Americans," he said. "It was lucky that I could fix it."

The green car was on the road ahead of us as we went through the crossing point and through the frontier zone, where trees and bushes have been cleared and mines sowed. "They'll stay with us."

"Will they?" I said and tried to sound pleased.

We followed them into the Moravian countryside. Eventually their green car turned off the main Prague road. The track was poorly maintained, and to keep behind them Staiger had to engage the four-wheel drive.

This is a strange and baleful landscape: a sinister legacy of history. Until a generation ago, some of these border regions were as prosperous as any in the whole land. Since the time of the Empire, German-speaking people lived in these lovely little towns with tree-lined thoroughfares and baroque houses set around grand squares. But Adolf Hitler used the *Volksdeutsche* as an excuse to add these borderlands to his Third Reich. This was the "faraway country" that Britain's Prime Minister—having contrived the modern world's first summit meeting—would not go to war for. This was where "appeasement" got a new pejorative meaning and "Munich" became a way of saying surrender. Here lived the Czechs who waved swastika flags and welcomed the German invaders in their own language.

But after Hitler was defeated, a Stalinist government in Prague ruthlessly pushed the three and a half million German-speaking Czechs out of the country. Given only a few hours' notice, the exiles were permitted to take only what they could carry. They hiked across the border to find a new homeland. The vacated homes were ransacked by authorized officials and looters too. In a gesture more political than practical, the houses were eventually turned over to vagrants and gypsies. Now few of even those residents remain.

We drove through villages that reflected the ambivalence the authorities showed toward this old "German region." Stop and go; push and pull; here were the fits and starts of a ponderous socialist bureaucracy burdened by its own historical perspective. Old buildings were half demolished and new ones half built. Piles of rubble spewed out into the roadway, and abandoned cinderblock frameworks waited for roofs and windows that would never come.

We bumped through a little ghost town, disturbing a slumbering pack of gaunt dogs that slipped away without even barking. There were no people anywhere. The houses on the main square—their regal "Maria Theresa–yellow" stucco faded into a pox of chalky scars—were boarded up. So were the shops.

I pushed at the heating control again. "For the last time, Staiger. When are you going to tell me what this is all about?" In London I had been told to do whatever he said. I was doing so, but I did not enjoy being kept in the dark.

He shifted in the driver's seat, as if his spine were becoming stiff. "I cannot do that," he said affably, as he'd said it so many times before on this endless and uncomfortable journey. "My orders are to take you to the place we have to visit: nothing else."

"And bring me back?"

He smiled. "Yes. Bring you back too. At four o'clock. That's all I know."

Until now the few bits of conversation we'd exchanged had been only Viennese gossip, mostly concerning people I knew only slightly or not at all. Even worse, I'd heard Staiger's detailed observations on Vienna's confectionary, in particular its *Torten*. He'd explained exactly why he preferred the single-layer simplicity of the *Linzertorte* to everything else at Sacher. He revealed every last secret of Demel's delicate *Haselnusstorte* and told me which of their vast selection of *Torten* benefited from the addition of a portion of whipped cream, and which would be spoiled by such a garnish. He even gave me the address of a little café where the extraordinary quality of the apricot filling they put in their *Sachertorte* made it preferable to the one they served at Sacher.

"What do I have to do at this meeting? Did they tell you that in your orders?"

He wrenched his mind away from the cakes. "They said you would know."

"Is it a Russian?"

"I say I don't know. This is the truth; I don't know. Soon we will be there." He was disappointed that his thesis on pastries had been so coolly received. Perhaps at some other time I would have enjoyed his dissertation, even joined him for a *Kaffeeklatsch* tour of the city. But not today.

The clouds were dark, and in the dull light the distant mountains loomed unnaturally large. Everything was gray: the sky was gray, the mountains were gray, the farm buildings were gray, even the snow was gray. It was like a poorly printed snapshot: no black or white anywhere. Life in Eastern Europe was like that nowadays. Belief had gone. Communism had faded, but capitalism had not arrived; everyone muddled along, complying but not believing.

On and on we went, slower now that the road was bad. We came to a road junction where two khaki-colored trucks were parked at the roadside. Three men in camouflaged battle smocks and netted helmets stood by the tailboard of the rearmost vehicle. As we got closer, I could see one of them was an officer and the other two were NCOs with automatic rifles slung over their shoulders. They turned to watch us pass.

It was at this junction that we turned onto an even worse road. Soon the green car stopped and pulled aside so that we could pass. As we overtook it, the men inside stared at us with a curiosity seldom displayed by such people. Staiger seemed undismayed. The road climbed, and we bumped and rattled along a pot-holed path where muddy pools were glazed with patterned ice. In the fields, islands of ancient snow had shriveled to reveal the hard earth. Birds circled in the sky, already deciding where to spend the night. Snow remained everywhere. Alongside this remote and narrow track, drifts of it piled high, its surface shone with tiny diamonds of ice and showed none of the accumulated carbon stains that passing traffic deposits.

"They're there," said Staiger. "See the tire tracks?"

"Yes," I said.

"Or perhaps it was the debugging team."

"Did you bring anything to eat?" I asked.

"I thought we'd have time to stop on the Austrian side. I didn't expect we'd be this late," he said with solemn regret. He lifted his hand from the wheel to indicate another farm ahead.

Built in some ancient time when a farmer's life was punctuated with the role of warrior, it was sited to command a field of fire upon the full extent of the wide valley behind us. The cluster of buildings included two enormous barns, their roofs covered with snow. There was an entrance gateway of considerable grandeur; its sculptured coat of arms had been deliberately chiseled away but not entirely obliterated, so that a decapitated lion clung precariously to half a shield. Tucked away from the wind on the leeside of the ruined gate lodge there were two Czech traffic policemen sitting astraddle motorcycles. They watched us pass.

After the gate, a long approach road led past wooden troughs, which steamed gently, and corrugated-iron pigsties, to what once had been the central building of a fortified farmhouse.

The car only just squeezed through the low, narrow archway, bumped over the cobbles into an enclosed yard, and stopped at the back door of a farmhouse upon the walls of which the floral patterns of folk-art paintings could barely be discerned. The yard was big, a huge piece of farm machinery was quietly rusting away in the corner, and some chickens—flustered momentarily by the car—resumed their search for sustenance between the stones. There was a smell of rubbish burning, or perhaps the stove needed cleaning.

Scrambling about on the roof were two men, each equipped with powerful binoculars. Two more men, in short leather overcoats and large boots, sat on a bench in the yard. Hats tipped forward over their eyes, they sprawled like drunken sunbathers, but I noted the relaxed posture of men who remained still for long periods. And I noticed the undone top buttons that would make it easy for them to pull something from a shoulder holster in a hurry.

Without moving, they watched us from under lowered eyelids. I got out and waited for Staiger as he carefully locked the doors of his car.

Suddenly a large black mongrel dog came flying out from a doorway, barking and snarling. With reckless speed, and suicidal disregard for its leash, the hound threw itself at my throat. But as the long chain reached its fullest extent the dog choked and toppled sideways, its bark strangled. Tugging ferociously at the chain, it crouched low and continued to snarl and bare its teeth, making an exaggerated display of aggression, as many creatures do when their anger is constrained.

The men seated on the bench had hardly moved during this display of canine fury. Now Staiger laughed nervously and made sure his hat was balanced on his toupee. "Go in," said Staiger. "I will be waiting for you."

By that time I had begun to guess what was to come. Inside, the farmhouse was dark, its tiny windows set low in the thick walls. The floor was rough, worn tiles, and there was not much furniture except a refectory table, pushed back against the wall because it was so big, and some old chairs with rush seats.

She was standing in the gloom. She spoke in a whisper. "Bernard!" My first impression was that Fiona was shorter and thinner than I remembered. Then, with a twinge of guilt, I realized that this was because I'd been with Gloria so long.

"What bloody mad game are you up to now?" I said. The words emerged as a mumble, revealing, I suppose, my confusion. I still loved her but I was wary of her, unable to decide what she wanted of me, and unwilling to provide for her another chance of duping me in some way or other.

"Don't be angry."

"Don't be angry," I said wearily. Her deliberate passivity fueled my rage and suddenly I shouted, "You stupid, devious bitch. What are you up to now? Are you raving mad?"

She looked me up and down and smiled. Who knows what kind of animosity lay concealed within her? If she was equally angry with me, she disclosed no sign of it. She waited for the steam to go out of me, as she knew it would, and smiled again.

She still had that wonderful smile that had devastated me the first time I met her. It was a humorous smile, with a trace of mockery in it, but it was an invitation to join her in her view of the world about us, and it was an invitation I never could resist. "There is nothing to eat here. Nothing at all. I knew you'd be hungry." Her voice was flat, perhaps deliberately so, and even though she was my wife I could not tell what emotions she was feeling. It had always been so. Sometimes I wondered whether this enigmatic quality was what made her so attractive to me, and I wondered to what extent she failed to understand me in return. Not much, I think.

"Bernard, darling." She tried to put her arms round me, but I shrank away.

She said, "How are the children?" and I was burning from the warmth of her body and overwhelmed by a perfume I'd almost forgotten.

"They are fine. They miss you." I amended it: "We all miss you." Her eyes mocked me.

"Billy is so big. As tall as you, perhaps. He has a craze for motorcars: posters, models, and even a big plastic engine that he keeps taking to pieces and reassembling."

"Was that your Christmas present?" she asked, demonstrating her remarkable intuition. It was madness to try to keep any secret from her, and yet I still tried.

"Yes. It was labeled 'educational toy,' " I said. She gave a little laugh, recognizing our long-standing joke that I fell prey to anything so labeled. "Sally's been chosen to play Portia at school. I believe Billy's a bit jealous."

She smiled. "Yes, he would be. Billy is the actor. Portia—*The Merchant of Venice?*"

"*Julius Caesar.*"

"Of course.

"Am I yourself,
  But, as it were, in sort or limitation,
  To keep with you at meals, comfort your bed,
  And talk to you sometimes? Dwell I but in the suburbs
  Of your good pleasure? If it be no more,
  Portia is Brutus' harlot, not his wife."

"What a memory you have," I said.

Fiona said, "You're supposed to reply,

You are my true and honorable wife,
As dear to me as are the ruddy drops
That visit my sad heart.

Didn't you learn any Shakespeare at school?"

"I learned it in German," I said.

That amused her. "I read a lot nowadays: Dickens, Jane Austen, Trollope, Thackeray, Shakespeare."

A note of alarm sounded somewhere deep in my mind. The books were all English ones. Most security people would be alarmed at what smelled awfully like homesickness. But I didn't say that; I said, "Portia will have a lovely costume—blue with gold edging."

She held out her hand to me. I took it. I found an amazing intimacy in this formal gesture. Her hand was small and warm; she'd always had warm hands. She said, "How absurd that it should be like this," and then hurriedly, as though to preclude other discussions which she wanted to avoid, she added, "There were so many difficulties about my leaving Berlin, and then suddenly I had to go to a conference in Prague and it was easy." There was an unconvincing gaiety in her voice as she said it, the tone I remembered from times when she tried to make a joke about Billy getting flu and spoiling his birthday, or her opening the car door angrily and scratching the paint-work. "How much have they told you?"

Holding her hand, I stood back to look at her. She was as lovely as ever. Her hair was drawn back tight in the severe style she'd adopted since going to the East. She wore a simple dark-green suit that was almost Chanel, but I guessed it had been made by some wonderful little woman she'd found round the corner. Fiona could always find some "treasure" to do things she wanted done. On her finger she had our wedding band. She looked down at our clasped hands as if in some renewed pledge of her vows. This was the ravishing girl I'd married so proudly. But that was a hundred years ago, and the changes that the recent, stressful years had brought were evident too. I could see within her something I'd never seen before: some weariness, or was it apprehension? Perhaps that's what at first I'd mistaken for smallness of stature.

She turned her hand in mine. I said, "You've lost our engagement ring."

"We'll get another."

I said nothing.

"I was working in Dresden. A man was killed. It was a terrible night. I washed my hands at the infirmary. It was careless of me. I turned the car round and went back, but it wasn't there and no one had seen it."

She was clenching her hands, as if telling me about the lost ring had been a fearsome ordeal. But I could also see that Fiona was as undaunted as she'd ever been. I knew the way she contained her fear by means of willpower, as some brilliant actress might play a role and bring an unconvincing character to life. Giving me no time to reply, she added, "They are not the trousers for that suit. The new lady in your life is not looking after you, dearest." She was cool and relaxed now, the gruesome memories locked away again.

"I'm all right."

"Does she iron your shirts? You were always so fastidious about your shirts. Sometimes, away from you, I have found myself worrying about the laundry. It's silly, isn't it?" There was bitterness there. A trace of the real Fiona showing through. It was all jokes, of course: the laundry and these exploratory probes about other women. Everything was a joke until Fiona blew the whistle and joking ended.

"She's decent, she's loyal, and she loves me," I blurted out in the face of Fiona's sarcasm. No sooner was it said than I regretted it, but it was what she wanted. Once I'd revealed my feelings, Fiona was ready to proceed. "How much have they told you?" she asked again.

"Nothing," I said. "They told me nothing." I thought back to Stowe's furrowed brow and guarded answers. Obviously Stowe had been told nothing either. I wondered who the hell did know exactly what was going on.

"Poor darling, but perhaps it was the best way."

"You're coming out now," I said, confirming by my words what my eyes found it hard to believe. "I was right, wasn't I?" Even now I was not unquestionably sure that she'd been working for London all the time.

"Not long now," she said.

"You're not going back to Berlin?"

"Just for a little while."

"Why?"

"You know how it is. . . . There are other people who would be in danger. I'll have to tidy things up. A few weeks, that's all. Perhaps only days."

I didn't reply. The dog in the yard barked as if at an approaching stranger. Fiona looked at her watch. I suddenly remembered how much I'd hated the way Fiona's dedication to the Department came before everything. Competing with her career was worse than having to compete with an irresistible lover. She must have seen those feelings in my face, for she said, "No recriminations, Bernard. Not now anyway."

I knew then that I had handled the whole thing wrong. With grotesque misjudgment I had taken her at face value, and all women hate that.

Some other kind of man would have swept her off her feet, made love to her here and now, and damn the consequences. Some other kind of woman might have provided such an opportunity for me to do so. But we were us: two professionals discussing technique man to man.

She stepped away from me and, while studying her wedding ring, said, "I'm the only one who can make that sort of decision, and I say I must go back."

"Why come here? Why take the chance?" I said. I'm sure she'd found a convincing excuse for this meeting with the enemy, but it was madness for her to risk her life meeting me.

I could remember so many good men who had been lost because of such foolishness. Men who had to see a girlfriend for the last time. Men who couldn't resist a meal in a favorite café, or men like poor old Karl Busch, who hid me for three agonizing days in Weimar, then, after we'd got away, went back home to get his stamp collection. They were waiting for him. Karl Busch was taken down to the security barracks in Leipzig and was never heard of again.

"Oh, Bernard." There was a sigh.

"Why?"

"Because of you. Don't be so dense."

"Me?"

"You were raking through everything . . . about me. . . ." She made a gesture of despair with her open hand.

"Are you telling me that you've made this reckless side trip just to tell me to stop digging out the facts?"

"London Central tried everything to reassure you, but you carried on."

"They tried everything except simply telling me the truth," I said emphatically.

"They hinted and advised. Finally they couldn't think of any way to persuade you. I didn't know how far they would go. . . . I said you must hear it from me. We put together this official—but off-the-record—meeting. London has already made concessions: I go back looking like a skillful negotiator. It will be all right."

"The bloody fools! Didn't you tell them how dangerous it is for you, sitting out here talking with me?"

"They know it's dangerous, but you kept snooping into everything. You were putting together a picture of the whole operation. Leaving a trail too. That was even more dangerous."

"Of course I was snooping. What did you expect me to do? You are my wife." I stopped. I was exasperated. Although my theory had been proved correct, I couldn't accept the enormity of it: London Central had sent Fiona to be a field agent in the East and decided not to confide in me. "For God's sake . . ."

"It seemed a clever idea at the time," said Fiona calmly. Despite the phrase, there was nothing in her voice to suggest it wasn't a clever idea now.

"Who thought it was a clever idea?"

"Your surprise, or—let's rather say—astonishment . . . your anger, indignation, and obvious bewilderment protected me, Bernard."

"I asked you, 'Who thought it was a clever idea?' "

"I wanted to tell you everything, darling. I insisted upon it at first. I wanted you in at the briefings and the preparation. The original idea was that you would be my case officer, but then it became obvious that there couldn't be a case officer in the ordinary sense of that term. There was no question of frequent, regular contact."

"So who decided otherwise?"

"At the beginning the D-G was against the whole scheme. He gave it no more than a twenty-five-percent chance of coming off."

"I would have given it less than that."

"The D-G made it a condition that you would not be told."

"The D-G . . . Sir Henry?"

"He has his good days as well as his bad ones."

"So the more fuss I kicked up the better?"

"At first, yes. And it certainly worked," said Fiona. "In the first few weeks, Moscow put you under their priority surveillance; they watched you with the greatest interest. They even had one of their psychological-behavior experts write a report on you. Erich Stinnes got hold of a copy and I read it. It said that no actor could have put on a performance like yours. And of course they were right. It was your behavior that finally convinced them that I was really theirs."

"Didn't they guess the truth? That you acted without telling me?"

"The Soviet Union may have women fighter pilots and crane operators, but marriage is a sacred institution here. Thanks to the millions of war casualties, Marx's views on marriage—like his views on a lot of other things—have been shelved indefinitely. Wives in the U.S.S.R. do as their husbands say."

I looked at her without speaking. She smiled. I wondered why I had been surprised by this whole business. Fiona: cultured, privileged daughter of philistine nouveau-riche father; exceptional Oxford graduate who studied Russian at the Sorbonne. She joins the Department and marries a man who never went to college and whose sole claim to any sort of respect was his reputation as a field agent. Why wouldn't such a person prove to be the ultimate exponent of woman's emancipation? Why wouldn't such a woman want to be an even better field agent, at whatever the cost to me and the children and everyone else around her?

"When did all this start?" I asked.

"Long ago," she replied airily.

"September 1978?" That was the night of one of those "Baader Meinhof" panics. The content of a Soviet Army signals intercept got back to Karlshorst so quickly that everyone thought we had a superspy sitting in Operations. She nodded. "You leaked that intercepted signal to them? So you were working both sides already." I took a moment or two to recollect what had happened. "Joe Brody was called in to handle the subsequent investigation, just in order to calm the anxiety in American hearts. In some way or other you slipped past him. But with you in the clear the blame was put upon Werner Volkmann, and he wasn't even given a chance to defend himself. Frank wouldn't use him any more, and Werner took it badly."

"That's right," she said and bit her lip. She'd always

disliked Werner, or at least dismissed him as something of a simpleton. Had some feeling of guilt, at the part she'd played in framing him, seeded that dislike? She said, "Then, when they opened an orange file on Trent, the blame was put on him."

"Trent was killed," I said.

She had her answer ready. Her voice was calm and conciliatory. "Yes, killed by your friend Rolf Mauser. With a gun he borrowed from you. You can't implicate the Department in Trent's death."

"But how convenient it was. Trent took his secret to the grave, and the secret was that he *didn't* give that intercept to the Russians."

She said nothing.

I said, "Were you approached at Oxford? Was it that long ago?"

"By the Department? Yes."

So that was it. Those stories of her joining Marxist groups at college were true, but it had been done to try her out. Of more personal concern was the way she'd let me recommend her for a job with the Department. That had all been a ruse: a way of covering her previous service. She must have been in regular contact with the KGB by then. Getting the SIS job would have made her case officer feel ecstatic. I could see the long-term planning that had made her so convincing as a Russian agent. It made me feel a damned fool, but I controlled my anger. "Who else knew?" I asked.

"I can't tell you that, darling."

"Who else?"

"No one else. Not Coordination, not Central Funding, not Internal Security, not even the Deputy."

"The D-G knew," I persisted.

"No one working there now," she said pedantically. "That was the condition the D-G made. No one!"

"You made my life hell," I told her gently.

"I thought you'd be proud of me."

"I am," I said, trying to put some feeling into my words. "I really am. But now is the time to pull out. Come back to Vienna with me. Your KGB identification plus my special identity card would get us through the control. We could catch an evening plane to London."

"I'm not sure that it would, Bernard. The crossing points are all on the computer nowadays. Believe me, it's something I know about." I knew that tone of voice; there was no arguing with it.

She'd heard me say a million times that field agents have to have the last word in such matters. I'd always used my experience as a field agent to have the final decision. Now my wife had proved to be the most amazing field agent of all. She'd moved into the top echelon of the East's espionage network and fooled them all. I was in no position to argue with her.

Lightly, as if to turn the conversation to trivial matters, she said, "I will have to make sure the computer gives the okay when I come. London have promised me something special in the way of papers."

"They have good people here," I said without really believing it. I wondered if her forged papers were being prepared by Staiger—done by the same crooks whom he got to fake his stamps and covers.

"I know."

"And Erich Stinnes too?" When the history of the Department is written, no fiasco of the recent past will demonstrate its capacity for vacillation and confusion better than the way in which Stinnes was handled. Stinnes was a slippery customer, a real old-time KGB officer. He'd said he wanted to defect to us; then doubts arose on both sides, until Stinnes was categorized as hostile and imprisoned by us. He eventually went back to the East as part of an exchange.

"Stinnes is kept entirely separate. That's the way it was

planned." She paused and changed the subject slightly. "When you got rid of that brute Moskvin you removed my greatest danger. He suspected the truth."

"He took a Russian bullet too. One of your people shot him. Did you know that?"

She gave a frosty smile.

I didn't want to leave it like that. "I wish . . ."

She raised a hand to silence any recriminations from me and said, "We've only got a few minutes. The car must leave at four. I must be back in Prague. There's this damned security conference tomorrow, and I have to be briefed." The dog barked again, more fiercely this time, and the barking stopped with a shrill yelp, as if the dog had been dealt a blow.

"Yes, four o'clock. I understand."

"So they did tell you something?"

It was a feeble joke, but I smiled and apologetically said, "We left Vienna early, but there was the Haydn Festival, and the road . . ."

"I know," she said. "It's always like that when it's really important. You used to say that."

"When I was late?"

"No, I didn't mean that, Bernard." She took a quick look at her watch. "There is another thing . . ." she said. "My fur coat. I left it with my sister Tessa. I'm worried she might sell it or give it away or something. . . ."

I remembered the coat. It was a breathtaking birthday present from her father at a time when he was very keen to establish his love for her, and his wealth and success. The huge silky sable coat must have cost thousands of pounds. Fiona had always been vocally opposed to the wearing of things made of animal fur, but once she'd tried on that coat her moral reservations about the fur trade seemed to dwindle. "What do you want me to do?"

"You must get it back from her."

"Well . . ." I said hesitantly, "I can't tell Tessa I've talked with you."

"You'll find a way," she said. Now it was my problem. I could see why she was so good at management.

There was the sort of awkward silence that only an English couple would inflict upon themselves. "And everything's all right? The children are well?" she asked again.

"Wonderful," I said. She knew that, of course. It would have been part of the deal that she had regular reports on the children. And on me. I wondered if such reports would have included news of my living with Gloria. For one terrible moment it flashed through my mind that Gloria might have been assigned to live with me and monitor everything I did, said, and thought. But I dismissed the idea. Gloria was too unconventional to be an informer. "The children miss you, of course," I added.

"They haven't grown to hate me, have they, Bernard?"

"No, of course not, darling." I said it so glibly and quickly that she must have sensed the reservations I had. It would not be easy to rebuild her relationships with the children: it would not be easy.

She nodded. "And you?"

I don't know whether she was asking whether I was all right or whether I'd grown to hate her. "I'm all right," I said.

"You've lost weight, Bernard. Are you sure you're quite well?"

"I went on a diet so I can fit into my old suits."

"I'm glad you're still the same," she said somewhat ambiguously, and there was more affection in that banal phrase than in anything she'd said up to that time.

I suppose I should have said all the things that were bottled up inside me. I should have told her that she was as beautiful as ever. That she was as brave as anyone I'd ever met. That I was proud of her. But I said, "Take care of yourself. It's so near the end now."

"I'll be all right. Don't worry, darling." I could hear in her voice that her mind was no longer devoted to me or to the children. She'd already started thinking of the next stage: it was the way of the professional. The only way to stay alive.

There came the sound of a big V-8 engine. Through the window I saw her car moving out from where it had been parked in the barn. A black official car. A big shiny machine like that, with official license plates and motorcycle outriders, would attract attention. And surely it was impossible to get it through that archway and down that pot-holed track.

Well, Fiona was good at doing the impossible. She'd proved that over and over.

Chapter 11

Once I was back in London, it was easy to believe my trip to Central Europe had all been a dream. In fact, I suppressed all thought of my meeting with Fiona from my mind. Or I really tried to do so. When Gloria met me at the airport, she gave a whoop of joy that could be heard across the concourse. She grabbed me and kissed me and held me tight. It was only then that I began to see the full extent of the terrible emotional dilemma I had created—or, should I say, dilemma that Fiona had created for me.

Gloria had left her new car—an orange-colored Metro—double-banked outside Terminal 2, a place where the parking-warden charm school invigilates its ferocity finals. But she got away unscathed: I suppose it was teatime.

The car was brand-new and she was keen to demonstrate its wonders. I sat back and watched her with delight. The awful truth was that I felt relaxed, and truly at home, here in

London with Gloria in my arms. She was young and vital, and she excited me. My feelings for Fiona were entirely different and more complex. As well as being my wife, my colleague, and my rival, she was the mother of my children.

Werner Volkmann's caustic wife, Zena, once told me that I'd married Fiona because she was everything that I wasn't. By that I suppose she meant educated, sophisticated, and moving in the right circles. But I would have claimed otherwise. My education and sophistication, and the circles I moved in too, were radically different to anything Fiona had known, but not inferior. I'd married her because I loved her desperately, but perhaps it was a love too colored by respect. Perhaps we'd both married believing that it was the combination of our talents and experience that really mattered; that we would prove to be an invincible combination and our children would excel in every way. But such reasoning is false; marriages cannot be held together solely by mutual respect. Especially when that respect depends upon inexperience, as respect so often does. Now we knew each other better, and I had discovered that Fiona's love for me was sober and cerebral, like her love of learning and her love of her country. Gloria was not much more than half Fiona's age: Lord, what an oppressing thought that was! But Gloria had an irrepressible energy and excitement and curiosity and contrariness. I loved Gloria as I loved the exhilaration she'd brought to my life and the boundless love she gave both me and the children. But I loved Fiona too.

"Good trip?" She tried to demonstrate the self-seeking radio and the auto-reverse tape player while overtaking a bus on the inside. She was an unrestrained driver, as she was an unrestrained lover and an unrestrained everything else.

"The usual routine. Salzburg and Vienna. You know." I felt no pang of conscience at saying that the trip had been routine. This was not the right time to sit down with Gloria and hear what she thought about Fiona. I hadn't yet worked out what I thought myself.

"I *don't* know! How would I know? Tell me about it."

"Salzburg: von Karajan held up rehearsals while we had a cup of that awful coffee he brews up under the rostrum. Then on to Vienna: a private view of the Brueghels and a boring little cocktail-party reception for me; then a private dinner with the ambassador and that uncomfortable box the embassy subscribes to at the opera. The usual stuff." She bared her teeth at me. I said, "Oh, yes, and I was attacked by a fierce dog."

"We're invited to the Cruyers'," Gloria told me as she got to the traffic lights near Hogarth's house. "Daphne phoned me at home. She was terribly friendly. I was surprised. She's always been rather distant with me. Long dresses, would you believe? And black tie."

"You're joking."

"No, I'm not."

"Black tie? Long dresses? At the Cruyers'?"

"On Saturday evening. Your sister-in-law, Tessa, and her husband are going. I don't know who else."

"And you said yes?"

"Dicky knew you were expected back today."

"Good God."

"I sent your dinner suit to the cleaners. It will be ready Saturday morning."

"Do you know these trousers don't match this jacket?" I asked her.

"Of course. I'm always telling you. I thought you did it to annoy Dicky."

"Why would my having mismatched trousers and jacket annoy Dicky?"

"It's no good trying to put the blame on me. You should keep your suits on proper hangers and not leave everything draped around. Of course your trousers get mixed up. Did someone remark on it, then?"

"I just noticed."

"I'll bet someone remarked on it, and made you feel a fool." She laughed. "What did they say—'Have you got another suit like that at home?'—is that what they said?" She giggled again. Gloria loved her own jokes: they were the only ones she saw the point of. But her laughter was infectious, and despite myself I laughed too.

"No one noticed except me," I insisted.

"It's about time you had a new suit. Or what about gray flannels and a dark-blue blazer? You could wear that outfit to the office."

"I don't want a new suit or blazer and flannels, and if I did buy new clothes I wouldn't buy them for the office."

"You'd look good in a blazer."

I never knew when she was serious and when she was goading me. "Wouldn't I need a badge on the pocket?"

"Alcoholics Anonymous?" she said.

"Very droll."

"I've bought a lovely dress," she confessed. "Lilac with big puff sleeves." So that was really it. That little preamble about me having a new suit was just to assuage her guilt about spending money on a dress.

"Good," I said.

That wasn't enough to put her at her ease. "I didn't have a long dress, and I didn't want to rent one."

"Good. Good. I said good."

"You are a pig, darling."

I kissed her ear and grunted.

"Don't do that when I'm driving."

The Cruyers' dinner party must have been planned for weeks. At previous dinners Dicky's wife, Daphne—an unenthusiastic cook—could be seen dashing in and out of the kitchen, sipping champagne between stirring the saucepans, referring to cookery books, and hissing instructions to Dicky. But this time they had some gravelly-voiced old fellow to open the door and breathe alcohol fumes upon all arriving guests; and an elderly lady, attired in full chef's outfit, complete with toque, to do whatever was happening in the kitchen. There was a smell of boiled fish as she peered out of the kitchen to see us in the hallway. Whether she was counting the dinner guests or checking on the old man's sobriety was unresolved by the time the doorbell sounded behind us.

There was soft guitar music trickling out of the hi-fi. "We tried to get Paul Bocuse," Dicky was saying as we moved into the crowded drawing room, "but he sent his sous-chef instead." Dicky turned to greet us and said, "Gloria, *chérie!* How spiffing you look!" in the fruity voice he used to tell jokes. He gave her a deferent, stand-off kiss on both cheeks to avoid spoiling her makeup.

"And *Bernard,* old sport!" he said, his tone suggesting that it was an interesting coincidence that Gloria and I should arrive together. "No need to introduce you to anyone here. Circulate! It's chums only tonight."

Most of the people must have already consumed a glass or two of wine, for there was that shrill excitement that comes from drinking on an empty head. Daphne Cruyer came across to greet us. I'd always liked Daphne. In a way, I shared with her the problem of putting up with Dicky every day. She never said as much, of course, but I sometimes thought I detected that same fellow feeling for me.

Daphne had been an art student when she first met Dicky. She had never entirely recovered from either experience. Tonight the drawing room was elaborately decorated with Japanese lanterns and paper fish. I guessed it was Daphne's purchase of her amazing rainbow-patterned silk kimono that had prompted this formal gathering. I would hardly think it was prompted by Dicky's new white slubbed-silk dinner jacket. But you could never be sure.

Daphne asked me how I was, with that unusual tone of

voice that suggested she really wanted to know. In an effort to reciprocate this kindness, I didn't tell her. Instead, I admired her kimono and her Madame Butterfly hairdo. She'd bought the kimono on holiday in Tokyo. They'd gone on a ten-day trip to Japan together with their well-traveled neighbors. I would never have guessed how much you pay for a cup of coffee on the Ginza, but Daphne had adored every moment of it, even the raw fish. She said Gloria was looking well. I agreed and reflected upon the fact that it had taken over three years for the Cruyers to decide that Gloria and I were socially acceptable as a couple, and that this momentous decision had coincided with the moment I learned that my wife was about to return.

"Dicky said everything in the office got into a terrible muddle when you went away," said Daphne.

"I think it did," I agreed.

"Dicky became awfully moody. Awfully withdrawn. I felt sorry for him."

"I came back," I said.

"And I'm glad," said Daphne. She smiled. I wondered how much Dicky had told her about my time on the run in Berlin. Nothing, I hoped; but it wouldn't be the first time that Daphne had wormed information out of him. She was awfully clever at handling Dicky. I should get her to give me a few lessons.

"We built on to the attic," said Daphne. "I have a little studio upstairs now. You must see it next time you're here."

"For painting?"

"Still-life pictures: fruit and flowers and so on. Dicky wants me to go back to doing abstracts. But he was always adding blobs of color to them. I got so angry with him that I finally went back to fruit and flowers. Dicky is such a meddler. I suppose you know that."

"Yes, I do."

When Daphne had moved on, I said my hellos to everyone, including Sir Giles Streeply-Cox—a retired Foreign Office man—and his wife. "Creepy-Pox," with his sanguine complexion and bushy white sideburns, might have been mistaken for a prosperous farmer until one heard that baroque Whitehall accent. Nowadays he grew roses between visits to London, where he chaired a civil-service interview board and prowled around the more languorous latitudes of Whitehall spreading alarm and despondency. Like all such senior officials and politicians, he had a prodigious memory. He remembered me from another dinner party not so long before. "Young Samson, isn't it? Saw you at that gathering at that girl Matthews' little place. Nouvelle cuisine, wasn't it? Ummm, I thought it was. Don't get enough to eat, what?" The Streeply-Coxes certainly got around.

He leaned close to me and said, "Tell me something, Samson. Do you know the name of this damned tune?"

"It's called 'Córdoba,' " I said. "Albéniz; played by Julian Bream." I answered authoritatively because after purchasing his hi-fi Dicky had played it over and over to demonstrate the track selector.

"Catchy little piece," said Streeply-Cox. He looked at his wife and nodded before adding, "My wife said you were a know-all."

"I try, Sir Giles," I said and moved away, murmuring about getting another glass of wine.

Once clear of the dreaded Streeply-Cox, I decided that finding another glass of champagne wouldn't be a bad idea. I waylaid the old man with the drinks and then took a moment or two to look around. The same rather battered painting of Adam and Eve dominated the fireplace. Dicky always called it *naïf* in an attempt to give it class, but to my eyes it was just badly drawn. The framed color photo of Dicky's boat had gone. That rather confirmed the rumors I'd heard about him putting it up for sale. Daphne had never been happy about that boat. She was rather prone to seasickness, and yet if she didn't join Dicky on his nautical weekends she knew there was a risk that some other female would share the captain's cabin.

The antique cabinet that had once held a collection of matchbox covers now held a Japanese dagger, some netsuke, and an assortment of other small Oriental artifacts. On the wall behind it there were six framed woodblock prints, including the inevitable *Breaking Wave*. They'd fitted a fine mesh screen across the artificial coal fire. I suppose too many people threw litter into it. Dicky was always on his knees, clawing cigarette butts and screwed-up scraps of paper from the plastic coal.

I reflected that every decoration in the room was new except the Adam and Eve that Daphne had found in a flea market in Amsterdam. It was a sign of the Cruyers' widening horizons and deepening pockets. I wondered how long Adam and Eve would last and what they'd be replaced with. Adam was already looking a bit apprehensive.

It was while trying to decide about the expression upon the face of Eve that I spotted my errant sister-in-law, Tessa, and her husband, George Kosinski. They were both dressed up to the nines, but even Tessa in her Paris-model-gown didn't excel the stupendous Gloria, who looked more enchanting than ever.

Tessa came over. She must have been getting on for forty, but she was still vibrantly attractive, with her long fair hair and bright-blue eyes, and she still had that breathless way of speaking that made you think that she'd been waiting anxiously to see you again. "I thought maybe you'd been sent to the bloody moon, poppet," she said, giving me an uncharacteristically coy kiss. "I've missed you, darling."

I confess to a frisson as she kissed me: I'd never noticed before how much like Fiona she could look. Tonight especially so. Perhaps it was just an accident of her dress or makeup. Perhaps it was something to do with Tessa getting older; or Fiona getting older; or me getting older. Whatever it was, for a moment it made me stare at her, deprived of words, until she said, "Fuck! Is my lipstick smudged or something?"

"No, Tessa. You're looking more lovely than ever. Just stunning."

"Well, that's really something, coming from you, Bernard. All we girls know that being noticed by Bernard Samson is the ultimate accolade."

The old fellow—whom I heard Daphne address as "Jenkins"—came round with a big silver tray of champagne. Tessa selected one unhurriedly and held her glass up to the light as if silently offering a toast, but I knew she was trying to identify the champagne from its color and the bubbles. It was one of her party tricks. Her mastering it must have cost George a fortune.

Having approved of what she saw, but without naming it, she drank some. "Did you ever see such a darling butler?" said Tessa as Jenkins moved away. "How sweet of Daphne to find an evening's work for some poor old pensioner."

I wondered how I was going to persuade Tessa to return Fiona's fur coat. What was I going to use as an excuse? And where was I going to put the damn thing without having to go into a lot of discussion about it with Gloria?

"I was thinking about Fiona's fur coat," I began.

"Oh, yes, darling. Do tell."

"I thought perhaps I should put it with all the other things."

"All what other things?" She swung her hair back from her face.

"Some bits and pieces that Fiona liked especially."

"It's a beautiful bit of fur, you know. Daddy paid the absolute earth for it."

"Yes, it's something of a responsibility for you."

"I'm not wearing it, poppet, if that's what you're on about."

"No, I'm sure you're not, Tessa, and it's kind of you

to look after the damned thing all this time. I just thought that . . ."

"No trouble at all, darling. It's with my own furs, and when summer comes—if it ever comes—they'll all go into refrigerated storage together."

"Well, you see, Tessa . . ." I started. She tilted her head as if very interested in what I was going to say but let her fair hair fall forward so that she could hide behind it. At that moment we were interrupted by an old acquaintance of mine: Posh Harry, a CIA troubleshooter from Washington. A short thickset man of vaguely Polynesian appearance, he was of that mixed Hawaiian and Caucasian ancestry that in his birthplace is called *hapa haole*. He was in his middle thirties, always carefully groomed and of pleasing appearance. It would be easy to imagine him, suitably costumed, singing baritone in *Madame Butterfly* or, more credibly perhaps, *South Pacific*.

"And who is this glorious young lady you're talking to, Bernard?" said Harry.

Tessa put an arm through his and said, "Have you forgotten so soon, Harry? I'm mortified." Posh Harry smiled and, before he could start an explanation, the sonorous voice of Jenkins announced, "Ladies and gentlemen. Dinner is served." I caught Tessa's eye and she smiled sardonically.

Tessa's husband was talking to Gloria. He was fortyish. Born in London's East End of impoverished Polish parents, he had become rich selling cars and, later, property. George put himself in the hands of the most expensive tailors, shirtmakers, outfitters, and hairdressers he could find. So he was to be seen in a succession of dinner suits cut to ever-changing fashions.

This evening George seemed to notice Gloria for the first time, for he fell deep in conversation with her soon after we arrived. I was somewhat surprised by this, for George had always seemed ill at ease with women, except the ones he knew well. Sometimes I wondered how he ever came to get married to Tessa; and why. Fiona used to say that it was Tessa's inexhaustible infidelities that had driven George to making so much money, but George was on the way to riches long before Tessa married him.

George was a man of irreproachable integrity, something I wouldn't have thought of as a prime asset in the secondhand-car business. Once I'd said this to him. Characteristically, George had given me a short lecture upon the probity and goodwill of his profession.

George and Gloria were talking when dinner was announced. Because George was very short, she had perched herself on one arm of a sofa so he didn't have to look up to her. George liked her, I could see that in his face, and when others came to join them in conversation he was determined to keep her attention. Jenkins repeated his announcement in a louder voice. Now they all looked up.

After a couple of false starts, Jenkins heaved open the doors of the dark, candlelit dining room to reveal the long polished table set with flowers and gleaming tableware. The assembled company paused for a moment to gaze at the spectacle. This, I felt, was the beginning of a new age of Cruyerdom, a bid for the better life, a home background that would suit a man destined to rub shoulders with the mighty, brilliantly administer the secret dimension of political affairs, and retire with that coveted K. The only question that remained was why I had been invited.

"Daphne! How picturesque!" called Tessa as we moved in. *"Un véritable coup de théâtre,* darling!"

"Shush!" I heard George say to her as we circled around to find our name cards. He said it in a quiet, impersonal way, as a member of a theatre audience might react to a latecomer without interrupting the action on the stage. As we sat down, George, with his enviable memory, recalled a meeting with Posh Harry a few years previously, when Harry visited

George's used-motorcar emporium in one of the less salubri-
ous parts of Southwark, South London.

Posh Harry smiled without either confirming or denying
it. That was his way. Harry could be inscrutable. He was
dressed in a remarkable shiny black dinner suit with a lace-
trimmed shirt that Beau Brummel might have worn except
that it was a bit too frilly. Harry was always a fancy dresser, and
it had to be admitted that he could carry it off. With him, and
wearing a strapless satin gown cut very, very low, was the same
American woman I'd seen him with in Southwark. She was in
her middle thirties and would have been pretty except for her
rather plump features, which gave her a look of unremitting
petulance. This impression was heightened by the strident
candied-yams-and-black-eyed-peas accent she affected. At
dinner she was sitting next to me. Her name turned out to be
Jo-Jo.

I was interested to watch the interaction between Posh
Harry and our host. I wondered when it was that they first met,
and I wondered if Harry's presence in London signaled some
CIA development that I should find out about. I knew that
there was a new Station Chief in London. Maybe Harry was his
troubleshooter.

"What's your new boss like?" Dicky casually asked Posh
Harry, once we were all seated and the wine was being poured.

Harry, who sat across the table from me, replied, "Say,
Dicky, what does *die neue Sachlichkeit* really mean?"

Dicky said, " 'The new realism.' It means realistic painting. Isn't that right, Bernard?"

Constitutionally incapable of answering such a question
in any way but fully, I said, "And poetry. It's nineteen-twenties
jargon . . . a reaction against Impressionism. Also against
beauty in favor of functionalism."

Dicky said, "You see, Bernard isn't just a pretty face." He
laughed and so did Jo-Jo. I could have banged their heads
together.

Posh Harry smiled and said, "My new boss keeps talking about *die neue Sachlichkeit* like he's going to be a new broom and give everyone hell."

Dicky smiled. I suppose it was Harry's prepared answer to an expected question. Posh Harry spoke damned good German. I'd be surprised if he really didn't know what it meant.

Posh Harry added, "Never mind Bernard's 'pretty face.' I want to know where he's been hiding this gorgeous little girl all this time." He was sitting next to Gloria, who sipped her wine to conceal her self-satisfied smile.

The first course was a crab soup with garlic bread. While Jenkins ladled it out with studied care, there was the usual small talk. Daphne Cruyer, relieved of her kitchen duties and with Jenkins to serve the food, was for the first time a guest at one of her own dinner parties. She seemed to thrive on it. Dicky too seemed delighted with this chance to play host. He was beaming the whole evening except when Jenkins—offering a second helping of crab soup from a heavy Japanese bowl—poured some of it over him. Even then Dicky only said, "Steady on, Jenkins man!" albeit rather loudly.

It was at this stage of the proceedings that I overheard Daphne's loud whisper that told the evidently unsteady Jenkins not to try to dish up the salmon. Instead he was to put the whole fish in front of Dicky. It must be said that Jenkins didn't do this with good grace. He slammed the platter down with enough force to make the cutlery jingle.

"I'm totally with Jefferson's interpretation of the Tenth Amendment," Dicky was saying as the fish arrived so dramatically before him. He'd been treating his end of the table—which is to say, me and Harry, for the ladies each side of him were trying to hear Daphne at the other end—to his views on federal government.

Dicky stared at the newly arrived salmon as if bewildered. His confusion might have been partly due to the huge pale-green scales the fish wore, although on closer inspection these proved to be wafer-thin slices of cucumber, laboriously arranged in overlapping rows. Dicky looked up and saw Daphne—at the other end of the table—staring at him and making energetic sawing motions with her hand. He looked at Posh Harry, who gave an inscrutable smile and murmured something about his position as a government employee making it inappropriate for him to voice any opinion on states' rights.

Dicky had to be satisfied with this, because he was, by that time, struggling to divide up the poached salmon. I don't know what persuaded Dicky to try slicing through it rather than fillet it from the bone; perhaps he took Daphne's mime too literally. But he soon discovered that even an overcooked salmon's spine is not easily severed with a silver serving spoon. Yielding to considerable force, for Dicky was nothing if not strong, the head seemed to slide off the platter, hide under the flowers, and look at Dicky reproachfully.

Daphne, while watching Dicky, got everyone's attention by suddenly beginning to describe a place in North London where she was going for skiing lessons on plastic snow. Everyone turned to face her. There was a certain shrill note in her voice, perhaps because the skiing season was over. As if suddenly remembering this, she said she was going to lessons there all through summer and winter so that next year she'd be really good. Only Tessa—sitting on my right—turned to see what had happened when the head came off. She said, "What a gorgeous fish. Did you land him yourself, Dicky?"

Dicky smiled grimly, and so did the indomitable Jenkins, who I now noticed was leaning slouched against the sideboard and watching Dicky's efforts appreciatively.

"It's not farmed salmon," said Daphne. "It's wild."

"So would I be, darling," said Tessa, turning back to her.

Daphne gave her a frosty smile. Tessa was suspected of a torrid affair with Dicky some years previously, and Daphne had not forgotten it.

"Jenkins," said Daphne in a trilling nursery-school voice, "would you pour the wine, please." And because Daphne had spent so many years monitoring Dicky, she was able to add in time, "Not the Chambertin, Jenkins; the white Hermitage." And this time her voice was less composed.

As Dicky said afterward, the wonderful *beurre-blanc* sauce completely concealed the broken pieces of fish. But Tessa's stated view was that it was like eating darning needles wrapped in cotton wool. Tessa was one of those ladies who didn't like finding fishbones in their fish. Anyway, there were plenty of second-helpings.

Moreover, there was hare cooked in red wine to follow. It came ready-sliced on plates. The little old lady in the kitchen was working miracles. And rhubarb pie followed by a huge Stilton cheese with vintage port.

Fully recovered from his contest with the salmon, Dicky was in top form, which meant attentive and charming. There was never a time when I more easily understood Dicky's success in everything he did. He told jokes—good jokes—and laughed at his guests' stories. He made sure everyone had what he or she wanted, from aperitifs to cigars, and was even cordial with Daphne.

George and Sir Giles were sitting each side of Daphne, but I noticed that Tessa had been distanced from Dicky. I wondered if Daphne had chosen the place settings. The cards were in her handwriting. And it was Tessa whom Daphne looked at when she stood up and called upon the ladies to retire. I thought Tessa would make a fuss and say no—as I'd seen her do before when she was feeling Bolshie—but she got to her feet meekly and left the room with the rest of them.

As if on cue, Sir Giles then told three rambling anecdotes about his time in Whitehall. Coming near enough to indiscretion to keep our attention, he made sure no beans were spilled.

It was toward the end of this port-and-cigar session that Dicky got Sir Giles and George into a discussion about interest rates—no fashionable London dinner party being complete without an examination of the Treasury's fiscal policy—and, turning aside from it, Posh Harry said to me, "Did you hear about your old buddy Kleindorf?"

"No, what?"

"Dead!" He stopped. He must have seen how much the news affected me. "The Babylon is closed."

"What happened?"

"He overdosed. You saw him recently, somebody told me."

"By mistake?"

"Mistake? And followed it with a whole bottle of brandy just to make sure?"

"Brandy?"

"French vintage brandy, the best from his cellar. I suppose he figured he couldn't take it with him."

"Poor old Rudi."

"He was old enough to have loyal friends both sides of the Wall. Not many people like that left. 'Der grosse Kleiner' was the last of the Berlin old-timers," said Posh Harry.

"Damn nearly," I said.

"Who else is there? Lange, you mean? He's American. That old swine Rudi Kleindorf knew where the bodies are buried. And he's taken his secrets to the grave, Bernard." He chewed a piece of water biscuit: Harry didn't like cheese very much. "He never got over losing his son. And he went the same way: OD. Holy cow! Where will all those deadbeats go, now that the Babylon is no more?"

"Poor Rudi," I said again. "Why would he do that?"

"I heard he was in trouble with the authorities."

"He was always in trouble with the authorities," I said.

"His father was some kind of war hero. Name of Rudolf Freiherr von Kleindorf. Career officer. Made his name in the winter fighting on the Eastern Front. The First Panzer Army was chopping its way out of Tarnopol. One after another he carried three of his wounded joes to safety. Under fire the whole time: the Russkies should have dropped him, but a blizzard made visibility tough for them. Recommended for the Knight's Cross with diamonds or some damn trinket, but he didn't get one. Maybe that's why the story went around and made him into a legend among the other ranks. An aristocratic Prussian officer who risks his life saving enlisted men has got everything going for him." He grinned. "Get saddled with a reputation like that and you've got to keep it up, right? I guess he was one of those brass-gutted guys who figure they'll never get killed. We've known a few like that, eh, Bernard?"

"And?"

"He was right. They often are, aren't they? Kleindorf senior survived the war, and went to bat for his corps commander, who was accused of war crimes. And, darn it, he noticed that some deskbound zombie in the war-crimes commission had written 'Australian Division' in the indictment instead of 'Airborne Division,' and Kleindorf senior got the charges thrown out of court on that technicality. A sharp cookie! They say that, when Kleindorf attended any of those postwar veterans' gatherings, he was cheered to the echo for fifteen minutes. Rudi grew up in his father's shadow: I guess the old man was a tough act to follow. That's why he never mentioned anything about him."

"You know the devil of a lot about the Kleindorfs," I said.

"I had to run a check on him a few years back. I went

through all the files, including his dad's. It was kind of fascinating."

"I see why Rudi wanted his son to go into the army."

"To keep up the family tradition, you mean? Yeah, I guess we are all a little inclined to have other people make up for the things we didn't do for our folks, don't you think?"

"I don't know," I said.

He didn't press me, but when he next spoke he leaned forward slightly, as if to emphasize the importance of what he said. "These krauts stick together, Bernard. You can't be in Europe ten minutes without noticing that. We could learn from them. Right?"

I didn't know what the hell he was getting at, but I said, "You're right, Harry." My brother-in-law, George, was watching Posh Harry with great interest. George was the only complete outsider there, but he knew that Harry had some sort of connection with the CIA. Harry had virtually told him so the first time they met. That was a time when Harry was very pushy; now he'd quietened a lot.

It was then that Dicky took his cigar from his mouth, blew a little smoke, looked at me, and said, "Harry would like you to go for lunch with his people next week, Bernard."

"Is that so?" I said and wondered why Posh Harry hadn't proposed this culinary rendezvous himself. I looked at Harry. He was looking at Dicky.

Dicky said, "I said okay."

"Does that mean you're going to lunch?" I said.

Dicky smiled. "No, Bernard. They don't want a rubber-stamp wallah like me: they want an ex–field man to sort out their worries." He ran the tip of a finger along his lips, wondering, I suppose, if I was going to respond in kind.

Perhaps I would have done, except that Posh Harry hurriedly said, "We'd appreciate, Bernie, we really would."

Streeply-Cox looked at me and sanctimoniously boomed, "We've got to cooperate as much as possible. It's the only way; the only way." He brushed crumbs from his flowing white sideburns.

"You took the words right out of my mouth, Sir Giles," I said.

"Splendid, splendid," he replied.

Dicky jumped to his feet and said, "Methinks 'tis time we joined the ladies."

When I entered the drawing room, Daphne seemed to be demonstrating some dance step, but she stopped awkwardly as Dicky ushered the men in. Gloria was sitting next to Tessa, and she looked up and winked as she met my eye. I went across to her, as I knew I was expected to do. "Oh, Bernard," Gloria whispered. "Tessa wants us to go on with them to a lovely party. Can we go? Do say we can."

"When?"

"Now. After this."

I looked at my watch. "It will make a very late night by the time we get home."

"But we're all dressed up, aren't we? Do let's go."

"If you'd like to," I said.

"They're wonderful," said Gloria. "I love George, and Tessa is so funny."

"That depends upon where you're sitting," I said. "Do you know where this party is?"

"George says we should go in his Rolls. There's plenty of room."

"And leave the car here?"

"I'll come back and get it."

"And how would I get home? Walk?"

"Don't be so mean, Bernard. We can both come back and get it. Or we could get a cab home and come to get it in the morning."

"The meters start at eight-thirty."

"Can we go, Bernard, or can't we?"

I looked at her. "I'd sooner go home right now with the most beautiful woman in the room."

"Do let's go," said Gloria, who obviously was not in the mood to be flattered into doing what I wanted.

"It sounds wonderful."

"I do love you, Bernard."

"You're a horrible wheedling female," I said.

"A Bavarian prince and princess!"

Oh my God, I thought, what have I let myself in for? But, on the other hand, it would provide another chance to talk to Tessa about that damned fur coat.

Chapter 12

The prince and princess had their house in Pimlico, a corner of central London around which the Thames bends before getting to Westminster. When, long ago, Thomas Cubitt had finished selling large stucco-fronted houses with balconies to the rich of Belgravia, he built the same designs on the cheaper land of neighboring Pimlico. Pimlico was said to be coming up; it still is. For it never became another Belgravia, despite the similarity of its gardens, squares, and grand-looking houses. It was, and to this day remains, an area of mixed fortunes: a plight not assisted by the local government's seemingly random arrangement of one-way streets and barriers, which makes the district a notorious maze for motorists.

Cubitt's large houses are now divided into cramped apartments or, as the adverts put it, "studio flats" and "roof terraces." Seedy hotels and boardinghouses with crudely lettered signs offer accommodation in convenient proximity to London's only cross-country bus station and the busy Victoria railway terminal.

It was in one of the quieter streets of this region that our host had purchased a large house and refurbished it at considerable expense. It was, George explained to me while driving there, a shrewd investment. The sort of investment that he admired so many other German businessmen for making, now that the deutsche mark was so highly valued. The prince would use the place for his visits to London, entertain his business associates there, and save money on what it would cost him to do those same things in hotels and restaurants. Property prices in that area were certain to keep rising, and the chances were that in twenty years he would end up with an excellent profit on his investment. This made me ask George why he himself had bought an apartment in Mayfair— London's most expensive residential area—rather than do the same sort of thing.

"Ah," replied George, "because I am the son of poor parents. I want to enjoy the pleasures that money can bring. I want to go home each night and sleep amongst the richest men in England. I need that reassurance." He chuckled.

"It's not true," said Tessa. "It's my fault. We live in Mayfair because I wouldn't go and live in Pimlico." We laughed. There was an obvious element of fact in what both of them said. But the truth behind the rationale was that childless Tessa and George had no one to make a good investment for. In the silence that followed, I wished I hadn't asked him about house values.

All the nearby parking places were full, but we stayed with George while he parked his Rolls a block or so away. It was a cold night, and the streetlights tinted the empty streets with a grim blue that made it seem even colder. Entering the house brought a sudden change. The heated exertion of the guests, the bright lights, the crowded rooms, the warmth of the bodies, and the noise and excitement were electrifying. And so was the idea of a drink.

It was a big party: perhaps a hundred people were drifting through the house laughing, chatting in loud, confident voices, and tipping back their drinks. In the largest room there were a dozen or so people dancing to the music of a small band, and there was a buffet table with shellfish, smoked salmon, and sliced beef being constantly replenished by waiters in white jackets. "This is how the other half live," said Gloria as we made our way to where our young and glamorous hostess was standing by the fireplace talking to a well-dressed bearded man who proved to be the caterer.

Gloria was right. Prince Joppi's world was quite different from our more secret world, where, for various reasons, men drank and conversed with studied caution. Neither was this the ordinary world of supply and demand; it was a world of abundance. All around me there were the "over-" people: overanxious, overweight, overbearing, overeducated, overrated, overweening, overachieving, overselling, overspending, and overproducing. They ate and drank and noisily celebrated their good fortune. Never mind tomorrow, there would always be people like me and Fiona and Bartholomew H. Johnson to look after that.

The princess gave a welcoming smile as she caught sight of George and Tessa. She was petite and very slim, with dark hair that was in that state of rattailed disorder that takes very expensive hairdressers many hours to arrange. Her makeup, specifically the way in which her eyes were elaborately painted with green, blue, and black shadow, was stagy. Most striking of all was her dark suntan. Germany is a notably sunless land, and there is a type of German for whom a sun-darkened skin is an essential status symbol, no matter that health warnings advise against it.

The music stopped. The dancers waited to resume, but the musicians put down their instruments and departed for refreshments. "Tessa, darling!" said the princess as we got to her. They embraced in that perfunctory way that women do when they are wearing makeup and jewelry and have their hair done. "Promise me that you'll never let George take my husband away again."

"Whatever did they do?" said Tessa, a laugh in her voice, as if the answer might be both shocking and entertaining.

"That beastly scuba-diving school. Joppi can't talk about anything else, ever since they went there."

"But that was ages ago," said Tessa. "That was in Cannes."

"I know. I thought it would go the way of the oil painting and the computers—forgotten after a week or two—but Joppi has been absolutely demented. . . . He's bought all the equipment: air bottles and . . . I don't know . . . even books about it. He wants me to do it too, but I can't swim."

"Poor darling Ita," said Tessa with no hint of sincerity.

Further indicating her distress, the princess fanned herself, a mannerism more that of a schoolgirl than of a grown woman. "George," she said, "do something to get Joppi out of the billiards room." To Tessa she petulantly added, "It's always the same at parties: Joppi hides away in there and doesn't help at all."

Tessa said, "How lucky you are, Ita. George helps me, and it's absolute hell." George smiled and then said, "Let me introduce Gloria and Bernard, my brother-in-law."

"Are you really Tessa's brother?"

"No, I'm married to her sister."

"And you are Gloria," said the princess somewhat condescendingly, and smiled to show the sort of satisfaction women get from uncovering what might be illicit relationships.

After a few more pleasantries, Tessa took Gloria under her wing and they disappeared together upstairs, while

George took me to meet our host in the billiards room. From George's description I was expecting someone old and fat—a rotund wurst-gobbler likely to be found in a beer hall swaying to the melody of *"In München steht ein Hofbräuhaus—eins, zwei, gsuffa!"* But the prince turned out to be a tall, thin, sleek man of about thirty-five. A cosmopolitan tough guy who spoke English with no trace of an accent. Suntanned like his wife, he had unnaturally black hair that was shiny and brushed close to the skull. His dinner suit was conservatively cut by some expensive tailor. Like George and many of the other guests, he wore it in the casual manner of men who spend a great deal of time in such costume.

He was standing by the marker, drinking wine and studying the position of the cue ball. He looked up as we entered. "George!" he said with what appeared to be genuine pleasure.

"All alone?" said George. "Perhaps you'd prefer . . ."

"No, George. I was hoping you would come." He snapped his cue into the rack with an excess of force, as a well-drilled soldier might place his rifle somewhere close at hand.

George said, "This is Bernard, a very good friend despite being my brother-in-law."

"Brother-in-law and friend too!" the prince said, grimacing in mock surprise. "That's surely a tribute to the grace and generosity in both of you."

As I went through the formalities, the vague feeling of recognition snapped into focus. I'd seen the activities of this "playboy prince" in some of the less serious German newspapers and magazines.

George said, "Quite a dressy crowd here tonight, Joppi."

"Not many real friends. They're people my wife feels we owe favors or hospitality to," said Joppi as if his wife were suffering a strange and troubling delusion, an affliction from which he hoped she'd eventually be released.

"Ita tells me you've become an expert diver, Joppi," said George.

"Yes, next time you'll find I'm even better than you," said Joppi. "It is a matter of fitness, George. And practice." To ask any German to undersell such hard-earned achievements is to ask a great deal. "We spent Christmas in my brother's beach home near Rio, and the water was perfect. Now I'm good, damned good."

"Lucky man," said George.

"You're guests, and not drinking," the prince said. "We must rectify that immediately." He smoothed his perfectly smooth jacket and began to move toward the door as if guessing that his wife had asked George to prize him out of the billiards room.

He snapped his fingers, German style, at the nearest waiter and conjured up drinks for us. But before I could get my hands on one, Tessa—bright-eyed and smiling—had grabbed my arm. "First you dance, Bernard. I insist."

I hadn't danced for so long that it required all my concentration not to tread on her toes, but soon I was managing well enough to try talking too. "When can I pop over for that fur coat?"

"Joppi's a lovely dancer, isn't he?" Tessa said as if she'd not heard me.

I turned my head to see our host with Gloria gripped tightly in his arms. "Yes," I said.

"I knew he would be interested in Gloria. She is just his type."

"But will Gloria find him interesting?" I asked.

"That doesn't matter half so much," said Tessa. "He will find *her* interesting, and that's what attracts any woman."

I didn't argue with her: probably she was right. I'd never understood women and given up hope that I might ever do so. Anyway, it would do no good to argue with Tessa. She handled her life in her own way and made no concessions to anyone, not even to her husband.

"He's like that," said Tessa. There was the hint of a joke in her tone. She was being provocative and made no secret of it. "He has quite a reputation with the ladies. He'll proposition her; you see if he doesn't."

"How do you know?"

"You silly man!"

I steered her sharply round to avoid bumping into another couple and said, "When was that?"

"Me and Joppi? He wanted me to leave George, but that was just his machismo. He would have left me high and dry after a few months. I knew that."

"Does George know?"

"There is nothing to know, darling." We danced without speaking for a little while, and then Tessa said, "Gloria is awfully worried about you, darling."

"Gloria is worried?"

"You're not looking your best, Bernard. Surely other people have mentioned it to you."

"No, they haven't."

"Don't get snotty. You're looking bloody rotten, if you want to hear the truth of it. Gloria thinks you should see the doctor, and I agree with her."

"See a doctor? What am I supposed to be suffering from?"

"Stress can do strange things, Bernard. You're probably overworked. . . . I don't know. But you're damned jumpy and suspicious all the time. And apart from that you don't look well."

"I'm one hundred percent," I said.

"My man in Harley Street is really wonderful, Bernard. Would you go and let him give you a checkup, as a personal favor to me?"

"I do believe you're serious."

"Of course I am. And I promised Gloria to talk to you."

"I'll think about it."

"No. Say you'll go. I'll make the appointment."

"I said I'd think about it."

"I'll phone you next week. I'm going to keep on at you until you go."

"For God's sake, Tessa." Then, realizing that I was being inappropriately rude, I gave her a kiss on the cheek. What I didn't tell her was that even a routine checkup like that would have to be reported to the Department. I didn't want anyone there asking if I was sick. All kinds of complications would follow. They were just looking for an excuse to put me on the shelf.

I saw Joppi again. He was a skillful dancer, and Gloria was loving every moment. She gave no sign of thinking that the prince should go and see a doctor. As they went gliding round the floor, I regretted that I hadn't made more effort at Frau Brand's dancing classes back in Uhlandstrasse when I was twelve years old. "And he's a friend of George's?" I said.

"Friend? George can't stand him. George detests Germans; you know that, Bernard. George turned away the offer of a Mercedes agency. He won't even buy a secondhand German car for resale."

"So why do you come here?"

"Ita is one of my best friends. She's a sweet girl. We go shopping together. And when it's my turn to arrange one of my charity lunches, you'd be amazed how many of those ladies want to meet a princess."

"I was wondering when I could collect that fur coat," I said, having given up hope of being able to introduce the subject with more subtlety.

"It was George who first met them," said Tessa. "He met Joppi at Mass; George always attends Mass, you know. You'd never guess that's where they met, would you?"

"No, I wouldn't have guessed that." I watched Joppi

laughing with Gloria and hugging her as they danced together and said, "Perhaps you'd like to visit us out in the sticks, and have dinner one evening?"

"We'd love that, Bernard, my sweet. But please don't say, 'Bring that bloody coat,' because the answer is no."

"It's just that—"

"Your Gloria is a nice girl. I don't know her very well, but from what I see of her I like her. And I like the way she worries about you: you're a lucky man. But I'm not going to deliver Fiona's fur coat for you to give to her. It's just not on, Bernard. It's wrong, and I'm surprised you don't see that."

"Come to dinner anyway," I said.

"It's almost summer," said Tessa.

"Yes," I said as the music stopped.

"Do look," said Tessa, her amused voice not concealing the malicious pleasure that colored her view of the world. "He's probably propositioning her now. He'll invite her to go to Rome for the weekend, or to the penthouse they keep in New York. It must be very tempting."

It was no use showing anger. No one was exempt from Tessa's *Schadenfreude.* "It's getting late," I said, "and I have to be up early tomorrow."

Generously George insisted upon us going back to his Mayfair apartment for a nightcap. And then, leaving Gloria and Tessa to chat, he drove me back to collect the car near Dicky's house. "That house of Joppi's," said George suddenly, "it's full of rot."

"Is it?" I said.

"I went upstairs to use the bathroom. My God! You should see the woodwork. And it's established in the walls . . . the plaster. You didn't notice?"

"No," I said.

"To get rid of that, the whole house will have to be gutted."

"Did you tell him?"

"And be the bringer of bad news? No. Poor fellow. I couldn't bring myself to spoil his evening."

"Didn't he have it surveyed?"

"He listened too much to that fancy architect—all stainless steel and indoor plants—I can't stand those fellows."

"No chance of redress?"

"Suing the builders, you mean? Compensation? No chance at all. They were right cowboys. Those people form a new company for every job, and go bust as soon as they are paid. Those people work like that."

"Poor Prince Joppi," I said.

"Yes, poor devil," said George solemnly. Had Tessa not told me George's real feelings, I might have thought he meant it. He was a good driver, careful, alert, and considerate of other road-users. When a young fellow in a dented Ford came roaring past him on the wrong side and gave a toot on the horn to reprimand George for driving too safely, George just pulled over and made more room for him.

"Stupid bastard!" I said angrily.

"Perhaps he had a bad day," said George mildly. Sometimes I wondered whether it was his piety that provided him with such remarkable tolerance. If so, it was a convincing argument for Roman Catholicism. "You're a man of the world, Bernard," said George suddenly.

I was about to give a flippant answer, but I realized that George had something on his mind. So I grunted and said I would like to think so.

"Any experience of drug addiction? Cocaine, heroin, that kind of thing?"

"I'm not an expert."

"There's a fellow hanging around Tessa. . . . She was talking about drugs the other night, saying that there is a lot of nonsense talked about them, and I don't doubt there is."

George went silent. I said, "I'd better get this clear, George. You think this fellow is selling drugs to her?"

"Yes, Bernard, I do think so," he said cautiously.

"Give me his name and address."

"I don't want to overreact," said George. "That could bring about the very thing I'm so anxious to avoid."

"There's no harm in checking," I said. "I know good people who would give you some answers within a couple of days."

"Calls himself Bill Turton, but I wouldn't give too much importance to that. He's a prosperous-looking American; not young." Having started to confide in me, he stopped and thought about it for a moment. "It wouldn't be so easy, Bernard. He's one of those people without a fixed address: hotels, clubs, rented places, one country to another. Never stays long anywhere."

"Is this what Tessa tells you?"

"She invited him up for drinks the other evening. I didn't like him at all. I could see he was charming and friendly and all that, but I had an instinctive reaction."

"You may be worrying unnecessarily."

"He was there at the Joppis' tonight."

"Was he?" I was surprised and wished George had brought the matter up when there was an opportunity for me to see the man.

"Always lots of that sort of muck available at the Joppis'. Did you go upstairs?"

"Upstairs? No."

"One of the rooms upstairs . . . They think it's very smart and sophisticated."

"I noticed that there was a mood . . . a sort of hysteria."

" 'Hysteria.' Yes, that's the word, isn't it? I can't imagine how people can bear poisoning their own bloodstream with chemicals. Do you know that Tessa won't eat processed food because of the chemical additives? And yet she . . ."

"I'm sorry, George."

"That's why she wanted to go. Did you notice how animated she became?"

"Not any more than usual. She's always in high spirits; you know, that, George."

"A big fellow, gray wavy hair and glasses."

"There were a lot of people like that," I said.

"This fellow has a little rim beard and no mustache. Curious-looking cove."

"I didn't see him," I said truthfully. It could have been a description of Mr. Bart Johnson, but Bart Johnson was dead.

Chapter 13

It was the morning after Prince Joppi's party that I was walking along South Audley Street and bumped into Rolf Mauser. Rolf was about seventy years old, a wartime artillery captain who didn't let anyone forget that he'd won the coveted Knight's Cross. He was an unprincipled rogue but he had an engaging manner, and when he worked for my father, and later as the barman in Lisl's hotel, I saw a lot of him. It was Rolf Mauser who'd shown me how to pick a lock and how to hold a playing card out of sight while shuffling the rest of the pack. When I was a child I'd been devoted to him, and even though I'd long since seen him for what he really was I'd never completely shaken off some of that awe. Although for me Rolf had become an elderly figure of fun, underlying the fun there was something ruthless and frightening.

I was surprised to see him here in London, for the last I'd heard of him he'd settled down to live permanently in East Berlin.

"You're looking well, Rolf. What are you doing in London?" He was a big fellow and wore one of those heavy brown leather overcoats with plenty of straps and buttons. Its tight fit made him look as if he were about to explode out of it. This impression of impending detonation was heightened by the rosiness of his cheeks and nose.

"Bernd! Hello! I'm visiting my relatives. I have a cousin who lives in Luton."

"Where are you living nowadays?" I asked.

He bent his head and touched his green loden hat as if to ease the constriction of its band, but it would be possible to read into this physical gesture a hint of apology. "I'm still in the East. When you get to my age, Bernd, you're looking for peace and quiet. And, what's more, it's cheap."

"Still in the same apartment?" He'd put me up there once. His apartment was large, comfortable, but somewhat neglected, rather like Rolf himself.

"Prenzlauer Berg, yes. Fifty-five marks a month! The rent of my apartment is the same now as it was twenty-five years ago. Can you say that about any apartment in the West?"

"No."

He lowered his bushy eyebrows and defensively added, "Sometimes there are shortages, but basic foodstuffs—bread, milk, meat, and eggs—are cheap. So are restaurant meals, and fares and theatres and concerts. I'm comfortable in the East, Bernd. Very comfortable." It sounded like a little speech he'd rehearsed.

"And a little money goes a long way over there," I said.

His face stiffened. Mauser had worked for the Department and was probably in receipt of some small pension through the good offices of Schneider, von Schild und Weber, the bank which discreetly handled such delicate financial affairs in Berlin. Social-security payments for the old—unlike almost all other types of benefit—are not high in the DDR. Only a dedicated cynic like Rolf could be extolling, even to me, the wonders of this regime under which he'd chosen to retire, while he was largely living on the proceeds of the pension he'd got from trying to overthrow it. "That's what I was saying, isn't it?"

"It's good to see you, Rolf."

"So I have to line up for groceries and meat sometimes; I don't mind lining up. I have time to spare. And when I walk home from the shops I don't have to worry about being burgled or mugged."

"You're lucky. Where are you going?"

"Yes, I am lucky," he asserted as if he weren't quite sure of my sincerity. "No matter how tough they are with the youngsters, old fellows like me can come and go as we like. I don't have to climb over the Wall, Bernd." He grinned.

If I knew anything about Rolf Mauser—and I knew quite a lot—he would never see eye to eye with any socialist regime. He was a rebellious loner. The communists, like the Nazis and indeed the Church, had always welcomed converts to their cause, but it was difficult to imagine Mauser acquiring *sozialistisches Staatsbewusstsein,* that unquestioning enthusiasm for the regime that the DDR expects of its citizens. Mauser was a pragmatist and a self-centered one at that. Long, long ago I'd heard my father describe Rolf Mauser as the sort of arrogant, bellicose German who earned for his race the civilized world's contempt. Calmly my mother had asked him why he went on employing him. Because he'll do things no one else will even attempt, replied my father.

"Come and have coffee?" I suggested. I guessed that he would be very short of hard currency, and casual cups of coffee are one of the first things such indigents sacrifice.

"I'd like that, Bernd. That's the one thing I can't get at a reasonable price. Luckily my son sends me a packet every month. I can't live without a cup of good coffee in the morning."

There was a smart little coffeehouse nearby, and we

walked there quickly, with Rolf complaining at great length about the weather. "It gets right into my bones," said Rolf as we sat down. It was the dampness, of course. Rolf, like most Berliners, found the marginally warmer English climate poor compensation for the penetrating chilly moisture that most natives don't even notice.

The coffeehouse was a chintzy place that I knew well. I used to have coffee here with Fiona when we worked in a nearby office. That was before we were married. I ordered a big pot of coffee prior to finding a table. It was the best way to get things moving.

"How is Axel? I haven't seen him for a long time." I was at school with Mauser's son. At one time we'd been close friends.

"They live in a nice house in Hermsdorf, but his marriage is not too smooth. Ever since that wife of his got that wonderful job and started earning big money, she's become a monster." He shrugged and reached for a Danish pastry.

"I'm sorry."

"Work work work—that's all she thinks about. She's a career woman," he said contemptuously. "But Axel won't hear a word against her. I don't see the attraction she has for him. He needs a real woman." I'd heard Rolf railing against his daughter-in-law for many long years. The way he spoke of her, you wouldn't think the marriage had lasted a couple of decades and that they had a teenage son.

"Axel was one of the brightest boys in the school," I said. Rolf had always been smug about the way Axel was consistently top of the class. He especially liked to tell my father that Axel had done better than I had.

He tore the wrapping from a sugar cube. There was a ferocity—if not to say malignity—to everything he did. Hellos, goodbyes, even thank-yous were a part of this belligerent spirit. I wondered if it was a pose he'd cultivated to maintain his authority as a young army officer, a pose that eventually devoured his true nature. "And now he's working as a clerk in the Polizeipräsidium. I know, it's a waste of a good brain, but he won't listen to me." He tossed the sugar into his coffee.

"I suppose he's worried about his son."

"His son? What is there to worry about?"

"I didn't mean that," I said. "I meant that Axel probably works hard to keep his marriage going so that his son has a mother and father and a settled home life."

"Nonsense!" said Rolf Mauser. He chewed his pastry, his mouth moving as if in anger.

"Axel loves the boy," I said. "I remember how he assembled a racing bicycle for him. He put it together with such loving care."

"I know, I know. The kid had an accident: some fool in a Porsche. Broke his leg, kept driving, didn't stop. He'd had a few drinks, I suppose. Axel blamed himself. That's stupid, isn't it?"

"I don't know," I said. In fact, of course, most fathers would have felt equally guilty. It was only roughnecks like old Rolf who saw things in such a simplistic light. I suppose it was the war. I remember Rolf telling stories about the last days of the Berlin fighting. Hauptmann Rolf had been sent off on patrol with a "flying court-martial," and they summarily executed anyone on the street who couldn't give a proper account of himself. They shot him there and then and hanged the body with a sign saying, "I deserted my post." Axel had said he couldn't imagine his father doing such things, but I knew that Rolf could be a cold-blooded killer if he thought it necessary.

Perhaps some of my thinking was communicated to him, but if so it arrived in a distorted form, for he said, "If Axel had served in the army, he might have kept a better sense of proportion."

"Is that what the army gave you, Rolf?"

He furrowed his brow, and his eyebrows bristled so that he looked ferocious. I remembered being frightened of such grimaces when I was a child. "Ever dream, Bernd?"

"Of being rich, or a film star?" I knew what he meant, of course, but I couldn't resist jollying him along. The fact was that I didn't want to hear his dreams; I didn't want to hear anyone's dreams. I had enough of my own.

"I don't sleep so well nowadays. I went to the doctor; he said it was my age. Stupid little schlemiel." He leaned forward. "I always dream about my time in the army, Bernd. I remember things I haven't thought of for years. And such detail! I got command of a self-propelled artillery battery when the battalion was out of the line. My battery commander went down with some kind of fever; I didn't know you could get fever in the middle of a Russian winter, but I learned a lot in Russia. It was Christmas, and we were refitting in Krasnograd. Ever heard of Krasnograd?"

"I don't believe I have," I said.

"A godforsaken dump in the middle of nowhere. But there were trees; a lot of trees, considering that the region had been fought through. The men liked the trees; it reminded them of home. Heavy snow and wooded countryside: with an effort of imagination it could almost have been the homeland. The peasants remained there, of course—they always did. Russian peasants would sooner die than leave their village, they were all like that. I couldn't understand it. Then, in the middle of my daily bowl of pea soup—that powdered muck, but the cook had found some ancient potatoes to go into it—the signals lieutenant came back from headquarters and told me that the battery was mine. Wow! Did that soup suddenly taste good!"

He sat back and gave a half-smile, but not at me. He didn't even see me at that moment: Rolf Mauser was miles away, and decades back in time, fighting his war in Russia. He rubbed his face. "Taking command of six huge fifteen-centimeter heavy howitzers mounted on tank chassis was quite an event in the life of a young man. I took it very seriously. I went round and spoke to every officer and man under my command: two officers, twenty-nine NCOs, and ninety-two enlisted men. Most of them were newly arrived replacements: green kids, not long out of school. The other night, in my dream, I recalled every name and face. I even remembered the equipment I signed for." He looked at me and wanted me to see how important all this was to him. "I could even taste that damned *Erbsensuppe.*"

"And when you woke up?"

"Still remembered everything. Twenty-eight lorries, two motorcycles, sixteen light machine guns, twenty machine pistols, forty-eight handguns, and seventy-eight rifles. I even remembered the names and ranks. Every one of their stupid faces."

For a moment I thought he was about to recite all their names and numbers and give me the specifications of the hardware and its state of readiness. Perhaps the consternation showed on my face, for he said, "Take my word for it. I can see those men now. Every face, every accented word they spoke. We left most of them deep under the ice and snow. By summer, only half a dozen of those men were still serving with me."

For the very first time I saw that Rolf Mauser had spent his life entertaining dreams of military glory. An absurd ambition, perhaps, but no more absurd than the dreams of most men. And, if the statistics were to be believed, no more unlikely than ending up with a happy marriage and a loving family. "General Rolf Mauser" had an implausible ring to it, but the award of a "tin tie" must have provided new impetus to his hopes of promotion, and certainly he had the necessary ruthlessness.

"Everyone dreams, Rolf," I said. "It's nothing to do with getting old."

"So what do I do?"

"Get another doctor."

He gave a humorless smile before giving all his attention to the coffee and what remained of his pastry.

For a brief time neither of us spoke. Then, "Der grosse Kleiner is dead," said Mauser as he stuffed down the final mouthful of his Danish pastry.

"So I heard. What do you know about it?"

"Don't tell me it was suicide."

"I don't know anything about it," I protested.

"Kleindorf wasn't the type." He used the tip of his tongue to remove a crumb from his teeth.

"So what was it, then?"

"He was a dope dealer. He was behind the refining, and he was the contact between East and West."

"Who says?"

"Regular consignments of it were coming through Schönefeld, arriving in the West for repackaging and then going back there again. There were DDR officials taking a cut. It's all being hushed up. Even the West Berlin authorities are keeping *stumm.*"

"Why?"

"The official word is that the relationship between the two Germanys must not be threatened by such crimes."

"And the unofficial word?"

Rolf let a slow smile spread across his big round face. "That officials on both sides are deeply implicated. Big shots, I mean."

"Sounds a bit farfetched," I said doubtfully.

"Does it, Bernd? We've known each other a long time, haven't we? Are you seriously telling me that you've never heard rumors or stories about such dealings?"

"Rumors, yes." I wondered if he'd heard the sort of stories Larry Bower had got from Valeri, the double agent. "Even so . . ."

"Kleindorf had a massive dose of heroin; that's what he died of. You know that?"

"I thought it was sleeping tablets."

"Yes. That's the story that's being put around." He nodded. "Do you happen to have a cigarette on you, Bernd?"

Having stopped smoking for a long period, I'd lately been accepting offered cigarettes. This morning my nerve had cracked and I'd bought a packet of cheroots. But I suddenly resolved to try harder. I handed the unopened packet to him. I said, "Isn't that more to your taste?"

"It's very kind of you, Bernd. Are you sure?"

"I've stopped smoking."

He lit one immediately and continued. "But the real story is that Kleindorf died while in bed with one of his young dancing girls, a woman with a strong Silesian accent who disappeared long before the police arrived and has never been traced."

"What are you getting at?"

"She'd worked for him for only a few days. The name and address she gave to his secretary at the Babylon were false." He blew smoke.

"Do you think the woman murdered him?"

"She arrived in town with an American. They flew out together: two first-class tickets to Rome. There were no needle marks on Kleindorf. Except for the marks of the needle that killed him." He waited for me to absorb that fact and then said, "He'd never take hard drugs: he was a health freak. Jogged every morning without fail."

"What did the autopsy say?"

"No autopsy. The certificate said death was due to an overdose of sleeping tablets. An accident. Hurried burial; a demand for an inquest summarily refused."

"I heard he'd drunk a whole bottle of vintage brandy."

"There was an empty bottle in the bedroom. Who can say how much he'd drunk unless they open the stomach? Probably he'd had a drink with the girl. Did you ever see Kleindorf drunk?"

"No," I said.

"Exactly. It's a cover-up. It sounds perfectly credible unless you know what Kleindorf was really like."

"Okay," I said. "The stuff comes from Asia. They bring it into East Berlin. The Schönefeld Airport customs let it go through because it's official policy to help the decadent West mainline its way to oblivion. Okay. What I don't get is why it does a turnaround and makes a journey back East again."

"The consignments they are tapping into are brown, raw stuff. You have to be pretty desperate to float that shit into your bloodstream. None of the people at that end of the dealing has the know-how, the resources, or the equipment to refine it, or the guts to risk it. That was Kleindorf's contribution to their game."

"Have another coffee, Rolf." I signaled to the waitress.

"This is a good place for coffee," said Mauser appreciatively. "I'm glad I met you, Bernd."

"What sort of people in the East would be buying this stuff?" I said. "And where would the money come from?"

Rolf Mauser knew he was being pushed, but that was better than confessing his ignorance. "You know how these things work, Bernd. The transaction was drugs for paperwork."

He paused as if he'd said something self-evidently significant. Perhaps he had, but I wasn't going to let him stop there. "Would you enlarge on that notion?"

"Permissions. Imports. Contracts. A signature and a rubber stamp on a desk over there can mean a lot of money over here. You know that, Bernd. So does your friend Werner Volkmann." He puffed smoke. It was a subdued gesture of aggression. He looked at me and waited for a reply.

"You're not saying Werner was implicated?" Before taking over the running of Lisl's hotel, Werner had made a lot of money from avalising: putting together import and export deals so that the DDR didn't have to part with hard currency. In that respect Werner's livelihood had depended upon East Berlin signatures and rubber stamps.

"I don't know." He waved a hand. "But if he was, he got out of that business at exactly the right time. He doesn't go over there any more."

"He's busy with Lisl's," I said. I watched Rolf tap ash from the cheroot. All my desire to smoke had gone: the smoke, the smell, the ash, the very idea disgusted me.

"Of course he is," said Mauser. "And if I were you, Bernd, I'd find myself something to be busy with." A meaningful look. "Because there are a lot of people on both sides of the Wall who are looking for someone to lay the blame on. You would fit the role nicely."

"As a drug courier?"

"With evidence from both sides? It would be overwhelming. Who would believe anyone protesting his innocence if East and West put together a story?"

"How do you know all this, Rolf?"

"I know a lot of people and I keep my ears open."

I talked with him for almost another half-hour, but Rolf had decided to say no more, or perhaps knew no more, and the conversation turned to chatter about his family and other people we both knew. His aforementioned relative in Luton was not amongst the people he talked of. I wondered whether his cousin was not just a cover to hide the real reason for his visit. There were several chair-bound Departmental officials not so far away from here who would be pleased to have someone like Rolf Mauser to amplify their long, tedious, and tendentious reports about the DDR: writing which bore little resemblance to the reality. It would be rash of him to continue to work for us, but, given on the one hand the pressure the Department was always ready to apply to anyone who could be useful, and on the other hand Rolf Mauser's appetite for both risk and extra spending money, I guessed that he might be doing exactly that. An added dimension was provided by the possibility that he was playing a double game, reporting everything back to the other side. I hoped any Departmental person dealing with him had considered that and kept it in mind constantly.

When I left Mauser I found myself disturbed by the conversation we'd had. There was something about his words that unsettled me. I'd known that same feeling since I was a child. Mauser enjoyed alarming people.

Chapter 14

I dismissed Rolf Mauser from my mind as I walked up to Oxford Street and went into Selfridge's hardware department to get a new hinge for the garage door. It had to be big, for the door's timber was not in first-class condition. Eventually I'd have to fit metal doors, but that was not an outlay I wanted to face in my present circumstances. And when Gloria went to study at Cambridge I might decide to sell the place. One of the store assistants went into a stockroom and found the sort of long hinge I needed. I was carrying it with me—wrapped in brown paper—when I went to the address in Upper Brook Street, behind the American Embassy, to meet Posh Harry for his promised lunch.

"No need to have brought your Kalashnikov, Bernard," said Harry when he saw the parcel. "Strictly no rough stuff; I promised Dicky that." He laughed in that restrained naughty-boy way that Oriental people sometimes do. "Come and have a drink," he said and led the way up to a first-floor room. As always, he was neatly dressed in somewhat English-style clothes: gray flannels and a dark blazer with ornate metal buttons and, on its pocket, the gold-wire badge of a Los Angeles golf club.

Mayfair is an exclusive district of elegant residences, most of which are offices in disguise. It is a place of high rents and short leases, of private banks and property developers, art dealers and investment managers, all discreetly hidden behind simple brass nameplates. These houses are small, and the cramped, overfurnished upstairs room into which he showed me was designed for rich transients. The house had been given the style of refurbishment that my brother-in-law called "the gold-tap treatment." There were lots of table lamps made from big robust jars and sturdy shades, sofas with loose covers of glazed chintz, and the sort of carpet that wine doesn't stain.

However, any effect of gracious eighteenth-century living was marred by the "refreshment center" in the corner: a plastic-topped table held a hot plate with two big glass jugs of coffee, mugs, paper cups, and biscuits, and a handwritten notice about putting ten pence into the cashbox and not using mugs with names on them.

"Take the weight off your feet," said Harry as he unlocked a reproduction terrestrial globe, the upper hemisphere of which hinged at the equator to reveal a core of drink. "A martini, or name your poison."

"A martini will do nicely." I watched him select the bottles: Beefeater and Noilly Prat.

"I'll tell you this, Bernard," he said as he went across the room and pulled at a bookcase. "You can keep California." His exertions bore fruit as a section of antique leather books and shelving came loose in his hands to give access to a small refrigerator that was concealed behind it. "Yes, sir!" With commendable dexterity he threw ice cubes into a jug, and held two chilled glasses while gripping the gin bottle under his arm.

He removed the stopper from the gin bottle and mixed the cocktails with careless skill. "Take it easy on the gin," I said.

"I never had you figured for a guy who was heavily into vermouth," he said, ignoring my strictures. He held up the glasses as if judging the color of the concentration and then handed one of them to me. "Only one thing I can't tolerate, Bernard . . . a vermouth addict. Pass that across your tonsils—the perfect martini."

"I like California," I said.

"Not working for my outfit you wouldn't like it," he said. He went to the window and looked down at the traffic. It came from Hyde Park and into this one-way street like close-packed herds of shiny migrating animals, thudding past without respite. "They let me go. Can you believe it?"

I smiled and tasted my drink. Whatever failings Posh Harry had exhibited in California, mixing martinis could not be amongst them.

Harry said, "There are a couple of files I want to ask your advice about before lunch." He looked at his watch. "Our table is booked for one o'clock. Okay?"

"Sure."

"Am I glad we had this meeting today, Bernard. You don't know what a favor you're doing me."

"I am?"

"Providing me with an excuse to stay clear of the office. Joe Brody is in town and kicking ass like there is no tomorrow."

"Joe Brody?"

I suppose he saw my antennae wobbling. He said, "Yeah, Joe Brody! Joe Brody has flown in from Vienna and is lunching with the ambassador today, but that didn't stop him from coming into the office and raising hell with just about everyone working there."

"Is Brody such a tough guy?"

"He can be: unless you know how to handle him." He gave a foxy smile. "He needs the velvet touch, if you know what I mean. You must know Brody?"

"We've met in Berlin."

"Brody is itchy for a big promotion. The buzz is that he will go into Operations at a senior level."

"Brody is too old."

"In the CIA, old buddy, no one is ever too old. That's what keeps us all bright-eyed and bushy-tailed and breathing down the necks of our bosses."

"Brody?"

"And he's making sure Washington knows he's alive and kicking. Get the picture?"

"I thought Brody worked out of Vienna."

"Forget Brody. I can handle Brody. Let me show you these files. You tick some boxes and tell me anything we're getting wrong, then we go and write off the rest of this month's expenses in the Connaught. What about that?"

"It's a deal," I said.

"Look through this while I go and get the rest of the stuff from the safe upstairs." He handed me a colored file and a felt-tip pen.

I looked through the file. It had the expected pink addendum sheet at the back, arranged with a question-and-answer format that the CIA designed for "day-by-day turnaround" of urgent material. There was nothing very difficult about the framed questions, even though I was depending entirely upon my memory. But there were a lot of them.

Harry came back with two more files and slammed them on my knees. Noticing that my glass was empty, he went and mixed two more of his "perfect" martinis.

"There's another file but I can't find it. One of the clerks says it went to Grosvenor Square. Could be Brody wanted it. It might arrive with the messenger at noon. Anyway, do what you can, and then we'll go and eat. Leave your parcel here.

We'll come back after lunch, and if that damned file's arrived maybe you'd take a look at that one too."

"Okay."

My work done, we walked to the Connaught Hotel in Carlos Place, the cold air only partially undoing the effect of Harry's martinis.

He'd reserved a seat by the window, and Posh Harry did everything he'd promised. We struck into the à-la-carte side of the menu, and the wines he selected were appropriately excellent. It was the first time I'd ever had such a friendly conversation with Posh Harry. I'd known him for many years but met him only in the line of business.

If an agent's competence was measured by his personal cover, then Posh Harry was one of the most proficient I'd known. For years no one seemed quite certain if he was linked to the CIA. Even now I was not sure if he worked for them on a permanent basis. Harry's brother—much older than Harry —had died miserably on a CIA mission in Vietnam, and the way I heard it, Harry blamed the Company for his death. But that wasn't anything I'd ever mentioned to him, and if any trace of bitterness remained from that ancient episode there would be little chance of him revealing his feelings.

Harry, no less assertive and no less devious than Rolf Mauser, was everything the old man wasn't. Mauser was a bully who enjoyed the rough-and-tumble process of getting his own way. For Harry the end result was all that mattered. It was, I suppose, the fundamental difference between Europe and the Orient, between the visible and the concealed, between force and stealth, boxing and judo.

It would have been wiser of me to have given more weight to such reflections before lunch, for by the time I got back to the house in Brook Street I was unprepared for the furious reception that awaited us.

"Do you know what time it is?" yelled Joe Brody, whose

lunch with the ambassador had apparently been a briefer and more austere refreshment than ours.

"I'm sorry, Joe," replied Harry, caught halfway up the stairs with a red-faced Joe Brody shouting at him from the upper landing. I looked at Brody with interest. Until now I'd never seen him in anything but a relaxed and gentle mood.

Brody was wearing a striped blue three-piece suit appropriate for lunch with the ambassador. He was old, a bald man with circular gold-rimmed glasses that fitted tight into his face like coins that have grown into the trunk of a gnarled tree. At other times I'd seen him smiling sagely while holding a drink and listening indulgently to those around him. But here was a frenzied little fellow who could even plow furrows across Posh Harry's calm features. "You're sorry. Goddamnit, you should be. Who's this? Oh, it's you, Samson, I almost forgot you were coming over here. Have you finished?"

By that time we were at the upper landing. Joe Brody ushered the two of us back into the room we'd been in before lunch. He strode across the room, took off his jacket, and tossed it onto a chair. Slowly, like some aroused reptile, the jacket uncoiled and slid to the floor. Brody gave no sign of noticing it.

I didn't answer. Brody looked at me and then at Harry. I felt embarrassed, as one feels when accidentally witnessing a blissfully married couple suddenly transformed by a savage domestic rift. In the silence one became aware of the traffic noise, which provided an unending roar, like distant thunder.

When Harry realized that I had decided not to tell Brody whether we had finished, he said, "Not quite, Joe."

"Jesus Christ!" And then, even more furiously, "Jesus Christ!"

"Just one more file," said Harry repentantly.

"Did you ask him about Salzburg?" Brody said, talking about me as if I weren't present.

"I wasn't sure if you wanted me to bring that up," said Harry.

"Sit down, Bernard," said Joe Brody. He gave a nervous, fleeting smile, as if trying to reassure me that I was not a part of his row with Harry, but some of his wrath spilled over.

"Do you want a drink, Joe?" said Harry, still trying to assuage Brody's wrath.

"No, I don't want a goddamned drink. I want to see some work done around here." Brody grabbed his nose as if about to take a dose of nasty medicine. Harry felt a sudden desperate need for a glass of club soda and went and poured one for himself. I'd never known Posh Harry even slightly discomposed, but now his hands were trembling.

Brody sank down into the armchair facing me and sighed. Suddenly he looked exhausted. His tie knot had loosened, his waistcoat was partly unbuttoned, and a lot of his shirt had become a rumpled lifebelt round his waist. His bad temper had made demands upon his attire and his stamina. But any expectations I had about his temper moderating were not encouraged by the harshness of his voice as he continued. "One of our people was blown away: in Salzburg. You hear about that?"

"I was there," I said.

"Sure, you were there. What exactly happened, Bernard?"

"So that was one of your people?"

"I asked you what exactly happened."

"I don't know what exactly happened," I said.

"Now, don't snow me, Bernard. I haven't got a lot of time and I'm not in the mood."

"I can't tell you anything that the police investigation hasn't already revealed."

"You saw the police report?"

"No," I admitted.

"So how the hell would you know?" He grabbed his nose

again, then finished the gesture by rubbing his mouth fiercely with the flat of his hand. I decided it was a gesture of self-restraint by a man who was on the verge of a real tantrum.

"Take it easy, Mr. Brody," I said. "It was an explosive charge triggered by electricity. Your man Johnson died. That's about all I can tell you."

"Would you please describe Johnson."

"Pleasant manner. Tallish, in good physical shape, but slightly overweight. Gray wavy hair; rim beard, no mustache, gold-rimmed bifocals—"

"That's enough. Who set it up, kid?"

"I've no idea."

"I think you have," said Brody, letting his voice go a bit nasty.

"Then give me a clue," I said.

"I'm asking the questions," said Brody. "Think again."

"I've told you all I can tell you, Mr. Brody."

He sat there glowering at me.

"I'm going to ask you again, Bernard. I want to put this on a formal footing."

"You can put it on any kind of footing you choose," I said. "I've told you once and I'll tell you again. I don't know."

"Our guy," he said and paused. I'd forgotten the way senior CIA men always said "our guy." When he continued he spoke in that disjointed way people do when they are upset. "Our guy was named Bart Johnson. He was a good man . . . worked out of Frankfurt. I've known Bart twenty years. We were together in Moscow: a long time back. Toughed out some bad ones. I lunched with the ambassador today. I wanted him to know that Washington has authorized me to follow this one as forcibly as my resources permit."

"I'm gratified to hear that, Mr. Brody, because, if I should get blown away like your friend Johnson, I'd like to be up there knowing that someone is following me up as forcibly as resources permit."

"Okay, Bernard, we know you were in contact with Bart Johnson. No one is saying that you were implicated in the killing, but I want to know exactly what was going on in that damned hotel right up to that explosion."

"The only thing I can tell you that was going on in that hotel up until the explosion was a stamp auction." I was trying to keep my voice calm and polite but not entirely managing it.

"Try harder."

"Try easier questions."

"Okay. Here's an easier question: why are you being such an asshole?"

I got to my feet and went across the room. Inconspicuously fitted into the oak paneling, and flanked by two horse-racing prints, there was a door. In front of the door there was an occasional table with an inlaid checkered top upon which chess pieces had been arranged by some interior decorator. I turned. Brody was standing up. I kicked the table aside, chess pieces and all, and tried to open the door. It was locked. "Will you open the door, Mr. Brody, or shall I do it?"

Perhaps, without that bottle of Château Talbot and the double measure of malt whisky with which my meal had ended, I would have had neither the rashness nor the force to do what I did next. I raised my boot and kicked the door almost off its hinges. It swung into the next room with a noise like thunder.

For a moment I thought I'd made a terrible miscalculation, but I hadn't. Standing up blinking in the sudden light were two shirtsleeved men with headphones clamped over their ears. Their faces were set in an expression of horror. Beyond them there were some TV monitoring screens shining in the gloom. The operators had jumped to their feet. One of them leapt back so that his headphones' lead pulled a piece of equipment from the table. It fell to the floor with a crash. Then the heavy door, with a prolonged squeaking noise, twisted on its remaining hinge and sank slowly to the floor, landing finally with a resounding bang. Neither operator said anything; perhaps it happened to them frequently.

They were of course putting me on videotape. I suppose it would have been stupid of them to hear what I knew without having some sort of record of it, but that didn't mean that I had to sit there and cheerfully confess to anything that might later be construed as making me an accessory to a murder.

"Okay, smart ass, you've made your point," said Brody calmly. It was a different sort of voice now. I still don't know how much of his former bad temper was feigned. And, if it was feigned, to what extent it was a device to intimidate me or to intimidate Posh Harry. "Come and sit down again. We'll talk off the record if that's what you want." To the two video operators he said, "Take off, you guys. We'll cut the crowd scene," and he smiled at his own joke.

Posh Harry hadn't moved. He was still standing near the refrigerator sipping his soda water.

"Could we go downstairs and talk in another room?" I asked. "The kitchen, for instance?"

"With the water running and the fluorescent light on?" offered Brody sarcastically. He went and picked up his jacket from the floor, frisking it to make sure his wallet was still in place. "Sure. Anything that will make you feel good, Bernard." His manner was warmer now, as if he preferred the idea of talking about his friend Johnson's death to someone who could kick doors in.

We went downstairs to the tiny kitchen in the basement. It had the same well-preserved look that the rest of the house had. Here was a kitchen where no meal was ever cooked. There were wet cups and saucers in the sink and some glasses on the draining board. On the shelf above it there were packets of coffee and a huge box of tea bags and a big transparent plastic container marked "Sugar." A gray slatted blind obscured the window.

Joe Brody opened a refrigerator filled with canned drinks. He helped himself to a Pepsi, snapped the top open, and drank it from the can. He didn't offer anyone else one: he appeared to be lost in thought.

I sat with Harry at the circular kitchen table. Brody gripped an empty chair, rested his foot on a bar of it, and said, "Were there two Americans, or just the one?"

"Two," I said, and I described Thurkettle and the way he'd come out onto the terrace and talked about sharing an office with Peter Underlet, and the way in which Johnson had approached me after the auction. I didn't say that I'd bid in the auction, and I left out any mention of my wanting the cover.

Brody sat down and said, "We know about the auction."

"Why don't you tell me what you know, Mr. Brody. I'll try and fill in the spaces."

"Thurkettle, you mean?"

"That's what I mean," I said.

"Well, now you see why I wanted to leave a few of the details out," said Brody. "We're trying to establish that both men were there at the time of the explosion."

"I heard Johnson speak to Thurkettle as he went into his room. At the time I thought he was talking to himself. Afterward . . . well, I don't know."

"When was that?" said Brody. He upended his Pepsi and drained the last of it with obvious relish. I suppose he needed the sugar.

"Maybe half an hour before the explosion," I replied.

"What did he say?" Carelessly Brody tossed the empty can across the room. It landed with a clatter in the rubbish bin.

When Brody's eyes came back to me I said, "I think he said, 'What about that?' It was the sort of remark a man might make to himself. But it might have been a greeting."

"To someone already in his room?"

"He knew Thurkettle was there the previous day."

"How do you know that?"

"He talked about it. He asked me if I knew who he was."

"He asked you that?"

"He said he'd met Thurkettle before but didn't know who he worked for or what he did."

"Do you know who Thurkettle is? Really know?"

"I do now," I said.

"Let me ask you a speculative question," said Brody. "Why would Thurkettle come back to the hotel and go to that room? The bomb was already in the razor. Why didn't he keep going?"

"Ummm," I said.

"Don't ummm me. You must have thought about it," said Brody. "Why didn't he keep going?"

"I don't know," I said. "But when I went back to warn him who Thurkettle was . . ."

"Hold the phone," said Brody. "Are you expecting me to believe you were going to tip Johnson off about Thurkettle? You? The guy who sits here stonewalling all questions about the death? No, sir, I don't buy that."

"I'm not sure what I was going to do. I went along to his room to find out what the hell was going on."

"Okay, keep talking."

Posh Harry got up and went to the refrigerator and, after looking at everything on offer and selecting a tumbler from the cupboard, poured himself a drink of soda. Harry must have been very fond of soda. Or perhaps he was trying to sober up. Brody glared at him to show that such movement disturbed his concentration. Harry sipped his soda and didn't look at Brody.

I said, "I went into his room and spoke with him just before the explosion. He said I was to come back in fifteen minutes. Right after that the damned thing exploded."

"Let me get this straight. You spoke with Johnson in his room a few minutes before he died?"

"He called from the bathroom."

Brody said, "The bathroom door was closed? You didn't see him?" He tugged his nose as if in deep thought.

"That's right." I began to understand what was going on in Brody's mind. He waited a long time. I suppose he was deciding how much to tell me.

Eventually Brody said, "When that voice told you to come back in fifteen minutes there were two men in the bathroom. Johnson was probably just about to be murdered."

"I see," I said.

"I don't think you see at all," said Brody.

"Who was Thurkettle working for?"

"He's a renegade. He's been a KGB hit man for two years. We've lost at least four men to him, but this is the first time he's come so close to home. Johnson and Thurkettle knew each other well. They'd worked together back in the old days."

"That's rough," I said.

Brody couldn't keep still. He suddenly stood up and tucked his shirt back into his trousers. "Damn right it is. I'll get that bastard if it's the last thing I do."

"So he didn't die as a result of the explosion?"

"You worked that out, did you?" said Brody sarcastically. He went over to the sink and turned to look at me, leaning his back against the draining board.

"Thurkettle murdered Johnson and after that blew his head off with explosive. Why? To destroy evidence? Or was Johnson too smart to go for the razor bomb? Was Thurkettle caught switching razors? Did he kill Johnson, then use the bomb with a timing device?" Brody, still staring at me, gave a contemptuous little smile. "That way he wouldn't get spattered with brains and blood."

Posh Harry had regained his customary composure by this time. Still holding his glass of fizzy water, he went over to where Joe Brody was lounging against the kitchen unit and said, "You'd better level with him, Joe."

Brody looked at me but said nothing.

Harry said, "If you want the Brits to help, they have to know the way it really happened."

Brody, speaking very slowly and deliberately, said, "We think Thurkettle killed Johnson and then blew his head off to destroy evidence. But the guy who told you he was Johnson was really Thurkettle."

"The hell it was!" I said softly as the implications hit me.

Brody, enjoying my consternation, added, "The dead body you saw in the bathroom was the man who spoke with you on the terrace."

"I see."

"You don't see much, Samson, old buddy," said Brody. I'd earned that rebuke: I should have looked more closely at the dead body on the floor.

Posh Harry said, "Thurkettle changed identity with his victim on a previous occasion. It had us real puzzled for ages."

"So what are you going to do about it, Bernard?" said Brody.

"I'll stick with the soap-and-water shaves," I said. Brody scowled. I got to my feet to show them that I wanted to leave. He turned away and leaned across the sink to prize open the slatted blind and look out of the window. There was a minuscule yard and a whitewashed wall and large flowerpots in which some leafless stalks struggled for survival. From the front of the house, through the double-glazing, came the traffic noise: worse now that the end of the working day was so close.

"Don't forget the Kalashnikov," said Posh Harry.

Joe Brody was still looking at the yard. He seemed not to have heard.

I went upstairs to get my parcel. Harry came with me and added a few snippets to what I knew about Thurkettle. Other

U.S. government departments, resentful at the way the CIA had got Thurkettle released from prison and provided with false documentation, had proved singularly uncooperative now that he had, in Harry's words, "run amok." The CIA had sought a secret indictment from a federal grand jury in the District of Columbia and it had been thrown out of court on the grounds of lack of identification. An application to the Justice Department had also failed, and so had the attempt to have Thurkettle's citizenship revoked. Harry explained that there was now a desperate need to link Thurkettle with a crime. Everyone—by which I suppose he meant Brody—had been hoping that my evidence would supply the needed link. Until it was obtained, Thurkettle was thumbing his nose at them and walking free.

"I still don't get it," I said. "If you find out why Thurkettle blew Johnson away, things might become clearer."

"We know why," said Posh Harry smoothly. "Johnson had the goods on him."

"On Thurkettle?"

"That was Johnson's assignment. They were buddies. Joe Brody told Johnson to find him and get pally. Last week Johnson phoned Brody and confirmed that Thurkettle was peddling narcotics. He couldn't say much on the phone, but he said he had enough evidence to put Thurkettle in front of a grand jury."

"But Thurkettle was a jump ahead of all concerned."

"Joe Brody blames himself."

"Narcotics."

"The prevailing theory in Grosvenor Square," said Harry, "is that Thurkettle blew poor old Kleindorf away too."

"Why would he do that?"

"I was hoping you'd tell me. We think Thurkettle is doing business with London Central." He laughed in a way that said it might be a joke. I decided not to get angry: I was too old to get angry twice in one day.

I nodded and thanked him for lunch and felt pleased that I hadn't mentioned Tessa's new friend with his rim beard and no mustache. They would have been all over George and Tessa. Anyway, by now he might have shaved it off.

We talked for a few minutes more, and then I said good-bye to Posh Harry and went home. I hadn't brought the car into town that day; I was using the train. Standing all the way in the shabby, crowded compartment, I had a chance to reflect on what had happened. Had I been set up, I wondered? Brody's fury had been all too convincing, and Posh Harry's reaction to it could not have been entirely feigned. But had the powerful martinis, and the big lunch with lots to drink, been a way of getting me softened up for Brody's grilling? And to what extent had Dicky guessed what I was walking into?

Chapter 15

I'd known "Uncle" Silas all my life. He'd been my father's boss from a time before I was born. I remembered him in Berlin when I was a child. He was young Billy's godfather and distantly related to my mother-in-law.

He had long since retired from the Department, and he now lived at his farm in the Cotswold hills. He was old and becoming more exasperating every time I saw him, but I knew there had been times when I'd exasperated him more than he ever had me. To look truth right in the eye, I suppose I'd only kept my job this long because my father had made good friends; and Uncle Silas was one of them.

So, when I had a phone call from an agitated Mrs. Porter, his housekeeper, and was told that Silas Gaunt was seriously ill and asking for me, I went to him. I didn't ask for permission, or tell Dicky I needed a day off, or even send a message to the office. I went to him.

The day began with unabating heavy rain, and the wet roads persuaded me to drive cautiously. It was a long drive, and so I had plenty of time to reflect upon this precipitate action during the journey. As I got to the Cotswolds, the hills were lost in gray silken skeins of mist, and the trees on the estate were entangled in it. "Whitelands" consisted of about six hundred acres of fine agricultural land and an assorted clutter of small buildings. There was a magnificent tithe barn, large enough to hold the parson's tribute of corn, and stabling for six horses. The tan-colored stone farmhouse itself had suffered a couple of hundred years of depredations by philistine occupiers, so that there was a neo-Gothic tower and an incongruous wing that housed the large billiards room.

I was used to arriving here to find a dozen cars scattered in the front drive and—on sunny days—parked in the shade of the three tall elms that marked the limits of the lawn. On such days the house was noisy with appreciative guests. It was not like that today. The front drive was empty except for a muddy Land Rover from which three young men in faded denim were unloading equipment, including, I noticed, three bright-red hard hats and three sets of earmuffs. The rain had stopped, but the water dripped from the drenched trees and the lawn squelched underfoot.

The metal grating in the porch rattled as I stepped on it, reminding me to scrape the mud from my shoes. I pushed open the front door and went into the hallway. The house was silent and, like all such farmhouses, dark. The tiny windows, set in the thick stone walls, allowed only small rectangles of daylight to cut colored rugs out of the Oriental carpet. Suddenly, from the drawing room, through several closed doors, Lohengrin began singing "In fernem Land."

Mrs. Porter, his ever-cheerful, ever-dependable cook, housekeeper, and general factotum, came from the kitchen to say hello and take my coat. Still holding it, she went past me to look out of the front door. She sniffed the air with relish, as a submarine commander might savor the night after a long spell submerged. Over her shoulder I saw that one of the forestry men had donned a red helmet and ear covers and was climbing one of the trees. He was getting very wet.

She came back to me. "Yes, I thought I heard your car," she said. "I'm so pleased you are here, Mr. Samson. I was worried. . . . I still am. He becomes so listless when he is ill."

"Really?" I said. I didn't find it easy to visualize a listless Uncle Silas.

"He got up and dressed when he heard that you were coming. I phoned the doctor about it, but he said it would be all right as long as he stayed indoors, rested, and kept warm."

"That sounds like the doctor," I said.

She smiled uncertainly. Women like Mrs. Porter become alarmed if their faith in medicine comes under attack. "The doctor said that Mr. Gaunt could be taken from us anytime," she said in a voice that seemed intended to remind me of the leading role Silas' physician played in a drama where I was no more than a walk-on. I assumed a suitably sober face and she said, "He's writing his memoirs. Poor soul! He seems to know his time is coming."

His memoirs! Political careers would be ended; reputations in shreds. It was unthinkable that Silas would ever get permission to write such a book, but I didn't contradict her.

"He puts it away when I go in there. I'm supposed not to know about it, but I guessed when he smuggled the little typewriter downstairs. Before the last bad turn, I would hear him tapping away in the music room every day. That's where he is now. Go in, I'll bring you tea."

The "music room" was the drawing room, into which Silas had installed his hi-fi and his record collection. It was where he sat each evening listening to music. He didn't care much for television. I was reluctant to interrupt his opera, but

Mrs. Porter came up to the door and said, "Do go in," and added, with an almost soundless whisper which her exaggerated lip movement helped me understand, "He's probably asleep; it's the pills."

At Mrs. Porter's insistence, I barged into the room. I didn't see him at first, for his back was to me as he faced the log fire. He wore a dark shirt and a plum-colored velvet smoking jacket, complete with cream silk handkerchief flopping from the top pocket. It was the sort of outfit an Edwardian actor might have chosen to go to the Café Royal. A tartan car rug was beside him on the floor. It had fallen from his knees, or perhaps he'd pushed it aside when he heard me arrive. His feet—in vermilion carpet slippers—were resting upon the fire irons. The music was loud, and there was a smell of wood smoke. As if in response to a draft from the doorway, the fire burned bright, so that yellow shapes ran across the low ceiling. "Who's that?" he growled. He wasn't asleep.

People who knew Silas Gaunt well, amongst whom my father was certainly numbered, spoke of his exquisite courtesy, old-world manners, and compelling charm. My mother had once described him as a boulevardier: it was the first time I'd ever heard the word used. To hear them speak of Gaunt, you would have expected to meet one of those English eccentrics in the mold of Henry Fielding's Squire Allworthy. But the Silas Gaunt I knew was a devious old devil who paradoxically demonstrated the skin of a rhino and the sensitivity of a butterfly, according to his long-term plans.

"I hope I'm not intruding," I said very quietly.

"I'm listening to *Lohengrin,* damnit!" he said. I was somewhat relieved to find that, whatever his corporeal condition, his bellicose spirit was alive and well. Then, as he turned his head to see me, and the fire flickered brighter, he said, "Oh, it's you, Bernard. I thought it was Mrs. Porter again. She keeps pestering me."

During my childhood Silas had always shown affection for me, but now he was old and he'd withdrawn into his own concerns with aging, sickness, and death. There was less affection in him now. "She's concerned about you, Silas," I said.

"She's in league with that damned pill-pusher," he said. He switched the record player off in a way that simply lifted the stylus. The record under the transparent lid kept turning.

I found a place to sit. He'd lost a lot of weight. His clothes were loose, so that his wrinkled neck craned from his over-sized shirt collar. The shadowy room was cluttered with his bric-a-brac, antiquarian curios, and mementos from far places: scarabs, an African carving, a battered toy locomotive, a banderilla, an alpenstock carved with the names of formidable climbs, a tiny ivory Buddha, and a broken crucifix. Once Silas had told me that he didn't want to be buried in the earth. He didn't want to be in a tomb or consecrated ground. He'd like to be put in a museum surrounded by his possessions, just as so many of Egypt's kings were now to be found.

"We're all concerned about you," I said. It was a somewhat feeble response, and he just glared at me.

"That damned doctor wants my grandfather clock," said Silas.

"Does he?"

"That's all he comes here for. Never takes his eyes off it when he's here. The other day I told him to go and put his bloody stethoscope on its movement since he was so interested in asking me if it kept good time."

"Perhaps he just wanted to make polite conversation."

"That marquetry work is what attracts him. But he's got central heating. It would dry out and crack in six months in his place."

"It's a lovely clock, Silas."

"Eighteenth-century. It was my father's. The front panel has warped a fraction. Some of the inlay work projects just a shade. It has to be polished very carefully by someone who understands. Mrs. Porter doesn't let anyone else touch it. She winds it too."

"You're fortunate to have her looking after you, Silas."

"That damned quack wants to have it before I die. I know what he's after: a written statement about the clock's condition and history. That sort of provenance affects the price in auction. He told me that."

"I'm pleased to see you looking so well," I said.

"His house is filled with clocks. Skeleton clocks, carriage clocks, balloon clocks, clocks riding on elephants, clocks in eagles' bellies. I don't want my lovely clock added to a collection like that. It would be like sending a child to an orphanage, or Mrs. Porter to the workhouse. He's a clock maniac. He should go and see a psychologist; there's something wrong with a man who wants to live in a house filled with clocks. I couldn't hear myself speak for all the ding-donging and carry-on."

There came a light tap at the door. Silas said, "Come in!" in the jovial booming tone he used for Mrs. Porter. But it proved to be one of the young men. "All ready to go, Mr. Gaunt," he said, his voice enriched with the local accent.

"Very well," said Silas without turning to see him.

The man looked at him as if expecting some more earnest response. "We'll go ahead, then."

"I said yes," said Silas irritably.

The man looked at the back of Silas' head, looked at me, rolled his eyes, and then withdrew. I waited to see if Silas would account for the interruption, but he just said, "I've rediscovered Wagner in my old age."

"That's gratifying."

After a long pause he said, "I'm losing the elms. They've got that damned disease."

"All of them?"

"The ones at the front." He bit his lip. "They've always

been here: my father loved them. I suppose I shouldn't let myself become upset about those stupid trees, but . . ."

"You can put in others," I said.

"Yes, I'm going to put in six oaks." He smiled. It was understandable that he identified so closely with the trees that had always framed the house from the drive. There would be more trees, and more people too, but Silas Gaunt will have been felled, fired, and forgotten by the time they matured. He brought out a bright-red cotton handkerchief, dabbed his eyes, and blew his nose. "Is it too smoky for you? Open the window if it is."

"I'm fine."

"Fledermaus went well? You saw Fiona?" Outside there came the sound of the chain saw being started up. His face stiffened, but he pretended not to hear it.

"I saw her," I said.

"It's clear to you now?"

It was still far from clear, but there was little or nothing to be gained from saying so. "So we're pulling her out?" I said, wanting him to confirm it.

"In due time."

"It's a miracle she's lasted so long."

"She's a damned good girl," said Silas. "A wonderful woman."

"And Erich Stinnes is coming too?"

Silas looked at me blankly. He must have been momentarily diverted by the racket of the chain saw. The sound of it came in longer and longer bursts as they severed larger and larger branches prior to the felling. A tree is like a network, of course, and that's how the old wartime training manuals always depicted it. And, like a tree, a network is destroyed beginning with a twig. Then a small branch, until it is uprooted and eradicated. "Stinnes . . ." said Silas. "Yes, I suppose so. Does Stinnes matter?"

"Matter?" I said. I was as puzzled as he seemed to be.

"Enrolling Stinnes . . . getting him to go back there and work for us was brilliant. It was the master touch," said Silas. His eyes were bright and alert now. "If Stinnes eventually comes back intact, the Department will break every rule in the book to get a K for Bret Rensselaer."

I looked at him carefully. So Stinnes *was* working for us. Surely what he really meant was if *Fiona* eventually comes back intact, but he didn't want to be that candid with me. "Was that Bret's doing?"

"No. But sending Stinnes back was originally Bret's idea. Bret pushed and pushed for it."

"It was madness," I said. "Maybe Stinnes pulled it off; maybe they are playing with him. Who can be sure? Either way, sending him back was reckless. It endangered Fiona."

"Can't you see it, even now?" said Silas. He shook his head at my slowness. "We didn't care a jot what happened to Erich Stinnes, and we still don't. Stinnes was sent back there for one reason and for one reason only: to reinforce the story that Fiona was a genuine defector."

"Not to work alongside Fiona?"

"No, no, no. That was the beauty of it. No one revealed to Stinnes that Fiona went back to work for us—because virtually no one there knows. Every one of our people believes that Fiona's defection was the worst blow the Department ever suffered, and whatever suspicions passed through his mind, Stinnes went back believing that too."

I said, "Do you mean Stinnes was told to report and defuse what Fiona was supposedly doing to us?" It was beautiful. It had the symmetry that distinguishes art from nature.

Silas smiled contentedly as he watched me thinking about it. "Yes, 'Operation Damage Control'—that's what Bret told Stinnes he was. Stinnes was just a means to an end."

"And so was I," I said bitterly. "I've been made a fool of, right from the start." The revelation that my wife was a hero-ine, rather than a traitor, should have made me rejoice. In some ways it did, but on a personal level I felt bitter at the way I'd been used. My anger extended to everyone who knew about Fiona's long-term commitment and had kept it from me. Everyone included Fiona. From outside, the sound of the chain saw was now continuous. They must have been cutting through the trunk.

"You mustn't look at it like that," said Silas. He sighed. It wasn't one of the histrionic sighs he'd used in the old days. It was the sigh of a sick old man who finds the effort of living too much for him. "You played a vital role in what happened. What sense was there in having you worry about the operational side?"

"That's what Fiona said. Was this what you wanted to see me about?" I asked.

"That damned quack says I could go anytime."

I nodded. He looked ill. Mrs. Porter wasn't worrying unnecessarily.

"I suppose Mrs. Porter told you that. She tells everyone. I can see from the look in their face when they come in here to talk to me."

"She's very discreet," I said to calm his anger.

"What will happen when I go, I've been asking myself. Bret is sick, and anyway Bret doesn't know the whole story. The D-G knows, but no one will listen to him because they say he's batty. What do you think about him?"

These were dangerous waters, and I navigated away. "I haven't seen him for a long time," I said.

"The rumor is that he has Alzheimer's, but my quack says the only certain way they can confirm Alzheimer's is by means of a postmortem." There was a sudden silence, and then a soft thud and a muddle of voices as the felled tree hit the wet lawn. The sounds of its death saddened me. Silas gave no sign of having heard it, but I knew he had. "Do you know what I think?" He shifted restlessly. A man as big and as powerful as Silas was apt to resent infirmity in a way that other men did not. He eyed me to make sure I was giving him my full attention. Then he said, "The old man's deaf."

"Yes," I said. "Everyone knows that."

"Even more deaf than he admits," said Silas. "They all think he's crazy because he's too damned vain to get himself a modern hearing aid. I think the D-G is as smart as you and I."

"I'd like to think you are right," I said, and then tried to get back to the point. "So you, Bret, and the D-G are the only ones who know that Fiona is one of ours?"

"That's exactly right. Even the Vienna team who arranged the meeting for you last week think she was acting for Moscow."

"I'm relieved to hear it."

"If all three of us—me, Bret, and the D-G—go at once, and that's not beyond the bounds of credibility, you and Fiona will be the only ones who know the true story. Even the case officer processing her reports is not really a case officer; he doesn't know where they come from."

"And so I'd have little chance of convincing anyone that she's one of ours."

"And Fiona won't dare try." He gave a little cough to clear his throat. "Yes, that's the position, Bernard. That's why I sent for you."

"What do you propose we do?" I said.

"Wait." I looked at him. His face was white and bloated but, ill or not, he still displayed the fierce determination that he'd always shown. "We can't pull Fiona out until the time is right."

"Don't wait too long, Silas," I said. "Agents get overconfident, we both know that. She'll have to be ordered out. I wanted her to come back with me."

"And undo everything she's worked for? Bernard, your wife is a perfectionist. Surely you must have realized that during your married life with her."

"No," I said. All I'd discovered about my married life with Fiona was that, although I'd shared with her just about every idea, thought, and emotion I had, she'd guarded her own secrets with a discipline that was no less than obsessional. I felt as if I'd been swindled. Not bilked, burned, or ripped off for a short-term loss, but systematically deceived for years and years by the person who had vowed to love me and care for me. Fiona Kimber-Hutchinson, do you take this bachelor? Yes, I was taken.

"She wants to stage her own death, so that they won't be alerted to what she's been doing over there. Stage her death and then go to ground somewhere for six months or so. We could continue using her material for ages if they are not alerted to what she's been doing."

I followed the reasoning, but the implications made my head swim. If Fiona was to be hidden away somewhere, would I be there with her? And what reason could Gloria be given for my sudden disappearance? Telling her the whole truth would be out of the question. And what about the children?

Silas added, "She's given us all sorts of wonderful stuff that we haven't used for fear of endangering her. Once she was safe, we could really pull all the stops out."

He might have said more, but Mrs. Porter came and set out tea for us. She had excelled herself today: homemade sausage rolls and a *Kugelhopf,* a sweet bread she'd learned to make after discovering that it brought back to Silas happy memories of times long ago.

"I can't eat all that, woman," said Silas fiercely.

"Don't fuss! Mr. Samson will eat it. It's a long drive; he must be hungry."

Silas reached in his pocket for the keys that were on a ring at the end of a gold chain. He held one key up. "You see this fellow, Mrs. Porter? If anything should happen to me, you take this little item and you give it to Mr. Samson. You phone him and tell him to come here, and you give it to him and to no one else. You understand that, don't you, Mrs. Porter?" In a carefree gesture, worthy of a boulevardier, he swung the keys round on the end of the chain before tucking them back into his pocket. Outside, the chain-saw noise began again.

"I can't bear to think of such a thing, Mr. Gaunt."

"You'll do as I say now. I can depend upon you, can't I?"

"You know you can, sir."

"That's good. Now, toddle along. I don't want you weeping all over me."

Mrs. Porter arranged the cups and lifted the lid on the vacuum jug to show me it was filled with hot water. Silas grunted to indicate his impatience. She gave me a brave smile, sniffed, and withdrew.

"I saw that fellow Dodo in Vienna," I told Silas casually as I poured tea from the magnificent silver teapot. There was a date engraved on it. Silas had been given it by his staff when he left Berlin.

"Ah, yes. We had to do something about him," said Silas vaguely.

"So what happened?"

"They gave him an MBE or something and supplemented his pension."

"They did what?"

"Don't get excited, Bernard. It was probably the best way of handling it. He was getting to be rather disgruntled, and he knows too much for us to let him go around talking his head off. He got the stick-and-carrot routine."

"He's a drunk."

"He's settled down, Bernard. He knows what's good for him."

"An MBE was the carrot?" Even a cynic like me was appalled.

"No citation, nothing like that. For services rendered to the intelligence community. All very vague. An MBE will disqualify his revelations. That award will make Moscow think

we're pleased—that he is acting on our orders." His com-
pressed lips moved in what might have been a fleeting artful
smile to celebrate the cunning of it. "It doesn't cost anything,
Bernard, and it's Fiona's safety we have to think about."

"Yes." How very English! When the peasants become
troublesome, throw a title to them.

"Give me that big brown packet." I took it from the table
and passed it to him. From it he got a legal document: the
curiously ornate sort of thing that—along with wigs and
gowns, and the world's most autocratic trade union—English
lawyers find indispensable to practicing the law. It consisted
of about forty pages of typed material bound together with
green tape that passed through eyelet holes punched in each
sheet. "Here's a complete description of everything I know
concerning Fiona's assignment. Names, dates, and so on. It's
all here."

Thinking he was about to give it to me, I held out my
hand, but he ignored it. "Have you got a pen that works?" He
opened it to the back page and said, "I want you to witness
my signature. The solicitor johnny comes round tomorrow for
me to sign and swear in his presence. I want you as a witness
separately. You don't mind, I hope?"

"No," I said. "Of course not."

He signed his name and then showed me where he
wanted me to sign, pedantically insisting that my address be
written in block capitals in the appropriate space. "I want to
make sure that it is legally valid," he said. Where it said "occu-
pation" I wrote "civil servant." He inspected what I'd done,
blew on the ink to help dry it, and pronounced it satisfactory.

"Can I read it now?" I asked.

"No need for you to read it, Bernard. This is just for
'insurance' purposes. I have every reason to hope I'll be alive
and well when Fiona returns."

"Of course."

He heaved himself from his chair and went over to an

antique military chest. Using a key on his key chain, he locked the document away. He held up the key before putting it back in his pocket. "Understand, Bernard?"

I nodded. "She was recruited at Oxford, was she?" I asked.

"Let's, rather, say she was noticed there. It was a cousin of mine—a history professor—who recruited for us. He'd never put forward a female student before. Fiona was to speak at a debate, and he suggested that we both went over there to hear her. I'll never forget that evening. She was supporting the motion that Einstein's theory of relativity was a hoax. I wish you'd heard her: it was an impressive performance, Bernard."

"But Fiona doesn't know anything about mathematics," I said.

"That's perfectly true, but not many of the audience did either. She was clever enough to exploit that. The other speakers bored everyone with rational argument. When it came to Fiona, she was attractive and amusing. She made fun of her opponents and put together a loose but reasoned and coherent argument. She couldn't win, of course—everyone knew that—but she demonstrated some fast thinking. She assembled a few well-researched facts, a few half-truths, and a lot of absolute bosh and cobbled together a convincing whole picture from it all."

"I thought that's what everyone did at university."

"You're not far wrong, Bernard. But in Fiona I saw someone who could keep her own mind crystal-clear and far removed from the material she was handling. That is the essence of the work we do, Bernard. Failure in the art of intelligence comes to those who cannot distinguish between what they know to be facts and what they wish were true."

"Or *will* not distinguish," I said feelingly.

"Precisely. And your wife is a realist, Bernard. No flights of fancy for her, no romanticism, no wishful thinking."

"No," I said. "None at all."

"She was never recruited. I kept her to myself. It was the way things were done at that time. We all had our own agents: your dad, me, Lange, ran our own people by means of Central Funding's unregistered transfers. The sort of money you hounded Bret Rensselaer about not too long ago: remember?"

"Yes," I said.

"When Sir Henry became Director-General, I told him that Fiona was in deep cover. When she pressed for a chance at this big one, I brought Bret in too. We decided to keep it to that. Her name was never written down."

He relapsed into silence. I poured more tea for myself, but he didn't touch his. Staring into the fire, he seemed to be lost in thoughts that he was reluctant to share. "I miss your dad," he said finally. "Your father always had an answer for everything that came along. He hadn't had his brain pickled by bloody university lecturers. I don't think he ever sat an examination in his life." Silas looked at me; I didn't respond. Silas said, "Self-educated people such as your father—'autodidacts,' I hear them called nowadays—don't read in order to find accord with the answers predetermined by half-baked examining boards; they find an individual point of view." He sat back in his chair. "My word, Bernard, I've laughed to see your father demolish some of those young lads they sent us. He could quote from such diverse sources as to leave them gasping: Jung, Nietzsche, Suetonius, Saint Paul, Hitler, George Washington, statistics from Speer's confidential records, Schiller, and Einstein. It was all at your father's command. I remember him explaining to a scholarly old SS general that his great hero Arminius—who valiantly defeated the Romans in a way that the Britons, Celts, and the rest of them had failed to do—deprived Germany of the benefits of civilization, kept her in a state of barbaric chaos so that for centuries they didn't even use stone for building. 'You Germans have a couple of centuries of civilization to catch up with,' said your father patiently. It was difficult to know how much of it was to be taken seriously." Silas chuckled. "We had such good times together, your dad and I." For a few moments Silas was his old self again, but then, as if coming to terms once more with the fact of my father's death, he relapsed into a solemn silence.

"What happened at Berchtesgaden, Silas? What happened there that seemed to destroy my dad's career?"

"And cast a shadow on my career too," said Silas. "Ever wonder why I didn't get my K?"

"No," I said, but in fact it was a question that I'd heard asked many times.

"How much do you know?"

"A German, a man named Winter, was shot. Dad was blamed. That's all."

"Two Germans: a prisoner in the direct custody of your dad and the fellow's brother, who, technically at least, had a U.S. Army commission. It was the American Zone. The war had ended. The men involved were all waiting to go home. They weren't front-line soldiers. They were middle-aged family men, supply clerks, warehouse men, misfits in low medical categories—not used to handling weapons: nervous, drunk, trigger-happy. . . . Who knows how it actually happened? Your father was the only Englishman there, and he'd ruffled a lot of feathers. The Yanks dumped all the blame on him. Max was sorry afterward. He told me so more than once."

"Max?"

"Max Busby. Lange's man." Seeing my blank look, he added, "The one who was killed when you came over the Wall with him. He had been a captain in the American army. He was in charge of the search party that night when the Germans were shot. You didn't know that? Max didn't ever tell you?"

It took me a little time to get over my astonishment. "No, Max never told me that. He was a damned good friend." It was a mealy-mouthed description of a man who had been shot dead while giving me a chance to get home safe and sound. But I didn't have to say more: Silas knew the story.

"To you he always was. Max liked you, Bernard; of course he did. But I often wondered to what extent he was trying to make up for the injustice he helped to bring upon your dad. It was Max's evidence that convinced the inquiry that your dad accidentally fired the shots. That story suited them. It enabled the soldiers to go back to civilian life almost immediately, and it deprived the U.S. newspapers of a story that they were planning to make into headlines. But your father's reputation never recovered from it. They were going to get rid of him to some rotten liaison job, but I insisted that he stayed with me."

"So that's why Dad hated Max," I said.

"Max—yes; and Lange too. He didn't have much time for any American after that. It was a childish reaction, but he felt bitter and frustrated."

"Didn't he want the inquiry reopened?"

"Of course he did. Your father wanted that verdict quashed more than anything in his life. But the Department couldn't permit the publicity that would have come with it. And the official policy, of both us and the Americans, was to avoid anything that might engender bad feeling between the Allies." He sat back. The memories had invigorated him for a moment, but now their ghosts had invaded the room and he seemed not to know that I was there. I drank some of my lukewarm tea.

When Silas spoke his voice was strained. He said, "I think I'd better have some of that damned medicine. Mrs. Porter knows how much to give me."

"I'll go now, Silas," I said finally. "You must get some rest."

"Stay to lunch, Bernard."

"I must get back," I said.

He didn't put up much argument. Now that his task was

done, all the energy was sapped from him, he wanted to be left alone.

"I'm sorry about the elms, Silas."

"The oaks will look fine," he said.

I declined Mrs. Porter's invitations to stay for something to eat. I had the feeling that Silas wanted me to leave the house and go away, rather than have something by myself in the kitchen. Or was that my paranoia? Whatever the truth of it, I wanted to get away and think my thoughts to myself. At the quiet little church, on the narrow road that goes from Whitelands' gates to the village, a line of parked cars gave notice of a service in progress. It was a funeral. Perhaps two dozen dark-garbed people were standing around an open grave, huddled under their umbrellas while the priest braved the elements, his vestment whipped by the wind and his face radiant with rain.

Crawling along behind a tractor, I was given a chance to study this solemn little ceremony. It depressed me further, reminding me that soon—very soon—Silas, and Whitelands and all they meant, would have vanished from my life. My mother was old and sick. Soon Lisl would be gone, and the hotel would be unrecognizable. When that happened I would no longer have any connections with the times that meant so much to me.

Perhaps Silas was right: perhaps a shelf in a museum, with all the rubbish of our lives surrounding us, would be the best end of us all.

Suffering from this somewhat irrational melancholy, I stopped at the next little town for a drink. No pubs were open, and the only restaurant was full of noisy housewives eating salads. I went into the grocery store and bought a half-bottle of Johnnie Walker and a packet of paper cups.

I drove down the road until I reached the main road and a lay-by where I could pull off the road and park. The rain continued. It was the ideal sort of day, place, and time to commit suicide.

As soon as the windscreen wipers were switched off, the glass became a confusion of dribbling rain, and there was the steady patter of it on the roof. I reached for the bottle, but before I took a drink from it I relaxed back upon the headrest and must have gone straight to sleep. I'd known such instant sleep before, but always until now it had accompanied danger or great stress.

I don't know how long I slept. I was awakened by the sound of a car pulling up alongside me. There was the buzz and slap of windscreen wipers and the resonant babble of a two-way radio. I opened my eyes. It was a police car. The uniformed cop lowered his window and I did the same.

"Are you all right, sir?" The suspicious look on his weathered face belied the courtesy of his address. I pushed the whisky bottle down between the seats, but I couldn't get it completely out of sight.

"Yes, I'm all right."

"Mechanical trouble of any kind? Shall I call a breakdown service?" The rain continued; the cop didn't get out of his car.

"I just thought I'd look at the map."

"Very well, sir, if you're fit and well, and able to drive." They pulled away.

When the police car was out of sight, I got out of the car and stood in the rain. It refreshed me. Soon I felt better. I got back into the car and switched on the heater and the radio. It was tuned to the BBC Third Programme: Brendel playing Schubert. I listened. After a few minutes I tossed the unopened whisky into the ditch.

I wondered if the policemen had been told to keep an eye on me but decided it was unlikely. Yet even the doubt was a measure of my distress; in the old days I would never have given it a moment's thought. Perhaps there was something wrong with me. Maybe all these people who kept telling me I looked ill were right.

I thought about everything Silas had said. I was particularly disturbed by the idea of Fiona going to ground, so that the KGB would not realize that she had been working for us all the time. It would be difficult to arrange such a deception.

There was another way for the Department to achieve the same objective: by killing Fiona while she was still working over there. It would be simple enough to arrange, there were plenty of Thurkettles around, and it would be complete and effective. Even if the KGB detected the hand of the Department in such a killing, that would only "prove" that Fiona's defection was genuine. Expedient demise. Such a ruthless solution would be unthinkable and unprecedented, but Fiona's unique position was just as unthinkable and just as unprecedented.

Chapter 16

I didn't go into the office that day. As I drove back from Silas Gaunt's farm, the weather got worse until, near London, I found myself driving through a spectacular electrical storm that lit the sky with blue flashes, made the car radio erupt static noises, and provided long drumrolls of thunder. I went straight home. It was early evening. The house was cold, empty, and dark, a chastening reminder of what it would be like to live alone. The children were eating with friends. I lit the gas fire and sat down in the armchair and watched the flame changing color until the whole grid was red. I dozed off.

I was wakened by Gloria's arrival. She switched on the

light and, although she must have noticed the car outside, she raised a hand and gave a little start of surprise at seeing me sitting there. It was a very feminine reaction, contrived perhaps, but by some magic she could get away with such childish posturing. She was very wet. I suppose I should have gone to the station and collected her, but she didn't complain. "There's only frozen *Székelygulyás,*" she said as she took off her soaking-wet raincoat and got a towel to dry her hair.

"Only frozen *Székelygulyás,*" I said reflectively. "What a colorful life we live."

"I didn't get to the shops," said Gloria. I heard a warning note in her voice.

"We can go to Alfonso's or the little Chinese place," I offered.

"What has made you growly tonight, teddy bear?"

"I'm not growly," I said and managed a convincing smile to prove it.

"A soft-boiled egg will do me," she said.

"Me too," I agreed.

She was standing in front of the mirror, combing her wet hair. She looked at me and said, "You say that, Bernard, but when I give you just an egg you always end up at bedtime rummaging through the larder and opening tins or having shredded wheat."

"Let's have the frozen *Székelygulyás,*" I said, having suddenly remembered that it wasn't some new packaged line from the supermarket; it was her mother's Hungarian home cooking. Criticizing such a meal could lead to a tangle in the psyche that only a Freudian gourmet could hope to unravel. "It's my very favorite! Is that the chicken in sour cream?"

"It's pork with pickled cabbage," she said angrily, but when I pulled a face at her she grinned. "You are a bastard! You really are."

"I knew it was pork and cabbage," I said.

"Or there's the new fish-and-chip shop, the one we haven't tried."

"What kind of wine goes with *Székelygulyás?*"

"You hate Hungarian food."

"No I don't."

"You said the caraway seeds got in your teeth."

"That was my other teeth."

She knelt down beside my chair and put her arms round me. "Please try, Bernard. Please try and really love me. I can make you happy, I know I can, but you must try too."

"I really love you, Gloria," I said.

"Is Silas very ill?"

"I'm not sure," I said. "One moment he seems on the point of collapse, and the next moment he's shouting and laying down the law."

"I know he means a lot to you."

"He's old," I said. "We all have to go sooner or later. He's had a good innings."

"Is it something I've done, then?"

"No, darling. You're perfect. I give you my word on that." I meant it.

"It's this house, isn't it? You've hated this house ever since we moved here. Is it the journey? Your other house was so central."

She kissed my ear. I held her. "The house is fine. It's just that I'm trying to work out a few problems at the office. You'll have to make allowances for the growly factor."

"Dicky Cruyer, you mean?"

"No. Dicky is the least of my worries. Without me to do ninety percent of his work, he'd probably be shifted off somewhere where he could do less damage."

"But?"

"A lot of people would like to see Dicky booted out of the German Desk. Deputy Europe, for instance. He detests Dicky.

If getting rid of me meant getting rid of Dicky too, Gus Stowe would do it and throw a party to celebrate."

Gloria laughed. The idea of a celebratory party given by Gus Stowe was not easy to imagine. "Let me put the food into the microwave," she said. The way she chose to say "Let me," instead of using some more assertive syntax, was the essence of our relationship. Despite what others may think, my love for her was not of any paternal sort: but what was the nature of her love for me? "And I'll bring you a glass of wine."

"I'll get it."

"You sit there and take it easy. When dinner is ready, I'll tell you the latest about Dicky. It will make your eyes pop."

"Nothing Dicky could do would surprise me," I said.

She brought me a glass of chilled wine. There was no Scotch. No gin, vodka, or anything else. We'd run out of such stuff, and she'd never bought more. She wanted to rescue me from hard booze. I sat back and drank the wine and took it easy while listening to the electronic squeaks of the timer on the microwave. The oven was her newest toy. I'd overheard her talking to the cleaning lady about it. She'd boasted of cooking delicious braised liver in it, although in fact the liver had exploded and covered the inside of the oven with a garlicky film of pulverized goo. She'd ended up in tears.

But now I could hear her singing quietly to herself, and I knew I'd done the right thing in choosing her mother's Hungarian cooking, prepared by Gloria in her new machine. It gave her a chance to play at housekeeping. The particular pleasure she got from it was demonstrated by the elaborate way she'd arranged on the table our tête-à-tête meal. There were candles and even a long-stemmed rose, albeit an artificial one.

"How wonderful you are," I said when I was permitted into the kitchen to eat.

"I've forgotten the pepper mill," she said, reaching for it

hurriedly. There was a nervousness in her voice, an anxiety, so that sometimes her earnest desire to please me made me uneasy. It made me feel like a tyrant.

"Tell me your news about Dicky."

"I don't know how Daphne puts up with him," said Gloria. She liked to begin with a preamble that set the mood. "Daphne is such a clever woman. You know she's painting leather jackets?"

"Painting leather jackets? Daphne?"

"She's an artist, Bernard."

"I know she went to art school."

"Same thing."

"On leather jackets?"

"Dragons and psychedelic nudes. You haven't seen them? I know you'd love to have one, darling."

"Having a psychedelic nude, even on a leather jacket, might prove a bit too much for me these days."

"They take hours."

"I would imagine."

"Stop it!"

"What?"

"I'm serious. Daphne works very hard, and Dicky doesn't understand her."

"Did he tell you that?"

"Of course not. I wish you'd listen instead of trying to be so smart."

"I like this pork and cabbage. A bit too much salt, but it's very good."

"Last time you said it was tasteless. I put the extra salt in."

"It's delicious. So what about Dicky?"

"He's going to Berlin on Friday. He's booked a suite at Kempinski's; he's taking a girl with him. Poor Daphne. If she ever finds out . . ."

"What girl? Someone from the office?"

"I don't know," she said.

"Where did you hear these rumors?"

"They are not just rumors. He's got the suite booked."

"Did Dicky's secretary tell you?"

Gloria took a moment to swallow her cabbage and then drank some wine too. It gave her time to consider her reply. "No, of course not."

"She has no right to be gossiping about such things."

"You wouldn't tell Dicky?"

"No," I said, "of course not. But it's stupid of her to gossip like that."

"Don't be stuffy, teddy bear," she said, pouring more wine.

"Suppose there was no woman," I said. "Suppose Dicky was waiting for an agent coming through the wire? Suppose that agent's safety depended upon everyone keeping their mouth shut?"

"Yes." She thought about it and said, "Suppose it *was* a woman; suppose it was your wife?"

"Impossible," I said.

"Why impossible?"

"Because Fiona is one of theirs! Damn you, I wish you'd get that simple fact into your thick blond Hungarian head!" I saw the sudden alarm in her face and only then realized that I was shouting and banging on the table.

She said nothing. I could have bitten my tongue off as soon as I'd said it. But once it was said, there was no way ever to unsay such a stupid gratuitous insult.

"I'm sorry, Gloria. Forgive me, please. I didn't mean it."

She was crying now, the tears running down her flushed cheeks as if they'd never stop. But she managed a hint of a smile and said, "You did mean it, Bernard. And there's nothing I can do to make you see me any other way."

"Let's go and sit in the other room," I suggested. I poured the last of the wine.

"No. It's almost time for me to go and collect the children, and I must throw some clothes into the spin-dryer before I go."

"Let me collect them," I said.

"You don't know where it is, Bernard. It's all ill-lit one-way streets: you'll get lost."

She was right. She usually is.

Chapter 17

It was easy to know when Dicky was having a new love affair. I suppose it is easy for the casual observer to know when any husband is having a new love affair. There was that tiger look in his eye, that stiffened sinew and summoned-up blood that Shakespeare associated with Mars rather than Venus. His detailed evaluation of expensive restaurants had become even more rigorous. The *plats du jour* of some of the favored ones were now sent to him each morning on the Fax. And there were jokes.

"Ye gods, Bernard! As far as ethnic food goes—the less authentic the better!" He looked at the fingernail he'd been biting and gave it another brief nibble.

He'd been striding around his office, pausing sometimes to look out of the window. He was jacketless, with his waistcoat unbuttoned, a dark-blue shirt, and a white silk bow tie. His shoes were black patent leather of a design that simulated alligator hide.

Dicky had mentioned his planned weekend in Berlin several times. He said he was "mixing business with pleasure" but then immediately changed the topic of conversation by asking me if it would be a good idea if Penelope "Pinky" Canon came to work here in London. I found the idea appalling, but I didn't say so. Answering that sort of question in London Central was fraught with dangers. Almost everyone here was related to, or at school with, someone else in the building. It could easily turn out that Pinky was Dicky's distant cousin or shared nannies with the D-G's son-in-law, or some such connection. "Fiona said she couldn't spell," I told him.

"Spell!" said Dicky and gave one of those little hoots of laughter that indicated how ingenuous I was. "Even I can't spell properly," he said, which of course clinched the matter for all time.

I felt like saying, Well, you can't bloody well do anything properly, but I just smiled and inquired whether Pinky was asking for a transfer.

"Not officially, but she was at school with your sister-in-law." A tiny smile. "It was Tessa who mentioned it to me, actually." When I didn't react, Dicky added, "At my dinner party."

"It's a small world," I said.

"It is," said Dicky. There was an audible sigh of relief in his voice, as if he'd been trying to make me admit to that fact all the morning. "And, strictly between the two of us, Tessa is also going to be in Berlin next weekend."

"Is she?"

"Yes." He ran a fingertip around his mouth, as if showing me where it was. "As a matter of fact, she . . ." He looked at his watch. "Look here, can you hang on for a cup of coffee?"

"Yes, thanks." I'd enjoyed many cups of coffee with Dicky in his office, but that didn't mean that the *Kaffeeklatsch* was part of his everyday routine. Dicky usually cloistered himself away from the hurly-burly to have his coffee. It was, he said, a time for him to wrestle with his thoughts, to struggle with difficult ideas, a time to confront his innermost self. Invitations to join him in this spiritual melee were not extended lightly or without thought of recoupment. I can truly say that most of the worst experiences of my life sprang from some notion, order, favor, or plan that I first encountered over a cup of Dicky's wonderful coffee.

With coffee Dicky smoked a cheroot. It was a bad habit, smoking—a poison, really. He was trying to cut himself down to three a day. I suppose that's why he didn't offer one to me.

"The fact is . . ." started Dicky, sitting back in his swing chair, coffee in one hand and cigar in the other. "That is to say, an important detail of next week's trip is that I need your help and cooperation."

"Oh, yes," I said. This was an entirely new line for Dicky, who had always denied his need for anyone's help or cooperation.

"You know how much I depend upon you, Bernard." He swiveled an inch or two from side to side but didn't spill his coffee. "Always could; always can."

I found myself looking for the fire escape. "No," I said, "I didn't realize that."

Delicately Dicky placed his cigar in the cut-glass ashtray and used his free hand to tug at one end of his bow tie so that it came unknotted. On the wall behind him there was a framed color photo of Dicky and the D-G in Calcutta. They were standing at a stall offering a huge array of crude portrait posters. Lithographs of famous people, from the Ayatollah and all the Marxes to Jesus Christ and Laurel and Hardy, surrounded Dicky and his boss. They were all looking straight ahead: except Dicky; he was looking at the D-G.

"I don't want to hurt Daphne," said Dicky, as if suddenly deciding upon a new approach. "You understand. . . ."

He left it there and looked at me. By now I was beginning to guess what was coming, but I wasn't going to make it easy for him. And I wanted time to think. "What is it, Dicky?" I said, sipping my coffee and pretending not to be giving him my whole attention.

"Man to man, Bernard, old sport. You see what I mean?"

"You want me to go instead?"

"For God's sake, Bernard. You can be dense at times."
He puffed at his cigar. "No, I'm taking Tessa." A pause. "I've
promised and I'll have to go through with it." He added this
rider woefully, as if a call of duty prevailed over his personal
wishes. But then he fixed his eye on me, and, with a quick
glance toward the door to be sure he wasn't overheard, he
said, "For the weekend!" He said it fiercely, through almost
gritted teeth, as if my failure to understand was about to cause
him to run amok.

"We all go? Gloria too?"

He shot to his feet as if scalded and came round to where
I was sitting. "No, Bernard; no, Bernard; no, Bernard. No!"

"What, then?"

"You come along. You stay at Tante Lisl's, but for all
practical purposes you are in the hotel suite with Tessa."

"For all *practical* purposes? Surely, for all *practical* purposes, *you* will be there with Tessa."

"I'm not in the mood for your bloody comedy," he
barked. But then, remembering that I was designated to fulfill
an indispensable role in his curious scenario, he became calm
and friendly again. "You check into the hotel. Okay?" He was
standing by the lion's-skin rug, and now he gave the head of
it an affectionate little kick with the toe of his shiny patent
leather shoe. He'd always been an animal lover.

I said, "If it's just the propriety of it, why don't you check
in under an assumed name?"

He became huffy. "Because I don't care to do that," he
said.

"Or get Werner to let you have a room at Lisl's?"

I watched his face with interest. I don't think even Lisl
herself would put the hotel high on a list of Berlin accommo-
dations suitable for a lovers' tryst.

"Jesus Christ! Are you mad?" I saw then that he was
nervous. He was frightened that the desk clerk at some big
hotel would challenge him in some way and he'd be revealed

not just as an adulterer but as a bungling adulterer. Certainly Tessa in such a situation would not make it easy for him. She'd revel in it and make the most of it. "Lisl's," he said. "What a thought."

He chewed a nail. I suppose I shouldn't have been surprised at this aspect of Dicky; I'd discovered long ago that womanizers like him are often uneasy and incapable when faced with the minor logistics of such adventures: hotel bookings, plane tickets, car rentals. The sort of man who will boast of his doings to all comers at his club will go to absurd lengths in attempts to deceive the concierge, the waiters, or the room maid. Perhaps that's why they do it.

"Well," I said. "You won't . . ."

He cut me short. He wasn't going to let me give him a negative reply. Dicky was a grand master at squeezing the right sort of replies from people. Now would come the softening up: a barrage of incontrovertible platitudes. "Your sister-in-law is one of the most remarkable women I've ever met, Bernard. Glorious!"

"Yes," I said.

He poured more coffee for me without asking me if I wanted it. Cream too. "And your wife, of course," he added. "Two truly extraordinary women: brainy, beautiful, and with compelling charm."

"Yes," I said.

"Fiona took the wrong road, of course. But that can happen to anyone." By Dicky's standards this was an astonishingly indulgent attitude to human frailty. Perhaps he saw that in my face, for he immediately added, "Or almost anyone."

"Yes, almost anyone."

"Daphne is astonishing too," said Dicky, delivering this accolade with distinctly less emphasis. "Creative, artistic."

"And hardworking," I said.

He was less sure of that. "Well, yes, I suppose she is."

"Daphne was in good form the other night," I said. "Did I thank you for dinner?"

"Gloria wrote."

"Oh, good."

"I only wish I could give Daphne the sort of support and encouragement she needs," said Dicky. "But she lives on a mountaintop." He looked at me. I nodded. He said, "Artists are all like that: creative people. They live in harmony with nature. But it's not so easy for those around them."

"Oh, really? What form does this take? In Daphne's case, I mean?"

"She's only truly happy when she's painting. She told me that. She has to have time to herself. She spends hours up in her studio. I encourage her, of course. It's the least I can do for her."

"You won't find Tessa needs any time to herself," I said.

He smiled nervously. "No. Tessa is like me: very much a social animal."

"May I ask why you are going to Berlin?"

"Why *we* are going," Dicky corrected me. "You'll have to come along, Bernard. No matter what reservations you may nurture about my peccadillos . . . No, no." He raised a hand, as if warding off my interjections, but in fact I had not moved. "No, I understand your reservations. Far be it from me to persuade any man to do something against his conscience. You know how I feel about that kind of thing."

"I didn't say it was against my conscience."

"Ahh!"

"It's not against my conscience, it's against the German legal code. The old German law that made incest a crime still applies in the case of a man committing adultery with his sister-in-law."

"I've never heard of that," said Dicky, suspecting, rightly, that I was inventing this historic clause on the spur of the moment. "Are you sure?"

I turned slightly toward the phone on his table and said, "I can get someone in the legal department to look it up for you."

"No," said Dicky. "Don't do that for the moment. I might go downstairs and look it up myself."

I said, "You didn't explain why I had to go."

"To Berlin? It has been ordained that you, me, and Frank Harrington have a powwow in Big B to go through some damned stuff the Americans want."

"Can't it wait?"

"Written instructions from the D-G himself. No way to wriggle out of that one, Gunga Din."

"And you're taking Tessa?"

"Yes. She has these bonus tickets that airlines give to first-class passengers who fly a great deal. She has to use up the free mileage."

"So you don't have to pay Tessa's fare?"

"It was too good an opportunity to turn away."

"I suppose it was."

"I should have married someone like Tessa, I suppose," said Dicky.

I noticed it wasn't Tessa's unique attractions he wanted but only someone in her category. Whether this left Daphne wanting in brains, wealth, beauty, chic, charm, or sexual performance was left unspecified. "Tessa is already married," I said.

"Don't be so priggish, Bernard. Tessa is a grown-up woman. She's sensible enough to decide these things for herself."

"When is this meeting?"

"Frank is being difficult about precise times. We have to fit it in around his golf and bridge and his jaunts with his army cronies."

"You've booked the hotel?"

"They get so full at this time of year," said Dicky.

I heard a defensive tone in his voice. On a hunch I said, "Have you booked it in my name?"

"Yes . . ." Momentarily he was flustered, but he recovered quickly. "I told the hotel that we are not yet sure who will be using the suite. They think we are a company."

I was damned angry, but Dicky had played his cards with customary finesse. I couldn't see anything specific that I could complain about that Dicky wouldn't be able to explain away. "When do we leave?"

"Friday. Tessa insists on going to some bloody opera that's only on that night. Pinky is arranging the tickets. I'm hoping for a preliminary meeting with Frank and his people on Friday afternoon. We should be through by Monday evening. Tuesday evening at the latest."

There goes my weekend with Gloria and the children. Dicky saw my face and said, "You'll have days off to make up for the loss of the weekend."

"Yes, of course," I said, although it wasn't much fun to be monitoring the weeds in the garden, and fixing my own lunch, while the children were at school and Gloria was slaving in the office.

"You're getting to be very surly lately," Dicky observed while he was pouring the last of the coffee for himself. "Don't go off the handle: I'm just telling you that for your own good."

"You're very considerate, Dicky."

"I can't understand you," Dicky persisted. "You've got that gorgeous creature doting on you and still you go around with a long face. What's the problem? Tell me, Bernard, what is the problem?" Although the words were arranged like questions, Dicky made it quite clear from his tone and delivery that he didn't want an answer.

I nodded. It was best to nod with Dicky. Like the Japanese, he framed his questions in the expectation of affirmative responses.

"Brooding won't bring Fiona back. You must pull yourself together, Bernard." He gave me a "chin up" smile.

I felt like telling Dicky exactly what I thought about him and his plan to implement me in the cuckolding of George, but he wouldn't have understood the reasons for my anger. I nodded and left.

At the end of the working day, I drove homeward with Gloria, but we didn't go directly to number 13 Balaklava Road. She said she wanted to collect some clothes from her parents' home. The actual reason for the visit was that she'd promised to look in and see the house was safe while they were away on holiday. They lived in a smart, burglar-afflicted suburb near Epsom, a few stations beyond us on the Southern Railway's commuter routes.

The Kents—her parents had changed their name after escaping from Hungary—lived in a four-bedroom double-glazed neo-Tudor house with a gravel "in-and-out" front drive on which their two cars could be parked and still leave room enough for the tanker that delivered their heating oil.

This evening the front drive was empty, the cars locked away. Her parents were spending ten days at their holiday villa in Spain. Gloria went through an elaborate routine of unlocking doors and switching off burglar alarms within the prescribed sixty seconds. Then we went inside.

The house smelled of a syrupy perfume resembling violets. Gloria said their cleaning woman was coming in every morning and systematically "shampooing" the carpets. "I'll make you a cup of coffee," she suggested. I agreed. It was interesting to watch her in her parents' home. She became a different person: not a more diffident or childlike one, but vicariously proprietorial, as if she were a real-estate clerk showing the house to a prospective purchaser.

We sat in the kitchen. It was a designer kitchen: Marie Antoinette at her most rustic. We sat on uncomfortable stools at a plastic Louis Seize counter and watched the coffee dripping through the machine. The overhead light—bleak and blue—came from two long fluorescent tubes which buzzed.

It gave me a chance to look at her. All day she'd been her usual warm and good-natured self. It was almost as if she'd forgotten yesterday's clash. But she hadn't. She didn't forget anything. How beautiful she was, with all that energy and radiance that are the prerogatives of youth. No wonder people such as Dicky envied me. Had they realized that Fiona would soon be returning, perhaps they would have envied me even more. But for me it was a miserable dilemma. I couldn't look at Gloria without wondering if I was going to be able to handle the personal crisis that Fiona's return would bring. The idea of Fiona being kept in deep cover for six months made it even more irresolvable. And what about the children?

"I don't think you've been listening to a word of what I've said," I suddenly heard Gloria say.

"Of course I have," and with an inspired evasion tactic I added, "Did I tell you who Dicky is going to Berlin with?"

"No." Her eyes were wide open. She swung her blond hair back and held it as she leaned very close, so that I was conscious of the warmth of her body. She was wearing a crimson shirtdress. On most women it would have looked awful, but she brought a dash to such cheap, bright clothes, just as small children so often do.

"Tessa," I said.

"Your Tessa?"

"My sister-in-law. Yes."

"So Tessa is up to her old tricks. I thought the affair with Dicky was over long ago."

"Yes. That's been puzzling me too."

"It's hardly a puzzle, darling. People like Dicky, and Tessa too, are capricious."

"But Dicky was warned off last time."

"Warned off seeing Tessa? By Daphne, you mean?"

"No. The Department didn't like it. Clandestine meetings with the sister of a defector looked like a potential security risk."

"I'm surprised Dicky took any notice."

"You shouldn't be. Dicky may wear funny bow ties, and play the bohemian student, but he knows exactly how far to go. When the bugle sounds and the medals are being awarded, he toes the line and salutes."

"Except when it comes to Tessa, you mean. Perhaps it's love."

"Not Dicky."

"So perhaps he's had official permission to bed Tessa," she joked.

"That's what it must be," I agreed, and not long afterward I was to reflect upon her joke. "Perhaps what Dicky found irresistible was not having to pay her fare."

"What a swine he is. Poor Daphne." She poured the coffee and, in a dented biscuit tin, discovered a secret supply of chocolate biscuits.

"And he's booked his hotel in my name. What about that?"

She took it very calmly. "Why?"

"I suppose he's going to tell Daphne some story about me going off with Tessa."

"But you're not going?"

"I'm afraid I am."

"The weekend?" I nodded. She said, "I told the Pomeroys to come to dinner on Saturday."

"Who the hell are the Pomeroys?"

"The parents of Billy's friends. The children were eating with them last night. They are terribly kind."

"You'll have to put them off," I said.

"I've put them off twice before when you went on trips."

"It's an order from the D-G. You know what that means. There's no way I can get out of it."

"The weekend?"

"I go on Friday morning; back on Monday or Tuesday. Dicky's secretary will know what's happening over there."

"And on Sunday there's Billy's car-club meeting. I said you'd take him."

"Look! It's not my idea, darling."

For a long time she drank her coffee without speaking. Then she said, "I know it's not," as if responding to some other question that only she knew about. "But you said there was going to be a party at Werner's hotel. I know you wanted to go."

"It's just to promote the hotel. We'll go some other time. They are always having parties, and anyway it would be no fun without you."

After the coffee I went with her to the room she had when living here with her parents. They kept it for her as if they were expecting her every night. Toys, teddy bear, dolls, children's books, schoolbooks, a Beatles poster on the wall. The bed had been made up with freshly laundered linen. Taking her away from them was my doing, and there were times when I felt bad about it. And I hadn't even married her. How would I feel if one day my daughter, Sally, disappeared with a middle-aged married man? Sometimes I wondered how I would be able to deal with the inevitable separation from the children. Would I find myself keeping their bedrooms as shrines at which I could pray for a return of their childhood days with me?

Looking out from the bedroom window, I could see the

flat roof of a large single-story building that had been added to the house. Gloria said, "I cried when they ruined my view of the garden. There was a lovely chestnut tree there, and a rhododendron."

"Why did you need extra space?"

"It's a surgery and workshop for Daddy."

"I thought he had a surgery in town."

"This is for special jobs. Didn't you know?"

"Why would I know?"

"Want to see? It's where he does work for the Department."

"What kind of work?"

"Come and see."

She got the big bunch of keys that her father had left with her, and we went down into the neat little dental surgery. She opened the door, and while she searched for the light switches the room was only lit from a glass box in the corner where tropical flowers appeared under ultraviolet lights. When she switched on the light, apart from seeming unusually crammed with apparatus, it was like any other dentist's workplace: a modern fully adjustable chair and an elaborate drill facing a large window. There was a big ceramic spittoon, a swiveling cold-light and many glass-fronted instrument cabinets, packed with rows and rows of curiously shaped drills, forceps, scalers, and other spiky implements.

Gloria went round the room, naming the equipment and describing what it was for. She seemed to know a lot about dentistry, despite having resisted her father's wish that she should become one. This, she said, was her father's secret sanctum.

"Who comes here for treatment?" I asked.

"Not so many nowadays, but I can remember a time when Daddy worked more hours here than at his proper surgery. I remember one poor Polish boy who was in the chair for at least six hours. He was so exhausted that Daddy let him come and sit in the drawing room with Mummy and me, to take his mind off things."

"Agents?"

"Yes, of course. At university, Daddy wrote a thesis on the history of European dentistry. After that he began his collection of old dental tools. Now he can look into anyone's mouth and know where they had their teeth fixed, and when. Look at that." She held up a particularly barbarous-looking instrument. "It's very old . . . from Russia."

"I was lucky," I said. "My teeth were always fixed by a Berlin dentist, and my cover story was always German. I didn't have to have any of my dental work changed."

"I've known my father to completely eliminate all previous dentistry to give an agent a completely new mouth: Russian, Polish, Greek. . . . Once he did old-fashioned Spanish dental work for a man who was going to be using the identity of a Civil War veteran.

"Come and look at the workshop." She unlocked the door of an adjoining room, and we went inside. This was even more cramped, with filing cabinets and racks of tools and equipment. There was a tiny lathe, a bench drill, and even a small electric kiln. On a large table near the window was the work in progress. A desk light was centered upon something concealed under a cloth. Gloria removed the cotton dust-cloth and gave a little shriek as a human skull was revealed. "Alas, poor Yorick! We mustn't touch it. It's probably a demonstration piece that will be photographed for a textbook. He does replicas of old dentistry and sends them as examples to police pathologists and coroners' departments all over the world. This one must be a special job, from the way he's covered it over so carefully."

I went closer to look at the skull. It was shiny, like plastic, and there were gold inlays and porcelain crowns fitted into it. "Did you never want to be a dentist?"

"Never. And Daddy was always so considerate that he

never really pressed the idea on me. It was only recently that I've realized how much he'd always hoped I'd become interested in his practice, and his collection. Sometimes he had students work with him. Once I remember he brought a young, newly qualified dentist home for dinner. I've often wondered if he was hoping that a romance would blossom."

"Let's lock up and go home," I said. "Shall we take some fish and chips back for everyone?"

"Do let's."

"I'm sorry if I've been a bit bad-tempered lately, darling."

"I haven't noticed any difference," she said.

Chapter 18

Afterward I looked back and saw that weekend in Berlin as the beginning of the end, but I don't know how much of that view was hindsight. At the time it seemed unusual simply because of the hectic way meeting followed meeting and the way in which Frank Harrington—always something of a mother hen—became so flustered that he was phoning me in the middle of the night and then admitting that he'd forgotten what he was calling about.

Not that any of the meetings decided very much. They were typically casual Berlin Field Unit conferences, at which Frank presided in his inimitably avuncular style and smoked his foul-smelling pipe and indulged in long rambling asides about me or my father or the old days or all three together.

It was on Sunday morning that Frank first gave me an inkling of what was happening. Dicky was not there. He had left a message to say he was showing Tessa "round the town," although what Dicky knew about Berlin could be written on the head of a pin and still leave plenty of room for the Lord's Prayer.

It was just me and Frank. We were in his study in the big house at Grunewald. He had a secretary there, and some of the top-secret material was filed there. It gave Frank an excuse for a day at home now and again. That incredible and unforgettable study! Although I could not identify any single object as having its origins in the subcontinent, this room could have been the Punjab bungalow of some pukka regimental officer, some hero of the Mutiny just back from hunting the nimble black buck with cheetahs. Shuttered against the daylight, the dim lamps revealed a fine military chest with magnificent brass fittings, the mounted horns of some unidentified species of antelope, a big leather sofa with buttons, and rattan furniture, all of it bleached, creaky, or worn, as such things become in the tropics. Even the sepia portrait of the sovereign seemed to have been selected for her resemblance to the young Victoria. The room expressed all Frank's secret longings and, like most people's secret longings, they had no basis in reality.

Even Frank was at his most regimental, with a khaki safari shirt, slacks, and plain brown tie. He'd been tapping the map with his fountain pen and asking me questions of a sort that usually were the concern of other technical grades. "What do you know about the East Berlin Autobahn entrances?" he said.

He indicated the wall upon which two large maps had been fixed. They were a new addition and rather spoiled the "great days of the Raj" decor. One was a map of East Germany, or the German Democratic Republic, the rather Orwellian name its rulers preferred. Like an island in this communist sea, our sectors of Berlin were bridged to the West by three long Autobahnen. Used by motorists of both East and West, these highways were a favored place for clandestine meetings. Smugglers, spies, journalists, and lovers all arranged brief and dangerous rendezvous at the roadside. And consequently the DDR made sure the roads were policed constantly, night and day.

The second map—the one Frank was tapping upon—was a Berlin street map. The whole city, not just the West. It was remarkably up to date, for I immediately noticed the projected changes to the Autobahn entrances, including the yet-to-be-built turnoff which would—some time in the dim and distant future—provide the West with a new control point on the south side of the city. Rumors said the East Germans wanted the West to pay a great deal of money for it. That was the usual way that anything got done.

"I don't use them," I said. "I always fly nowadays."

"Pity." He looked at the street map and with his pen showed me the old Berliner Ring and the route that East Berliners took when joining the Autobahn from their side of the city.

"Remember that general directive about us using the Autobahn?" I reminded him gently. There was a fear that Departmental employees, with heads full of secrets, might be kidnapped on the Autobahnen. It was not a groundless fear. There was a whole filing case full of unsolved mysteries: motorists who started out on the long drive to the Federal Republic and were never seen again. There was no way for the West's authorities to investigate such mysteries. We had to grin and bear it. Meanwhile, those who could fly, flew.

"I want you to drive back down the Autobahn this time," said Frank.

"When?"

"I'm waiting to hear." His pipe stem was tapped against his nose in what I suppose was a gesture of confidentiality. "Someone is coming out."

"Through Charlie?" That would mean a non-German.

"No. You'll pick them up on the Autobahn," said Frank. I waited for some explanation or expansion, but he gave neither. He continued to look at the street map and then said, "Ever heard of a man named Thurkettle? American."

"Yes," I said.

"You have?" Unless Frank had been attending drama lessons since our previous meeting, he was completely taken aback by this revelation. Clearly he'd not heard about my escapade in Salzburg. "Tell me about him."

I briefly told Frank about Thurkettle, without going into detail about my task in Salzburg.

"He's here," said Frank.

"Thurkettle?" It was my turn to be surprised.

"Arrived by air last night. I told London, but I got only an 'acknowledgment and no further action' signal. I'm wondering if London knows all this you've just told me."

"Yes, they do," I said.

Frank frowned. "We both know how signals get spiked and forgotten," he said. "They should at least let me tell the Americans and the police."

"You can tell them off the record," I said.

"That might bounce and get me into hot water." Frank was something of an expert at finding reasons for inaction. "If Thurkettle has come here on some secret mission for the Yanks, and London has been informed in the usual way, well . . . !" He shrugged. "They might be displeased to find I've told all and sundry."

"On the other hand," I said, "if Thurkettle has come to town to blow away one of the CIA's golden boys, they might feel that one routine signal to London was an underreaction."

"It was a confidential," said Frank. "My informant was someone who I can absolutely not name. If London, or the CIA office, demand details of the identification, I will find myself having one of those wretched arguments that I hate so much." He looked at me and I nodded. "What do you think this fellow's here for, Bernard?"

"No one seems to be sure who Thurkettle works for. The prevailing wisdom—if Joe Brody is anyone to go by—is that he's a hit man who works for anyone—that is to say, anyone who comes up with the right target for the right price. Brody says the KGB have used him over the past two years. If Thurkettle was on his way to see our friends in Normannenstrasse, he'd fly into Schönefeld."

"You mean he's targeting someone here in the West?" Frank screwed his face up. "I can't put a tail on him. I don't know where he's gone, and even if I did know I simply haven't got the resources."

"West Berlin isn't on the way to anywhere," I said. "No one comes here en route to anywhere; they come here and go back again."

"You're right. Perhaps I should send London a reminder." He used his clenched fist to brush up the ends of his mustache. To the casual observer it looked as if he were giving himself two quick punches on the nose; perhaps that's what he thought London was likely to give him if he persisted. "I'll leave it for the weekend; they might respond again."

Good old Frank: never hesitate to do nothing. "Phone the old man," I suggested.

"The D-G? He hates being disturbed at home." He scratched his cheek and said, "No, I'll leave it for the time being. But I'm disturbed by what you told me, Bernard."

I realized that my description of Thurkettle's activities had put Frank into a difficult position. Until talking with me, he still had the chance to plead ignorance of anything concerning the man or the danger that he might present to Allied personnel here. I wondered if I should suggest that we both forget what I'd said, but Frank could be very formal at times. Despite the friendship that went back to my childhood—or even because of it—he might consider such a suggestion treasonable and insulting. I decided not to take a chance on it.

"One thing I still haven't got clear, Frank," I said. He raised an eyebrow. "You sent Teacher to get me, and had me sit in on Larry Bower and the old apparatchik. Why?"

Frank smiled. "Didn't Larry explain that?"

"No," I said. "Larry didn't explain anything."

"I thought it might be something that would interest you. I remembered that you were handling Stinnes at one time."

"Why not simply show me the transcript?"

"Of the debriefing?" Pursed lips and a nod, as if this were a novel and most interesting suggestion. "We could have done that; yes."

"Would you like to hear what I think?" I said.

"Of course I would," said Frank with that suppressed irony with which a doting parent might indulge a precocious child. "Tell me."

"I kept thinking about it. I wondered why you would give me a close look at a still-active agent. That's not the way the training manual says it's done."

"I don't always go by the training manual," said Frank.

"You are not contrary or perverse, Frank," I said. "What you do, you do with a purpose."

"What's eating you, Bernard?"

"You didn't invite me to that safe house in Charlottenburg to hear the debriefing and see Valeri," I said. "You brought me over there so that Valeri could see me. See me close up!"

"Why would I have done that, Bernard?" He found a stray thread on his sleeve, plucked it off, and dropped it into an ashtray.

"To find out if Valeri could identify me as one of the people mixed up in the narcotics racket?"

"There is such a thing as being too skeptical," said Frank gently.

"Not in this business there isn't."

He smiled. He didn't deny the allegation.

"You need a holiday, Bernard."

"You're right," I said. "Meanwhile, when do I start my trip down the Autobahn?"

"Not for a few days," said Frank. "Tuesday at the earliest." I suppose he thought I would welcome a few days idling around in Berlin, but I wanted to get back, and he must have seen that in my face. "Look on the bright side. You'll be able to enjoy Werner's costume party tonight." When I didn't respond to this he added, "It's out of my control, Bernard. We just have to wait for the message."

"When am I to be briefed?"

"There won't be a briefing. We're keeping it all very low-key. But Jeremy Teacher will be with you. He's waiting downstairs. I'll get him up here now and he'll tell you his plans." Frank picked up his internal phone and said, "Send Mr. Teacher up here, would you."

I wasn't delighted at the idea of having Teacher tell me his plans. "Let's get this straight, Frank," I said. "Is Teacher running this show, or am I?"

"No need to designate a boss," said Frank. "Teacher is easy to get along with. And it's a simple enough job."

"Never mind all that smooth London Central talk, Frank," I said. "If I'm picking up a DDR national on DDR territory and bringing him out, that's Operational. When did Teacher ever work in Operations?"

"He didn't," admitted Frank. "And he's never been a field agent either. I suppose that's the real thrust of what you're saying."

"You're damn right it's the real thrust of what I'm saying. I'll go alone. I don't want to be playing nanny to some penpusher who wants a glimpse of life at the sharp end."

"You can't do it alone. You'll have a passenger. Someone will have to drive. Who knows what unexpected things might happen. We can't risk it."

"Teacher?"

"He's the best man I've got."

"Let me take Werner," I said.

"Werner is a German national cleared only for noncritical employment," said Frank primly.

"And that bloody Teacher is . . ."

There was a knock at the door, and Teacher came in. Losing his wife did not seem to have done anything to improve his miserable demeanor. He brought a sulking broodiness into the room. The smile he gave as he shook hands was sour, and although the grip of his hand was firm there was something listless in the gesture. Perhaps he'd heard me before he came in.

"Tell Bernard what you've arranged," said Frank.

"Volkswagen van. Diplomatic plates. We meet the other car at a pull-off near the Brandenburg exit. It should be very straightforward. They don't stop diplomatic vans."

"Bernard says when will you go?"

"I'm waiting for diplomatic passports for all three of us. We can't expect those to come through until after the weekend."

"No," I said. "Don't let's ruin anyone's weekend."

Teacher looked at me and looked at Frank.

Frank said, "Are you armed, Bernard?"

"No," I said.

"Jeremy will have a nonferrous pistol," said Frank, unable to conceal his distaste. Frank had a dislike of firearms that ill-fitted his romantic notions of the army.

"That's nice," I said. Teacher pretended I wasn't there.

"It won't come to that," said Frank. "It's a straightforward little job. A drive down the Autobahn, that's all." I didn't respond, and neither did Teacher. If it was so bloody simple, I thought, why wasn't Frank doing it? "But there is one more thing. . . . I've been through this with Jeremy." A pause revealed that Frank was having difficulty; that's probably why he'd left it to last. "There must be no question of the field agent going into custody over there. You understand?"

"No," I said. "I don't understand. We'll be in a diplomatic vehicle, you said."

"That's not one hundred percent, Bernard. Remember poor little Fischbein? They dragged him out of that car right in the Alex."

"I've been briefed," said Teacher.

But I wasn't going to let Teacher get Frank off the hook. "Then brief me, Frank."

"If worst came to the worst, Bernard, the agent would have to be . . . eliminated."

"Killed?"

"Yes, killed." Frank looked again at the map, as if searching for something, but I think he was trying to avoid my eyes. "Jeremy has the gun for that purpose."

"Poor bloody agent," I said.

"All concerned are aware of what's at stake," said Frank stiffly. "Including the agent."

Frank turned and looked at me now. His blunt-ended mustache was completely gray these days. Frank was too old to be involved with Operations. Too old, too squeamish, too weary, too goodhearted. Whatever it was, the strain on him showed in his face.

"It's all right, sir," said the ever-helpful Teacher. "We'll do whatever has to be done."

Teacher's face was lined too, but Teacher was not old or weary. Teacher was a tough little bastard in a way that I'd not recognized before. They'd chosen him well for this job.

Frank seemed not to hear Teacher. It was as if it were just me and Frank in the room. "Okay, Bernard?" he said softly. I looked Frank in the eyes and I knew, beyond any shadow of a doubt, that it was Fiona who was going to be picked up on the Autobahn. It was Fiona who knew what might have to be done to prevent her being interrogated by the professional torturers at Normannenstrasse. And Teacher was there in case I hesitated when it was time to pull the trigger.

"Yes, Frank," I said. "It's okay."

On the Sunday evening there was a big party at Lisl's. The printed invitations said it was to celebrate the opening of the newly refurbished premises. On this pretext Werner had obtained the support of a number of his suppliers, and the invitations, like the paper napkins and some of the other objects in evidence, bore the trademarks of breweries and distillers.

Now that it was almost summer, and the evenings had lengthened, Werner's plan was to hold the party in a huge tent he'd had erected in the courtyard at the back of the hotel. But all afternoon the sky had darkened, and by evening there was torrential rain falling from an endless overcast. Only the most intrepid guests ventured into the chilly tent, and the inauguration was celebrated indoors.

But it was something more than the official reopening of the hotel. And it was Frank's presence at the party at Lisl's on Sunday evening that told me that he felt the same way. Frank was past retirement; soon he would be gone. Looking back on it afterward, I saw that he regarded it as his very own gala finale. Frank had never shared my love for Lisl, and despite all evidence to the contrary, he persisted in blaming Werner for an old security leak for which Frank had taken a share of criticism. But even Frank knew that Lisl's was the only place in Berlin to celebrate, and having decided that, he was at his most ebullient and charming. He even wore fancy costume: the Duke of Wellington!

"It's the end of an era," said Lisl. We were sitting in her little study. This was the room in which Lisl spent so much of her life, now that walking had become so painful for her. Here she had breakfast and played bridge and looked at the account books and gave favored residents a measured glass of sherry when they came to pay their bills. On the wall there was a picture of Kaiser Wilhelm, on the mantelpiece a hideous ormolu clock, and around the table where she took breakfast four carved Venetian-style figure-of-eight dining chairs, all that remained of her parents' grand dining room.

Now she never sat in her beloved chairs; she was in a functional steel wheelchair that she could maneuver at such high speed that Werner had fixed a small bulb-horn to it.

The noise of the party came loudly through the tightly closed door. I don't know whose idea it was to use Lisl's wind-up gramophone and her collection of ancient 78s to provide the music, but it had been hailed as the ultimate in chic, and now Marlene was purring "Falling in Love Again" against a honky-tonk piano for what must have been the fifth consecutive time. Werner had predicted that it wouldn't be loud enough, but it was loud enough.

Even Lisl had sought refuge from the dedicated and unrelenting playfulness that Berliners bring to their parties. Open on the floor there was a very old suitcase that had belonged to my father. It dated from the days before designer labels, when such things were properly made. The outside was pale-green canvas with leather for the handle, the binding, and the corners. The lining was calico. Inside it there were his papers: bills, accounts, newspaper clippings, a couple of diaries, a silk scarf, even the British Army uniform tunic that he so seldom wore. I was rummaging through it while Lisl sat in her wheelchair, sipped her sherry, and watched me. "Even his gun," she said. "Be careful with it, Bernd. I hate guns."

"I noticed it," I said. I took it from its leather holster. It was a Webley Mark VI, a gigantic revolver that weighed about two and a half pounds, the sort of weapon that the British Army had been hanging on its officers since the First World War. It was blue and perfect; I doubt if my father had ever fired it. There was a box of ammunition too; nickel jacket; .455-inch rounds "for service use." The label was dated 1943 and the seal was unbroken.

"That's everything. Klara made sure that all your father's things were packed in his case. So that's all, apart from the footstool, the mattress, and the set of Dickens."

"Thank you, Lisl."

"The end of an era," she mused sadly. "Werner taking over the hotel. The changes to the rooms. You taking your father's things. I'm a stranger here now, a stranger in my own home."

"Don't be silly, Lisl. Werner loves you. He's only done it all for you."

"He's a good boy," she said sadly, not grudging him her affection but reluctant to abandon the self-pity she so relished.

There was the sudden increase in the noise of the party as Werner came in and shut the door behind him. Werner was dressed as a knight in full armor. Expediently, the armor was fashioned entirely of fabric cunningly embroidered with gold-and-silver wire to reproduce intricate decoration on etched and gilt metal. He looked magnificent; even Lisl thought so. Lisl looked equally splendid in a long brightly patterned dress that—according to the rental company's label—was that of a thirteenth-century noblewoman, and was based upon the stained-glass figures of Augsburg Cathedral. It included diadem and wimple and a light but voluminous cloak. Whatever the integrity of the design, she made a fine figure alongside Werner, the wheelchair providing her with an imposing throne. I thought he might have chosen his costume and hers with filial congruity in mind, but he later confided that it was the only garment he could find in her size that was also bright crimson. Lisl loved vivid colors.

"It's a madhouse out there," said Werner as he stood against the door and caught his breath. His face was pink with excitement and exertion. "I brought you some more champagne." He had the bottle in his hand and he poured some for both of us. "Absolutely ghastly."

"It sounds ghastly," I said, although I had long grown

used to the way in which Werner organized this sort of frenzied fancy-dress party and then went around all evening saying how much he hated it.

He looked at me. "I wish you'd put on your costume," he said. He'd selected an amazing mid-nineteenth-century costume for me that was called "the Biedermeier gentleman" on the box. It came complete with a frock coat and high hat. I suspected that Werner had chosen it with a certain sardonic glee that I had no intention of sustaining.

"I'm all right like this," I said. I was wearing a battered gray suit. My only concession to the party being one of Werner's more colorful bow ties.

"You're so bloody English," said Werner, not unkindly.

"Sometimes I am," I admitted.

"There must be a hundred and fifty people out there," he told me. "Half of them gatecrashers. The word got around, I suppose; they're all in costume." It was typical of him that he should show a trace of pride that so many should want to gatecrash his party. "Do you want the Duchess to tell your fortune, Lisl?"

"No, I don't," said Lisl.

"They say she's a witch," said Werner, as if that were a recommendation.

"I don't want to know the future," said Lisl. "When you get to my age, the future holds nothing but heartbreak and pain."

"Don't be a misery, Lisl," said Werner, who dared to go much further with her than I would ever do. "I'm going to make sure you meet people."

"Go away!" said Lisl. "I'm talking to Bernd."

Werner looked at me and gave a tiny grin. "I'll be back," he promised and returned to the party, which was getting louder every minute. He stood in the open doorway long enough for me to see the crowded dance floor. There was a frenzied crowd of dancers all elaborately costumed—for Germans take fancy-dress parties as seriously as they take every other social activity from operagoing to getting drunk—and waving their arms in the air more or less in time with the music. Sequined chorus girls, a Roman senator, Karl May's Old Shatterhand, and two squaws danced past, wriggling and smiling. Jeremy Teacher—dressed as a thin, elegant, curly-haired gorilla—was dancing with Tessa, who was in a long diaphanous yellow dress with long antennae bobbing above her head. Teacher was holding her tight and talking; Tessa was wide-eyed and nodding energetically. It seemed an unlikely combination. The door closed.

"What time will they go home?" Lisl asked me.

"It won't go on very late, Lisl," I promised, knowing full well that it would go on very late indeed.

"I hate parties," said Lisl.

"Yes," I said, although I could see she had already decided to go and circulate. She preferred to be pushed round in her wheelchair. It gave her an added sense of majesty. I supposed I'd have to do it, but I knew she'd find a way of making me look a bloody fool while doing so.

I locked up the suitcase. "Come on, Lisl," I said. "Let's go and look round."

"Must we?" she said and was already looking in the mirror to inspect her makeup. Then the door opened again. There was a short, smiling man standing there.

At first I thought he was in a specially elaborate costume that included face-black. Then I recognized Johnny the Tamil. He looked different; he was wearing gold-rimmed glasses. He laughed. "How wonderful!" he said. "How wonderful!" I thought he must be referring to the party, but he seemed almost not to notice that the party was going on at all. Perhaps he was stoned. "Wonderful to find you, Bernard," he said. "I've looked all over town."

"I heard the cops got you," I said.

He looked at me over his glasses. "I was lucky. There was

the cruise-missiles demonstration. Three hundred arrests. They needed the space in the cells. They threw me out." His German had not improved, but I'd got used to his accent.

"I'll get you a drink," I offered. Behind him, through the open door, I spotted the Duke of Wellington holding tight to a rather gorgeous geisha. For a fleeting moment I thought it was Daphne Cruyer, but as she turned her head and smiled at Frank I knew it wasn't.

"No. I must go. I brought this for you." He gave me a large dog-eared envelope. I opened it. There was a plastic box that looked a bit like a small radio. "It's Spengler's . . ." said Johnny. "He wanted you to have it. It's his chess computer."

"Thanks."

"He always said that if anything happened to him I could have his glasses and you could have his computer. That's all he had," Johnny added unnecessarily. "The cops took his passport."

"For me? Are you sure?"

"I'm sure. Spengler liked you. I put new batteries in."

"Thanks, Johnny. Do the glasses suit you?" He looked quite different in the glasses.

"No, they make everything blurred. But they are stylish, aren't they?"

"Yes, they are," I said. "This is Tante Lisl. Have a drink?"

"Hello, Tante Lisl." He seemed baffled at the idea that Lisl might really be my aunt, but he didn't question it. "No. I must go, Bernard."

"Did they find out who killed Spengler?" I asked.

"They haven't even found out his real name or where he came from. No one cares about him, except us."

He waved and was gone. Lisl had made no attempt to follow the conversation. "You should be careful who you mix with in this town," she said. "It's not like London."

Lisl, who, as far as I knew, had never been to London, had been saying that to me since I was six years old and brought Axel Mauser back to see my Nazi medal collection.

Johnny's visit was over so quickly that I forgot to give him some cash. With people like Johnny, a few marks go a long way. Goodness knows what time and trouble he'd spent in tracking me down. He'd even stolen new batteries for me: long-life batteries, the very best. I suppose he'd got them from Wertheim. He liked stealing from Wertheim; he said it was a quality shop.

In the event, it was Werner who trundled Lisl around the party as she bowed graciously, offered her hand to be kissed, or gave a regal wave, according to the degree of approval she extended to these merrymaking guests.

I took my father's suitcase down to the cellar, but when I got there I sat down for a few minutes. I was aware of the absurdity of hiding away from Werner's party, aware too of the derision I'd face from Werner if he found me down here. But I didn't want to be upstairs, with 150 exhilarated people, most of whom I didn't know in disguises I couldn't penetrate, celebrating the end of something I didn't want to say goodbye to.

I went and sat in the little hideaway next to the boiler room, a place I used to come to do my homework when I was a child. There was always a bright light and a tall pile of old newspapers and magazines in here. Reading them, instead of doing my homework, was one of the reasons I'd become so good at German that I could often beat all the German kids in vocabulary tests and essay writing.

I did the same thing now. I took a newspaper from the top of the big pile and sat down on the bench to read it. There was a story about the discovery of buried nerve gas at Spandau. It had been there since the Second World War.

"Bernard, darling! What are you doing here? Are you ill?"

"No, Tessa. I just wanted to get away from it all."

"You really are the limit, Bernard. The limit. The limit."

She repeated the words as if she found some pleasure in saying them. Her eyes were wide and moist. I realized that she was stoned. Not drunk on alcohol. She was on something more powerful than that. "Really the limit," she said again. She extended her arms. The almost transparent yellow cloth was attached to her wrists so that she became a butterfly. The bright light made her a whirling shadow on the whitewashed wall.

"What is it, Tessa?"

"Your friend Jeremy is looking for you." She twirled around to enjoy again the fleeting shadows she made.

"Who is Jeremy?"

"You mean, Jeremy who, darling." She laughed shrilly at her joke. "Jeremy thing!" She clicked her fingers. "Jeremy the cultivated ape. Know you not the couplet: *He doth like the ape, that the higher he climbs the more he shows his ars.* Francis Bacon. You think I'm an untutored wanton, but I went to school and I can quote Francis Bacon with the best of you."

"Of course you can, Tessa. But you seem a little high yourself."

"And the more I show my arse? Is that what you mean, Bernard, you rude sod?"

"No, Tessa, of course not. But I think it might be a good idea to get you back to your hotel. Where's Dicky?"

"Are you listening to me, Bernard? Jeremy the ape is desperate to find you. He is going mad. He is in fact going ape!" More laughter, soft but shriller, and a suggestion that hysteria was not far away. "The signal has come and you must go."

"Is that what Jeremy the ape said?"

"The signal has come and you must away."

"Tessa!" I shook her. "Listen to me, Tessa. Get hold of yourself. Where is the ape now?"

"He was trying to get into one of Werner's three-piece lounge suits—blue with a pinstripe—but Werner got angry and wouldn't let him borrow any clothes. They were both shouting. Werner doesn't like him." She smiled. "And Werner's suits are too big."

I said it slowly. "Where is Jeremy the ape now?"

"You're not going without me. The car's here. Van. Ford van, a lovely shade of blue. Diplomatic plates. Outside in the rain. Jeremy the ape is driving. They make good drivers, apes. My father employed one for years. Then he started wanting extra bananas all the time. They can be awfully tiresome, apes. Did I tell you that?"

Outside, the rain was falling in great steel sheets, hammering the road, and pounding upon the roof of the Ford van. Jeremy Teacher, still in gorilla costume, was in the driver's seat. He was soaking wet. I asked him what was happening and had to shout to make myself heard above the sound of the rain and thunder. "Get in," he said.

"What's happening?" I said for maybe the fourth time.

"What the hell do you think is happening?" he said furiously. "The bloody signal came through three and a half hours ago!"

"You said a VW van." He shot me a poisonous look. "I haven't got my passport," I said, my mind racing as I thought of all the other things I didn't have.

"Get in! I've got the passports here." The prospect of going through the checkpoints dressed as a gorilla had obviously put him in a foul temper.

It was then that I noticed that Tessa was dancing about in the rain. She was drenched, but she seemed oblivious of the arresting sight she offered as the thin material clung tightly to her body.

It was Tessa dancing round the Ford Transit—added to the sight of a gorilla gunning it while arguing volubly with a civilian who might have been his keeper—that brought other revelers out into the street. They made an astonishing sight in their costumes, and although some of them had umbrellas, many were as indifferent to the downpour as Tessa was.

Werner came too, struggling under the weight of my father's suitcase. He opened the rear door to put it inside, and as he was doing so Tessa pushed him aside and climbed into the van, slamming the door with a crash that made the metal bodywork sing.

"Let's go!" shouted Teacher.

"Tessa's in the back," I said.

He looked round and shouted, "Get out of there, Tessa."

"I'm coming with you," she cooed.

"Don't be silly. You haven't got a passport," said Teacher with a calm politeness that was commendable under the circumstances.

"Oh, yes, I have," she said triumphantly. She had produced it from somewhere and was holding it up in front of her to show him. "Dicky said I was to carry it everywhere while I was here."

"Get out, you stupid bitch!" He revved the engine as if hoping that would persuade her, but it didn't. It simply confirmed that the engine was not firing properly. I had doubts that it would ever complete the journey.

"I won't. I won't."

"For Christ's sake, get her out of there," shouted Teacher to me.

"Who the hell do you think you are?" I said. "You get her out." I recognized one of Tessa's bloody-minded moods and decided to let the intrepid Mr. Teacher earn his pay.

He looked at his watch. "We must go." With a string of curses he opened his door and got out, but as the rain hit him and soaked his hairy gorilla outfit he changed his mind and climbed back into the driver's seat again.

"Come on, Tessa. We're leaving."

"I'm coming too," she said.

"No, you're bloody not!" said Teacher. He switched the heater on to full. His damp costume was obviously chilly.

Then Dicky arrived on the scene. He was dressed as Harlequin, the carefully decorated face, checkered costume, and imposing hat a favorite for Germany's Fasching celebrations. He spotted Tessa and dutifully told us that she was in the back of the van. Teacher gave a loud and angry sigh. "Then get her out of it," he said, abandoning his usual respectful attitude to those set in authority over him.

By now there seemed to be dozens of people in bizarre costumes milling around the van, although in the darkness and the relentless rain it was difficult to be sure who they really were. But they formed such a crush that getting through them, getting the door open, and getting Tessa out would be physically difficult even if no one objected to Tessa being manhandled. And if I knew anything about the effects of alcohol on the male psyche, any sort of struggle with Tessa would be enough to start a riot.

There was a flash of lightning. Hordes—in ever more amazing garb—spilled into the street. The commotion round the van had become the party's new attraction. A rain-soaked Frederick the Great was waving both hands in glee, while Barbarossa, his false beard bedraggled, offered his hat to a Roman maiden to protect her coiffure.

I saw the Duchess. She was dressed as a witch, in a pointed hat and a long black gown with occult symbols on the skirt of it. That damned cat was with her, despite the heavy rain, its eyes glowing angrily in the darkness. The Duchess was standing in front of the van and began making solemn gestures with her wand. A roll of thunder came in on cue.

"What's that old cow doing?" Teacher asked.

"I think she's casting a spell," I replied.

"Jesus Christ!" said Teacher, aggravated. beyond control. "Has everyone gone insane?"

Before the Duchess had finished her incantation, Harlequin stuck his painted face through the window of the van and said, "Teacher is in charge. Remember that, Bernard." I ignored him. He grabbed my shoulder and, in the voice of a provoked parent talking to a naughty child, he said, "Look here, Bernard! Do you hear what I said?"

I looked at Dicky's elaborately made-up face and his cold little eyes. Years and years of repressed resentment welled up in me. The way in which he'd been promoted over my head, the pompous things he said, his pretentious life-style, his readiness to cuckold poor old George and make jokes about it. Now emotion took precedence over common sense. Whatever the consequences, now was the time to react. I pulled my fist back and gave him a solid punch on the rouged nose. Not hard, but it was enough to send him reeling back into the roadway just as another car came past. With incredibly quick response, the driver swerved with a sharp squeal of brakes and avoided him. I turned to see him through the window. Dicky still staggered back, hat askew, feet splayed wide apart. His arms were flailing to keep balance, but he fell backwards into the road and his big cocked hat came off.

"Go! Go! We'll sort it out at the checkpoint," I yelled.

Teacher let in the clutch and there was a squeak of rubber and a sickening bump, followed by a woman's scream. I knew immediately what had happened. That bloody cat Jackdaw had gone under the van to shelter from the downpour. Now it was flattened under the rear wheels. We might have hit the Duchess too, but Teacher spun the wheel and narrowly missed her, and we sped out into the traffic of the Ku-Damm.

The wet streets shone with the colored light of the neon signs that summoned tourists to meet the junkies, winos, and dropouts who had made the Europa-Center their home. "Is she still in the back?" said Teacher as we passed the Gedächtniskirche, preserved to remind the nostalgia-prone that old Berlin had its fair share of ugly buildings. Even at this time of night there was plenty of traffic. Teacher gunned the motor a couple of times and after that the engine began firing more efficiently. I suppose the rain must have been afflicting it.

"I'm here, darling," said a voice from the back. "I can guess who you are going to meet. If you dare to try throwing me out at the checkpoint, I'll scream it aloud to the whole world. You wouldn't like that, would you?"

"No, we wouldn't like that," I said.

"This bloody heater's not working," said Teacher and slapped it with his hairy hand.

"That's a damned convincing costume, Jeremy," I said admiringly. Tessa giggled softly, but Teacher didn't answer.

Chapter 19

Traffic leaving West Berlin for the Autobahn to West Germany goes through the Border Control point at Drewitz, in the southwest corner of the city.

The procedures are efficient and, for a car with diplomatic plates, minimal. On the DDR side of the controls it is customary for the drivers and passengers of vehicles so marked to flatten their identity papers against the glass of the window, where they are examined by the flashlights of the communist officials who work with that studied slowness that in the West is usually the modus operandi of trade unionists in dispute.

Eventually the guards grudgingly waved us through. They gave no sign of noticing that one of us was a gorilla. Teacher tossed the diplomatic passports into the glove compartment, and we began the long and monotonous journey to the West. In keeping with the DDR's siege mentality, there are no cafés or restaurants on this road. There's nowhere to savor those sixty-eight different flavors of ice cream that punctuate long, wide American Freeways, none of the *bifteck et pommes frites avec Château Vinaigre* that mark the expensive kilometers of France's Autoroutes, not even the toxic waste and strong tea so readily available on Britain's motorways.

At first there was a great deal of traffic on the road. Lovers and husbands, returning from blissful weekends, passed each other on the way home. Trucks starting out at the stroke of midnight after the weekend embargo on heavy vehicles slowly and laboriously overtook other heavyweights. In the fast lane Germans roared past us at top speed, flashing their lights lest they be inconvenienced in their public demonstration of German mechanical superiority. *"Deutschland über Alles,"* said Teacher as one such Mercedes driver, who'd come tailgating close behind us, pointed his finger to his head as he overtook, and sprayed us with dirty water.

"Tessa's gone to sleep," I said.

"Something good had to happen," said Teacher. "It's the law of averages."

"Don't bet on it," I said. The wipers squeaked and squealed at the rain. Teacher reached for the radio switch but seemed to have second thoughts about it.

We came up behind a line of heavy trucks, the wind whipping the covers of the rearmost vehicle, and stayed there for a bit. "Keep awake. We'll check *all* the exits," said Teacher. "The message may have got it wrong."

"No comment," I said.

These East German Autobahnen were in poor condition. Little had been done on this stretch since it was first built, in Hitler's time. Subsidence here and there had caused wide cracks, and hasty patches of shoddy maintenance had failed to cure the underlying fractures. All over Europe the motorways were pocked with signs, and littered with the equipment of construction gangs, as the Continent's roads succumbed to an arteriosclerosis that had every sign of proving fatal.

There had been roadworks at several places along the route, but after the turnoff for Brandenburg—a town that

forms the center of a complex of lakes to the west of Berlin—
the westbound side of the Autobahn was reduced to single
lane working. Teacher slowed as our headlights picked out the
double row of plastic cones, some of them overturned by the
gusts of wind that accompanied ceaseless heavy rain.

The road curved gently to the left and began a downward
gradient. From here I saw ahead of us the ribbon of highway
marked by pinpoints of light that climbed like a file of insects
and disappeared suddenly over the distant hill only just visible
against the purple horizon.

This section of the Autobahn was being widened. Lining
the road were colossal machines: bulldozers and towering
power shovels, spreaders, graders, and rollers, the bizarre
toys of a Gargantuan world.

"Look there!" I said as I spotted a car parked amongst the machines, its parking lights just visible through the
downpour.

"That's them," said Teacher, the relief audible in his
voice. He swung the wheel. We bumped off the edge of the
roadway and down onto the mud, picking the way carefully
past metal drums, steel reinforcements, abandoned materials,
broken wooden fencing, and other undefinable debris. We
were about fifty yards from the other car when Teacher judged
us close enough. He stopped and turned off the engine: the
lights died. The noise of the rainstorm was suddenly very
loud. It was dark except when passing cars, coming round the
curve, swept the site with their headlight beams. The light
came swinging across it like the revolving rays of a lighthouse.
There was no movement anywhere.

"Careful," I said. "When you open the door we'll be lit
up by the interior light. We'll be sitting targets." I slid into the
back of the van, opened the suitcase, rummaged to find the
ammunition and the pistol. I loaded it carefully. It wasn't
the sort of thing you could tuck into the waistband of a pair
of cheap trousers, so I kept it in my hand.

"I'm getting out," said Teacher. "You two stay here."

"Whatever you say."

It was no time to start a row, but as he opened the door and got out of the driver's seat I slid out the back and into the darkness and pouring rain. Outside, there was the sort of stink that roadworks always exude, the smell of disturbed earth, feces, and fuel oil. But the road here runs through a tall forest, and the felling of the trees had added sap to the medley of odors. The rain soaked me to the skin before I'd taken more than two steps through the sticky mud. I kept the gun under my coat and out of sight, and watched the dim figure of Teacher walking cautiously toward the car. Some traffic swung past, driving carefully along the prescribed lane, their beams dulled by the steady rain.

While Teacher moved forward, someone got out of the car, which I could now recognize as a Wartburg. The other side had taken the precaution of taping up the interior light switch. The Wartburg's interior remained dark, and the glare of the parking lights was enough to make it impossible to see whether it was a man or a woman standing there. Nearer to me—and directly behind the nearest of the big yellow machines—there was a barrier. It fenced off the deep excavations where the foundations were being extended.

"Please walk forward, one at a time," I heard Teacher call, his uncertain German evident from only those few words.

Suddenly the full beams of the Wartburg came on. This light was hard and brilliant. It cut through rain that shone like glass beads, and exposed Teacher as an absurd and soaking-wet gorilla. Teacher was alarmed and jumped aside into the darkness, but I could still see his outline.

From the bulldozer closest to me I heard a movement, a soft metallic click that might have been the safety catch of a gun. A figure had shifted position from behind the bulldozer's tracks in order to see where Teacher had gone. I moved closer to the line of earth-moving machinery, which would provide me with the sort of cover that the other side had taken advantage of. Now I could see more clearly in the darkness. There seemed to be a woman standing by the Wartburg, and possibly others still inside it. The metallic sound I'd heard had come from someone standing near the barrier. It was a man holding a gun with a long silencer attached. All their attention was on Teacher.

It was like watching a performance on a fully lighted stage, its backdrop the tall trees of the immense forest while to one side there were the twin lines of traffic—one red, one white—flickering away into the far distance. Now I could see Teacher, but he couldn't see the figure with the gun, who was silhouetted against the mud and puddles which shone like silver in the beams of the Wartburg's headlights.

I heard a shout—almost a scream—a woman's voice—and there was someone running through the squelching mud behind me. I turned to see, but our Transit van was in my field of view. Then came the first shot: the sort of soft plop you only get the first time from a gun with a brand-new silencer. It wasn't Teacher. The woman called again. She was shouting, "Do as you were told!" In German, Berlin German.

Then came another shot, a loud report from an unsilenced gun, and the smashing of glass. It was a single shot from somewhere to the left of me. Now came a confusion of darkness, pierced by pistol shots and the sudden beams of passing headlights. Traffic rumbling past gave light enough to show that the Wartburg had suffered a broken windscreen, its shattered glass scattered around like snow. In that brief flicker of light I saw Teacher standing crouched with a pistol held at arm's length, the way actors stand in TV movies about cops. I couldn't be sure whether he'd fired the shot. Had he, I wondered, tried to hit someone inside the car, and if so had he succeeded?

Then something came fluttering out to make a glowing pattern between me and the light of the Wartburg headlights.

Until that moment I thought Tessa was still in the back of the Transit van, but there could be only one person who would go whirling through the mud, twisting and turning, oblivious of the rain and the gunfire.

Whoever shot her was standing near the front nearside wheel of the Wartburg. She was very close to the gunman when she was hit and lifted in the air. Bang. Bang. Two rounds from a shotgun floated her through the headlight beams with her skirt and draped sleeve shining and translucent yellow. As she fell back to earth, she metamorphosed to crimson and the cloth wrapped round her like some beautiful flying insect that in fast playback becomes a twitching chrysalis. Illuminated by the headlights, she was full-length in the mud. The rain beat down. She moved again and then was still.

"You bastard!" said someone in English. It must have been Teacher. And then he fired; I recognized the pump-pump sound of the 9mm Browning I'd seen him carrying. Two shots, very loud and very close together. One of them hit the steel frame of a big earth-moving machine, and was deflected into the sky with the piteous little cry that spent rounds give. But the other shot hit the Wartburg's nearside headlight and it went out with a secondary explosion and much hissing as the rain found the hot metal of the light.

Bang. Bang. Bang. Bang. Bang. There were men with guns in the darkness over beyond Teacher. No silencers. They returned the fire immediately. Several shots, so close together in time that they sounded almost like one. Teacher ran, stumbled, and then went down with a loud scream. I could just see him in the gloom beyond the light provided by the Wartburg's solitary beam. He writhed and shouted, hugging himself with both arms like a man trying to escape from a straitjacket of pain.

But under cover of the attention he was getting I was able to slide round the back of the bulldozer and scrambled up onto the wide track. The blade was elevated and I used it for cover, as I climbed as high as I could.

I was rewarded with a view of the whole site. More traffic moving slowly past in single file provided light to see the wide trench of the excavations, the line of earth-moving machines, and at the end of it the Wartburg. In the center of the stage there was the Transit van parked askew, and to the left of it Teacher's body. Two men came from the direction of the shots and stood over Teacher. One of them prodded the body with the toe of a shoe. There was no sign of life. "It's all safe now," he said. I recognized the voice of Erich Stinnes.

From behind the Wartburg there came the woman. She walked carefully, so as not to put her shoes into the worst of the muddy pools. It was Fiona, my wife.

"How many did they send?" said one of the men.

"A man and a woman," said Stinnes. "They are both dead." Fiona walked past Tessa's body and looked down at Teacher without giving any sign of recognizing him. I realized then that she'd not recognized her sister either. Stinnes turned to look at the Transit van. He was probably considering the smashed windscreen of the Wartburg and what it would be like to be behind it driving through the rain that was still falling.

At that moment I had many alternatives. I suppose the textbook would have wanted me to negotiate with them, but I wasn't a dedicated reader of textbooks and training manuals, which is the principal reason that I was still alive. So I raised my big revolver and, resting the barrel on the dozer's heavy steel blade—the sort of position considered unsporting by the instructors supervising the Department's outdoor firing range—I fired at the one who was farthest away, aiming for the center of the body. The heavy Webley round hit him like a sledgehammer slamming him into the darkness, where he remained still and silent. The second man—Stinnes—stepped back in alarm, but his training overcame his fear and, without seeing me, he immediately raised his gun and fired three times, aiming in my general direction. The bullets buzzed past my head and one plucked at my coat. It was the right thing to do, the prevailing theory being that your adversary stops shooting and seeks cover. But my reactions were far too slow for such theories, and by that time I'd hit him with my second round. It struck him in the neck.

It was a sight that was to interrupt my sleep, a finale to nightmares that awoke me sweating in the middle of so many dark nights. For Erich Stinnes spurted blood like a fountain, high in the air. And with blood spurting—hands to his throat—he stumbled backwards with a gasping noise and went slipping and sliding along in the mud until he hit the barrier around the excavation. There he stayed for a moment, and then slowly he toppled and went headfirst down into the waterlogged trench with a loud splash.

Fiona, frozen in fear, and now spattered with fresh blood, stayed where she was. I waited. There was no sound from anywhere. There was a pause in the passing traffic, and the forest absorbed the sounds of the wind and rain.

Then Fiona ran back to the Wartburg. As she did so the heel of her shoe broke and she twisted her ankle, stumbling, so that as she reached the car she was down on one knee and sobbing with the pain of it. From the assumed security that the darkness gave her—and unaware of how close I was—she called, "Who is it? Who is there?"

I didn't reply, make a sound, or even move. There was someone with a silenced gun somewhere out there, and until I settled with him it wasn't safe to climb down to the mud.

I waited a long time. Then Fiona hobbled to the Wartburg, leaned in, and doused the headlight beam. Now the site was entirely in darkness except for the occasional lights from passing traffic as it swept round the bend and started down the hill.

Fiona tried to start the car, but the bullet that had smashed the headlight must have done some other damage, for the starter motor screamed but didn't turn the engine over. In the silence of the forest I heard her curse to herself, gently and softly. There was desperation in her voice.

It was then that I saw the other one. He was creeping very slowly along the line of the barrier. I caught only a glimpse of him, but I could see he was wearing a trench coat and the sort of waterproof hat that Americans wear when golfing. I guessed who it was: Thurkettle.

For a long, long time I saw and heard nothing except the sounds and light of the passing traffic. Then I heard a man's voice call, "Are we going to wait here all night, Samson?"

It was Thurkettle's voice. I remained silent.

Thurkettle called again: "You can take the woman and take your transit van and go. Take your gorilla too. I don't want any of you."

I didn't respond.

"Do you hear me?" he said. "I'm working your side of the street. Get going. I've got work to do."

I called, "Fiona! Do you hear me?"

She looked around but couldn't spot me.

"Get to the Ford, start up the engine, and roll on a yard or two. Then keep it ticking over."

Fiona stepped forward and then kicked both shoes off and went squelching through the mud. Nervously, and pained by her twisted ankle, she made her way slowly to the transit van. She got into it and started up the engine. After a moment, finding the controls, she drove forward a little way and cut the engine to idling softly.

"Now you owe me one, Bernie."

"Give my regards to Count Zeppelin," I said. I still had the edge on him. I knew where he was but he hadn't located me. I clambered down to the ground and estimated how many paces I would need to get to the other side of the van. If Thurkettle started shooting, I'd have the van as cover.

I waited for a few minutes, so that Thurkettle would start looking round to see if I'd got away. Then I ran across to the van. A heavy truck came crawling round the curve and caught me in its headlight beams. I kept running and threw myself down into the mud just as I reached the rear of the van. I stayed there for a moment to catch my breath. No shots came. I moved to the front and put a hand to the glass to get Fiona's attention. "Can you see him?" I whispered.

"He's behind the Wartburg."

"Is he one of yours?"

"I know nothing about him."

"Didn't he come with you?" I asked her.

"No. He's on a motorcycle."

"Are you fit to drive?"

"Yes, of course," she said. Her voice was firm and determined.

"We'll get out of here and leave him to it. Slide down low in the seat, in case he shoots. I'm going to climb in. When I say 'go,' start driving. Not too fast, in case you stall."

I slid my hand around the door seating until I found the light switch, and then I pushed it to keep the light off. I opened the door and scrambled inside. "Go!" I said softly. Fiona revved the engine and we went bumping forward over the rough ground. There were no shots.

In the darkness the van bumped over some planks of wood, and then we rolled up over a high ledge and onto the Autobahn. It was very dark: no traffic in sight either way. We started westward. We were about half a mile down the road when there was a great red ball of light behind us.

"My God!" said Fiona. "Whatever's that?"

"Your Wartburg going up in flames, unless I miss my guess."

"In flames?"

"Someone is destroying the evidence."

"Evidence of what?" she said.

"Let's not go back and ask."

The flames were fierce. We could still see them from miles away. Then, as we went over the brow of a hill, the light on the horizon vanished suddenly. Very little forensic evidence would be salvaged from such a blaze.

I asked Fiona if she wanted me to drive. She shook her head without answering. I tried in other ways to start a conversation, but her replies were monosyllabic. Driving along the Autobahn that night gave her something to concentrate upon. She was determined not to think about what she'd done, and in no mood to talk about what we'd have to do.

My arm began to throb. I touched it and found my sleeve was sticky with blood. One of the bullets had come closer than I'd realized. It was not a real wound, just a bad extended graze and an enormous bruise, of the sort that bullets make when they brush the flesh. I wadded a handkerchief and pressed it against my arm to stanch the dribbling blood. It was nothing that would put me in hospital, but more than enough to ruin my suit.

"Are you all right?" There was no tenderness in her voice. It was as much admonitory as concerned, the voice of a schoolteacher herding a class of kids across a busy street.

"I'm all right." We should have been talking and embracing and laughing and loving. We were together again, and she was coming home to me and the children. But it wasn't like that. We weren't the same carefree couple who'd honeymooned on a bank overdraft and got hysterically drunk in the registry office on one half-bottle of champagne shared amongst four people. We sat silent in the darkness. We watched the traffic crawling to Berlin, and saw the Porsches scream past us. And I dribbled blood, and the unspoken dreams that keep marriages going bled away too.

The rain stopped, or perhaps we drove out of it. I switched on the car radio. There was a babble of Arabic, Radio

Moscow's news in German, and then that powerful German transmitter that during the night effectively overwhelms all opposition throughout Central Europe. A big schmaltzy band: *We could make believe I love you, only make believe that you love me. Others find peace of mind in pretending. Couldn't you? Couldn't I? Couldn't we . . .*

Behind us a strip of sky gradually lightened and colored to become a contused mess of mauves and purples.

"All right, darling?" I asked. Still she didn't respond to my overtures. She just concentrated on the road, her lips pressed together and her knuckles white.

The unbearable uncertainties that gave me severe stomach pains as we got nearer and nearer to the frontier proved unfounded. When we stopped, she looked in the driving mirror and wiped some spots of blood from her face with a handkerchief moistened with spittle. Her expression was unchanging.

"All all right?"

"Yes," I replied.

She drove forward. An indifferent border guard, seeing the diplomatic registration plates, gave us not more than a glance before going back to reading his newspaper.

"We made it," I said. She didn't answer.

There was a reception committee waiting for us on the other side of the control point. It was dawn with that uncertain light that soldiers use to start their battles. Some army vehicles were parked by the roadside: an armored personnel carrier, a staff car, and an ambulance—the complete panoply of war. From the empty roadside two soldiers suddenly materialized. One was middle-aged, the other in his twenties. Then came a cheerful young colonel of some unidentifiable unit with his khaki beret pulled tight upon his broad skull and a battle smock with no badges other than parachute wings, and his rank stenciled in black.

"We have a helicopter here," said the colonel. He affected a short swagger stick, wielding it to give Fiona a mock salute. "Are you fit enough to travel to Cologne?" His voice was loud, his manner almost jubilant. He was clean and freshly shaved and seemed oblivious of hour.

"I'm all right," said Fiona. The colonel opened the door to let her out of the driver's seat. But Fiona sat tight, and didn't even look at him to explain why. She held the steering wheel very tight and, looking straight ahead, she gave a little sniff. She sniffed again, loudly, like a child with a runny nose. Then she began to laugh. At first it was the natural charming laugh that you might expect from a beautiful young woman who had just won the world championship in espionage and double-dealing. But as her laughter continued, the colonel began to frown. Her face became flushed. Her laughing became shrill and she trembled and shook until her whole body was racked with her hysterical laughter, as it might be afflicted with a cough or a choking fit.

The laughing still didn't stop. I became alarmed, but the colonel seemed to have encountered it before. He looked at the blood spots that covered her; and then at me. "It's the reaction. From what I can see, she's had a rough time." Over his shoulder he said, "You'd better help her, doc."

As he stood aside, the younger man behind him stepped forward. The middle-aged soldier handed him something. Then the boyish-looking doctor reached in through the window, grabbed her, and with a minimum of fuss—in fact, with no fuss at all—he put a hypodermic needle into her upper arm, right through her sleeve. The army is like that. He kept hold of her arm and watched her while she quietened down. Then he felt her pulse. "That should do it," he said. "A sedative. No alcohol. Better if she doesn't eat for an hour or two. There will be an RAF doctor waiting for you at Cologne Airport; I'll give you a message for him. He'll go with you all the way."

"All the way to where?" I asked.

The young doctor looked at the colonel, who said, "Didn't they tell you? It's always the same, isn't it? They never tell the people at the sharp end. You're transferring to a transatlantic flight. It's a long journey, but the air force will look after you."

Fiona was relaxing. The laughter had completely stopped, and she looked around her as if waking from a deep sleep. She let the colonel help her down from the car. "Where are your shoes?" he asked her gallantly and tried to find them.

"I've lost my shoes," she said flatly and pushed back her hair as if becoming aware of her scruffy appearance.

"That doesn't matter a bit," said the colonel. "They have lovely shoes in America."

Chapter 20

Summer is not the best time to be in southern California. Even "La Buona Nova," the big hillside spread in Ventura County where Fiona was hidden away for her official debriefing, had long energy-sapping days when there was not a breeze off the Pacific. Bret Rensselaer was in charge. Some people—including me—had said he was too old ever to become a full-time Departmental employee again. But Bret was officially considered as Fiona's case officer. Bret had been a party to Fiona's long-term plan to defect to Moscow since that time when she first confided it to him. He'd monitored her progress. There was really no one else who could debrief her.

Bret Rensselaer was determined to make a big success of what would obviously be the last job he'd ever do. The prospect of a knighthood was never mentioned, but you didn't have to be a mindreader to know what Bret thought would be an appropriate thank-you from a grateful sovereign. No worries about Bret bowing the head for that one: he'd walk coast to coast on his knees for a K.

No one ever mentioned any kind of thank-you for me. When my salary check was paid, I noticed that all the allowances and extras had been trimmed off it. I was down to the bare bones. I mentioned this to Bret, and he said that I should remember that I wasn't having to pay for my food and keep. Good grief, I said, what about the way I'm being deprived of contact with my children? I didn't mention Gloria, for obvious reasons. It was Bret who brought Gloria into our conversation. He said that she had been told that I was on a special mission too secret for details to be revealed. The Department was making sure my children were happy and well cared for. He said it as if his words contained some not very veiled threat for me: I had the feeling that what Gloria was told would depend upon my good behavior.

One day I noticed amongst the papers on Bret's marble-topped table a colored postcard. It was Van Gogh's portrait of a blue-uniformed postman, a picture of which Gloria was inordinately fond. "Could that card be for me?" I asked him.

"No," he said immediately and without hesitation.

"You're sure?"

"It's my private correspondence," said Bret.

I felt like grabbing it to see, but the table was big and Bret reached it before I did. He put it in a drawer. I knew it was a card from Gloria to me. I just knew it.

After that I was seldom allowed into Bret's "office," and when I did go in there his table was always cleared. And in all that time the only correspondence that was forwarded to me was a picture of Paul Bocuse. It was postmarked Lyon and was from Tante Lisl describing the meal she'd eaten.

They put me and Fiona into a comfortable guest house set apart from the main buildings. It was complete with kitchen, dining room, and a young Mexican girl to make breakfast and clean and tidy. Fiona spent four—sometimes five—hours almost every day with Bret. Neither of them emerged to eat a proper lunch. Sandwiches, fruit, and coffee were sent in to them, and they carried right on talking. Bret had a part-time secretary, but she wasn't with them during these sessions. His large and very comfortable office, with its window grilles and security locks, had maps and reference books and a computer that would feed into his screen and/or print out anything he required from all sorts of data banks. Everything Fiona said was recorded on tape and locked away in a huge safe. But there were no transcripts; all that would come later. This was the first run-through, so that Bret could alert London and Washington to anything urgent.

Sometimes I went in and listened, but after a few days Fiona asked me to stay away. My presence made her too self-conscious, she said. I was hurt and offended at the time, but one-to-one was the usual form for such debriefings, and I'd never much liked having someone sit in when I was doing one of these deep-analysis stunts.

So I swam in the blue outdoor pool, caught up on my reading, and listened to twenty-four-hours-a-day classical music on KSCA-FM or to cassettes on the big hi-fi. Most days I swam with Mrs. O'Raffety, the artistic old lady who owned the place, and who had to swim on account of her bad back. And most days we took lunch together too.

I would have liked to go into Los Angeles, or, failing that, go for a beer in Santa Barbara, which was much nearer. Walk along the beach, drive up the Pacific Coast Highway, do the tour of the Hearst mansion: anything to break the monotony. But Bret was unyielding; both of us were confined inside La Buona Nova's compound, surrounded by the chain-link fences, the armed Mexican guards, and the dogs. It was a prison—a nice, comfortable prison, but we were sentenced to stay there as long as the Department decreed. I had the nasty feeling that that would turn out to be a very long term indeed. But what could I do? It was for Fiona's safety, said Bret. There was no arguing with that.

One night, soon after arriving, I'd tried to talk to Fiona about her time with Stinnes and his merry men. We were preparing for bed. She answered normally at first, but then she grunted shorter replies and I could see she was getting very upset. She didn't weep or anything as traumatic as that. Perhaps it would have been better for all concerned if she'd done so: it might have helped her. But she didn't weep; she climbed into bed and curled up small and pulled the bedsheet over herself.

Each evening we'd eat dinner with Bret, our hostess, and her son-in-law, an amiable lawyer. They were dull affairs at which the Mexican servants hovered all the time and the rest of us made small talk. Sometimes I'd see Bret Rensselaer at the pool and exchange pleasantries with him. His only response to anything I said about Fiona seeming unwell was bland reassurances. The doctor had given her a physical the day following her arrival and she had lots of vitamin pills and sleeping pills if she required them. And he told me that she'd been through a tough time and generally treated me like a neurotic mother worrying about a child with a grazed knee. But the changes I saw in Fiona were perhaps not evident to those who didn't know her so well. The changes were all small ones. She seemed shrunken and her face was drawn, and she didn't walk absolutely upright in the attractive way that I remembered so well. There was the soft and hesitant way she spoke, and the diffidence she showed to everyone from me and Bret right through to the Mexican house servants.

One evening at dinner she spilled a couple of drops of barbecue sauce on the tablecloth—the kind of thing I do all the time—and she slumped back in her chair and closed her eyes. No one round the table gave any sign of noticing it, but I knew she was close to screaming, close perhaps to breaking point. The trouble was that she'd confide nothing to me, no matter how I tried to get her to talk. Finally she accused me of harassing her, so then I stopped and left it all to Bret.

Two days later Bret asked me to sit in with them for the morning session. "There are a few things unexplained," said Bret.

"From where I'm sitting, there are a lot of things unexplained," I said.

Fiona sat slumped in a big armchair. Bret was behind a table—an elaborate modern design of pink marble with polished steel legs—with his back to the tinted window. The garden was packed with color. Against the whitewashed wall of the yard there were orange and lemon trees, jasmine, roses, and bougainvillea. There was no perfume from them, for the window was tightly closed and the air conditioning fully on. Bret looked at me for a long time and finally said, "For instance?"

"The traces of heroin in the Ford van." It was a bluff, and it didn't work.

"Let's not get sidetracked," Bret said. "We're supposed to be establishing the identities of the other people there."

"Fiona can tell you that," I said. "She was in the car with them."

"Erich Stinnes," said Fiona somewhat mechanically. "Plus a Russian liaison man. And there was a man I had never seen before. He arrived on a motorcycle."

"Good! Good!" murmured Bret as he laboriously wrote it down in case he forgot. He looked up. "Three men," he said and gave a quick nervous smile. Bret Rensselaer was one of those slim, elegant Americans who, whether sick or healthy, always look well cared for—like a vintage Bugatti or a fifty-carat diamond. Sitting behind his desk, golden pen in hand, he looked like a carefully posed photo in a society magazine. He was wearing tailored white designer slacks and a white tennis shirt with a red stripe at the collar. It all went well with his white hair and made his tanned face seem very brown.

I wondered if the mysterious "extra man" was going to be identified as Thurkettle. I didn't volunteer that idea, and I noticed that Fiona said nothing of his American accent.

"Have the monitors picked up anything?" Fiona asked.

"Nothing in any of the newspapers or periodicals, and certainly nothing on the radio." He gave another of his crisp little smiles and fidgeted with his signet ring. "It would be surprising if there was."

"And even more surprising if you told us about it," I said.

Bret wasted no more than a moment on that one. He grunted and turned to Fiona again. "Why would they burn the car, Fiona?"

"Bernard says it was to destroy the evidence," she replied.

"I was asking you, Fiona."

"I really have no idea. It might have been an accident. There was still one man there."

"Ah! The man on the bike?"

"Yes," she said.

"I wish you could tell me more about him." He waited in case Fiona said something. When she didn't he said, "And you didn't talk with Stinnes or this liaison guy during the car journey?"

"No, I didn't."

"Did they talk together?"

"I don't think there's much to be gained in this line," said Fiona. "I've told you all I know about them."

Bret nodded sympathetically. He looked at his yellow legal pad and said, "This 'other man' came by motorbike? Unusual, that, don't you think?"

"I really don't know how unusual it was, Bret."

"But if the car was set on fire after you left, it has to be the biker who did it?"

"I assume so," said Fiona.

"So do I," said Bret. "Now we come to the final stage of this strange business—him letting you get away so easily."

Fiona nodded and wet her lip as if she was distressed to think about it. "Strange, yes."

"What would be the motive for that? Bernie here had just shot his two buddies. Then he let you go. Does that sound a little crazy?"

Fiona said, "It was a stalemate. He couldn't move without getting shot. He knew Bernard couldn't get to the van without offering a target. Some kind of compromise had to be reached."

"No, it didn't, honey," said Bret. "These people were in their own country. Let's say Mr. X holds out until it's daylight. Passing traffic will see what's happening. The construction workers will arrive. Just about anything that happens will resolve things his way. Right?"

"I don't know who he was," said Fiona as if she hadn't listened to Bret's question.

"What does that mean?" said Bret.

Fiona looked at me, needing support. I said, "Fiona means that if some CIA agent was in a shootout on the Pacific Coast Highway, along the road from here, how keen would he be to have himself discovered by the local cops and passers-by when daylight comes?"

"Well, okay," said Bret in a voice that conceded nothing. "But this is the U.S. of A. Liberal newspapers who are looking for ways to take a swipe at the government, crackpot senators ditto. In a situation like that, maybe some CIA agent might want to keep a low profile at whatever cost. But in the DDR . . . I don't see it."

"Why don't you just tell us what you want us to say, Bret," I said.

"Come again?" said Bret, the frayed edge of his temper showing through.

"We all know you're writing a fairy story," I said. "It's a

scenario that was probably all settled months, maybe years, ago. You don't want to know what really happened; you just want to find excuses for saying everything went as planned. I know what the report will be: fifty pages patting all the desk men on the back and saying what a wonderful job they did. The only decisions still to be made are who gets the knighthood and who will have to make do with an MBE or a CBE."

"You're a rude bastard, Bernard," he said softly.

"Yes. I know. Everyone tells me the same thing. But what I say is true, all the same."

He looked at me and conceded just a fraction. "Wasn't it Goethe who said, *Der Ausgang gibt den Taten ihre Titel*—how's that? 'The outcome decides what the title will be'? Sure. This is a phenomenal success story. It's Fiona's success. She won't ever get a proper credit for it, because that's not the way the Department handles these things: we all know that. What she will get is the report. Would you rather I write it up as some kind of turkey? You want me to say she screwed up?"

"No," I said. Bret could always find a way of putting his opponents in the wrong.

Fiona said nothing. Her contribution to the talking was minimal, and yet she was not uncooperative: she was like a sleepwalker. She knew her sister was dead—Bret had told her—but she avoided mention of Tessa. It was as if Tessa had never been there, and Bret left it like that. There were a lot of things that Fiona would not talk about; she seldom even mentioned the children. I didn't envy Bret his task.

Bret looked at his watch. "Well, let's move on to a few easier questions. We'll get some of those rare roast-beef sandwiches sent in and break early. How about that?"

The sandwiches were lousy too.

A couple of days later we had a visitor. James Prettyman was an Americanized Englishman who used to work alongside me.

Since then London Central had sent him to Washington in some deep-cover plan that enabled him to do things for them at arm's length. At one time we'd been close friends. Now I wasn't so sure, although I suppose I owed him a favor or two.

Jim was in his early thirties. He had the wiry form and presence of mind that are associated with the pushier type of door-to-door salesmen. His complexion was pale and bloodless. His head was domelike and he was losing his silky hair, but sometimes a strand of it fell across his eyes. I think he was glad to see it.

It was early in the morning when he arrived. He was wearing a blue striped suit, the lightweight cotton you need in Washington, D.C., at this sweaty time of the year. There was a paisley silk square in the top pocket, and the trousers were very rumpled, as if he'd been strapped into his seat for a few hours.

"Good to see you, Bernie," he said and gave me a sincere handshake and fixed me with his eyes, in that way that Americans do when they are trying to recall your name. "I'm sitting in." He looked at his watch. "Later this morning. You, me, and Bret: okay?"

"Good," I said, uncertain of what was expected of me. I thought he must have come to talk with Fiona, but she was taking breakfast in bed, having been given a morning of "free activity."

Bret Rensselaer went into secret session with Jim Prettyman, and I was summoned to join them at ten o'clock. The remains of their breakfast were still distributed around the room. Bret couldn't think without striding round the room, so there were plates with half-eaten corn muffins, cups, and unfinished glasses of orange juice on every side. I poured myself coffee from the vacuum jug and sat down. I reached for the cream jug, but when I poured from it only a drop or two remained.

Bret Rensselaer said, "Jim would like to hear your version of what happened."

I looked at Bret and he added, "On the Autobahn."

"Oh," I said. "On the Autobahn."

"Who was this man on the motorcycle?" said Prettyman.

"No one seems to know," I said.

"I told Jim you had theories," said Bret. "And I told him you wouldn't open up."

Jim said, "Off the record, Bernie."

"It was a dark night, Jim," I said.

He leaned forward and switched off the tape recorder and said, "Off the record."

"Oh, that kind of off the record," I said. I drank some coffee. It was cold. "I think your vacuum flask is on the blink," I said. "Yes, well . . . He had an American accent."

"They've all got American accents," said Bret. "It's the teaching machines."

"So I hear," I said.

"Did you recognize the voice?" said Prettyman.

"Are you putting me on?" I asked. "Do we have to go through with this nonsense?"

"Who was it?"

"Jesus, Jim! You know who it was. It was a thug named Thurkettle, a renegade American. A hit man the Department brought in to make sure Tessa Kosinski was blown away."

"Why you dumb . . ." started Bret, but Prettyman waved a hand that silenced him.

"Tell me more," said Prettyman. "Why would the Department want to kill Fiona's sister?" It was casually put, but in his voice there was that specially kindly tone with which psychiatrists coax maniacs.

"The car burned," I said. "Tessa Kosinski's remains— no more than a few bone fragments and ashes—will be identified as her sister, Fiona. Fiona is hidden here: Moscow won't know that she is alive and well and spilling everything to you guys."

"You're forgetting the teeth," said Bret. "They are sure to find some jawbone. Fiona had dentistry—a crown and a filling—while she was over there in East Berlin." If anything was needed to convince me that my theory was right, it was Bret's remarkable knowledge of Fiona's dental chart.

Prettyman looked at Bret and then at me and then sneaked a quick look at his wristwatch.

"I'm forgetting nothing," I said. "Let's suppose a skull, sufficiently like Fiona's, was fitted with dental work that exactly matched hers. That would have been put into the car."

"Two women's skulls in the car?"

"That's why you need a madman like Thurkettle. Hacking a head from a body is covered by his all-inclusive fee."

"Thurkettle is the one who wasted the CIA man in Salzburg," said Prettyman, as if remembering the name from something in the dim and distant past. Then he said, "It would need a lot of planning . . . a lot of cooperation. Who would put him in position and so on?"

"There was drug trafficking: officials on both sides. A scapegoat was needed. All concerned were desperate to close the file. That spot, with the construction work on the highway, would provide a chance to bury any inconvenient evidence."

"Where did you get all this?" said Prettyman.

"It's the only feasible explanation."

"You'll have to do better than that, Bernie," said Prettyman in a voice that seemed truly friendly. "I'll listen to anything you have to say. I learned what I know from you: all of it. But you'll have to do a rewrite for that cockeyed script."

"So what the hell was Tessa doing there?"

It was Bret's turn to speak. "Isn't that a question for you to answer, Bernard? You took her there with you. Remember?"

"Will you go and see Gloria?" I asked Prettyman on a sudden and desperate impulse. "Tell the children I'm well and that I love them?"

Bret said nothing.

Prettyman calmly said, "There's not much chance of me getting a trip to London anytime in the foreseeable future, Bernie."

I drank my tepid black coffee and didn't answer.

"I'll be back," Prettyman told me like a dutiful son visiting a difficult octogenarian. "But I have to be at Camarillo Municipal Airport by two. Next month, maybe . . . Good to see you, Bernie. Really good! I mean that sincerely."

"Get stuffed!" I said.

Prettyman looked at Bret. Bret responded with a tiny shrug as he was showing Prettyman out. I remained where I was, but I could hear them in the next room. As they parted I heard Prettyman say, "What a tragedy. Both of them."

I heard Bret reply, "It's not too late. Let's see what happens."

It was a week afterward that I learned that Camarillo Municipal Airport used to be a fully equipped U.S. Air Force operational base and that the runways are still in good order. So when Prettyman went there he hopped back into the supersonic military jet that had brought him, and he was in Washington for happy hour. I suppose it was something that Fiona had said to Bret, and Washington had to be told double-quick.

We'd been at the house for over a month before Fiona began to open up to me. Even then what she said was fairly banal stuff about her day-to-day work in Berlin, but it was a start. It became routine for us to talk for half an hour or so. Sometimes we'd talk over a drink in our sitting room, and sometimes we'd take a walk around the perimeter fence. Once, while walking, Fiona almost trod upon a big gray rattlesnake, and after that we kept to the paths and the terrace. It was a big property, and high enough so that on a pitch-black night the California coastline shone like a diamond necklace laid out all the way to Los Angeles.

"What really happened?" she said one night as we were standing there looking at the view and listening to the ocean.

"They got you out," I said. "That's what happened."

"What was Tessa doing there? That's what I can't understand. What was Tessa doing there, Bernard?"

"I told you," I said. "She was having an affair with Dicky. She thought it would be fun, I suppose."

"I loved you so much when I married you, Bernard. I loved you because you were the only man I'd ever met who had a real respect for the truth. You never lied to me, Bernard. I wanted my children to be like you."

I was holding her hand, staring into the darkness, and trying to recognize the distant coastline.

She said, "You wouldn't be working against me, would you, Bernard? You wouldn't do that?"

"What do you mean?"

"They haven't even told George that Tessa is dead."

"Why not?"

"Poor George. He'd never do harm to anyone."

"Why haven't they told him?"

She turned to look at me. "He's been sworn to secrecy and told that Tessa went to Berlin with you and that you've run away together . . . run away somewhere where no one can find you."

"So that's the story," I said. It fitted so neatly: the hotel room that Dicky had shared with Tessa was registered in my name.

"They want Moscow to believe that Tessa is alive. The story is that it was me who was killed at the Brandenburg exit."

"The burning car. Yes, that would be it."

"Could anyone get away with such a deception, Bernard?"

"There was trade in heroin. Could Erich Stinnes have been involved?"

"Erich? No!"

"A lot of people think he was," I persisted. "And he was working for the Department. Do you see how he could have been set up?"

"Stop worrying about Erich."

"Who says I'm worrying about him?"

"You identify with him . . . the way he grew up in Berlin with a father in the army . . . you identify with him."

I didn't deny it: she knew. I suppose I'd been shouting in my sleep. I'd had a couple of nightmares. "I killed him."

"It's all over, darling. Stop torturing yourself. Why was Tessa there? That's what I want to find out."

"Tessa was an addict, you know."

"That's what Bret said."

"That might have been the reason she went to Berlin. There was a man named Thurkettle who probably supplied her. I think he might have cut off her supply to make her follow him there. There were a lot of people involved. A scapegoat was needed. You can bet the official explanation is that you were bringing it in."

"That I was bringing it? Heroin? Whose explanation? East or West?"

"Everyone. It was a chance to close the file," I said.

"How far would the Department go with that?"

"This is an unprecedented situation. We can't be guided by past examples."

"Uncle Silas knew what I was really doing."

"Yes, I know, I talked to him. Uncle Silas said they needed six months with Moscow still believing you remained loyal. They'll be using all the material that they were frightened of using before in case you were compromised."

"You're saying someone deliberately planned it so that Tessa would die?"

"I don't know." My answer came too pat, and she thought I was not telling her all I knew. "I really don't know, Fi."

She put her arm round me. "I have no one to trust any more. Sometimes that frightens me."

"I understand."

"Was it like that for you?"

"Sometimes."

"Who would plan such a terrible thing?"

"Perhaps I've got it all wrong," I said.

"Bret?"

"I wouldn't start going through the possibilities. Probably it was a mixture of planning and opportunity. Maybe it's nothing like that. As I say: maybe I've got it all wrong."

"I suppose Tessa did look like me. Daddy always said so."

"I have no evidence one way or the other," I said. "The most important thing is to give Bret the sort of answers he wants. We have to get out of here. The children need us."

"I abandoned them," said Fiona. "They must hate me."

"Of course they don't."

"Why wasn't it me? Tessa so loved life, and you and the children can manage without me. Why wasn't it me?"

"You've got to start again, Fi," I said.

"I didn't even recognize her," said Fiona. "I left her there in the mud."

I could hear the ocean, but I couldn't see anything there but darkness. I said, "Why don't we see if Bret would let the children come here for the final three or four weeks?"

"Bret says we'll be here for a long time," she said casually, as if she didn't care.

I shivered. I was right. We were imprisoned here. Maybe for years. Maybe indefinitely. I knew of defectors, needing protection, who were tucked away out of sight for a decade or more. "Tell Bret you insist upon seeing the children," I suggested.

She didn't reply immediately, and when she did her voice

was listless. "I love the children, and I desperately want to see them. But not here."

"Whatever you say, Fi."

"I need time, Bernard. I'll be that lucky, joyful girl you married, and the good times will come round again. We'll live happily ever after. But I need time."

From the Pacific Ocean there came that smell of salt and putrefaction that is called fresh air. The sky was very dark that night: no stars, no glimmer of moonlight. Even the lights along the waterfront were being extinguished.

A Note on the Type

This book was set in a digitized version
of a type face called Baskerville.
The face itself is a facsimile reproduction of
types cast from molds
made for John Baskerville (1706–1775)
from his designs. Baskerville's
original face was one of the
forerunners of the type style known to
printers as "modern face"—a "modern"
of the period A.D. 1800.

Composed, printed, and bound by
The Haddon Craftsmen, Inc., Scranton,
Pennsylvania

BASED ON A DESIGN BY CLAIRE M. NAYLON

DATE DUE
